Ashley Franz Holzmann Presents

Vices and Virtues

Cover design and interior design by Ashley Franz Holzmann

Edited by Ashley Franz Holzmann and Amber Whelpley

Front cover font is Credit Valley, *provided by Larabie Fonts*

First Printed in the United States of America

First Printing, 2017

ISBN-13: 978-0692960097
ISBN-10: 0692960090

As For Class
PO BOX 70692
FT BRAGG, NC 28307

www.asforclass.com

To the people of the Nosleep community.

You have given us all so much.

Table of Contents

My Time Is Very Valuable 175

By J.D. Patrick

Birthmarked 201

By J.L Spencer

Given Form 215

By S.M. Piper

Dammit, Janet 229

By Ashley Franz Holzmann

Heart Full of Love 255

By L Chan

Sesshoseki 269

By Kristopher J. Patten

The Sand Quarry 313

By Manen Lyset

Chaucer's Horses 335

By Christina Ferrari

Biserka 355

By Kristopher J. Patten

The Girl Who Died

By C. K. Walker

She was a painfully ordinary girl. Anyone who had the pleasure of meeting her walked away retaining neither the memory of her face nor her name. She was simply forgettable—a transparent background character even in the play of her own life. She was plain, quiet, and weak, and perhaps worst of all, the girl knew all these things about herself.

Having little in common with the mature, coquettish girls at school, she instead preferred the company of the forest animals that dwelled on her family's property. Every day she would walk the two miles home from school, throw her backpack on the front porch and run off into the woods until sundown to play with her Forest Family. Squirrels, raccoons, foxes, frogs; she considered them her brothers and sisters. Her real family, her legal family, meant little to her.

Her mother was cold and dismissive. Her father, cruel and demanding. And as for her four brothers, well, they never noticed her until they wanted something. Her mother had told her to never say no to a man.

No, the girl much preferred her life in the woods, away from the people that either hated her or, perhaps worse, had never noticed her at all. None of her classmates ever talked to her and most didn't even know her name. Sometimes they would run into her and cry out in surprise as if they had been brushed by a ghost. These interactions always made her sad. She didn't want to be famous or even popular. The girl just wanted to be noticed.

And then, on a day as ordinary as she was, everything changed. It was a hot, sunny April afternoon and the girl had skipped her last two classes wagering that she wouldn't be missed anyway. She was a solid C student with perfect attendance—not because she attended school every day but because no one noticed when she wasn't there.

On this particular Wednesday, her fourth-period class had been covering notable people in America throughout the 20th century. Their great deeds and household names made the girl feel even smaller and less important than usual. So, after the class ended, the girl had simply left school and walked home.

The closer she got to her family's property the faster she walked, slowing only slightly when she crossed the acreage of her cherished neighbor Dr. Danner. When the long driveway of her family's homestead finally came into view, a smile broke across the girl's round, homely face and she ran as fast as she could up the drive. When she reached the house, she threw her backpack up on the porch and sprinted into the woods toward her favorite grove of trees.

She came upon it loudly, breath heavy and chest heaving from her sprint. Though she couldn't see them, the girl had heard the animals scatter as she crashed into the clearing. She knew that in the woods her presence was noticed; she could not be ignored. No longer small and insignificant, rather she was strong and imposing. She was alive.

The girl spent most of that particular afternoon as she usually did: trying to coax her woodland friends from their holes and burrows to play with her. It was a hot, humid day and the sun was unrelenting. The sweat made her skin slick and her hair fall flat upon her head. Her human scent was more potent than usual and so she had little luck finding members of her Forest Family that day.

Shortly before sunset, the girl gave up. She walked home in tears, feeling small and rejected, and all the while getting closer and closer to the thing that would violently hurl her from obscurity into the spotlight of the world's stage. She plodded on, making tiny whimpering sounds and long, thin marks in the dirt where her feet dragged behind her.

She was twenty yards away from it. She was twelve yards away from it. Now only eight yards. And then two.

It was just before the tree line that the girl saw finally saw the thing. Its body was rotting in the sun, feet fully extended in the air where they'd likely succumbed to rigor mortis after its death throes. The smell was pungent but it wasn't a scent that was totally unfamiliar to her. The girl had attended many funerals for her Forest Friends. And, even though she didn't want to admit it to herself, she was pleased to have found a friend that couldn't run away from her that day.

The girl knelt down next to the dead animal, unaffected by

the sick smell of viscera and rot. She was sad, for even though she hadn't met him before, the animal was part of her Forest Family and she knew he deserved a proper burial as the others had had.

The girl grabbed a nearby stick and began digging a hole next to the dead creature. As she worked, sweat dripped off her brow and onto the hot, decaying body of her friend. She noticed a drop fall onto the creature's nose and roll down into its eye—and she swore she saw it blink. The girl stopped digging with the crude stick and used it to gently prod the animal instead. When it didn't flinch, she pinched its belly with her finger. There was no reaction.

Deciding she hadn't seen it blink after all, the girl finished digging the makeshift grave and picked up the rotting body, placing it gently into its grave. As she covered the animal with dirt the girl sang it a song that she'd heard her mother sing to her brothers when they were little and feeling sick. She cried for her Forest Friend.

The girl found a nearby rock, which she thought was smooth and pretty, and placed it near the mound to serve as a headstone. She wiped her face then and stood up, looking toward her house. The girl was hot, wet and miserable and she left the woods walking toward the hose on the side of her house. She quickly rinsed off, grabbed her bag from the porch, and went inside.

The girl went into the kitchen to get some water and grabbed half a cantaloupe from the fridge, weaving her way between her family members as if she were a ghost. The girl ate the cantaloupe in her room and completed her homework for the day. When it was done, and she should have been full, the girl found that she was still hungry. No, not hungry—starving.

She went to the kitchen and grabbed an entire package of Ritz crackers and two cans of soup. She went back up to her room and consumed it all in minutes. When she found that she was still hungry, she curled up and cried on her bed. Her father would surely notice if she took more food and he would become angry. She got hurt when her father was angry.

The girl cried herself to sleep, waking several times in the night to intense hunger pains. Just before the sun rose the next morning—when the house was still quiet and she was sure everyone was asleep—the girl crept back into the kitchen and took from the cupboard two cans of SpaghettiOs and half a leftover casserole from the fridge. She ate it on her bed and then hid the cans and casserole dish underneath it. She went to sleep then, finally satisfied.

When the girl awoke again, it was late—very late—and she was cold. She dressed quickly in a long, khaki-colored skirt and a brown flannel shirt. She then all but ran the two miles to school. And though it was already hot (and even more humid than the previous day) the girl still felt very cold.

When she arrived at school the girl tried to sneak into her third period class. No one noticed until the door shut behind her. The girl watched her teacher furrow her brow in confusion and glance down at the attendance sheet.

The girl watched the metal clock on the wall count the long, slow seconds as she eagerly waited for the class to be over since next period was her lunch hour. And though she usually ate very little at school—if at all—the girl got into the lunch line and filled her tray high. Then she sat in the corner of the cafeteria and ate her lunch so quickly she didn't bother to open the plastic utensils. And when she was done, she felt embarrassed and looked around to see if anyone was laughing at her. But no one was paying attention.

She stood up then, and walked over to place her tray on a dirty dish cart nearby. She very suddenly felt a spasm in her stomach and even though she knew what was coming, she had no time to react. The vomit splattered onto her empty lunch tray and, to her horror, splashed two popular girls that were walking by. They cried out in disgust and yelled at the girl. People around them started laughing as they hurled insults at her while wiping the sick off of their faces.

The girl had never been the center of attention before and didn't know what to do. Tears welled in her eyes and when the girls started demanding she tell them her name, the girl dropped the tray splattering watery vomit onto the floor and ran from the cafeteria.

She didn't stop to grab her backpack or run for the bathroom to clean herself; instead she ran down the hall, out the front doors and onto the street that led her home. She couldn't bring herself to take the shortcut through Dr. Danner's property and by the time she slammed her bedroom door and threw herself onto her spongy twin bed, the girl's body was wracked with violent shudders and her skin was ice cold. She buried herself under her blankets and, when that didn't warm her, she tore every piece of clothing in her closet off its hanger and threw it over her bed.

The girl didn't move again that night and she didn't leave her room the next day either. She was hungry, completely ravenous really, but too cold to leave the warmth of her bed. And then, when the hunger would finally have driven her into the chilled air of a hot May afternoon, the girl found herself too weak to get out of bed. She tore strips of fabric from her clothing and chewed them until they were small enough to swallow.

The pain she had felt the first few days had matured into an intense, throbbing agony which rode a wave from her toes to her head and then back again. Within a day she could no longer move her limbs and the pain was approaching its crescendo while the hunger drove her insane. And though she tried to remain quiet and not disturb her family her efforts were in vain. She awoke one day writhing in her sweat-covered sheets and moaning loudly. Within minutes her mother came into the room, throwing open her door and screaming, threatening her father's punishment.

The girl moaned louder and her mother came over to her bed and slapped the girl hard in the face. And then, when her mother raised a bony hand to hit the girl again, she froze. The blood drained from her impossibly pale face and Mrs. Moore

began screaming for her husband. The girl's father arrived
then, more annoyed than angry, with four curious teenage sons
in tow. They all piled into the room and immediately began
coughing and complaining of the awful smell.

The family crowded around the girl's bed and though her
mother was horrified at what she saw, the girl's four brothers
laughed. Mr. Moore ordered his sons from the room then and
closed the door behind them. He and Mrs. Moore had a short,
urgent conversation about whether to call a doctor and cough
up the fee for a house call or to leave the girl sequestered in
her room and wait to see what happened. They couldn't be
blamed, after all, if she succumbed to a sickness that wasn't
their fault.

And as they argued the girl tried to offer them a third
option, but all that came from her was a wet, rattling breath of
air. *Kill me*, she tried to beg them while they spoke as if she
wasn't there. *Please, Mama, it hurts so much.* In the end, Mr.
Moore decided to fetch their neighbor, Richard Danner, who
was a veterinarian. The girl's father wagered that the good
doctor would be neighborly and look over his daughter for
free, thereby fulfilling Mr. and Mrs. Moore's legal
responsibilities to their child's welfare.

Though the girl was frozen solid through there was a
warming in her stomach at the mention of Dr. Danner. He was
a nice man, the girl could tell, and she thought that when she
grew up she may marry him. Though they'd never exchanged a
word between them, Dr. Danner always smiled at her. He

always saw her. And she knew that he loved animals as much as she did. The girl used to sneak onto his property as often as she could to watch him service his livestock or birth a foal. *He must know that they were meant to be together. He must feel it, too.* The girl spent a considerable reserve of her remaining energy to painfully reach up and smooth her hair. It burned like her arm was on fire. The girl's mother noticed her efforts and sneered then spat out a cruel word.

Dr. Danner, for his part, was hard pressed to remember that the Moores had a daughter at all. And when he entered the girl's bedroom and encountered the potent smell of decay, he briefly wondered if the simple Moores simply hadn't realized their daughter had died in her sleep some time ago.

The child was surely dead. Her skin was yellow and her hands and arms stiff with rigor mortis but when he approached, her glassy eyes followed him. He felt a quickening in his heart and knew that the creature before him was wholly unnatural and medically impossible. There was nothing that could save her, but he wondered in a panic if perhaps a call to the CDC could save others. Though he felt for the living corpse lying before him, Dr. Danner knew he couldn't touch her.

"Hello, I'm Doctor Danner. Do you remember when you first got sick?"

She did. The girl knew that her condition was mirroring that of the creature she buried in the woods a couple weeks before. The sick smell coming off of their bodies was identical.

She coerced her stiffening tongue to move in her mouth and forced air out of her lungs. Yes

"Do you remember who got you sick?"

Again she tried to tell him but nothing resembling the English language came out of her mouth and she blinked away the tears that strangely didn't come. She was horrified that her future husband was seeing her in this state and embarrassed that she couldn't answer his questions. She could see Dr. Danner was disappointed in her and that he was trying hard not to choke on the smell of her rotting body.

"Was it a person? One blink for yes, two blinks for no."

She blinked twice.

"Good. Was it something you ate?"

The girl again blinked twice.

"Do you know what it was?"

She blinked once and forced the word 'animal' through her slowly hardening lips.

"What kind of animal?"

The girl stared at him and Dr. Danner knew he didn't have much time left.

"Where is the animal that got you sick?"

Her mouth was almost stone now and her lungs were only pulling in tiny wisps of cold air. But the girl couldn't let him down, she wouldn't. With the last bit of strength and breath her body possessed, she managed a broken 'buried him' and then could move no more.

Dr. Danner watched the young girl slip into the ether and

then stood up and left the room. He found no concerned relatives hovering outside the bedroom door. When he descended the stairs, he saw the Moore family going about their daily routines. Mr. Moore nodded to him but didn't inquire about his daughter and the doctor slipped out the back door of the Moore home and pulled out his phone as he walked back to his property.

The conversation with the CDC was short and ended with their promise to send someone out to the Moore homestead the following day. The woman on the phone asked Dr. Danner to keep the body quarantined and Dr. Danner said he would try. Just before the call ended, Dr. Danner remembered to mention the dead animal the girl had been in contact with in the days before her illness.

At the Moore household, the girl waited for God to either ferry her away from the mortal plane or heal her body through miracle. She could not decide which she preferred. The girl could no longer move any part of her body, nor draw air into her lungs—yet she was decidedly still alive. She stared at the door, the last place she had moved her eyes before the stiffness had taken them, and waited for something to happen. She waited many long hours.

And then, after night had fallen, the pain drained away from her like sand in an hourglass. And as it left her limbs one by one she felt parts of her body moving again. First her fingers, then her hands, her arms and legs and finally her eyes and mouth. She tried to yell for her parents but found there was no air to push out of her chest. She was no longer breathing.

Then, through no voluntary action of her own, the girl's body sat up. It turned its head and looked around the room. It got off the bed and walked to the door and stopped. And then it opened the door.

The girl was screaming inside her mind, frightened and imprisoned in her own body. Who was controlling it? What did it want? She could see and feel and hear but the actions of her body were not her own. She felt hungry and thirsty and very alert. There was an unfamiliar dominating necessity in her cells and this new hunger was governing the movements of her body.

It walked down the stairs and when her brothers saw her, they laughed. They laughed. The girl wondered what she must look like to make them laugh so hard and then her body was moving very fast. It reached one of her brothers and her teeth tore into the soft skin of his neck and ripped the muscle from it. The girl was horrified but she couldn't stop her hands and mouth from ripping through her brother's flesh. At first she experienced his death from the outside, as if she were merely a spectator at a gruesome play. But then she realized that she could feel it and that it tasted good… it felt good.

Her brother fell to the floor in a puddle of flesh scraps and viscera. To her horror the girl found she was savoring the taste of his meat. She tried to spit it out in disgust but she was merely a passenger in her own corpse and it continued to chew and swallow its food. The girl's body had barely finished what was in her mouth when it lunged at another of her screaming brothers. When it had finished with him, it bounded up with surprising agility and followed the smell of her mother's flesh into the sewing room. When it found her it lunged like a predator and tore the skin from the woman's arms. The girl felt something hard hit the back of her head and heard the bones crunch in her skull though there was no pain. Her body turned around and leapt onto her father's chest, biting into his cheek and tearing the greasy fat of his face away. He threw her across the room and the girl realized as it rose to its feet that she was cheering for her body and the flesh it was consuming. *Escape! Run! Eat!*

From down the hall she heard the screen door slam and she saw another of her brothers running away from the house. The hunger washed over her, never satisfied, and the body was running, faster than she had ever run when it was hers, sprinting toward the boy. She tackled him and bit into the thin skin that covered the back of his skull. Her body took its time with that one and had eaten quite a bit of his back before the force of a bullet catapulted her off of the body and into the dirt.

The girl's eyes looked down as her body stood up and she noticed the long, slimy tubes from her insides hanging down from her stomach, swinging in the dirt. She screamed at her body to shove them back into her stomach but it didn't heed her. She was still a prisoner.

The girl's body let out a guttural wail and ran into the woods. As her body ran past the crude grave she had made for the creature days before she noticed the dirt was disturbed. Perhaps her Forest Friend had escaped death as well. Perhaps they could form a new family. A stronger family. She wanted to call out to her Forest Family that she was locked away in her own mind, conscious to bear witness to all the horror her body wrought upon human flesh.

The CDC arrived two days later to a town under martial law. They were everywhere, the dead bodies that ate living bodies. They were spreading to other towns. And then, they were spreading across the state.

No one remembered the two popular girls, who ate their families the day after Dr. Danner called the CDC. No one even remembered Richard Danner himself. But everyone across the world knew the girl's name. And though they looked far and wide for her, no one identified her body in the hordes. She was out there, somewhere, rotted to an unrecognizable state. But her name and her legacy lived on and the ordinary girl no one ever saw became the person that everyone on the planet was trying to find.

Her name was Emily Moore and she was patient zero.

Remembrance

I Loved You So Much

By Christopher Bloodworth

I found you on the last day of fifth grade. It was recess and I was playing with Brock on the swings. We took turns jumping from the swings at the crest of their arc.

I used to love jumping from swings, working my way to a decent height and then letting that floating speed take me. There's nothing like that feeling when you're little.

On the last jump I ever took from a swing, I found you.

Brock told me that I was stupid. He said that you were just a rock, that you weren't an egg. I knew better so I slipped you into my pocket.

I took you home and looked at you under the big magnifying glass Papa Joe got me for Christmas. It was a huge thing he'd held on to from his time selling antiques. It clamped onto the side of my desk and a large arm extended out to a bended elbow.

Papa Joe told me that it was used to perform autopsies on aliens, but Mom told me it was an old watchmaker's magnifying glass.

I liked the alien story better.

I put you under the glass and turned on the light.

I could've sworn you shook on my desk. Just a little

tremor, but you shook. Your egg was a dark shade of red with little shiny black flecks dotting the surface. The flecks reminded me of my sister Mandy's freckles.

I looked at you under the magnifying glass for a long time that night, wanting so badly for you to hatch.

You didn't.

You waited until the next day.

I was at swim practice when it happened. I was finally old enough that I didn't have to go to the earliest session of summer league.

When I got back, I ran straight to my room to find you. Your egg was still under the magnifying glass, but you weren't.

Your shell was shattered on my desk, little jagged shards everywhere.

I tried to pick one up and accidentally cut myself.

It stung.

I searched my room for you, but I couldn't find you anywhere.

I found you in the bathroom I shared with Mandy. You hid in the trash can, burrowed under a tampon bundled in toilet paper. I didn't know what a tampon was then. I just knew it was some weird girl thing.

I pulled you out. I had to be careful because you were all legs. Twelve spindly legs with six joints on each. At the center of all those legs was your body. It looked like nothing more than a little red pebble with shiny black flecks, just like your egg.

I picked you up, and you climbed up my arm. I giggled, because it tickled.

You ran up and down my arm several times before you got tired, then you perched on my finger, the one with the cut.

The joints of your legs all bent at once and you touched your body to the place where the egg shard cut me.

You stayed there for a few seconds. It tickled. Then you lifted your body away from the cut. Pulsing up and down several times.

I giggled again. Pulsing was how you purred.

Summer stretched out in front of us. I kept poking my finger and feeding you every day. You got bigger.

I loved you so much.

Do you remember how I taught you to fetch?

I would go into the backyard and lift up the bricks that lined our planters. Underneath each brick would be grub worms, caterpillars, and the occasional earthworm. I would put them all in a jar and come back up to my bedroom. I would spend hours tossing those bugs across my room, watching you race after them and bring them back.

When you started getting bigger, I started bringing home even bigger things for you to fetch.

The neighbor's canary, a baby squirrel I found. I even had my parents buy me a hamster so you could retrieve it.

* * *

I loved you so much. You killed the hamster.

It was the first thing you killed. The first thing I saw you eat.

When I tossed the hamster across the room for you, you went completely still.

Usually you went sprinting after whatever toy we were playing with.

That time you didn't though. You just froze. I was scared that you were sick for a second, but then one of your legs lifted up from the carpet. A shiny, black fang slipped out from the tip.

Three other legs lifted and three more fangs slipped out.

Then you slowly started moving toward the hamster, your movement fluid as you held the four fangs in front of you.

You crept close to the hamster and froze again, not moving until the hamster moved.

Then you were a flurry of activity. The fangs shot down multiple times, piercing the hamster over and over until all that was left was a bloody mess of fur.

The four fangs brought a ruined mess directly under your body. I watched as the underside of your belly split open, hundreds of black fang tipped arms snaking out from inside, ripping off pieces of the hamster and taking them into your body before coming back for more.

After the hamster was gone, your belly closed and the fangs at the tips of those four legs slipped back inside. You skittered across the carpet and pulsed up and down on your legs, purring at me.

I was so proud.

I pet the greasy-looking fur on your back and smiled, thinking we were going to need a bigger hamster.

You found one the next morning.

Actually you found three.

Mom. Dad. Mandy.

I saw the bloody mess you left in their beds and started to cry. I'd never felt a loss so pointed that it ached. People were going to take you. They might even kill you and that sent me right back to tears.

I wasn't about to let that happen.

I took you to the forest by the neighborhood pool that Brock and I used to play in. You let me put you in a duffle bag. We went there and I hugged you. You wrapped all your legs around me and I felt your belly split open. All those fangs inside you caressed my face and neck. It reminded me of how a puppy will lick you when it knows that you're sad.

By this point I was crying again. I think you knew I was crying and didn't want me to feel bad.

I turned my back on you and listened to you skitter off into the forest.

I still miss you every day. You were the best friend I ever had. I loved you so much and if they ever let me out of here, I'm going to come live with you in the forest forever.

Pride

In The Throes

By Rona Vaselaar

When I was a kid, my mother and I saw a homeless man sitting in the gutter outside of our house. My mother made the mistake of turning away from me while she called the police, intending to report him. Imagine her shock when she looked out the window to describe his appearance to the officer and saw me chatting with him. She ran out practically screaming at me to get away from him. Fortunately for me, he was a nice man—just a little down on his luck. When she yanked me unceremoniously away from the street, the man responded by thanking her.

"Your little girl just gave me her allowance money," he said with a smile, holding out the four little coins my dad had given me that morning. "You're raising a very generous, kind little girl, ma'am."

When my mom tells that story now, she laughs, although I can sense the slight exasperation hiding behind her words.

"After all, you've always been my sweet, compassionate little girl," she says, before adding, "if just a little too trusting."

What I've never told her is that I went out to the man because I could feel his pain—the depression, the cold, the gnawing hunger—as though it were my own, and I desperately wanted to get rid of it for him. For me.

* * *

My life was stable, predictable, up until a few months ago. It looked a little something like this:

I would walk to school each morning with my best friend, Stephanie. Some mornings, I'd feel nothing out of the ordinary. Other days, I'd feel marks smarting on my arm. They weren't really there, and if you looked at my skin, it would be smooth and unblemished. But I could feel them—the cuts. Stephanie's cuts. And I knew that if I lifted up her sleeves on those mornings I'd see fresh blood.

My morning would go by otherwise unimpeded, breezing through my Spanish, Math, and Biology classes.

At lunch, I'd sit with Stephanie, Matt, and Hyacinth. Sometimes, my head would begin to throb and the harsh fluorescent lights of the cafeteria would stab my eyes, so I'd take Hyacinth to the nurse's office to get something for her migraine. Sometimes, I would feel aching bruises covering my back and torso, and I'd know Matt's father had come home drunk the night before.

Afternoon classes—P.E., English Lit, Psychology, Homeroom. My favorite teacher was Mrs. Hill, for Homeroom. When her depression was particularly bad, I could feel my own spirit grind to a halt and the colors begin to fade out of life's expressions. I tried to spend a little extra time talking to her on those days, leaving once I felt the terrible weight of her illness lighten just a bit.

I'd go home. I'd stay home. Because it's hard spending my days feeling other people's pain.

I try to use it as best I can. Maybe it's because I feel guilty —after all, a person's pain is private, and I shouldn't be privy to it. So, when I am able, I try to take responsibility for the pain I shouldn't be seeing.

I would draw butterflies on Stephanie's arms so she wouldn't mar them with cuts. I would buy Matt chocolate bars from the vending machines during lunch because they're his favorite. I would give Hyacinth back rubs when I felt the strain coming on.

Mostly, I just tried to make it through the day.

* * *

Once, when I went to Stephanie's house after school, she spoke up as I was cleaning her new cuts and said, "How do you do that?"

"Do what?" I asked.

"When I'm around you, my cuts just don't hurt as much anymore. Why?"

I considered that carefully before answering her. She'd known some of the truth for a long time, might as well tell her the rest.

"I don't just feel your pain... I share it."

She didn't seem surprised by that. She simply asked, "Do you want to?"

I thought for a moment before shrugging in response. I didn't want her to know how I really felt.

No, I don't want this. I wish I weren't this way. But I'll bear it, because I think someone has to.

* * *

I don't always have to be next to the person to feel their pain. If it is intense enough, if it is visceral enough, it can break through the space separating us and make itself known.

When Stephanie slit her wrists, I could feel the blood ebb out of me, the darkness flooding in on the heels of her ragged skin. I barely managed to call the police before I passed out. The thing is, they traced the call to my house and arrived there instead.

Yes, I felt death. It was like something was being pulled out of me. Perhaps it was a thread. A thread that kept my insides sewn together in some sort of cohesion. Death pulled it out, my insides collapsed, and the pain was unbearable, but only for a moment.

Then it was darkness.

And then it was gone. Everything, I mean.

That's death.

* * *

After Stephanie died, my pain overwhelmed me. That can happen when there's no one to share it with you. It's funny—I share the pain of others all the time, but no one shares my pain.

My grades dropped and depression crept up on me. Blame lurked dark in the background, sneaking out to claw at me in quiet moments. I wasn't much like myself, I admit. I tried to be.

One morning when I came downstairs for school, I got a flash of pain. From my mother, that time. It was a different kind of pain, one that wasn't usually strong enough to be felt. That day it was.

Regret.

I felt her regret for having me, raising me. Because watching me pained her, and she wanted to get rid of that pain. She didn't want to share it. So she regretted me.

Of course, it was only a moment. And then it was replaced, I presume, by love. But I can't share love.

I left the house without revealing what I'd felt. I didn't go to school that day. Instead, I walked. For hours it seemed. I walked until I didn't recognize the streets and neighborhoods. I didn't respond to anyone who saw me, didn't return any of the vapid greetings that fluttered around me. I just walked and wondered why I was fated to the kind of life I lived. A life of pain that I didn't deserve.

I walked.

The day faded into twilight. Traffic began to pick up as people went home from work and school.

I walked.

The stars began to peek out of the sky, giving me strange looks that I dared not return. A few people catcalled me. Someone brushed a hand through my hair.

I walked.

A few cops whispered as I walked by, but didn't stop me. The empty alleys lining the streets began to look inviting.

I stopped walking. Because my feet hurt, because my dry throat hurt, because my heart hurt.

I sat at the edge of an alley, not really caring what happened to me, so long as the only pain I felt was my own.

I sat there for my own little eternity, unaware that I was being watched by someone just outside my line of sight. I became aware of the gaze when I felt a light tapping on my shoulder.

An elderly man, at least in his late 60s, maybe early 70s, with thick wire-rimmed glasses and white hair that clung in wisps to his skull.

"Excuse me, young miss, are you lost?" he asked.

I didn't know how to answer that. In truth, I'd walked so long that I didn't really know how to get back home. But I didn't want to go home anyway, so did it matter?

"I guess," I answered.

He continued to watch me as my mind drifted off into space again, searching my memories for answers to questions

I'd always been too afraid to ask.

He interrupted me again, saying, "If you don't have anywhere to go, why not come home with me? I live just a few miles away from here."

As my mother says, I am, by nature, a trusting person, perhaps because there is so little that people can conceal from me. For the first time in many years, I closed my eyes and extended my power willingly, feeling for the man with whom I had no prior connection. Usually, I don't feel someone's pain unless I reach out for it, the exception being for those with whom I'm extremely close. I could feel myself connecting to him in that moment, and he was blissfully, perfectly devoid of pain.

Perfect.

I stood up and he took my hand. I followed him, not knowing or caring where he led me, so long as all the pain in my body was solely my own.

* * *

I spent four days with George Harris.

When he first opened the door to his townhouse, a rickety, decaying structure with absurdly bright furniture, I wondered what sort of person he might be. I should have cared that he may be some type of social monster, but I didn't. My grief and my power had ruined me and I didn't care much whether I lived or died.

He was very kind to me.

There was a guest bedroom on the first floor, one that I thought must be for grandkids because it was filled with little toys and trinkets such as children would find amusing. I ran my fingers over them and wondered what special pains they, too, had seen. When he showed me my lodgings, he told me I was free to stay as long as I liked.

"My family doesn't come to see me much anymore," he admitted as I looked questioningly at the trappings of the room, "and I like having young people in my home."

I spent my days with him in quiet bliss, finally relieved of what I thought to be a curse. He liked to garden, and so I spent hours with him in his backyard, a veritable meadow boiling over with flowers and greenery and life. He wasn't much of a cook, so I cooked for the two of us, and he enjoyed chatting with me while I did it. He didn't ask me much about my life or why I'd been sitting in the alley that day. He seemed content to give me a sort of reprieve from the life I'd left.

Those were nice days.

In that time, I felt no pain, no suffering. It was almost strange, that wonderful absence of feeling, and I had to wonder if this was how most people felt all the time. If so, I envied them.

For four days, I didn't make use of my power. I spent most of my time in the spare bedroom, in the kitchen, or out in the garden. I left the rest of the vast house in peace, not caring much to expand my universe in any way, shape, or form.

And then, on the fourth night, I had a terrible dream.

As if in spite of my days of rest, I was besieged by an awful nightmare. It seemed to me that all the pain in the world came knocking at my door, crashing into my body and wreaking havoc as revenge for trying to escape it. I woke up with a strangled cry, the pain still radiating from my body.

It was everywhere, like hellfire in my nerves and I couldn't breathe through its ferocity.

George, I thought, racing to the second floor where he'd said was his bedroom.

After a few moments of searching, I found it. I peered into the room, my bumbling steps somehow failing to wake him. He was sleeping peacefully, and I knew then that the pain I felt wasn't coming from him.

But it was coming from somewhere inside the house.

Once again, I closed my eyes and took a deep breath, focusing my power. Using it willingly. I stepped softly down the stairs, letting it lead me to the source, feeling it become stronger as I got closer. I tried to compartmentalize the pain, focusing. Focusing. The thrum in my body led me to the stairs that descended into the basement.

When I tried to door, I found it locked. I searched the first floor, but no matter where I looked I couldn't find the key. All the while, the sensation of agony was growing until my body could barely take it anymore.

In desperation, I grabbed the landline and phoned the police. I choked out the address to them over the phone before my breathing cut off and the world went dark once again.

* * *

It's funny how one experience can completely change the way we think.

For so long, I kept a secret that killed me just a little in its keeping. No, it's not the power—not in and of itself, anyway. The thing is, I always thought of myself as a monster, someone to be feared and avoided. After all, if you knew that I could feel you so intimately, so secretly, wouldn't you be afraid? I thought that nothing in the world could be more hideous than me.

I was wrong.

I don't remember the police arriving. By the time they were there, I was in the throes of unconsciousness, and I could feel that thread pulling apart my insides once again. When I woke up, I was in the hospital, only to have my fears confirmed that somebody had died.

Well, not somebody. Somebodies.

George liked young people. He liked them a lot. So much, in fact, that his basement was full of them, some dead, some dying. All of them hideously disfigured under the weight of months of torture.

That night as I stuttered over the phone, two of them died. There were six still alive that were saved. The number of bodies is hard to tell, because there were so many pieces scattered here and there. There were even more in the garden. It pained me a little that they ripped apart the flowerbeds to search for bodies underneath. Death on top of death.

The police don't know how I found the bodies. I could give them no real explanation. I only said that George had been acting strange and I felt in my gut that something was wrong. My fear made me pass out. All of that, of course, is untrue.

The police returned me to my parents. They cried and screamed, vacillating between relief and rage. They wanted to take me to see a doctor, but soon they saw there was no need. I was different when I came back. Better, even.

I know now that I am not a monster. My power has only ever served on the side of good, and I wouldn't know how to make bad use of it if I tried. After all, my natural inclination is to help people, and my power has always been a manifestation thereof. When I returned home, I put Stephanie's death behind me. It was painful and difficult, but it had to be done. I went forward with my life, taking solace in the fact that I could help other people.

Now I know that I'm not so scary, not really, not after I've seen the face of true terror.

George felt no pain. Not just physical pain, but no remorse, regret, or conflict. I've come to believe that he lacked the capacity.

It is incomparably terrifying to me that some people in this world can feel nothing.

Empathy

The Compliant

By J.L Spencer

"You're nuts if you don't see this as our only out," Trevor breathed. It might have been crazy—no. It was purely crazy, he was sure. But over the course of the last few days, it was the best plan they'd come up with. Trevor knew it was their last hope. "You want to live to use that scholarship?" he barked, interrupting the silent debate he saw going on between Zach and Corey as they exchanged glances.

The three of them came to a complete stop on the sidewalk. Huddled in a circle, as if to keep warm.

"We can at least entertain it. We don't have many options here," Zach said persuasively to Corey as Zach's hand nervously found its way up his jacket sleeve. "We don't have any options here."

Corey sighed.

Zach had always been high strung. When he was younger, his hyperactive anxiety caused him to develop nervous habits like picking his skin. His left forearm had scarred so badly it resembled a burn victim's, and sometimes that was the story he told. Sometimes it was that he was out camping and got mauled by a black bear. Other times he saved his four-year-old nephew from a wild dog. The story changed depending on who he was talking to and how badly he wanted their attention. And he'd be picking at his arm the entire time he'd tell it. As if he were acknowledging how gullible people were right to their faces.

Corey sucked in a deep breath. "You do realize this might be one of the dumbest things we've ever done?"

"I'd argue it may be one of the smartest," Trevor said with a laugh.

"You would." Zach playfully nudged him. After a collective silence, the boys peered up at the large sign that loomed above them, announcing that they were standing in front of the same nightclub they went to every weekend.

Except for this time, they hadn't come to gamble in the basement. This time, they wouldn't enter with a mission to come out with swollen pockets stuffed full of their winnings. Instead, they would enter with absolutely nothing but prayers, hoping to be able to exit at all.

* * *

A man in a champagne button-down led the boys past the bartender and toward the basement of The Green Room. Corey recalled the first night they'd visited the place and how off-putting it was that there was nothing green at all about The Green Room. In fact, it was dimly lit with all sorts of neon light fixtures and strobes and not one of them was green. Eventually, Corey satisfied his curiosity by convincing himself the place got its name for the gambling in the basement. The lounge areas were decorated with black leather sofas and the carpet beneath was some kind of gray Berber. Even in the afternoon, the nightclub was entirely devoid of light. Opening the front door was like setting off a bomb.

Corey drifted with the foot traffic and reached the bottom of the staircase after everyone else. It was too dark to see much, but he could make out some worn posters stapled to a wall. 'The Vodka Project' one of them read, with two-for-one drink specials advertised. The place was dusty. He started to wonder if his trouble seeing had been from the lack of light or the amount of filth. *It always seemed cleaner before,* he thought. Or maybe he just never noticed.

The man in the champagne button-down shoved past the boys, making a gesture for them to stay put and disappearing through a dark doorway. The three of them flocked closer together, taking advantage of the privacy.

"I think Trevor is right with all this. If we're going to do this, we tell Marcus we have a plan, not what the plan is." Zach looked over his shoulder as he said this, but not at anybody in particular. Warm air had begun pouring in from a vent overhead, making a large clicking sound as it did, causing a synchronized jump between them. Trevor felt his face get hot.

"You don't think we should maybe be a bit more descriptive?" Corey asked, his tone nearing sarcasm.

Zach waved his hand dismissively. "Just… follow my lead." This ignited Corey. What was once a spark next to a gas line had suddenly become a roaring fire. *How was Zach so nonchalant? How was he so easily rejecting the danger?* Death looking them square in the face, ready to pounce as soon as they walked up to Marcus. Corey tried to stifle his panic, but it rose in his throat. Only to be worsened by the sadistic chime of Marcus's voice as he emerged from the dark threshold.

"Well, if it ain't the three little pigs!" Marcus said.

The majority of Marcus's demeanor was derived from little characteristics he'd picked up by watching gangster movies and years of sitting courtside to the big timers he answered to. Marcus had a lot to prove, and Corey knew be wary of those types of men, where Trevor and Zach didn't. The types of men who feared not being feared more than they feared death, dying or prison. Corey also knew Marcus fit well within that category. Killing the boys would make Marcus look hard to the people he wanted to look good for. Corey knew enough to fear Marcus, and it petrified him.

"We don't have the money, but we can get it to you. Not by Sunday, but we can—"

Marcus held a hand up and flashed Zach a smile. His mouth looked crowded. Every tooth seemed to overlap another except for a single gold incisor. He was wearing an untailored suit which covered a Rolex on his left arm and his hair was unkempt.

Zach's hand crept up his jacket sleeve, desperately fidgeting at his scars to provide himself with a moment of security.

"I want to show you something," Marcus said calmly.

He led the boys to the same poker table they had lost money at the week before. Each of them uneasily settled into their chairs to face Marcus, who now had his hands poised neatly in his lap. The air was heavy with the smell of paint or something else chemical. It made Trevor lightheaded.

Marcus leaned back in his seat, kicking his feet up onto the battered green felt. "I know you want more time."

Marcus reached into the inside of his jacket. Trevor and Corey tensed, wide-eyed and regretful. *He's going to kill us. Right here. Right now,* Trevor thought.

Sweat dripped from Zach's forehead as he held back his urge to urinate. Marcus pulled out a cell phone.

"A buddy of mine, right? He has these fish." Marcus tapped at the screen until it came to life and a picture displayed. He slid the phone across the table. "You know what that is?" The boys started to shake their heads, but Marcus continued. "It's an Oscar. They're mean as all hell and they eat anything you drop into their tank. Worms, bugs, mice, Twizzlers—they don't give a shit. They don't think about what it is, they just eat it. Oscars are driven by hunger, so if you put them in a tank together you have to keep an eye on 'em. 'Specially if they don't have anything to feed on; they'll eat each other." Marcus paused, grabbing the phone and putting it back into his inside pocket. "My guy has a few of them and I just ordered a 525-gallon tank for them today. Hoping to pick them up by the end of this week." He pulled the cigarette that had rested behind his ear, putting it between his lips and quickly lighting it. Exhaling a plume of smoke, he shook the Newport in his fingers at Zach. "You know what I think? I think there's something fucking beautiful about the hungriest one surviving. And I think it'll be fucking beautiful to have a piece of National-fucking-Geographic in my living room." He brought the cigarette to his lips again and Zach nodded, resisting the urge to dig at his arm.

"Sunday. You will have my money by Sunday."

* * *

They reached Corey's by seven o'clock. The entire trip home had been spent rehearsing every detail of their newly decided plan. It would happen. They would stage a kidnapping.

Corey stood dead center of the concrete floor in his garage, readying himself to rummage through the stacks of oddities in hopes of finding their summer camping equipment. The place reeked of heavy mixtures of gasoline and cedar; strong and distinct. Corey's mind mechanically sorted the boxes while Zach pulled out his phone to check his texts and the time.

"We're going to have to do this first thing tomorrow morning. There's no way we can do it Saturday," Zach said.

"Why can't we do Saturday?" Trevor asked, still visibly shaken. His nerves were all surely remnants of their encounter with Marcus.

"The best way to do this, and do it right, is to leave first thing tomorrow morning," Zach rambled on. The plan was clear. They would leave like they were headed for school, treating it as an average day. He went over how long he suspected it would take for Trevor's dad to get the money. He talked about the trek they'd make through the woods the following morning to get to the old abandoned cabin that lay desolate and decrepit out in what could be considered the middle of Nowhere. He explained the expected time they'd arrive and the expected time it'd be over and the boys listened intently to all of it, receiving each instruction and tucking it all into memory, until Zach mentioned the gun.

"What gun? Who said anything about a gun?" Trevor barked.

Zach was confused, as if he hadn't expected that reaction. "You said we needed to make it look as real as possible, right? Isn't that what you said?"

"Yeah, I said rope and masks. Not a fucking gun!" Trevor was yelling. His fear masquerading as anger, hoping to conceal his vulnerability.

Zach moved in closer, studying Trevor. "This was your idea. Yours. I didn't say we were going to use it. I said I was bringing it. Relax, chief." Zach gave Trevor a hard pat on the back and picked up right where he left off. Rambling on about where they would get the phone, where they'd instruct Trevor's dad to drop off the money and what to pack.

They decided on two large duffles. In one bag were bottles

of water and some coils of polyester rope. The rope's color and texture made Trevor think of the kind he'd climbed on in elementary school gym class: bright yellow and frayed; tinged with dirt. In the other duffle were a few changes of clothes, a first aid kit and a bottle of bourbon from Corey's father's liquor cabinet.

It was on their drive to the cabin to drop off supplies that Trevor felt the weight of reality. All that time Marcus had been responsible for his anxiety. Trevor knew what he felt before going to The Green Room and what he felt when he left it. It was all linked to Marcus. Marcus, who knew exactly what he had been doing from the moment he set his eyes on the three of them. Marcus, who knew his best chance at getting what he wanted was to take advantage of the trust-fund children. The types of children who came from neighborhoods that were gated labyrinths of luxury. Except right then, those trust funds and fortunes were nowhere within reach. Right then, it was nothing but holes in a plan with no safety net. Right then, Trevor's fear sprouted and bloomed amid all the possibilities, all the what-ifs of the plan. The risks, the poor probability, and the gun.

Trevor couldn't begin to think about what he'd be putting his mother through, much less to imagine the look on his father's face when he'd first read the text. *We have your son. We will kill him. These are our demands.* Trevor's mind began flashing torturing images like a flipbook of suffering, cutting from one scene to the next. He pushed it all away, trying to find small measures of comfort in watching the pines blur past the window.

When they finally approached the tree line, Corey couldn't make out a path. The ground was a feathery carpet of opal fluff. The dusty kind of snow that got carried in swirls by the wind.

It's kind of beautiful, Trevor thought as he remembered the trips he'd taken with his cousins out to that same stretch of pine in the fall. He recalled the darkness of the woods and how the temperature plunged to near freezing once the sun was lost under the horizon. He recollected the forest's depth and the way the trees curled above them, swaddling everything from harm, like a nurturing mother. And then, in the same instant, Trevor remembered the coyotes.

"We can't do this right now," Trevor muttered, nearly silent.

"What? What do you mean?" Zach asked.

"I mean there's no way we're going to make it in there and back before dark."

"Day, night, what does it matter? Scared of the dark or something?" Zach tried to joke, but his voice was unsteady.

Trevor didn't respond right away, his eyes fixed on the endless shadow of balsam firs in front of him. "Coyotes," he finally said.

"So what does that mean?" Zach was restless.

"It means we're not dropping anything off until tomorrow morning. And definitely not without the gun," Trevor said.

"C'mon, man. You can't be serious," Corey whined. "What happens if someone looks in the bags? What are they going to think? How would we explain that?"

"No one's going to look in the bags." Zach rolled his eyes.

"How do you know?" asked Trevor.

"Because I'll stash 'em at my fuckin' place! Jesus, Trev. Would you lay off?" Zach said.

That caught Trevor completely off guard. Every nerve in his body was like a live wire. Adrenaline pumped and each hair on his arms stood up. It was clear to him that he wasn't the only one afraid. "Look, man. I trust you. I just don't want to mess this up."

Corey offered reassurance, giving Trevor a pat on his back. "Zach's a smart cookie. He always finds a way."

* * *

Things seemed to move quickly the next morning. By the time Trevor reached the cabin, everything was set to go. He stood outside for a moment, taking in his surroundings.

First was the smell. Coyote urine, he was sure. The thick stench made Trevor's head hurt. Some mysterious outdoor sculpture lay chipped and broken under one of the warped windows. The cabin was so worn it looked like it had at one time begun to melt and the freezing temperatures had stopped it dead in its tracks. Suspended in disfigurement, as if it were tirelessly waiting for summer to kick it back into its decay. He could have sworn the last time they had been out there the cabin had stood at least ten feet higher. A stone bird sculpture was half submerged in the snow, so that only its neck and head were showing. Trevor looked like he was going to be sick, peering through the windows and watching Zach and Corey waiting anxiously. *Now or never.*

Trevor walked in to find that Zach had put everything ready to go. A single chair nestled tightly against a wall toward the back of the shack; rope and masks sitting neatly beside it. Trevor could see the gun tucked away securely in the waistband of Zach's jeans.

"The man of the hour!" Corey said as he pulled himself to his feet, the bottle of bourbon grasped tightly in his hand.

"I see you've already started the party without me," Trevor said.

"Nah. Just a little pre-gaming," Corey joked. Trevor didn't want to risk embarrassment, so he turned his attention to Zach.

"Everything in order?" asked Trevor.

Zach nodded. "Yep. All we need is you, buddy." He patted the chair.

Trevor removed his backpack, setting it down with a thud on a pile of glass shards. There was still time to turn back. He could walk out of the cabin to be followed by disapproving glares from the boys and patiently await whatever fate Marcus had plotted for them. But he didn't. Instead he took his seat, positioning his arms and legs to be restrained against the oak chair. His throat was dry and his stomach ached.

Zach got right to work, wrapping the rope around Trevor's wrists and making taut knots. When Zach was finished, Trevor tested their strength by using all of his, twisting and writhing against the twine. Strapped in and immobile, it was clear he wasn't going anywhere without one of the other boys cutting him free.

Once that was finished, Zach slipped the black mask over his own face and adjusted it around his eyes. He blinked a few times to ensure his lashes were free and tossed the other mask to Corey as Corey made his way over to check the ropes. He laughed and took another swig from the bottle. "Good god, Zach. They taught you a ton of shit in Girl Scouts, huh?"

Ignoring Corey, Zach pulled the gun from his hip and in an instant everything changed.

A breeze poured through the broken window kicking up dust in its path and swirling it around. Zach took his place behind Trevor, positioning the gun to Trevor's temple. Beads of nervous sweat trickled onto the iron as Trevor's teeth forced together brutally in his mouth. He could feel the bulk of the gun and how much it weighed by the nudge it gave upside his head.

It took Corey a second to get the camera working. He could tell the others were growing impatient. He snapped a few photos and Zach walked over to see the results, eyes squinted as if he were studying them for imperfections. "Take another." He walked back behind Trevor, but had changed his position.

Zach's hands were against Trevor's shoulders. The gun's barrel slightly pointed upward in his right hand, which reeked of cigarette smoke.

Several photos later, they had what they needed. The demands were sent. They weren't just setting it up, they were actually doing it. It wasn't happening, it had happened. There was no turning back.

Zach paced while waiting, gripping the gun in his hand and kicking battered splinters of wood as he walked. All of them on edge, alert, and saying nothing. Just wallowing in their personal purgatory, listening to each other's labored breathing.

The response came shortly after noon. Zach sported an embarrassingly large grin reading the message.

Corey seemed enthusiastic but was too drunk to find his feet.

Trevor didn't want to know what it said at all. "Does this mean I can be untied now?" he asked.

Zach pondered for a moment. *What if Trevor's dad demanded more pictures, ensuring his son's safety?* It would take them some time to fully secure Trevor back into the chair, just as it had that morning. They were on borrowed time. Between the temperature dropping, the wind chill rising and the howls they'd heard nearby, they were racing against the clock. Untying Trevor meant risk, and they were already risking a lot as it was.

"Sorry, bro. I can't do it. Not until we have the cash," Zach answered. "Work smart, not hard."

There was a distinguishable prod in the hollow of Trevor's gut. He wondered if the fate they were headed toward was any worse than whatever it was that Marcus had had in store for them. Not only was he physically immobile, so were his thoughts. An endless refrain of the same sequences over and over: Marcus, his parents, the gun, the cops, jail. There was more opportunity for failure than success, even though everything had been going according to plan. Up until that point Zach was right. It gave Trevor some peace of mind, but not nearly enough.

Zach was speaking on a tangent about why he should go to the drop-off when Trevor spoke up. Regretting his words before they were even out of his mouth. "Maybe going to jail isn't so bad," he said, both boys turning to face him in genuine confusion, as if Trevor had spoken in tongues.

"What?" Zach said slowly, almost menacing.

Trevor explained, "I mean, maybe we should just call this off, you know? Just turn ourselves in. It can't be any worse than Marcus sending his goons after us." His voice was sheepish.

"You pussyin' out on me?" Zach quickly stepped forward. Trevor's weathered fingers were shaking.

"No, I just mean—"

"You mean you're going to man up and keep quiet. This was your idea. The money is there. We're nearly finished and you want to bail?" Zach was waving the gun around now carelessly.

Corey's eyes widened and he made an attempt to decelerate the tension, practically pushing Zach out of the door. "There's twenty-five thousand out there in a bag somewhere with our names on it. You're the one with the gun. You have protection from the wild mutts. Just go get the money. I'll handle Trev. We're all good here."

Trevor didn't feel like they were all good. Zach wore a pained expression. Zach's hand crept up his coat sleeve while he was shoved through the threshold of the door. The dynamic had changed. The trust broken.

Zach felt it, too, while making his way through the pines. But he wasn't just worried about Trevor. He saw the look on Corey's face when Trevor had mentioned jail. Zach could see that Corey saw something in the idea. There was a spark behind Corey's eyes. Zach tried to convince himself he was paranoid and that twenty-five thousand and risking their freedom would affect anyone. He stopped under a large birch tree to collect his thoughts. There was no way he would let either of the others spoil the opportunity. They had come too far. He had come too far.

* * *

Things had been eerily quiet in the cabin. Trevor awoke from a nap to find that Zach still hadn't returned. His surroundings faded into familiar view and within moments Corey was waving the bottle of bourbon under his nose. Trevor tilted his head back and gaped his mouth, preparing for the small bit of amber warmth to hit his throat.

Corey couldn't help but to feel sorry for Trevor. It was bad enough that he was experiencing a completely different side to everything. Trevor was a victim, as far as Corey was concerned. Trevor had to face his parents, the police, give statements and answer questions. Nothing ended when he went home like it did for Corey and Zach. Corey couldn't think of anything to say, despite the reality of the situation. The best comfort he could offer came in the bottle he had been nursing throughout the day.

Corey moved to check the time on his phone and it was as if performing this action summoned Zach. At 4:32 PM, Zach came barreling through the front door, out of breath and slumped over.

"We fucking did it!" he gasped, dumping the contents of the duffle bag onto the depressed floorboards. Zach's smile was unrelenting as he panted through his teeth. "It was that easy! That fucking easy!" After exhaling a large huff of air from his overworked lungs, he laughed.

"Zach…" Corey practically whispered, hoping to pardon Trevor's feelings. Zach started digging through the money, counting each sliver of crisp paper in one of the bricks. They had been stacked neatly and tied nearly perfect. Each bill looked like it had come right off the printer.

"Zach!" Corey hollered, immediately getting Zach's attention. Then he spoke softly, as if to cushion the reality.

"Zach, this isn't ours."

Zach went whey-faced. Corey was right. They had the money in hand, but none in their pocket. The walls of the cabin seemed to understand, too, as they were washed of their glow and the sky turned the color of spoiled milk. Zach did what his instincts told him to. He didn't even look up from the bag when he said, "We're going to demand more."

"You can't be serious!" Trevor shouted, the chair fighting him. "Do you know what you're doing right now? There's a limit, Zach. A limit!"

"Yeah, there is. And we ain't at it."

Corey debated on jumping in. Instead, he let his eyes dance between the two of them. There was no way Zach was going through with it. He couldn't possibly. Not after everything Trevor had been through and still had left to endure.

"We've been at it. We're in over our heads at this point," said Trevor.

Zach ignored Trevor. He looked at Corey with a pleading expression. "You have to see what I'm saying here. Look at this, man." He waved his arms over the heap of cash. "Just five more thousand and we can use it to try and win some of this back. Just five more, that's all I'm saying." But Zach wouldn't ask for five more. He had already made up his mind. He would send the texts himself, demanding a much larger amount. *It's all or nothing,* he thought.

Corey didn't like it, but he nodded in agreement, which

sent Trevor into a fit of rage. The blond ropes pulling at his
wrists until they dug into his skin.

"You know what this is now, don't you? You've turned
this into an actual kidnapping!" Trevor screamed at Corey,
who could only turn away. "Please, dude, don't do this to me.
Don't do this to me, Corey."

The smirk on Zach's face hadn't wavered. There was no
way Trevor would talk about the plan. Even under the stress of
the moment. He wouldn't be able to without incriminating
himself. Once they received the last installment and untied
Trevor, everything would be fine. Trevor would have his debt
paid and cash to play with. He'd get over it in the end.

* * *

Corey's stomach grumbled. The sun had started to set and
everyone was nearing twelve hours without food. He cradled
the nearly empty liquor bottle in his arms and wondered how
much longer it would be. The howling they had heard
sporadically throughout the day had intensified in both
frequency and volume. It was more like a crooning, and he
understood it. The coyotes were hungry, too.

Corey glanced at Trevor in the corner, noting that his head
was slumped over tucking his chin into his chest. He looked
exhausted. His eyes were sunken inward, his tawny hair looked
like dead pine needles atop his head, and on his waxy cheeks
was a residue left behind from tears. And then he looked up at

Corey. Both of them exchanging glances of pity.

That did it. Corey wasn't sure if the amount he'd drunk had played a role in the moment, or if the sheer potency of reality did, but he had decided that he had enough. He couldn't go through with the plan any longer. Five grand or fifty, it wasn't worth it. He was leaving.

He pulled himself upright without saying a word and collected his bag.

"Where are you going?" Zach snapped.

"I'm done. I'm out. I'll keep my mouth shut, you keep your money. I don't want any part of this anymore." Corey started for the door and Zach stood up, quick as lightning.

"What do you mean you're out?" Zach's paranoia washed over him like a hard wave. His mind reverted back to the thoughts he had mulled over earlier that afternoon under the birch tree and the world suddenly became a reservoir of doubt.

Zach launched himself between Corey and the door. Zach was shaking. Combating the urge to dig at his forearm. The adrenaline coursed through him, hungry for a fight, and he embraced it.

"You're not leaving. We all leave together." Zach's voice trembled, but not in fear. It shook from security, knowing what Corey's response would be. It shuddered in certainty of what was about to happen, helping to coax him to do whatever needed to be done.

"No. I played my part. I pretended to be a monster and now, because of you, I'm actually becoming one," said Corey.

Corey wanted to turn and give Trevor an apologetic glance before pushing his way past Zach. Instead, he shoved Zach aside and walked through the door. Zach let him go for a few feet as he stood studying Corey a moment before reaching into his waistband and pulling the gun steady out in front of him. Trevor screamed and Corey's body jerked before he had fully spun around. The sound was deafening and Zach's ears rang as he watched Corey's body fall against the pallid snow.

At first, Zach thought he missed. It happened so quickly, he didn't know where he'd shot Corey. It wasn't until Zach trudged up closer that he saw the bullet hole in Corey's coat, dead center of the back.

Trevor never stopped screaming. Not when Zach inspected the body, not when Zach tucked the gun away, and not when Zach grabbed Corey's legs and started dragging him toward the melted cabin. The screams gradually morphed into malformed sobs. Trevor's frigid blue eyes searched Corey's body from the other side of the room, hoping he'd see a sign of life left, but there was nothing.

Zach's stiff-legged movements became increasingly more difficult to make as he yanked the body through the threshold. "You know, I didn't see this happening today," he said, trying to pull Corey's face over a cracked concrete step. Trevor's sobs had moved to whimpers. "Of all the outcomes we considered, this…" Zach paused to grunt on another yank. "This was not one of them." Corey's face traveled the splintered floor as Trevor looked on. Once far enough in, Zach dropped Corey's feet with a thud. "But you know, I did a lot of thinking on my way to pick up the money," Zach pulled the bag of cash and the bottle of bourbon from the floor. Sucking the last bit of bourbon down before adjusting the weight of the duffle on his shoulder. "And I think I found my out," Zach said as he stepped over Corey and walked through the door without closing it behind him.

Trevor cried out as he realized what Zach meant. "Zach!" he screamed. "Zach!"

Zach didn't stop. Trevor was so loud that Zach thought Trevor's throat might begin to bleed.

Zach moved through the woods in the direction of the drop-off, thinking of the Oscars that Marcus has told them about the day before.

As the sun set amid the overcast sky, Trevor heard the howling of the coyotes getting louder. Closer than they had been all day.

Obedience

Constance

By Adam Gray

Lids opened wide and blinked once. The sides of Constance's chair were blocked in by piles of deteriorating cardboard boxes stacked nearly to the ceiling. Sunlight shone through Constance's missing blinds and warmed her cheek. The strip of light crept across her face. She sat up and heaved herself out of the recliner with a practiced roll.

She took note that the locks on the door were still bolted and chained. Voices echoed and screamed in the hallway. The residents of the other apartments in the building never slept.

Constance shuffled through the kitchen, past the tiny dining room table and into the bathroom. After relieving herself, she stood and studied her face in the mirror. New crease lines and patches of dark-colored veins had sprung up overnight. Flecks of dry skin and makeup stuck out at all angles. She dabbed her finger in the stick of butter sitting on the edge of the sink. Constance liked the soft way that it felt, but was careful not to use too much. She applied it to her face, smoothing as she went until the crow's feet were hidden. A beauty magazine she'd read in a waiting room once had recommended olive oil to make skin look younger. She smiled at her ingenuity.

Behind her in the bathroom, the shower curtain rod held her clothes for the day, with the outfit she'd worn the day before still drying. Rent included access to on-site laundry but Constance wouldn't use it. She disliked the way that people outside would huddle around the warm exhaust and stare through the windows. Constance worried that if they broke in they would steal her clothes.

She pulled on her slacks and blouse and noted a new hole in her threadbare black jacket. Pulling the sleeves along her arms dislodged a Band-Aid. It tugged painfully at the small hairs. Constance pinched it between her fingers and pulled. Seeing the red-brown spot underneath made her heart flutter. She took a new Band-Aid from the cupboard and threw away the empty box before applying the adhesive to the swollen insect bite on her forearm.

Back inside the kitchen, she opened the cupboard which was empty except for a can of lima beans and stiffened bag of flour. The refrigerator held nothing but cold air.

The kitchen window—the only window in the apartment not totally obscured by boxes—sat over the dining table. Sometime before the kitchen sink had stopped working but after the bedroom door had jammed, the window had gotten stuck open. Constance pondered the view for a moment: a gray slab of concrete on the other side of the alley, just a few feet from her own building.

That concrete building was the regional headquarters of the Kensington Foundation. Through the concrete and rebar was Constance's cramped office cubicle. Lisa, her clump-mate, would be there already. Constance thought that she might prefer the laundry-watchers to Lisa, but they both made her shiver.

She sighed and shuffled her feet over the patchy, dusty carpet of her living room, unlocked the door and stepped out of her apartment.

* * *

Annie's eyes fluttered open as her ears filled with rushing radio static. Her thin hand shot out from the covers and slid the alarm clock's switch to *off*. She sat up and checked on the twisted lump of blankets on the other side of the room. Still sleeping. Ben was three years old and had never been a good sleeper. Especially since moving to Smithfield last spring.

It was the noise. The other residents in the building never seemed to quiet down.

Annie always did her best to put on a smile for Ben. She didn't sleep well herself. Instead, she'd watch the door at night. A few times, someone had tried to turn the handle, and once it had even been unlocked. Money was scarce, but Annie'd scraped enough together to re-key the door and add two door chain locks high enough that Ben couldn't reach them.

The plug had to be jiggled just right in the outlet to give power to the plastic coffee maker. After brewing passable water for her instant oatmeal, Annie put in the grounds and started the coffee. A slight, cool breeze blew in through the kitchen window. Annie breathed in the fresh, coffee-scented air and almost smiled. It was rare that Ben would sleep long enough to give her a morning to herself.

They'd have the day together. There was no hurry.

The lack of work kept her smile in check. She'd worked 36 hours this week. In order to keep her food and childcare benefits she'd have to bring the average up to 40 or fall into a different bracket, but Joy Burger didn't like to give full-time hours to hourly employees.

Annie removed a lighter and a pack of cigarettes from her jeans. She put one in her mouth and lit the little flame. She stared at it for a while, admiring the way that it danced— nothing better to do with the time. Once the cigarette was lit, she'd stop between puffs to look at the glowing embers. It was hypnotic. She took a receipt from the corner of the table and pressed the cigarette through it. She waved her hand through the lighter's flame.

Not for the first time, she wondered what would happen if she just… *dropped it.* She heard a noise from behind her and snuffed the cigarette hurriedly.

Ben's little voice groaned and he kicked the wall between the bedroom and the kitchen. Annie resolved not to think about work or about money. *Not today.*

* * *

Constance pecked at the yellow keys of her computer with her right index finger. With her left, she absentmindedly rubbed at something stuck in her eye. Neither hand was having much success.

She was distracted.

There was a lot going on at the ends of her appendages, but it was her nose that was giving her the most trouble.

Her client, Mary "Winky" Tindle, was a hooker. Constance had seen her before—and she'd be back again. Because Winky had gone from her particular work straight to snorting her breakfast and now to her appointment at Kensington's, she was still wearing a cloying concoction of ladies' perfume. It was a Band-Aid of sorts. Covering up an infection in her *downstairs* parts, along with the rest of the smells. Such a thing could have been bad for business, but for $3.69 at the gas station convenience store she'd found a solution.

If Constance had been aware of the alternative to the smell of perfume, she might have been more thankful. As it was, however, she was very annoyed.

The left hand finally prized a fleck of dried butter from Constance's eyelash. Her right hand managed to spell "Tindle" and bring up the appropriate profile. It was one of the longest records she'd seen. The words and entries populated the screen and with so much going on, Constance hardly noticed that she'd placed the fleck on the tip of her tongue. Winky saw, but said nothing.

"Okay, Mary—"

"Winky."

"Winky? Oh, that's an adorable name. So, you think that you might be pregnant, is that right?"

"Yeah."

"Okay, so what we do here is try to make you aware of all of your options."

"I'm having an abortion."

Constance hated the word. The surety that stood behind it. It was her job to help people. How could she, when they came to her with their minds made up. *Why come to her at all?*

"Um, well… um, do you have a primary doctor? You'll need to be seen for a wellness visit…"

"Dr. Zigler did one a few months ago. I think it's still good from last time."

"Oh. Well it's our purpose to make you aware that you have options. I really think you ought to think about what this means. Think about the baby."

"I don't need all that. They won't do it free unless I get all the signatures, so you just need to sign. Don't get all preachy."

"No, I—"

"Is there someone else here that I can talk to?"

Sweat was causing Constance's skin to itch and her blouse to stick to her. Winky had made eye contact with Lisa as she walked past the cubicle opening, rubber neck dangling over her shoulder.

"T-there's no problem. I'll sign."

Constance signed her initials in the block and held the

form for a moment. If she got even one more negative client feedback… well, she didn't like to think about that.

"Could you take these brochures? This one is for an excellent partner communication class at the community college—"

"Partner? Are you for real?" Winky stood and snatched the trifolds from Constance's hands. After slightly wobbling in her ten-inch heels and wiping a finger across her upper lip, Winky stormed off.

Constance deflated behind her desk. With her head in her hands and her eyes shut, she thought back to when she first started at this job. "Oh, and another thing!" Winky reappeared. "Your makeup? It's fucked up. I saw you eating it. That's nasty. You're a nasty bitch."

Constance closed her eyes again a bit longer. Lisa walked past two more times, concluding that she'd fallen asleep.

When Constance reopened her eyes, it was after ten o'clock. She still had Winky's paperwork to do. She started it.

Lisa should have been filling Constance's schedule with new clients so they could take care of walk-ins. First, Winky's paperwork.

Constance went to lunch.

* * *

Annie rushed in the back door of the Joy Burger. She entered her employee number and clocked in without looking at the time. It would only make her feel more anxious. She took off her hoodie and donned her red visor, then took her place behind the grill. A brown patty tumbled out of the broiler with a wet slap only she could hear.

The lunch rush was starting to come in. A man in tattered clothes sat near the window and tracked the movements of a fly by swiveling his head around. A regular—an older lady dressed in black—pushed through the front door.

Annie flipped some patties before she heard a voice behind her. "Annie bo-bannie!"

"Johnny."

She could see her supervisor through the heated pass-through that separated the register area from the kitchen. There was white powder on the collar of his manager's polo. His mouth beamed a smile of blackening teeth below a face that was too old to carry a faux-hawk.

"Late again, Annie. That's three times now."

"I'm filling in for Sharon, she just called. I got here as quick as I could."

"Hmph. Yeah. I know." His face said that he hadn't. "So… what are you doing after work tonight?"

"I can't. I'm busy."

Johnny swiped at his nose. "I didn't even say anything yet. What are you, on the fucking rag?"

A priest walked into the restaurant. Another regular on his lunch break.

"Something like that." Annie fidgeted and turned the

broiler settings all the way to low.

"Well, alright. Orders coming in. You got patties being cooked?"

"Yeah. I got it now, thanks."

Out in the dining area, Annie could see the fly-chaser now reaching with both hands, trying to pinch the fly out of the air.

Another patty dropped from the broiler, this one blackened and dry. The absence of another wet slap was relieving.

A lady had ordered ice cream. The priest ordered a cheeseburger. Annie piled wilted lettuce, mealy tomatoes and American cheese turning white around the edges onto the ashen burger patty. That would be it for the lunch rush. She wrapped it all sloppily and put the bags into the window, then went to the supply closet. She didn't want to be in the window when Johnny came back.

Annie sat next to the same bottle of watered-down bleach that she always sat next to, near a plastic bucket and a brown tattered rag had been used to clean the restrooms practically since the restaurant had opened.

"Oh, hi, Annie!" said a woman in black. Annie tried to remember the woman's name. Constance, was it?

"Hey! How are you doing today?"

"Doing fine." She held up a cup of chocolate vanilla swirl soft serve. "Got my rocket fuel. Help get me through the day. Did I ever tell you that you look like my daughter? She always liked to keep her hair short too. So cute."

Behind Constance, the fly-snatcher was now violently scratching at his face with his fingernails.

"Heh. Yeah. Well," Annie held up the bucket, "gotta get back to work."

"Alright, alright. Enjoy the rest of your day, Annie."

The fly-catcher sprinted into the women's bathroom, nearly knocking Annie down. She knocked on the men's room and entered. The smell of raw sewage pushed in on her senses. Annie locked the door behind her before smearing the urine and dirt in circles on the floor.

When it was as clean as it could get—which was still singularly filthy—she put the rag in the bucket and opened the door. Droplets of blood were splattered on the linoleum of the hallway every few inches.

Annie knocked on the women's room door and it swung open. Annie's relief that no one was inside was tempered by the pool of blood streaming down the porcelain toilet. She nearly left, feeling sick. Curiosity beckoned her forward, though, then brought her to standing beside the toilet, looking straight down to the bottom of the bowl.

Staring up at her from the pink water in the bowl, perched on top of a runny black bowel movement, a single eyeball stared back up at her.

Annie stumbled out of the bathroom and into the hallway. She ran into the priest and bounced off his round chest. He smelled cloyingly of marijuana.

"On the rag, huh?" he asked and let go of her.

* * *

"Connie? Connie?"

"Hm?"

"Are you alright?"

"Mm, yes. Just resting my eyes."

"Your eyes were wide open, Connie."

Constance blinked her eyes, which were as dry as the Sahara. Karen's face eased into focus.

"Really, what am I supposed to do with you?"

"Uh…"

"Are you going to take your one o'clock appointment?"

"Yes, I'll uh—"

"Because it's one thirty-six now."

"Sorry, Karen. I'll do it now."

"You know that you got another complaint, yesterday? Someone named… Winky? How you upset someone with a name like that?" Karen shook her head, her slack jaw wobbling. "I don't even understand."

"Sorry, Karen."

"'Hygiene and appearance,' it said. And I hate to say, but I agree."

"It's from *Cosmo*—"

"I mean, we're a charity, our services are free, but we don't want to drive people away."

"I know."

"And 'pushing personal beliefs on others.' Again, Connie?"

"It was just a misunderstanding."

Karen looked down. "What am I going to *do* with you?" she said as she walked away.

Lisa smiled lasciviously over the edge of Constance's cubicle. "Uh oh, Constance. Is that three complaints this quarter?"

"Four."

"Four? Really… *wooow*. Didn't Mr. Kensington say that if someone got more than three—"

"Shut up," Constance whispered.

"What was that, Connie?"

"Shut… *up!* I said, shut up, Lisa! I know what he said! I know what that means! I know. I've done this job for nine years and I *know* more about helping people than you'll ever forget in your life. So I said, *shut up!*"

"Excuse me, am I in the right place?" A small voice asked from the opening of Constance's cubicle.

"Yes!" Constance gave a withering glance at the place where Lisa's face had ducked behind the cubicle wall. "Sorry about that. Oh, Annie! Oh, what a blessing."

"Oh! You're… erm. I know you!"

Constance looked around the computer monitor. "Annie! Oh goodness. And this is your son?"

"Yep. This is him. Ben, say hi to Ms., um…"Annie searched the desk for a nameplate, "Hall."

"Hi, Ms. Hall."

"Please, call me Constance."

"Hi, Constance."

"Hi, Ben. Did you know that your mommy's work has the *best* ice cream in the whole world?"

The boy shook his head.

"I'll bet you like ice cream, too!"

"Yeah!"

"Well that's great. Now, I've got to talk to your mom about some grown-up stuff for a little bit. I've got some toys for you to play with though, and we'll be done in no time. How's that sound?"

Ben was already too busy looking through the plastic bin of stuffed animals and plastic cars to hear what she'd said.

Constance pushed back to her desk while she sang, "I scream, you scream, we all scream for ice cream." Then she began to rummage. "Okay, so, I've got your records here. Did you bring your most recent pay stub, Annie?"

"Yes, I, uh. Here it is."

Constance looked over the paper. "That's strange."

"I know that it says I'm under forty hours a week, but there just weren't enough shifts available at Joy Burger this month. Next time I'll do more and it'll average out."

Constance looked over Annie's form. "Well, you're not far off anyway. Thirty… thirty nine? Give or take? I'll tell you what we can do; how long does it take you to get to work? Round trip."

"About fifteen minutes? I don't have a car, so."

"Well, there you go. We'll add that fifteen minutes which brings you up above forty hours spent *devoted to* work. You can't do anything else with that time, so I don't see why we don't include it. So you'll stay in bracket 'A,' no change."

"That's... yeah. Oh, that's a relief!"

"Yes. Now, what was interesting is this address. Is this current?"

"... Yes?"

"Well this is funny—I live in this same apartment building. Just down the hall from you in 209."

"Oh, wow!"

"Funny thing. Anyway, as I was saying. The benefits include some food vouchers. Have you ever been to the food pantry on Le Blannes Street?"

"No."

"Well, they run a shelter for women there. I've heard that they have the *best* food pantry. It's completely free. You can go up to twice a week and fill a box. They even have desserts." Constance took a brochure from a disorganized stack next to her computer and initialed the inside page. "Just show them this, which shows that Kensington verified your need status, and the two of you could practically eat for free."

"Thanks so much!"

* * *

Annie and Ben left hours ago. Constance had let Ben take one of the cars home: a red one. Ben said that because it was red that it was the fastest.

Five o'clock was usually the end of the work day, but Karen—Constance's supervisor—had requested that Constance accompany Karen without saying what it was about. Now they inside the elevator, trailing up to the head office.

"It's bad luck to have a thirteenth floor, you know."

"Hm?"

"Well, most buildings don't have them. Even taller buildings like this one will skip thirteen. Eleven, twelve, fourteen."

"That's ridiculous, Connie."

"It's true. And it's not that I'm superstitious. It's just that if everyone else is doing something…" She trailed off. "Don't you think there might be a reason for it?"

The elevator dinged and Karen and Constance exited onto the thirteenth floor of the Kensington Foundation's Russel County headquarters. A receptionist welcomed them into the lavish lobby made of marble and glass. Constance turned her nose up at it all.

Mr. Kensington was waiting for them, they were told. She thought to herself that it wasn't *the* Mr. Kensington, but rather *a* Kensington that was president of this branch. She'd heard the rumors. Financial embezzlement. Family embarrassment. Sent to Smithfield to keep him hidden away and out of trouble.

The lobby's out-of-place luxuriousness continued into the

office. A pair of opaque black glass doors slid aside as the receptionist pressed her thumb against an electronic pad.

"Robert, Ms. Hall and Ms. White are here to see you."

The young red-faced man in a tailored blue suit held up a finger while pressing a mobile phone to his ear.

"Yeah, Jer. Look, I'm barely making out on this thing as it is. I'm giving you two good running backs… No, I hear you, but come on. As a favor to me? You can't be fucking serious. He's not *that* good. No one is that good."

He waved his hand to the women to have a seat as he paced behind his spacious desk.

"Jerry. You're going to make this trade. It's just a matter of time. I gotta go. No, I gotta go. I got work to do, or did you forget what that's like, you lazy son of a bitch?"

Kensington was extremely loud. He set his phone on the desk and sat on the front edge near the two women.

"Sorry. Fantasy football league. Your husband plays, doesn't he, Karen? You know how it is, then. Anyway," he shook his head as if to regain his balance, "what's going on here?"

"Ms. Hall here has received three customer complaints this quarter. They're quite severe."

"Complaints? And Ms. Hall, your position in our company is what?"

"I'm a ca—"

A small, dry fleck of something caught in Constance's throat. She choked. Then coughed. Constance vomited thick, chocolate-vanilla bile onto Kensington's desk, pants, and shoes. Kensington nearly kicked her as he leapt off the desk.

Karen screamed in shock. Constance was still coughing, unsure where to direct her head; she stared into her lap. Long strings of vomit streaked from her mouth to the floor. She was having trouble taking a full breath.

Kensington's receptionist came running in with a small handful of paper towels, which Kensington snatched. His eyes never left Constance. "I think it's safe to say that you shouldn't come back tomorrow," he said in that blaring voice.

Constance was just trying to catch a breath. Her vision was dark around the edges. She caught snippets of his words as Kensington ranted and paced around her.

"… not a charity. We're a business…"

Black.

"… without *standards*, we can only…"

Then he was screaming "Out! Out! Out!" directly into Constance's face.

Karen nearly got into the elevator with Constance, but looked over the mess down Constance's front and took the stairs instead.

* * *

Sunlight beamed onto Constance's cheek.

The old woman rolled off the recliner without even taking notice of the discomfort in her eyes. Her whole body ached and her eyes were so dry that she had yet to fully take measure of it. Her stomach muscles were sore from crying in a way that they hadn't been since her husband Max had died.

Was Max dead?

The mirror in the bathroom showed the toll that the afternoon of unemployment had taken on her. Tears had worn canyons in the improvised mask of dairy foundation. Her hair had thinned by the fistful. Those patches that had been spared hung in dark, greasy strings.

After relieving herself, she went to the kitchen. The refrigerator was full of just cold air, and she was afraid of what was in the cupboard.

The freezer was filled with stacked cardboard cups from Joy Burger. Constance found it easier to put the empty ones back into the freezer than to throw them away. She took yesterday morning's half-full cup and carried it to the table.

Tiny droplets of rain filtered in through the stuck window. She wouldn't look up at it, though. The only thing out that window was the gray concrete of the Kensington Foundation and she didn't like to think about that.

Constance ate a spoonful of hard soft-serve ice cream. As she used her tongue along the roof of her mouth to take in the chocolate vanilla swirl, her eyes were drawn to something on her wrist.

Slowly, she grabbed one end of the Band-Aid and lifted. A tiny brown spot was on the white gauze, but the insect bite was all but imperceptible now. Constance pulled up her sleeves, fingers tracing her loose skin toward her armpit. Her hunger was gone. Her heart beat in her chest.

She was suddenly taking inventory.

She felt something on her shoulder. Suspicious that it was a zit, she squeezed it. It was painful, but she held on.

Constance dashed to the mirror in the bathroom. There it was, a bit of clear pus oozing from the top of a tiny volcano. From a spider or a tick or a flea. She couldn't know. But it had chosen her. Constance Hall, the woman with so much to give.

A smile pulled at the edges of her face.

She took the tattered Band-Aid from the kitchen table and gently applied it to the bite. With a contented sigh, she finished her breakfast.

* * *

Someone was knocking at the door.

Something like this had simply never happened before. Constance was miffed. Occasionally, neighbors would pound on the door. Or the ceiling. Or the floor. Often times they would scream and then the screaming would stop. Police sometimes came knocking as well, looking for witnesses for one type of crime or another, but they didn't knock this way. And if Constance avoided them for long enough, they would simply leave.

At first the knocking had come in little, unsure bursts, then less often. Now the small pats were as consistent as a metronome.

Knock.

Knock.

Knock.

Knock.

Slowly, Constance rose and walked over to the door. After sliding open the first deadbolt with a click, the knocking stopped. Constance undid the remaining locks and opened the door gingerly.

A young boy was sitting cross-legged in the opposing door frame. In front of him was a woman in a red visor.

"Oh! Thank God," she said. "You're home! I almost gave up."

Constance said nothing.

"I'm… I'm Annie? From Joy Burger? We saw you the other day. Me and Ben?" She indicated toward the boy.

"Constance Hall," Constance said and put her hand out through the door. It took a few moments for Annie to realize why.

She peered at the Band-Aids peeling off Constance's exposed skin, but shook Constance's hand anyway. "Uh, well I'm really sorry to bother you, but my usual babysitter is… *gone* today, and I need someone to watch Ben for a few hours. Would that be alright?"

Constance smiled broadly. "I'd love to," she whispered.

"Oh my gosh, thank you so much. Ben? Be good for Mrs. Hall today, okay?" Annie turned back to Constance, and looked past her into the apartment. "He's a really good kid. I know you won't have any problems. Maybe he can even help you unpack some of those boxes."

* * *

Ben was very interested in the boxes in Constance's apartment. To him each one contained a mystery or priceless treasure. After a slight hesitation wherein he checked for a negative reaction from Constance, the boy dove into the first box.

Constance had to wonder how long it had been since someone had been into her apartment. She didn't feel particularly judged—he was just a child—but she was suddenly aware that she hadn't actually noticed the boxes in what felt like a very long time. Every day she passed by them, walked around them, slept next to them, but never once saw them.

Ben had found a toaster from the 1970s and was admiring himself in the dented chrome casing. The next item he pulled out was a large kitchen knife, and Constance thought that she'd better intervene.

Having spent her professional life working with young mothers and children, Constance quickly got the impression that Ben was left by himself a lot. Probably too much. He talked to himself with broken English and hardly even seemed to know that she was there.

"I'm sure that there is a box of my son's toys in here somewhere," Constance said. Box after box they opened and explored together. They never did find anything that resembled a safe child's toy.

Constance's entire life it seemed was spilling out of these boxes and filling the walkway in the living room. Most things reminded her of Max. She supposed that was why she'd never wanted to touch them.

"Can we play in there?" Ben asked.

Constance looked over to her bedroom. It had been a long time since she had gone inside. Max was always sleeping.

"No, Benjo. Max is very tired. He's also really stinky and we don't want to be around such a smelly man," said Constance.

They both giggled.

When they'd completely run out of free space, Constance suggested dinner and they moved to the kitchen. Constance had some chocolate vanilla swirl from the morning, which she gave to Ben at the table.

She opened her refrigerator which was filled with warm air and then the cupboards. The lone can of lima beans stared at her from the shelf. Beneath it—like a scene from a puppet show—were two animals that she had somehow never noticed. The first was a large black rat. The second, a brownish-orange tabby cat. It couldn't be surmised whether the cat had somehow tracked the mouse there to eat it, or if the mouse had come across the body of the feline and had died of an engorged stomach. The two lay facing each other, completely lifeless and rigid.

Constance looked at Ben, then looked back at their corpses. She picked them up.

"Ben, after dinner, you'll have a bath. Alright?" she said.

"Okay!"

* * *

As Constance waited for the cold water to run out of the pipes, she stroked her finger through the cat's oily fur. Ben did the same with the rat he was holding. Both animals were quite dead. Constance had found them below her cupboard? Perhaps she had put them there. She couldn't remember. But she liked to try, just the same. She was always running an ongoing review of the day's events through her mind. It kept her grounded.

She couldn't seem to remember much of anything specific since she'd left the thirteenth-floor office. Days blended into each other. She could count the cups in her freezer to tell how many times she'd been to Joy Burger, but even that wouldn't tell her how many times a day she'd eaten. It could be a dozen or she might not have eaten for a week.

Steam was fogging the bathroom mirror now as the warm bath filled up. Ben crawled over the edge and splashed the rat in the water. An eye fell out and floated toward the spigot where it was caught in the turbulence.

"These are excellent bath toys, Benny," Constance said as she set the cat in at one end of the tub. "Shush now, kitty. It's bath time, and I'll have no arguing from you."

The cat did not protest.

After a few minutes, Ben was looking quite a bit cleaner than when she'd seen him in the hall that afternoon. His game of cat and mouse had cleaned his bathfellows as well, each in their own way. The tabby cat was definitely worse for wear. It had lost much of its hair which now formed a ring around the edge of the bath and tickled the boy's stomach. The bald cat was pale and limp as Ben chased the floating bloated rat around the tub.

Knock.

Knock.

Knock.

Knock.

Constance stepped one foot out of her bathroom and stared coldly at the door. She looked at Ben, checking that he was okay for a moment before walking across the living room and unlocking the deadbolts.

The woman from before was standing in the doorway, hair soaked and makeup gone. *Was it the same woman? What was her name?* She'd changed her outfit into threadbare sweatpants and a hoodie.

"Hi, Ms. Hall. Is Ben ready to go?" she asked.

"Almost. Almost. You were right, he takes care of himself."

"Wh-where is he?" the girl asked. Annie was confused as to why no lights were on in the apartment.

"Oh, he's having a bath."

From the bath, Ben let out a loud cat's shriek and splashed water onto the floor. The girl pushed past Constance, through the living room, into the kitchen and stared into the orange-lit bathroom. She screamed and took an involuntary step backward from the tub, propping herself up against the dining room table.

With wide, scared eyes she looked again at Constance.

"He had a bath," was all that Constance could say.

"Stay the fuck away from me. Get the fuck away!" The girl ran into the bathroom, out of sight. She then reappeared a moment later with Ben, still dripping wet, in her arms. She sprinted past Constance and down the hall, never taking her eyes off the woman until she was out of sight.

Constance locked the door after her.

That had been unexpected.

She went to let the water out of the bath, but stopped short. The animals had ripped open, tinting the water a rusty red and leaving various entrails floating in the water, hugging the sides of the tub.

* * *

Constance sat at the empty table. All night she'd been up, replaying the evening in her mind. She beamed a smile at the wall as she remembered what a help she'd been. Babysitting, cooking, cleaning—*I used to be so useful,* she thought. Her smile drained away.

"More," she said. "I could help more. I could. I could give more. More."

Constance looked around the kitchen for what she could give, and her eyes settled on the oven. From the drawer beneath it, she pulled a small glass casserole dish. She took the can of lima beans from the cupboard and set it inside. Next she went to the bathtub, and fished out what she could save of the animals.

"The trick is to let the turkey sit overnight," she said as she scooped handfuls of intestine and bone into the casserole dish. "The trick is to *trick* the turkey," she said again and laughed her best impression of Julia Child. Once the dish was full, Constance took it to the oven. A layer of dust burnt off and created black smoke in the apartment. Constance put in her special casserole.

She then took a cup of ice cream from the freezer and sat at the table while she waited for it to cook. Before she knew it, her cup was empty and the apartment was smelling of smoke again. Constance took out the casserole and looked at it. At least three quarters of the casserole was black ash. The tin can in the center had burst and the label had burned off of it.

Constance went to the living room. Carefully she knocked on the bedroom door before gently pushing it open. It came unstuck from its frame easily.

Into the dark room she said, "Mm, Max. Can you smell that? I'm going to take it to the girls' house. I'll be back by supper. Of course, dear. Why don't you get some more rest?" Max hadn't been feeling well in some time.

All he did was lie in bed.

* * *

Annie stared as flames crawled across the bed. It was much faster than she'd pictured. One match and the whole thing had gone up. She took a step back as fire spilled onto the carpet and licked at her shoes. She shivered, skin tingling with the new sensual warmth, then turned and ran.

She thought of the day's events. Dropping off Ben. Getting groped early in her shift by Johnny. Then Johnny getting the balls to try for more a few hours into work.

Johnny was high. He had eyes similar to that Constance woman when Annie picked up Ben.

"What happened, Mommy?" Ben was waiting on the entryway stairs.

"We're moving, Ben. Somewhere better than before."

On her way out, Annie pulled the fire alarm.

* * *

The wind had blown Constance's hair in every direction but down and a blister had grown on one of her heels, giving her normal waddle a distinct lilting limp. She stopped and waited for a break in the cars in order the cross the street. The white fluorescent sign for Kensington Shelters glowed across the street. One couldn't help but notice that there wasn't a scrap of garbage or graffiti in sight in front of the building.

The lobby was similarly clean and empty. When she came through the front doors, a young woman in a glass box set down her cell phone and greeted Constance. "Hi, welcome."

"Hello. I brought a casserole. Can I go on back?" Without waiting for a response, Constance started walking toward the locked double doors to the ward.

The young girl looked positively surprised. "No! No, ma'am. Actually it's full back there, you can't…" She eyed the black casserole suspiciously. "Um, actually we don't allow just anyone—anyone who's not staying here with us, I mean. For the protection of some of the women."

Constance turned slowly in place and faced the young girl. "It's alright. I've done it a million times."

"I'm sorry, they just told me not to let anyone in…"

Constance took something from her pocket and slipped it under the glass and onto the desk of the young woman. It was her employee ID from Kensington.

"Oh! You're an employee? Sorry I didn't recognize you, sure, let me buzz you in."

Constance retrieved the ID badge and passed through the double doors. As soon as the doors cracked open, she was hit by the smell. Fecal matter and decaying food, as well as distinct body odor. The hallway was crowded with women in dirty sleeping bags. There were rooms on either side of the long hallway, but these seemed to be even more crowded with people and their collections of junk and garbage.

Few of the women even noticed Constance coming into the hall. Constance saw one body hanging out of a sleeping bag, so skinny and sick-looking that she wasn't even sure they were still alive. There was a syringe sticking out of the sleeping-bag-woman's arm.

Constance started to notice all of the other needles. Strewn all over. Absolutely everywhere.

The glass casserole dish crashed to the ground.

* * *

Annie walked around the corner from the bus stop to Kensington Shelters with Ben. She noticed the clean exterior.

The young girl at the counter was nervous, like she was waiting for something as she continuously glanced at the double doors that led to the rest of the building. She explained to Annie that the shelter was full, but that a shuttle would be along in a few minutes.

Annie then received some paperwork on a clipboard, explaining the steps and signatures that were needed to go to the other Kensington site.

Annie and Ben had just settled into a couple of the comfortable seats in the lobby when the front door to the building swung open. A red-faced man in a tailored suit stepped through. His face lit up when he saw Annie and Ben.

The double doors that led to the rooms also opened, and Constance Hall walked into the room. The same double doors that the woman behind the counter was unable to take her eyes off of.

"Ms. Hall?" said Robert Kensington.

"Annie?" said Constance.

"You," said Annie.

Kensington was the loudest. "What the hell are you doing here? Stacie! Stacie, why is she here?" The young girl behind the counter stuttered an apology.

Ben recoiled into his mother's lap at the sudden noise.

Kensington turned from the girl behind the counter and again faced Constance, face almost purple. "You should not be here. You don't work for us anymore."

"Annie," Constance said, ignoring Mr. Kensington. "Get out of here! What are you doing here?"

Through the front door came a mountain of a man in a suit like Robert Kensington's, but twice as wide.

Constance would have to go through the man if she wanted to leave the building, but that wasn't what came to her mind. What first came to mind was her need to help. All of the needles in the women behind her. She didn't understand, but she knew it wasn't good. And Annie and Ben were nice to her. Constance had to help.

"Somebody get her—Mike, there you are. Finally. Mike, get this woman out of here," Kensington said.

The mountain crossed the room toward Constance with

the grace of a linebacker. Constance stood frozen in place as he lifted her up by her shoulders and began to carry her out of the shelter. "Take Ben away. Go home. No, not here!"

"Stacie! What was she doing here?" Kensington asked.

"But she had an ID. She works here. She wouldn't have an ID if she didn't—"

"She still has her ID? Stop!" Mike stopped, but didn't do a thing to loosen his grip on Constance's arms. "Just tell me what she was doing back there," Kensington said to Stacie.

"Erm, she wasn't in there for long, I don't think she made it all the way to the back."

Constance was taken outside through the front the door.

* * *

"I'm so sorry, Miss…?" Kensington's face had begun to return to a normal color, though it was covered in beads of sweat.

"Brannon."

"Ms. Brannon, Robert Kensington, chapter president of the Kensington Foundation. I want to assure you that this is far outside the norm here. I'm really sorry that you had to see that."

"I-I know her. That's Mrs. Hall, she's my neighbor."

"Your neighbor?"

"Well, yeah. And I went to Kensington a few times. The office downtown."

"I see."

"So weird seeing her here."

"Yes. And I want you to know that she is no longer an employee of ours. We offered her help, but she refused."

"Don't worry. I don't feel bad for her situation. Some people aren't meant to be helped."

"Sad, more than anything. I think we'll have another chat with her once she's calmed down." Mr. Kensington stared at the closed doors thoughtfully. Annie thought that it looked rehearsed. "What brings you in here tonight?"

"Well, we're leaving." Annie stroked Ben's hair.

"Leaving?"

"It's time to go."

"I'm sorry to hear that. On to bigger and better things, though, I'm sure." Kensington tried to smile.

"Yeah…"

"And you're interested in staying in our shelters tonight?"

"Yes. We, uh, lost our apartment. There was a fire and…"

Kensington raised his eyebrow. "The fire? That was right near my office, actually, I could see it from my window. How horrible."

Annie didn't actually think that it was all that bad, and pondered what it must have looked like looking down from the top floor of the Kensington building.

"Now, I don't usually do this, but since you're only interested in staying for one night, I could set you up with a place to stay that's not a shelter." Mr. Kensington waved his hand toward the doors. "They do what they can here, but there's always more need. I'd love to have you and your son come back to our headquarters and stay in one of our business suites. It will be like a hotel; shower, internet, TV. No charge, of course. Get a good night's sleep, stay as late as you like tomorrow and then get a good start on your new beginning."

"Are you sure?"

"Positive," Kensington said, with a more natural smile.

* * *

Constance pulled herself to her feet and stood shakily, bracing herself against the nearby dumpster. She raised a hand and felt her jaw. Shocks of pain rose around her fingertips. The skin was swelling already.

The strong man named Mike had left her there. Constance wasn't sure which way he'd gone.

She closed her eyes and spat copper-tasting blood on the ground. In the darkness behind her eyelids she pictured her children. Melissa, with her short hair, just in time for senior pictures. Constance had been so angry. Why?

And Doug, always the ringleader, getting the other neighborhood kids together. Playing in the yard. They'd always had at least one extra boy over for dinner. Constance had loved that.

She remembered Max. The way he would always get fussy when Constance brought over people who needed a meal. Or the end. Was it the end, or was Max still sleeping in bed? Doug yelled. He had yelled at Constance about something the last time he visited. Maybe about the boxes.

Constance heaved a little, then let herself open her eyes. They burned a little and seemed dry like before. She didn't remember eating. Something dripped out of her mouth and she wiped it with her hand. Black.

She looked around and saw a pile of dried vomit speckled with cigarette butts blown there by the wind.

Maybe it was time. Had she been fired? Had everything stopped? There was still so much to do. So many people that needed help. She scratched at the red marks on her arms. It made her skin tingle.

Constance let go of the dumpster and walked carefully out of the alleyway. She wasn't done. Not yet.

She exited in time to see Annie and Ben being led into a blue BMW out behind the main building. Ben had liked Constance. Maybe he was a sign. Annie must be a sign, too. A boy and a girl. Just like her own children.

"Wait! Annie! Ben!" Constance yelled. Or tried to yell. Instead only a weak sound like <u>waa</u> and a dribble of blood and drool came out of her mouth. No one had heard her. She felt faint from her brief walk and her knees wobbled with the effort of standing. She put a hand out to grab hold of a nearby pickup truck.

Kensington's car pulled out of the parking lot.

Constance felt like she needed to sit. It was as simple as that.

Her decision was to get into the truck. Some truck. It was just sitting there. Once she was comfortably inside, she saw that the keys were in the ignition, so she started it. She pictured Annie in a dark hallway, Mr. Kensington tying surgical tubing around her arm and handing her a needle. More needles. More itching.

With a loud grinding and after lurching dangerously, Constance followed the BMW through the dark, empty streets.

* * *

Evening traffic was heavy. Eventually Constance got better at stopping and starting a stick-shift but never left second gear and managed not to lose the BMW. She let her mind wander on a short leash, it was even kind of fun. She hadn't driven in decades.

Buildings gradually became more familiar. Constance took note that they'd passed Joy Burger's half-extinguished neon sign.

Kensington's car pulled into a little private garage attached to the Kensington Foundation's headquarters where Mike swiped a security badge. A little striped wooden gate dropped down and Constance lost sight of Annie and Ben.

Constance got out of the truck, which slid down the hill, across the road and sailed through the glass storefront windows of another building.

Constance was busy thinking of a way to get inside and

hardly even heard all the commotion. She walked over to the front steps of the building. If she simply walked in as if she still worked there, the night-time security guard would recognize her.

Many people were passing her on the sidewalk as she made her way to the building, some of them rushing over to see what all the commotion across the street was about. She paid none of them any mind. However, Constance gradually became aware of a tall figure standing beside her.

"Hey," the figure said in a deep baritone.

Constance turned and was surprised to see a barrel-chested man. He was wearing all black.

"You know how this works," he said. "Go around the back. Knock four times, then buzz the intercom and do the drill."

"Well, what for?" she asked.

"What for?" The man chuckled. He tugged at Constance's sleeve and the Band-Aid, now weeks old and re-used, slithered out onto the ground. "Like *you* don't know what for. Heh."

Police cars were gathering around her temporary truck. With her head down, Constance trudged around the dead hedges and toward the alley. It looked different, even in the dark, and she came to a full stop when she realized that her apartment—the entire building—was now an empty black shell.

Constance didn't quite know what to feel about that. She wondered if she'd turned the oven off.

As she got past the initial shock, she found herself standing beside a door, an intercom next to it. She put her back to the burned frame of her former home and pressed the button.

"Name?" came a voice distorted by static.

"Con—Mm... Mary? Tin... der-dle? Mary Tindle—Winky!"

There was silent for a moment. Not directly into the microphone someone swore, "Fucking junkies," before asking again, "Name?"

"Mary Tindle, but everyone calls me Winky."

"Okay go on up."

A buzzer vibrated as the door was electronically unlocked.

Inside Kensington Headquarters, Constance found herself in a kind of pharmacy. Sprawled over the chairs and carpeted floors of a waiting room were two dozen or so people. Constance had to step over the legs of a thin man with a missing eye. The other was spinning wildly in his head. In his lap was a little white medical bottle and a syringe.

Something about the experience felt familiar, but she tried not to think about it. She decided to ignore the tiny blood splotches on her sleeves and instead think about how much Ben needed her. Annie, too.

Then she coughed a little and forgot entirely what had been going through her mind. The lights were nice and bright and she closed her eyes for a moment to soak it in. She had read somewhere that UV lights of the right color were just as proper for the skin and health as the sun.

Then Constance realized she was in a hallway that opened up to a waiting area and she got herself back to task.

She'd worked in the building for years and had never once come down to this wing. She wondered if she even could have if she'd tried.

Something about the buzzer outside was familiar. It didn't seem to matter.

No one was at the counter in front of her, and Constance made her way to the far side of the room, stepping over comatose bodies as she went. It took some effort not to step on a needle or the little white bottles, while trying to stay away from the few who were watching her with glazed eyes.

The doors at the other end of the room were locked, but she saw that the one that led behind the counter was propped open. She walked inside and at the other end of the clean white room, Constance saw a few people talking. She slipped through a side door and into a dark hallway.

She wasn't sure that no one had seen her, so she walked as fast as she could toward the center of the building. The hallways were not straight and seemed to turn left and right at random.

It was a maze.

She finally passed through a few sets of doors that locked behind her before she found herself in a familiar area. The main elevator showed its position as "13." Without an ID card, the button didn't respond to her touch.

It only took a few minutes, and Constance was able to get into Karen's office and root through her desk drawers. That's where Constance found an older ID in the drawer and took it, then sped back to the elevator. This time the buttons lit up and Constance was able to get on.

She pressed "13" and felt her added weight as the elevator sped upward.

Kensington's assistant wasn't at her post. Constance walked straight by and flung open the doors to his marble office.

Kensington wasn't there. The office seemed empty, but she could hear voices coming from another room.

Instead of the dark, hard marble, the adjoining room was dim and soft. Everything seemed to be carpeted. Sitting on the edge of the biggest bed that Constance had ever seen was Annie.

"Annie!" she whispered.

The young woman didn't open her eyes at the sound. Kensington was in the adjoining bathroom, probably talking on his cell phone. Next to Annie was a little white bottle and an empty syringe.

"Oh, Annie, no," Constance said as she fretted over Annie's limp body.

Constance wouldn't be able to carry her, and Kensington's voice was getting louder.

"Annie. Annie! Come on. Wake up!"

Annie didn't move. That's when Constance noticed the

blood coming out of Annie's mouth. That was it. Annie was dead.

* * *

There were so many rooms. All Constance could do was open all of the doors she could find and keep moving. She had to find a way to do more. To be more to at least one person.

Constance felt as if she had searched through every corner by the time she finally opened up a door on the eighth floor and a man was standing in front of her. It stopped Constance cold.

"Max? Max, you should be in bed."

"First floor, dear. First floor, broom closet. You know the place. And I'm plenty rested."

"Oh. But, how? Why?"

"It's too much to talk about here. Better hurry." And with that, the door closed without Constance touching the handle.

She decided to ignore the incident and continue on her journey. Except she would, of course, first examine the broom closet on the first floor. If the Devil himself had told Constance where Ben was she would probably pay enough attention and follow his directions just to check. You never know where solutions could pop up. Constance felt like she was thinking as clearly as she had in countless weeks. Maybe months or years, even. She could remember years again.

The broom closet did not disappoint. There was Ben,

crying on the floor with his arms around his knees.

Up until then Constance did not have much of a plan. The moment Ben was with her was the moment everything seemed to fall in line.

"Benny boy. We're leaving," said Constance.

* * *

Annie woke up with a headache and blood everywhere. Her nose and mouth were covered, and so were some of the other parts of her. Her hips were sore and she didn't understand where she was.

It took a moment, then she realized she was in a hotel room. It wasn't a very expensive one. Annie looked down at herself and saw all of the blood. She began to cry and did so for hours. Her arms itched and curled themselves around her until she was empty of everything.

She was in a daze when she finally got up and showered. There was a set of clean clothes in the restroom. The tags were still on.

As Annie stood in the shower, a single thought crept into her mind. *Ben*. Ben was out there somewhere and she needed to find her baby.

Ben.

Ben.

Ben.

Ben.

* * *

Constance first took Ben home with her. It seemed to make sense. Ben made a comment about the crashed truck in the street, but Constance was barely paying attention. She was busy thinking about why her stomach was hurting.

Max kept popping up on the street while they were walking. He never said anything, but he kept winking at Constance. Winking. Winking. *Winky?* Constance giggled and held on tight to Ben's hand. If only Winky knew how much her complaint had achieved. Constance would thank Winky the next time she saw her. All of the adventures were because of that complaint. Winky, in a way, gave Constance Ben, which made her happy. It felt good to be needed again.

When they finally made it to the apartment building that used to be their home Constance stood there in shock. Max was gone. The boxes were gone. The cats and rats and that really comfortable chair of hers.

Truly gone. Constance had not ever been able to confront the things she had lost. She either packed portions of them away or ignored it all. It was hard to ignore her burning life in front of her. It reminded her of the last job, and then of the accident with her children. The tragedies of it all. The bodies in the boxes. Now they all really were gone. She dabbed her mouth with the back of her hand, saw some black liquid and wiped it off on her clothes.

Constance began to scratch at her arms until she realized Ben was standing next to her. *No one likes a party pooper.*

"Come on, Ben-o."

"Where are we going?"

"Wherever we want to. How about we start at Joy Burger and then go from there?"

"Alright!"

"Ben, have I ever told you that your mother looked like my daughter? I forget her name right now, but she looked exactly like Annie. She was pretty like your mother was—I mean—is. She is pretty."

* * *

Annie searched for days.

Going back to work for that final paycheck was a mistake. She needed the money, though. Even if it meant getting harassed by Johnny and being talked to about her periods and what size her breasts were. Creeps. She was surrounded by them.

Then she found herself at another women's shelter in the city. It was late. Before she could walk in, a couple of men in long coats walked up to her. They were continuing a conversation amongst themselves. As they neared, Annie could see one was wearing an eye patch.

"You hear about the Kensington place up the street? Yeah, man. Place got ashed to the ground. Can you—Come on, lady, you know the drill. 'Round back is where you need to go. Knock four times."

Annie scratched at her arm and walked around to the back of the building. She would find him. She would find Ben.

Charity

The Lonely Man

By Kristopher J. Patten

Captain Grace Parnham didn't mind the games her confinement played on her. She kept her focus on the ultimate goal: to be the first Allied Western States spationaut to walk on Mars. To be the first woman, the second person to set foot in the red dust.

It was a long trip—even with the sleep-lengthening meds and meditation exercises. Sometimes a single sun salutation seemed to stretch out for centuries; other times, the entire strengthening routine streaked past at light speed.

Parnham's control console gave off several slow beeps. She rotated the command chair from where it faced her meager entertainment bay to bring the capsule's landing controls into easy reach. She prepped her systems for passage through Mars' minimal atmosphere and readied her reverse thrusters necessary for a soft landing on the Isidis Planitia. The capsule began to buck noticeably as it struck the first matter particulates it had encountered for millions of miles. The console's chirps increased in both volume and frequency, indicating it was time for Parnham to take over manual flight of the craft.

The first visitor to Mars had been Robert Bell, an

astronaut from NASA, a defunct organization belonging to a no longer existing host country. That was almost 120 years in the past. An outbreak of disease followed by wars over food and water had put space exploration on indefinite hold. Bell had been the pointman for a larger mission, a mission that never happened. A mission crewed by friends and colleagues who never went to Bell's rescue.

Parnham descended through the Martian atmosphere calmly, taking time to gaze out of her viewport at the rusty curve of the planet, the gentle slope interrupted randomly by jutting mountains and crater lips. She looked forward to exploring some of those features in her downtime. The confinement in her capsule had set her calves to aching for a good climb, protesting for a run. The strength training was a poor facsimile for real physical activity.

Like Bell, Parnham was a scout for a future mission, one scheduled to launch eleven months after her own. Unlike Bell, however, who had been tasked with waiting for his colleagues on Mars—biding his time by setting up hydroponic greenhouses—Parnham's landing capsule was equipped with a return vehicle. The design of the craft was not unlike those used by NASA's ancient Apollo program. If Parnham found Mars to be more inhospitable than the rovers and atmospheric scout drones indicated, she could leave. If launch of the six-person colony raft was delayed or scrubbed, Parnham wouldn't die of starvation or anoxia on an alien world.

As she descended, a conical white shape appeared on the

Isidis Planitia. Part of Robert Bell's X-72 rocket. The last rocket produced by man before the Dark Days. Aside from the dust that had accumulated to one side, partially burying it, the rocket capsule looked brand new. Part of her mission was to investigate Bell's capsule for supplies and design. A lot of classified NASA technology had been lost in the years of war; secret production and test facilities had either been destroyed or irradiated by foreign governments or, later in the wars, the US government itself. As such, the spaceflight programs of the new world had to hybridize their own designs from a combination of turn-of-the-millennium NASA designs and scratch. A look at what had been state-of-the-art when the old world died would push AWSSA vehicles ahead by at least thirty years.

Parnham also had an ulterior motive to investigate Bell's craft. Throughout her training, she felt they were kindred spirits. Even before she was chosen to be the Martian scout for her mission, Commander Robert Bell had been her professional idol. She relished the thought of seeing where the man lived and worked. Where he read, what he read, and where and what he ate; how he died: brave and alone.

Parnham set the capsule down on the flat Planitia without incident. She should have been more surprised than she was to see an atmosuited figure emerge from the angry cloud of red dust thrown up by her landing. No other space agencies had progressed as far as that of the Allied Western States; the Imperial Russian Kosmoburo had sent kosmonauts to the moon, but no further. Others hadn't even gotten that far.

The red and white striped patch with a blue field of stars in the upper right corner on the suit's shoulder and breast should have been even more alarming than the figure itself. Symbols of the Dark Days had been abandoned by all terrestrial governments; too many bad memories. War crimes everyone would rather forget. That old banner meant the atmosuit didn't belong to a secret launch by mission control in Topeka or a black flight out of Baikonur. Or maybe one of those secret missions had been sent up and found itself in need of one of Bell's extra suits. None of these were likely, which left Parnham with the realization that there was no good explanation for a living person to be on the surface of Mars.

A strange feeling of tranquility came over Parnham at the sight of a fellow explorer. Her muscles involuntarily relaxed, melting a sore spot that had been irritating her neck for the last two weeks. She made no movement, feeling as though she was welded to the chair. The figure raised its gloved hand and beckoned to her, looking for all the world like a child waving for a friend to come out to play.

As she stepped out of her capsule, the figure waved again, then gestured toward Bell's capsule; a classic, universal gesture of "go this way." Parnham smiled and walked toward the figure, her mind racing to figure out who could be wearing Robert Bell's atmosuit. Rationally, she knew the situation had the potential to be dangerous but, emotionally, she felt nothing but joy and hopeful curiosity. At that exact moment, the side of her capsule exploded and she was thrown violently to the gritty, rusty surface of the barren world.

* * *

Commander Robert Bell had aged, but did not look his 147 years. He barely looked a healthy 70. Long, alabaster hair flowed down his shoulders, lost on the white bodyglove that used to be standard issue beneath atmosuits. His stubbled face was surprisingly free of the deep, ravine-like wrinkles that cut across the familiar faces of Parnham's grandparents. Bell's offer of hot tea, however, did conjure up feelings she associated with her Gramma and Grampa. It was, apparently, a drink popular to people who had been born just before the Dark Days. Parnham smiled and reached for the mug, emblazoned with the shield of NASA, and winced as pain shot from her abdomen to her chest, shocking the air out of her lungs.

"Easy, Captain Parnham," Bell said, holding out a hand to ease her back down to a makeshift couch constructed from several acceleration chairs. "One of the explosive bolts that, I assume, holds your escape vehicle to your lander blew as you exited the ship. A piece of the bolt caught you in the stomach, here," Bell gestured to a spot about two inches up from where the waistband of her coveralls sat, the gray spandex-like material stained a dark rust with blood that had since been staunched. "I was able to get the shrapnel out and suture the wound, but I have no idea if there might be a punctured bowel, internal bleeding, or some other complication. I'm a pilot, not a doctor."

Judging by the smirk that accompanied Bell's last sentence, Parnham assumed it must have been a joke. She smiled, though she didn't get it.

"Bones McCoy?" Bell asked.

Parnham shook her head.

"Ah, well. Too bad," Bell said, lifting the bundle of gauze to check on Parnham's wound. "Just one more thing lost to the world down there, I guess. I knew it would change after the wars, but my communication systems went offline before I could tell how different things were going to be."

Parnham snuck a look at her wound, wanting to see the damage for herself. She thought Bell was probably giving her a slightly better report than fit the situation. Spationauts were trained to give appropriate assessments and Parnham guessed the same was true for NASA astronauts of old, but that was for mechanical situations. As Bell had pointed out, he wasn't a doctor. That was a different beast. The gauze pad hid an inch-long ragged tear in her flesh, sewn back together with a steady, though inexperienced hand. The wound was clean and a healthy pinkish-beige, with only the slightest reddening and swelling at the edges of the severed skin.

"You'll probably want to eat to regain your strength," Bell said, heading toward the airlock hatch of his capsule. "I'll break out the rations and we can have a proper feast."

"Wait," Parnham called. "Commander Bell, forgive me, but I have to ask…"

Bell chuckled. "How I survived?"

Parnham nodded.

"I'll answer your question with a question. Why didn't seeing me outside your capsule frighten you? Or at least startle you?"

Parnham thought for a moment before hazarding a guess. "It was just too unexpected. On Earth, you might feel like you're alone, but you know there are other people around so you startle. Here, I knew the planet was devoid of life." She paused, considering the bacteria one of the rovers had found. "Multicellular life, anyway."

Bell smiled at that. A warm smile. Then he nodded to encourage her to continue.

"By the time I had made sense of what I was seeing, I must have realized there was no threat."

Bell spoke through his smile, wider now. "Rational. Scientific. A true astronaut's answer." Bell spread his hand before him. "We are scientists, all. We're trained to think outside the proverbial 'box,' but that creative extraenvironment —fit a square peg into a round hole with only the objects at hand—that NASA nurtured still exists inside a bubble of convention. It took me a long time to pop my bubble, but I had no guide." Bell smiled at Parnham like a kind mentor. "Let's pop your bubble, Captain Parnham."

Bell pulled several metal boxes from their storage spaces,

announcing what each contained as he opened them. "Food; three years' supply remaining. Water; same. Medical supplies including a painless suicide cocktail; almost mint condition."

He looked up from the array of containers, each representative of his larger store. "These should have been empty 108 years ago. Maybe not the medicine and certainly not those silly half-inch Band-Aids they insist on sending us."

Parnham smiled at his joke, actually understanding the reference. The AWSSA also packed several nearly useless items in their first aid kits. "So what do my 'unshakeable calm' and your impressive rationing ability have in common aside from being two of the only human actions to ever take place on Mars?"

"That's an interesting way to put it, Captain. And, perhaps, when framed in such a way, there is no similarity." Bell studied Parnham's face. "All human actions on Mars are connected, but not simply by the virtue that they happen on Mars."

"Chaos theory?" Parnham offered.

"No, no. Nothing quite so abstract and mathematical. They are deliberately connected.

"When I got word that the instability on Earth had reached a point at which retrieving me was too much a strain on the effort to contain the Takahara virus, I despaired. I can't tell you the number of times injecting myself with the mercy cocktail crossed my mind, how many deadlines I set to wait until shooting up. Days would go by where I did nothing but sit here in this room, needle in hand, trying to work up the nerve to die. Then I'd wake up, having passed out from lack of food, water, or sleep, close the medkit, and weep over my own cowardice. I'd tell myself, 'The virus will run its course and then I'll be saved. Perhaps they'll need uninfected blood.' Then, of course, the wars began. I watched the nuclear explosions from my satellite feed and I could feel my heart shrivel and sink into my stomach like a setting sun. No rescue effort could be mounted in the aftermath of such destruction. I doubted NASA even existed after the first year of warfare; probably consumed by the war or the war effort. Washington, London, Beijing, Moscow. All gone. The entire Arabian peninsula a radioactive wasteland a hundredfold worse than Chernobyl."

Bell smiled sadly and Parnham could see the age in his eyes.

"You don't even know some of those places, though. Am I right?"

Parnham didn't answer, but Bell seemed to hear the truth in her silence.

"One night I came here and got the syringe. I was going to do it. Truly. And then a calm set in. A warm comfort like being a swaddled child with a full belly. I felt I should wait, that everything would work out fine. Really turn out for me in the end. A week passed and the feeling only intensified. And then I heard a voice, almost like telepathy. 'You are not alone. You do not have to be afraid.' Of course, I thought I had finally lost my mind, but even that was comforting; a split psyche still meant someone to talk to. The voice convinced me to do some computationally-intense estimates to discern the time I could survive under best and worst case conditions. Both were grim. The voice told me it could extend those estimates indefinitely. All I had to do, it said, was have faith and open my heart to the warmth I could feel surrounding me."

Bell sighed and placed his hands on his knees, easing himself down to sit on the food crate.

"Does that make sense to you?" he asked.

"Are you saying," she shook her head, unsure if she would even finish the question. She was a scientist, a pragmatist, one who required hard evidence. While scientists trained after the Dark Days were taught to be more humble and acknowledge that all questions couldn't be answered through rational scientific inquiry, she knew scientists from Bell's time were more cocksure. The natural laws were unbreakable confines of the universe. No ifs, ands, or buts. When Bell said he was going to 'pop her bubble of rationality,' she expected him to profess something that could still be rooted in an unknown physical truth. Perhaps some sort of psychic phenomenon. The tale he told her, though—indeed, the evidence of unused supplies before her eyes—had no scientific explanation. "God?" she finished in a hushed, husky voice.

Bell nodded slowly. "I think so. After all this time, even I don't know for sure. Perhaps God, perhaps a God."

"It never told you?" Parnham asked, her curiosity stifling the pain in her abdomen.

"No. We've shared memories, though it seems to remain an enigma. Perhaps what they say of God is true: mortal men cannot survive the sight of the divine countenance. If so, perhaps I would be driven mad by the true immensity of the divine mind. I've grown accustomed to not knowing for sure. There was a time I was angry with the voice, for years upon years after I let it in. Let it care for me. If it could save me, why not Earth? Why not my friends who asphyxiated in low-Earth orbit setting up a missile defense platform that stopped one measly nuke? 'Density,' was the voice's answer. Like a room of powerful electronic equipment surrounding itself in a cloud of electromagnetic energy, Earth is shrouded in a sort of psychic field, an impermeable barrier of collective unconscious so strong it cannot be breached even by the mind of God, itself."

Parnham propped herself up from laying onto one elbow in rapt attention. She always knew, no matter how ardently she argued against it, that there was something more out in the cosmos. Religion had thrived during the Dark Days and now—though rational thought was again growing in popularity—science was influenced by the trend. Scientific research had become more holistic, more pagan-like and nature-worshipful than ever. Despite that position, most scientists refuted the idea of a god. Parnham always felt that was a mistake.

"There is a reason," Bell continued after taking a sip of his tea, "that religious ideals take a jump during population lulls."

Parnham awed at the direction Bell's story took, paralleling her own thoughts. Was that the voice? Had it heard her?

"The story of Noah may be a mere parable, but there is definitive evidence of a cataclysmic event around the same time. In the aftermath of such a disaster, we get the Old Testament. A similar event happened in the ancient Indus civilization; warfare led to the wholesale destruction of several large cities, true metropolises of their day, and the Epic of Gilgamesh emerged from the rubble. When thousands of men lost their lives in the Second World War, the extravagance and glamour of the Twenties was replaced by the piety and solemnity of the Fifties. My communications systems have been offline since sometime during the wars so I don't know for sure, but I'm willing to bet something similar happened during your parents' and grandparents' generations."

Parnham nodded.

"The less intense the psychic field, the more likely it is that the spirit of redemption can visit the planet, walk the soils of Earth, impact the lives it watches over. That's why it found me," Bell said, raising his tone from somber to jovial at the last sentence. "One lone Martian who doesn't have much brain power, anyway."

Parnham and Bell shared a snigger over this.

"Get some rest, Captain. We need to contact your mission control tomorrow. Maybe get you in that escape pod so you can head for the ISS and get patched up." Bell walked toward the airlock again, then paused. Without looking back, he asked, "Do we still have the space station?"

"We have something like it," Parnham answered.

* * *

Parnham awoke to a dull ache around her wound. A quick peek beneath the dressing revealed swollen, hot flesh that looked more akin to a cow's flushed teats than a human abdomen. Parnham lay her head back on Bell's makeshift couch, teeth clenched in frustration. Infection.

There were probably antibiotic meds in Bell's medicinal cornucopia, though she wasn't sure she trusted medication that old, and she had three one-week antibacterial packs in her own ship. Still, there were two possible vectors for her infection and neither of them boded well. First, the infection may have been from Martian microbes. If that were the case, the meds might not be effective. Martian life could interact with drugs differently than terrestrial microbes. Second—and more troublesome—Parnham's bowels may have been damaged slightly, allowing fecal matter and blood to cross contaminate. She would need a real surgeon to repair that kind of damage. Communicating her situation to mission control wouldn't matter; they needed to repair her return pod ASAP.

Repairs went slowly as Bell's aerospace knowledge was built on foundations lost to time and buried in the irradiated bases of NASA. Parnham had to teach him on the fly as she worked and, as her condition worsened with the sun's arc across the Martian sky, even that became tedious.

When the sun finally set, Bell helped Parnham the short

distance back to his ship. He laid out the facts they both knew, but could pretend weren't true until they were spoken aloud.

"This task we've given ourselves is impossible. I simply don't have the knowledge to fix the capsule release on my own. And you need to rest if you're going to survive this."

"So, we're out of options, then. I radio for a rescue at daybreak."

"Captain, you know the length of a flight from Earth to Mars. You won't survive that. Is there an orbiting waystation that can get someone to us faster?"

Parnham swallowed, her throat bobbing hard at the friction of her suddenly dry mouth. "No."

The pair waited silently in Bell's capsule, neither making eye contact with the other. Parnham fought hard to keep her wet eyes from brimming over. She hated to look weak, especially in front of someone she respected as much as Robert Bell. She was also pissed, though she knew it was irrational, at Bell for having out-of-date knowledge. If he just knew enough to follow her direction, they could both return to Earth. Instead, she would die on Mars.

But maybe it wasn't Bell she should be angry at. Maybe it was the voice. The voice that kept Bell alive, but couldn't return him to safety. Was living in solitude for over a century really living? It seemed a life unfit for even the basest insect. And with the promise of returning to society hanging in front of him like steak in front of a starved dog, Bell's hope was dying from sepsis.

Parnham, given hope in the form of an impossibly alive and capable partner was injured in one of only a few ways in which Bell's skills were rendered useless. Instead of help, it seemed the voice had condemned them to a Hadean fate, not unlike that of Tantalus.

She felt a sudden pang of guilt at that line of thought. Those blasphemous accusations. Her Gramma wouldn't appreciate such talk. That realization gave her further pause, however; the voice could sustain Bell without food and water. Why not heal her wound? Had she been too vocal an atheist in her youth? Was this her punishment: to fade away knowing she could have been saved if she had more faith? Perhaps the reason Bell was saved was because he was more open to ideas beyond science. The bubble the voice had burst for him was more permeable during his developing years.

"There is one other option," Bell said quietly, seeming to sense he was intruding on Parnham's silent struggle, her mind running a marathon to find an explanation for her fate and a scapegoat for her anger. "The voice," he said before Parnham could ask. "It could help you just as it did me."

There, again, Bell had seemed to be on the same wavelength as Parnham. Could the voice sense her thoughts? Perhaps she needed to show remorse before it would save her.

Faced with salvation, she doubted its existence. Bell's tale had seemed like a revelation of truth the night prior, but she had graduated to a different mood. A more rational mood born out of sleep and a rested mind.

Bell's entire story seemed like the musings of a deranged castaway. Surely there was a more concrete explanation for Bell's unused supplies. For his incredible longevity.

Maybe.

But if there was, she thought, would it hurt to play into Bell's delusions? Parnham feared that confronting Bell about his beliefs could lead to a situation even worse than the one in which they currently found themselves. Giving in to Bell's 'voice' might make her time on Mars pass more smoothly until she either succumbed to her infection or her immune system fought it off.

And if it was real, she couldn't turn down the help.

"Let's do it," she told Bell.

He nodded.

"I've lived a long time. I wanted to go home, but my home doesn't exist anymore. It died with the United States. With LA and DC. Maybe I lived just long enough. Long enough to be here for you and to pass on what I know of the voice. To help you learn to live with this light inside you."

The hair on Parnham's forearms rose visibly. Bell's words —Bell's not-so-cryptic final monologue—were eerie. He actually believed he was going to die.

Parnham feared what would happen if he didn't. Would he break?

She feared what would happen if he did. Would she break?

Then, as suddenly as it overtook her in her capsule when she saw Bell in his atmosuit, a calm descended over her like a wave enveloping a beach. It seemed just as natural, just as correct. Parnham also began to sense a presence in Bell's capsule, as if the space was filled to brimming with a warm, velvety energy.

"Try to open yourself, Parnham. Outside the box, remember. Outside the extraenvironment. Exist in the ether of possibility."

"You have no reason to be afraid. I am here to help."

The first voice was Bell, but the second came from somewhere else. Everywhere else. As if the room itself were speaking. But it also sounded like it came in a whisper from right next to Parnham's ear. A booming whisper. A deafening hush. She couldn't really tell. And, she was surprised to notice, she didn't really care.

She could feel the truth. Bell was right. Gramma, too. That shred of faith she had buried under denial and rhetoric was rewarded. It grew, blossomed like a flower of life. Parnham let her shoulders relax, tense for far too long. She lay back on the couch, trying to open her mind to the voice. The painful pull of her wound was there, but she couldn't really feel it. Pain without pain.

Bell moved to her side and grasped her hand tightly, reassuringly. Parnham felt her mind rustle, as though it were nothing more than a collection of leaves in a breeze. She saw eons pass on Mars, supernovae and other celestial events watched from the peak of Olympus Mons, the Earth become green, fade to a sickly radioactive brown, then blossom verdant once again. She saw other worlds, other life forms. Great space battles that spanned several solar systems.

She felt a consciousness greater than hers, greater than Bell's. Something ancient. Timeless. She felt eternity enter her.

Bell's grasp tightened. Painfully so. Parnham willed her consciousness away from the melee that overwhelmed her like a sensory flash flood and focused her eyes. Bell clutched at his chest with his free hand, grimacing and struggling to breathe. His gaze would not leave hers. She felt he was trying to communicate with her.

"Cardiac arrest," the voice explained, whispering in the capsule and echoing in Parnham's mind. "When I left his body, the ravages of age rapidly took their toll. My being staved off his atherosclerosis and chronic obstructive pulmonary disorder. It is a necessary death, but it is a painful death. I feel remorse for that."

"No," Bell croaked, the tendons and veins in his neck protruding like termite trails on a decaying tree. "Not me."

The words chilled their way down Parnham's neck and into her arms. The icy fear reached the swelling shard of faith and snuffed it out. She initially interpreted the words to be that of regret. But Bell's eyes gave the subtext of the communication. Rationality prevailed. The voice was not God.

She gasped and tried to pull away from the voice, first physically then, realizing that was futile, cognitively. The effort was like trying to stand under a titanic waterfall; each time she found a foothold to gain her balance, the torrent beat Parnham back down or her toes slipped on mossy stones. She felt an icy bloating overtake her spine, like a shaft of chilled water had drilled its way through her scalp and was working its way to fill her completely.

"It's too late, Captain," the voice said.

Parnham's mind's eye conjured the image of an ancient motel room door being impotently shoved closed against a vastly more powerful muscular arm. With a lackluster flick of the fingers, the arm shot the door back at the figure inside, the chain latch snapping and catapulting pieces of brass-plated aluminum into the room. The figure inside cowed away from the now open portal. Parnham could see that the figure was an odd, 21st-century version of herself. Her hair was longer and curled and she wore a soft, purple cowl-neck top, but it was definitely her face that screamed in incessant hysteria at the open door. Instead of a physical manifestation of the voice, an inky, swirling darkness spilled into the motel room, enveloping the doorway, the nightstand, and—finally—the shrieking woman huddled against the queen bed.

Parnham understood. The voice was showing her what was happening. Or, at least, a metaphor of what was happening. Parnham had opened herself to the voice and now it flowed into her more rapidly than she could staunch. It was as though she had poked a hole through a dyke; the hole could have been patched if tended to quickly enough, but the rush of water had eroded the dirt beyond repair. It wouldn't be long until Parnham was completely submerged in the frigid control of the voice. And what would happen to her? Would she simply cease to be? Would it be like falling asleep and then waking once the voice had finally left for a new husk only to die an excruciating death as Bell had?

"No, Captain Parrnham," said the voice. "I'll need you. This body is the only you've ever known. You grew in it, lived in it, created the neural connections which govern this machine. More than anyone else could ever hope to, you know how to use this body. I need to learn from you. You also have access to the knowledge I need. Until I learn how you work, how you think, how you organize your information synaptically, I must rely on you to retrieve that information."

"I won't help you," Parnham said, though she couldn't tell if it was spoken aloud or merely thought.

"You will. I assure you, you will. Bell began just as stalwart, but I have memories just as you do. I can call them up at will. How long could you stand up to torture of this sort?"

With that question lingering between them, the voice filled Parnham's consciousness with a multisensory memory. It took place in what looked like an obsidian-walled room, though the joints between the slabs of rock seemed vitrified to create a completely solid cell.

Parnham was held on a cold slab of the same material, spread-eagle, by lashings of pure energy. Her legs, outside of her control, thrashed to get free. Each movement was met by a painful and constricting shock from the energy restraints. The air smelled sulfuric and heavy; dirty. Oily. The low rumble of engines clouded her auditory attention. It reminded her of being inside her landing module or a submarine but, somehow, she could picture she was inside an interstellar craft streaking through space.

Without warning, Parnham felt as though every millimeter of her body was doused in flesh-disintegrating chemicals, like she was being rent apart into the smallest components of matter. She, Parnham, ceased to be. All that existed was a being of pure agony, as if each cell was simultaneously burning and drowning. Shriveling from being deprived of energy and swelling to burst with poisons.

And then it was over.

"Or this?" the voice asked.

This time, the memory was not a sensory one. It was emotional. Wave after wave of agony flooded into Parnham. Her children, her spouse, her entire nesting brood had been killed. And not by an errant energy beam, but one by one by the bare hands of her enemy. She pictured their precious faces, saw their black eyes bulge and their sleek snouts open to bleat in fear as muscular hands compressed their necks. She wanted to die. This was too much pain.

And then, again, the memory faded away with surprising speed. It may have taken mere seconds to experience both instances, but she was left psychically drained. She couldn't handle much more.

"I can reminisce about those incidents whenever I want. But it won't always be those, what you could grow used to;

there are others. Pain you can't even imagine, both physical and mental. I lived a long life before being cursed with this partial existence. You will either succumb to my will or go insane. Or both, like Bell.

"No matter the result, we'll fix your capsule and return to Earth. I'll finally be able to walk on fertile ground for the first time in millennia."

"Is that it?" Parnham asked. "Your goal is just to walk the Earth?"

Parnham considered that the voice itself may have gone insane from isolation and was using its most intense tools to obtain such a simple wish. She also considered willingly aiding the voice if setting foot on the Earth was its sole purpose. She could return, then finding a terminal patient to pair with the voice, giving them both a better life. That hope was expediently crushed.

"No. My purpose is not something so banal. And I will not settle for the bicameral government for this or any body that you imagine. My people were once a force against which the galaxy had no defense. We conquered system after system, spreading our influence and bringing glory to our species. Then, we were stopped. An alliance of alien species coalesced into an undefeatable enemy. We chose to follow what Bell knew as a scorched-earth policy; we destroyed worlds and systems from whence we retreated. We poisoned atmospheres, detonated planetary cores, and set in motion apocalyptic seismic events. When our enemies eventually outmaneuvered us, we stood trial for war crimes. We were too dangerous for imprisonment, our crimes too heinous for a simple death. We were sentenced to roam this dark corner of the galaxy without corporeal form indefinitely, to an unending undeath. But, Captain, you have provided me with more. Much more. An entire planet of husks to be reaped. I will send out a radio signal to gather my brethren to this world. Then we will exploit your solar system for raw material. We will build a massive armada of warships stocked with your hearty species and retrieve our mantle as galactic conquerors."

"Do you think all the world leaders you'll need to influence to even get close to making that plan a reality will be injured like me? You seem to need voluntary subjects. You'll never find the numbers," Parnham said, feeling her own consciousness slip into the periphery of what used to be her body.

"We have learned to be patient since our fate was handed down. Did you forget the memories of passing time I showed you? If it takes 200 of your years to position ourselves in the correct political and military roles, that is but a blink of the eye to this damnable form.

"Still, Captain, I think we will not need two centuries. Your species is built for warfare. Truly a thing of beauty. You are far more powerful, agile, and adaptable than my own former body or that of other species. Beautiful and ripe for exploitation; humans have a need for faith, an irresistible desire to believe in something greater. That's how I convinced Bell.

How I convinced you. If we return to Earth and tell stories of your mortal wound miraculously healing after encountering an amorphous consciousness floating around the Martian surface, how long do you think until the already faithful line up to speak with the divine? And, as I heal lepers and raise the dead, do you honestly think there will be many who resist the opportunity to open themselves to the essence of a just and merciful God?"

Faith

Marina

By Rafael Marmol

Memorial Day weekend marked the start of the summer hunting season at the Jersey Shore. Our squad was packed and primed, ready to indulge ourselves in a summer of sweet debauchery. The two-and-a-half hour crawl down the Garden State Parkway was a nightmare of traffic. Accidents, construction zones, and the sheer volume of vehicles on the road made it an exercise in futility. Blasting music and talking smack made the ride tolerable for the first hour. The next hour was spent trying to maintain our sanity while rolling five miles an hour down the highway.

By the time we reached Point Pleasant, it was past dinner time. We were starving and ready to jump out of Ian's Explorer until we drove through the town on the way to the shore. All was forgotten while we drove past the crowded streets lined with small Mom-and-Pop shops, restaurants, and convenience stores. Traffic was slow moving since there were tons of people walking. It was a nice little town, alive with the excitement of the summer. It sucked us in right away. Anthony and Larry leaned out the window catcalling all the women passing. There were a few dirty looks from the uptight girls but for the most part it was all laughs and smiles. By the time we crossed over the train tracks toward the residential areas near the boardwalk, we were pumped up and ready to get the party started.

As soon as we got out of the car, we could smell the salt water and suntan lotion in the air. Our beach house was a two-story home right on the boardwalk. It was more toward the Manasquan Inlet than the Jenkinson's Boardwalk leaving us in relative peace while still being close to all the action. After Superstorm Sandy had turned the entire town into beachfront property a few years before, the house had been lifted and renovated from the ground up with new furniture, floor tiles, and state-of-the-art appliances. The odor of fresh paint still lingered in the air. We took a quick tour checking out the amenities like the home gym, billiards table, and indoor hot tub then dropped our bags off in the bedrooms we claimed at random. Ian got the master bedroom since he drove and more importantly, his father footed the bill for our luxurious headquarters.

"Yo guys, come check this out!" Ian shouted from the back porch. When we stepped outside, our backyard was the boardwalk. It was separated from the sand by only a few feet of wood planks and a tiny white picket fence. The public strolled past our porch. A few people noticed us standing there awestruck. They smiled and waved at us as they passed. There would never be a moment of privacy on the porch, and we were okay with it. We anticipated meeting new people, preferably girls in bikinis, but any manner of dress would do.

"What the hell is that?" Anthony asked referring to the music playing.

"It's Ol' Blue Eyes," I replied, recognizing the song playing was "Blue Moon."

"Old who?" Anthony questioned.

"Frank Sinatra, bro," Larry answered.

"Who's that?" Anthony asked, drawing a groan from Larry and me.

Ian laughed and said, "What kind of Italian are you? How do you not know Frank Sinatra?"

"If it don't got bass, I ain't bothering with it," Anthony stated, trying to save face. By the end of the summer, Anthony was able to belt out Frank Sinatra like it was no one's business. We invited all sorts of people to come over and hang out while the timeless sound of Ol' Blue Eyes played from the speakers of the semi-famous "Sinatra House" nearby. The owner had an outdoor sound system playing only Frank Sinatra music for the entire summer. It was a charming part of the locale and added to the ambiance.

South of our pad was Point Pleasant's main attraction, Jenkinson's Boardwalk. The half-mile stretch contained all the amenities we wanted. Bars and restaurants operated next to game stands and arcades. A small amusement park stood at the halfway point with kiddy rides and snack stands. While those were all fine and dandy, we were most excited about the nightclub on the boardwalk. The convenience factor of being able to pre-game at the house, walk to the club, and stumble back home with a couple of girls was priceless.

We were originally going to rent a place in Seaside Heights for the summer. Yeah, I'm referring to the same Seaside Heights where the Jersey Shore train wreck was filmed. Luckily, when Ian's dad heard we were going to spend a month at the shore, he offered to pay for our summer rental if he was allowed to come down with us for a couple of weeks for his vacation. As a bunch of ramen noodle-eating college students, we jumped at the opportunity of saving money. Ian's dad loved going to expensive places and paying for everyone. However, Ian's dad insisted upon Point Pleasant. He stressed the difference in the quality of rentals in both towns being leagues apart. After hanging out at a couple of beach houses in Seaside, I had to agree. They all stank of cheap beer soaked in carpets and musty mildew.

Point Pleasant also wasn't inundated with unruly college kids partying until the break of dawn and beyond. I don't think he quite understood we were going exactly for the purpose of being a part of the unruly college crowd but money talks and liquor isn't cheap, unless you are a sadist with a hangover fetish.

We accepted the offer after confirming all the hotspots we wanted to visit in Seaside Heights like Karma, Hemmingway's and Bamboo were only a twenty-minute drive away from us. Unfortunately, it required one of us to remain sober, which was a drag, but it's better to be safe than sorry or dead. Ian's dad offered to drop us off and pick us up from the bars while he was around, but unfortunately he never made it for his visit. Some unexpected problems arose in his business forcing him to cancel his trip, leaving us alone in luxury for the month.

Our first week passed in a blur of alcoholic bliss. The daylight hours were spent chilling at the beach, throwing around the football, and pounding down beers at the Tiki Bar. Oftentimes we'd meet girls and invite them back to the beach house for barbeques on the porch and some fun and games involving lots of drinking and the removal of clothing. We utilized the house's amenities with strip billiards and truth or dare in the hot tub. We did whatever it took to get the ball rolling in terms of getting the girls drunk, naked, and in the mood.

Our success during the day was nothing like the main event at night. Everyone got dressed in their best and we hit the town hard. We'd start off with the bar and grills on the boardwalk for pre-game. Once we were good and ready, it was game on and off to bar hopping. More drinking, more dancing, and more and more girls out and about for a good time. We were the freakin' unstoppable life of the party, often closing out the bars.

There was never a time someone went home alone. We couldn't even remember how many girls had come back with us but at the end of the first week, we were all feeling disgusted with ourselves. The sentiment only seemed to hit us in the morning when we couldn't even remember the name of the girls in our beds. It only lingered until they left on the walk of shame and we'd proceed to do it all over again. Good freaking times.

Of course, there were some weird moments, like finding Larry taking a dump while some girl was puking into the bathtub only a couple of feet away. It was hysterical. Anthony had managed to land a threesome notch under his belt with two girls he met at the bar. We were jealous but proud. Ian became a drunk den mother getting on everyone's case about picking up bottles and clearing our messes. We could hear him murmuring and tossing bottles into a bag in the early morning hours. After that first week, we decided it was best to slow down a little so we wouldn't tire out too much before the end of the hunting season.

In the second week, Ian and Larry managed to land the first of the clingers for the summer. One morning, while tossing around the football, Ian "overthrew" the ball where it "coincidentally" landed near a pair of blondes catching some sun. Larry broke the ice with them and after a few minutes of conversation, they came over to our spot to hang out. Alexis and Brooke introduced themselves. Larry made a quip about giving us fake names that sounded way too much like stripper names and they took it in stride, swearing that those were the names their parents had actually given them. I liked them although they were nothing special in the physical attraction department. Both were slim with flat tummies, long hair, and great personalities. Solid six out of ten on the Scale. Nothing worth busting balls over. There was plenty of tail to go around.

Our squad has only one rule: "Bros before Hoes." We didn't fight with one another because of a girl. When it came to chasing tail, all was fair. We thrived on the competition. If we got a girl stolen from us right under our nose, well, it was on us for losing her. We obviously didn't have her if we lost her. It was never personal. Just fun and games. If the squad was getting laid, it was no skin off my back if I didn't get it in with a girl. Always plenty of fish in the sea.

Anthony and I let Larry and Ian work their magic with the girls with stripper names. The conversation was mostly about partying, the college life at Rutgers, and a bunch of other meaningless small talk. It ended with the exchanging of numbers and promises to meet up later in the night at Bamboo in Seaside. The girls declined our invitation to come back our beach house, instead opting to get lunch somewhere else in town. They were smitten, of course, but wanted to make the boys work for it. I don't know who suggested going to Bamboo but I hated the place. I almost didn't go but some last-minute smack talk changed my mind. I was so glad I went.

The squad started dancing, taking shots, and trying to get groups of girls to come home with us. The stripper-named girls, Alexis and Brooke, hadn't arrived yet so Larry and Ian were hamming it up until their "dates" arrived. Everything was going fantastic until right in the middle of a conversation with this blue-eyed, busty blonde, I spotted the woman of my dreams dominating the dance floor.

Her dark, lustrous hair silenced me mid-conversation. It

bounced off her shoulders and appeared to float as she gyrated her hips to the music like a professional belly dancer. The white spaghetti-strap top she wore put on display the fullness of an hourglass figure. She could have been used as the model for the statue of an ancient goddess of fertility. She was stunningly hypnotic. I hadn't even noticed that the blonde girl left me standing there alone with my jaw on the floor. It was for the best; it freed me up to approach the dark-haired woman without having to brush off the blonde.

I don't believe in fate or divine intervention. Every man is responsible for his own destiny. It's his choice whether he takes the reins and makes the world his bitch or not. But there was a cosmic force pushing me that night. That woman was my destiny.

My heart pounded like I had sprinted a marathon. Sweat pooled underneath my armpits. It was hard to breathe. Nerves were never a problem. Rejection wasn't an issue. That moment was different. For once in my life, I actually cared about being rejected. The thought of taking a couple of shots to calm my nerves before approaching flashed through my head but I didn't want to waste a single moment longer. Diving into the deep end of the pool was the only option. It was sink or swim.

The dance floor was packed with drunken people fist pumping, grinding it up, and flopping around doing some sort of thing resembling dancing. The target was in my sights. We made eye contact. She smirked and the whole world ceased to exist. It was an invitation to Heaven on Earth. Unfortunately, halfway to meeting my destiny, there was a commotion coming from behind me where the squad had been standing.

A scrawny guy dressed in a pink button-up shirt shouted obscenities at Anthony and challenged him to fight like he was a drunken Kung-Fu master confident in his skill. Anthony would have ripped him to shreds if Larry and Ian hadn't dragged him out of the club. He shouted back, drawing the attention of everyone including the bouncers who were itching for a reason to crack some skulls. Knowing my friends were in a bad situation, I stole one more glance behind and couldn't find my goddess. Part of me wanted to kick my friends' asses for ruining my chances.

Outside on the street, Anthony calmed down, allowing Larry and Ian to rest a moment.

"What happened?" I asked.

"Skeletor wanted to fight me," Anthony answered still fuming.

"Why?" Ian asked.

"It was a misunderstanding. I hit on his girlfriend not realizing she was taken. Dude flipped out and started shit," Anthony explained.

"Damn, he acted like it was a crime against humanity," Larry stated. Anthony's phone notification beeped, he opened his phone, and laughed.

"Eh, let's hit up Hemmingway's. Bamboo was beat anyway," Anthony suggested with a grin across his face.

"Who's that?" Ian asked. A girl stood in the doorway of

the club, giving flirtatious glances to the group.

"Skeletor's girlfriend," Anthony replied and bellowed a laugh.

We laughed right along with him, even though no one really said a joke. We trooped our way across the street to Hemmingway's to resume the party. A few minutes after we arrived, Alexis and Brooke met with Larry and Ian, drawing their attention for the rest of the night.

At some point, Anthony headed toward the bathroom leaving me alone. The temptation to strike out on my own was overwhelming. No other woman at Hemmingway's even compared to the dark-haired goddess at Bamboo. It was a quick walk across the street. No one would miss me.

Skeletor's girlfriend passed me near the exit. She had followed us to Hemmingway's and was heading toward the bathrooms in the back, where Anthony was. There was no way I could leave. If Skeletor and his crew came cackling around searching for his girl, Anthony would need backup. He could take two of them at a time but there were five guys in total. With Larry and Ian being distracted, who knew what could happen if something went down? Hanging back to babysit made my heart ache. The most beautiful woman in the world was across the street and there was nothing to be done. I cursed Anthony's recklessness and ordered a Corona to nurse for the rest of the night.

Larry, Ian, Alexis, and Brooke found me a half hour later and stood with me making the situation less miserable.

Anthony and Skeletor's girl grinded each other to dust on the dance floor. Being sober for once made me realize how awfully inappropriate they were being. It was like two dogs in heat. They didn't care who saw what. It was all about them.

"Dude, what's wrong with you?" Ian asked, noticing my lack of enthusiasm.

"Nothing man, just tired," I replied, not wishing to discuss it.

"Do you need a wing man? I can totally wing woman for you!" Alexis shouted much louder than necessary.

"Nah, I'm cool. Just not feeling it tonight," was my response. Taking the hint, everyone dropped the conversation and went back to focusing on getting themselves laid. The idea of trying to find another girl seemed insane. How could anyone measure up to the level of the dark-haired goddess? She was Helen of Troy reborn. It would have been like settling for a White Castle cheeseburger when there was a juicy, mouthwatering New York strip steak with my name on it right across the street.

"Stop being a pussy!" Alexis shouted, bringing me out of my trance. She slammed a drink in front of me and raised her glass, downing the emerald green concoction in three sips. Following her lead was a mistake. The drink was straight up hard liquor.

"What the hell is that?" Larry asked.

"Irish trash can!" Alexis shrilled. She seemed incapable of speaking without yelling.

"What's in it?" I asked taking another sip and starting to feel the effects.

"A little of everything with a splash of Red Bull," the bartender answered, overhearing our conversation. "That'll be 24 dollars," she said. Alexis turned and pretended not to have heard her. I paid the tab, downed the rest of the drink, and allowed myself to have a good time. The dark-haired goddess never strayed too far from my thoughts.

After closing out Hemmingway's, Alexis and Brooke went home much to the disappointment of Larry and Ian. Alexis was white-girl wasted and Brooke was her ride home. We said our goodbyes and left Seaside with Skeletor's girlfriend in tow. We stopped at an all-night diner for a bite to eat before heading home. While we gorged ourselves on chicken fingers and disco fries, pork rolls, egg, cheese, and other assorted delights, Anthony smashed out Skeletor's girl in the parking lot. The Explorer rocked back and forth the entire time. It was one of the highlights of the summer. We still joke about keeping an ear out for His Boney Majesty's bones crackling as he haunts the Earth seeking revenge upon us. For me, it marked the end of a joyous summer and the beginning of some very strange events.

The next morning, Skeletor's girlfriend embarked on her walk of shame without a peep. No one ever got her name, Anthony included. With the wicked hangover he was nursing, it was no surprise he couldn't remember. He was out of commission for the day, choosing to stay indoors and under the covers. The rest of the squad decided a day of rest was in order. My liver cried out for a break from the constant stream of alcohol. The purple bags beneath our eyes were becoming a permanent fixture on our faces. Everyone agreed to taking it easy, at least until nightfall, when we would decide if it was going to be a full day of rest or not.

But who were we kidding? With the boardwalk and the beach at our doorstep, we were automatically thrust into the hustle of the summer hunting season once more. Alexis and Brooke joined us on the beach making me the fifth wheel once more. It didn't last long, since Alexis was hung over, too. She left for our beach house after vomiting in the ocean and needed Ian to assist her out of the water. Anthony was home so it wasn't a problem if she went to relax.

My thoughts remained on my dark-haired goddess the entire time. Dwelling over a woman was new for me, especially one I never formally met. Writing her off as a lost cause would have been for the best. Instead, I kept my eyes peeled for her, knowing it was a slim-to-none chance she'd come walking across the sands of Point Pleasant Beach to find me. It was pathetic.

Later in the afternoon, we returned to the beach house for some grilled hot dogs and hamburgers. Anthony and Alexis were hanging out together in the living room with a bunch of chips, pretzels, and a dozen doughnuts laid out. Wrinkly, alcohol-stained playing cards were spread out across the living room table ready for a game of Kings. The long table in the dining room was set up for beer pong with ten red cups on both sides of the table and clean water cups. Alexis was giddy from a glass of white wine she was drinking. Anthony wasn't imbibing. There was no taunting him for it. Red splotches covered the area around his eyes like freckles. He had vomited earlier in the morning. It echoed throughout the entire house. It sounded like a demon riding a freight train was trying to escape the bowels of Hell.

"Welcome back, pussies!" Anthony greeted.

"Someone's ready to party again," Larry said grabbing a Boston cream doughnut and shoving it into his mouth.

"Clearly, Alexis is ready," Brooke scolded her friend.

"You only live once, grandma!" Alexis declared and took another sip of her wine in response. Brooke rolled her eyes and sighed.

"Did she just YOLO us?" Ian asked rhetorically and laughed. We dug into the snacks while Larry cooked up the food. After we were good and ready, the party games started with a few rounds of beer pong. Larry and I annihilated Alexis and Ian at beer pong. It wasn't even close.

Kings took a while to start because no one could agree upon the rules. The girls argued about which cards meant what and who did what when and how. Alexis and Brooke demanded we play with Rutger rules which ended up being a couple of slight changes to the overall game but enough to throw the rest of us off our game. Anthony made sure the drinks continued flowing toward Alexis' direction. It wasn't necessary. It was obvious she wanted to jump his bones. She hung all over him and tried as much as she could to touch him. Larry seemed annoyed since he'd been the one trying to get it in with her and failed but he was a big boy and understood Anthony was in for the easy layup.

As the fun and games reached a climax, Brooke suggested we hit up the club on the boardwalk.

It made sense. There was no need for anyone to drive and if anyone wanted to leave early, it was a short walk back home. It was no surprise that Larry, Ian, and I were down to party. Brooke left to get changed and promised to meet us later.

An hour later, the smell of Cool Water, Georgio Armani, and Versace permeated through the air in a mixture of manly greatness. Everyone was in uniform with their button-ups and form-fitting t-shirts showing off the results of countless hours at the gym. We were ready to go and dressed to kill.

As we headed out the door, Alexis was stripped down to her bathing suit and inviting everyone into the hot tub with her.

"Come on guys! It'll be fun!" she invited, pulling on Larry's arm. He wasn't feeling it. He brushed her off to the side and told her he'd call her later to placate her.

"Make sure to clean the hot tub when you are done," Ian reminded Anthony with a smirk on his face.

"No worries bro. We won't make a mess," Anthony promised, grabbing Alexis by the waist and pulling her away from us. She giggled and squealed. "Have fun fellas," he said before turning the corner.

The walk from the beach house to Jenkinson's was short. Ian grabbed his to-go bottle of Captain and Coke before we left. We took turns taking drinks and shooting the shit with each other. Larry complained about Alexis playing hard to get with him while going to bed with Anthony the first chance she got. Ian and I took one look at each other and then proceeded to bust his balls for acting like a beta. True friends don't allow each other to fall into beta behavior. After thoroughly skewering him, we arrived at the club.

From the outside, the music was pumping. We could feel the bass pulsing through the floor. We paid the cover at the door and made our way inside pushing past the crowd of people gathered near the bar closest to the door. We did a quick lap around, checking what we had to work with. There was a gracious balance of tail ranging from the land whales to page one of the Victoria's Secret catalogue-quality girls.

We took our spot at the bar furthest away from the entrance with our favorite bartender. She was this scorching hot brunette we had gotten friendly with in the prior weeks. Our generous tips made us her priority. In return, she gave us some top-notch deals on our drinks. Remember to always tip your bartenders and they'll take care of you all night. Ian had tried to make it more than a business relationship one night and found out her boyfriend was the hulking man checking IDs at the door. She was beautiful but not worth the thumping.

As per tradition, the first order of business was getting through the "Opening Rounds." Larry stepped up first and ordered a round of Jäger bombs. It was my least favorite drink but there was no other choice. Opening Round shots are non-negotiable. Man up; pound it down. That was the only choice in the matter until it was your turn to pick. Ian ordered shots of Fireball next. Much better than Jäger. When my turn came, I ordered Jose Cuervo and was met with protest. The other guys couldn't handle tequila. Watching them cringe and make sour faces was worth the price of admission.

"Don't be a pussy!" I shouted at Ian, slapping him hard on the back as he recoiled from the aftertaste. He needed a chaser. When he turned to the bartender to order another drink, my eye caught a glimpse of the bodies twisting and twerking out on the dance floor. At the corner of my eye, the lustrous dark hair was floating through the air again. My dark-haired goddess!

"Dom!" Ian shouted and waving his hands in my face. He blocked my view of her and was nearly thrown to the floor as I shoved him out of the way. She was already disappearing in the thickening crowd.

"What the fuck, man?" Ian shouted.

"Sorry, guys, I just… I don't think you'll believe me if I tell you this…," I replied bobbing and weaving my head in search of her.

"What?" Ian replied still pissed.

"There is a ten over there on the dance floor," I replied,

pointing to where the dark-haired goddess had been standing only seconds before.

"You were right. I don't believe you. Tens don't exist. Maybe a nine and a half but never ever a full ten," Ian explained as if I hadn't known the rules of the rating system we'd been using since high school.

"I don't know. Dom don't grade so easy. If he says the girl is a ten, she has to be fucking outlandish," Ian vouched, handing us both Coronas.

"I'll be right back," I announced, pushing past my friends. Twisting and turning to navigate the crowded bar wasn't easy. People stood around forming little cliques and blocking others from passing. None of them realized they were the jerk-offs causing the blockage in foot traffic. The same people were the type who complained about getting bumped into and getting their shoes stepped on. Between the flashing lights, booming music, and the sea of bodies thrusting, gyrating, and grinding, there was no way to spot her. Pushing through the crowd of dancers was the only option. It took forever as no one was ever aware of their surroundings. Reaching the other side of the club and still not seeing my goddess was disappointing. I wanted to punch myself in the balls for missing her again.

Circling around back to the boys took a few seconds. Spotting Larry and Ian standing at the bar in conversation with my perfect ten goddess took me by surprise. My stomach jumped into my throat and my heart plunged into the empty void where my stomach used to be. Either the alcohol or the nerves made me nauseous. It was not like me to be afraid to approach a woman. It was something I'd done a million times. The room was spinning. All the blood in my body was going straight to my head. My only saving grace was the little voice in the back of my head with the presence of mind to cut through all the insecurity, fear, and garbage. It forced me to march up to my lifelong friends, ready to engage them in battle.

"What are we drinking next?" I shouted at Larry and Ian, walking up to them. Their replies fell on deaf ears. My dark-haired goddess laid jade-colored eyes upon me. They made me feel insignificant and like the weight of the world rested upon my shoulders. She smiled and it took my breath away. It was love at first sight. Fireworks exploded in my heart. Our souls connected. Doves flew and wedding bells rang. You get the picture, I fell hard. Dangerously hard.

"Marina said she wants sex on the beach," Ian joked with a laugh not reflected in his eyes. The icy gaze settled on me, telling me everything I needed to know. Camaraderie, friendship, respect, all be damned. It was one alpha male challenging another for supremacy. An open invitation to combat like nature intended. Only the fittest would survive. Ian wanted to throw down. I was willing to oblige.

Larry was also interested in Marina but recognized the fists were about to fly and wanted no part in the approaching bloodbath. He would stand outside the fighting pit and await his opportunity to strike. Allow his enemies to tear each other down and he could swoop in for the kill. A smart strategy. If it didn't present itself, he'd be thrilled to walk away with one of Marina's friends or pick up a random before closing time.

"Are your friends going to want some sex on the beach too?" Larry asked like a seasoned pro. He exaggerated searching for her friends to break the ice. What he really needed to know is if there was a Hero in the group. The Hero is the one friend out to crush everyone's enjoyment because no one else can have fun if they aren't. They're usually overweight or unattractive (both, most of the time) and no one gives them the time of day. Deep down, there is an inferiority complex stemming from jealousy since their much more attractive friends are getting attention they wish they were getting. They disguise it with this "never leave a man behind" attitude they think gives them the right to butt into other people's lives and make decisions for them. Heroes were like kryptonite to Supermen like us.

"Oh, I'm here alone. None of my friends wanted to come out but I wasn't going to waste such a gorgeous night," Marina replied, bestowing us with another lovely smile.

"Since your friends couldn't make it, you can hang with us. We're only here with each other so you can easily take the spot as the most beautiful one in our group," Ian flirted, caressing the small of her back. She smiled at him and accepted the invitation. There was a twinge of envy threatening to make me lose my cool. Those smiles were only for me.

"Hey guys!" Brooke greeted as she approached the three of us. Marina's expression changed. Her smile faded and she stared daggers through Brooke.

"Hey!" Larry greeted.

"Who's this?" Brooke asked, checking out Marina from head to toe.

"Marina. Nice to meet you," she greeted, extending a hand. Brooke took her hand and Marina leaned in. Brooke turned her cheek and Marina followed, planting a kiss on her lips. It wasn't a peck either. It lasted more than a three Mississippi count. Brooke didn't seem to mind it. I could have sworn she let out a moan when Marina broke the kiss off.

"Well, you certainly are friendly," Brooke said with a flustered gasp. She turned to the rest of us and there were no words.

"More drinks?" Marina asked, bringing everyone out of their bewilderment.

"Yes!" Larry replied guiding us to the bar and ordering another round of shots.

Marina was like a queen holding court. We hung on her every word like she was Jesus during the Sermon on the Mount. We laughed at her jokes all the while fighting each other for her attention, Brooke especially. She seemed uncomfortable in her own skin. Sweat dripped down her forehead in beads. Her face was red and her chest heaved like she was having trouble breathing. Asking her to stand still would have been interesting. Her hands were restlessly moving. If she wasn't touching herself, she was trying to touch someone else. She was loud and boisterous and leaned in close when speaking. There were a couple of times I thought she was going to kiss me. It was out of character for her. More like Alexis after a few drinks. What made it weirder was this was all happening while she was sober.

"Dude, Brooke seems kinda hot tonight," Larry said to me in the brief moment Marina wasn't speaking with us. "Look at her. She looks like she's down to fuck on the floor," he continued. Without being obvious, I glanced over at Brooke and she was running her fingers through her hair, twirling it around her fingers like a porn star pretending to be an innocent schoolgirl.

"How many has she had?" I asked, hoping to get Larry focused elsewhere. One less contender for Marina's attention would have been nice.

"None," Larry answered, taking the bait.

"Maybe she's letting loose since she doesn't have to babysit Alexis," I suggested, planting the seed further into Larry's mind. Ian was gaining the advantage with every passing second.

"Just seems out of character," Larry stated and broke off from the conversation with me and turned to Brooke. He said a couple of words and in an instant she was shoving her tongue down Larry's throat and reaching down to unbuckle his belt. Both Larry and I were taken aback by the sudden development. He pushed her hand away and her eyes went wide with madness.

"Come back!" Brooke screamed, offering herself to Larry

on a silver platter.

"How many drinks have you had?" Larry asked. He was making sure she wasn't taking drinks on the side somehow.

"I've only had two Coors Lights. What does it matter?" Brooke replied, biting her lower lip and looking over to Marina and Ian. She moaned and let out a gasp. A wave of confusion flashed across her face and quickly went away.

"You are acting a little different," I stepped in, taking the edge off Larry.

Brooke smiled and then pulled Larry to her and whispered into his ear. He nodded his head and a wide grin stretched across his face. Brooke turned her gaze to me and smiled, then whispered more until she let go of Larry and walked away in the direction of the exit.

"What did she say?" I asked knowing something awesome had forced the shit-eating grin across his face.

"She wants to go back to the house," Larry answered. "She said you could come too, if you wanted."

"A devil's three-way? Not a chance," I replied with a laugh.

"I'm out," Larry said and turned to follow Brooke into the night. At least Larry would walk away with a consolation prize. It was only me and Ian left with Marina. There was no consolation prize for the two of us. Just a winner and a loser going home to whack it alone with their tears as lubrication.

As the night progressed, Marina matched me and Ian shot for shot and beer for beer like a champ with no signs of drunkenness. In the end, the best man won. Ian conceded victory to me, red faced and almost collapsing where he stood. The last shot put him over the top and he refused a shot of Wild Turkey Marina had ordered. With eyes only half open and unable to form coherent words, he made a gurgling sound and ran for the bathroom. It was safe to disqualify him as a contender.

"Pussy!" Marina shouted at Ian as he ran away and pounded down both shots back to back. Not only did she have my undying love and admiration, she had my respect.

"You'd think by now he'd have built a tolerance," I stated, feeling my stomach turning too.

"And then there was one," Marina replied with a smirk. We stood next to the bar a little longer, talking. Thankfully, we stopped drinking and it gave me time to recover. Every joke I made was met with a cute little laugh and if it was dirty, a light slap on the arm as if offended. Each volley back and forth was a game of cat and mouse. It was beautiful, intense, and exhilarating. Absolutely beyond expectations until it was interrupted.

A hard shove came from behind me and sent me colliding into Marina. My body fell against her, crushing her against the bar. My blood boiled with the heat of ten thousand suns. Someone was going to die for hurting Marina.

"Where's your friend, faggot?" Skeletor shouted when I turned to face him.

"Probably still fucking your girl," I answered, not missing a beat. His face contorted in fury. "Let's take this outside," I challenged, knowing if we started a brawl inside the club, the bouncers would destroy the both of us regardless of fault.

"What's going on? Who is this?" Marina interrupted, breaking the tension.

"Some cuckold," I answered.

"What's that?" she asked.

"A guy who can't keep his woman in check," I replied. Skeletor lost it and took a swing at me. In one fluid motion, Marina caught his arm and pulled it behind him. She pressed up against him, hiding both their hands from the view of everyone around them. It looked like she was trying to whisper in his ear. With her free hand, she chopped him on the side of the neck softly like she was targeting a specific spot. Skeletor's eyes went wide and his mouth hung open like he was waiting for a dentist to examine him.

"Let's hit the dance floor," Marina demanded, releasing Skeletor and taking my hand. With no time to argue, I followed along turning back to see Skeletor collapse onto to the dirty nightclub floor.

"What did you do to him?" I asked, unable to believe she had taken him down so easily. A couple of bouncers carried Skeletor out of the club. Marina grabbed my chin and turned me to face her.

"Don't worry about it. It's a little something I learned in the Marines," Marina replied.

"A Marine named Marina?" I teased.

"Life has a weird sense of humor," she replied. "Come on,

let's dance."

"Yes, ma'am," I replied as she pulled me onto the dance floor for a sampling of each other's moves.

With each hip gyration, seductive smile, and sensual touch, we came closer together until we were inches away from kissing. Her body was hypnotic, the way it swayed with the music. Everything ceased to exist with the exception of Marina and the bass pulsing through our connected souls. We bumped and grinded against each other with the rhythm of the music guiding our bodies together as one. There were eyes on us from all around, watching our mating dance, radiating with sexuality. They were ravenous for the flesh, and the heat, and the sweat. The jealousy reflected in lustful eyes drove me nuts.

There was no holding back. I kissed the side of her neck, tasting sweat and skin along with a delicious-smelling perfume. There was a hint of something else there. A sour, bitter taste. The thought was interrupted when the song ended and the overhead lights flashed on, blinding everyone in the room. The DJ announced the bar was closing in ten minutes and directed everyone to close their tabs or head to the restaurant outside the bar.

It was the moment of truth for all the brave men and women hooking up with strangers in the dark. When the lights came on, all the butterfaces, acne scars, and blemishes were revealed. When Marina turned around a dazzling smile still beamed across her gorgeous face. Her face was symmetrical with a thin, short nose, a round mouth with full lips, and a tightly toned body to boot. She was perfection.

"Well, this sucks. I was having such a good time, too," Marina pouted.

"I have a beach house not too far from here. Why don't we go hang out there?" I invited.

"Aren't Larry, Ian, and Brooke going to be there, too?" Marina asked.

"Yeah but we can chill out in my room and watch a movie on Netflix or something," I replied, hoping she would accept the obvious ploy. It was no secret we wanted each other. There were no more moves to make. It was either close the deal or have my soul crushed.

"I have a better idea. Why don't we go to the inlet instead?" Marina suggested. The idea of rolling around in the sand didn't have any appeal. Sex on the beach wasn't the arousing, roll-around-in-the-sand sex scene Hollywood showed in movies. They never bothered to show the people trying to wipe the sand off their genitals or their faces when they felt sand crunching between their teeth. Did I say yes?

Of course I did. I wasn't about to let a little discomfort stop me from being with Marina.

"Let's get out of here," I agreed and took her hand. We filed out of the bar to the restaurant and found Ian sitting at a table with a beast of burden chowing down on a couple of slices of pizza next to him. He could have been mistaken for an extra in a zombie movie. His eyes were rolled into the back of his head and there was dried vomit on the collar of his button up shirt. Red welts covered the side of his neck. They would be purple the next morning. His pants were undone and halfway down.

"Is he okay?" Marina asked the stranger stuffing her face.

"Yeah, he's coming home with me," the girl answered.

"Ian, buddy, are you alive in there?" I asked, lightly slapping his face. He made a sound no one could understand. If he was lucky, the machinery inside his head would be disabled, saving my friend from the indignity of copulating with the creature sitting next to him.

"Maybe we should take him home," Marina suggested. Ian grunted in the negative. He wanted to be left alone with the beast which wasn't necessarily a horrible idea. This girl was in the middle of landing the sexiest man she'd ever get into bed. She had to strike while the iron was hot and very wasted.

"Well, get home safe guys. We're headed to the inlet. Call me if you need me, bro," I directed. Ian laughed and nodded his head.

It was my turn to lead as Marina and I walked out of the restaurant past the rest of the drunken crowd standing in line waiting for pizza and stepped outside into the chaos of gleaming light, music, and noises coming from the arcades and game stands. Not too many people remained on the boardwalk past two in the morning. As soon as the nightclub closed, everything else followed.

A chilling breeze came in off the surface of the Atlantic Ocean. It was refreshing after being in the heat of all those bodies crowding around in the restaurant. We turned and left behind the cacophony of ringing bells, blaring music, and the sea of human activities for the isolation of the Manasquan Inlet. It was a prime spot for tourists in the summer to relax and watch the million-dollar yachts float into the marina. In the early morning hours, it was a hangout spot for those wishing for privacy and isolation.

Our march down the boardwalk was going to be the perfect opportunity to convince her to come home with me. We were going to pass the house and she'd see it was a much better option than going on to the inlet. No sand. Guaranteed privacy. A nice warm bed.

As we approached, the Sinatra House was playing "Strangers in the Night."

"Isn't that appropriate?" Marina asked. She began to sing along with the song.

I sang back, doing my best Sinatra impression.

"It turned out right?" Marina responded gently.

"Come inside," I insisted. She came into my arms and kissed me. I melted. It was like every single cell in my body was on fire. My mind was floating over the clouds and into outer space. When she pulled away, I gasped for breath.

"Not yet. Remember, I wanted sex on the beach," Marina whispered into my ear. She pulled me back onto the boardwalk and past the Sinatra House which had moved on to another song I didn't know.

We walked the rest of the way to the inlet and found it

devoid of human life. The last person we passed had been sitting on the porch on the boardwalk half a mile back. We were alone in our own little part of the world.

None of my friends. No strangers. No Skeletor. Nothing could stop us.

Marina took a seat on a bench and pulled her skirt to the side, revealing more sun-bronzed skin and a flask holstered in a strap going around her thigh. She took a sip from it and then offered some to me. It tasted like alcohol, milk, and seawater combined. Spitting it out would have been rude. Plus, if she could handle it, I could, too. It was an Opening Shot. *You take the shot, she opens her legs,* I thought to myself, swallowing hard and fighting the urge to vomit.

"What was that?" I asked, and forced myself to laugh. Marina took another swig and passed it back. The sour taste mixed with salt and thick, milky substance was doing a number on my stomach. It was getting me drunk, too. The ocean, the beach, and the moon, everything seemed darker. The temperature dropped a few degrees. My teeth chattered. Everything went sideways. My head slumped to the side and my body followed. Marina grabbed the sides of my face in her hands and stared deep into my eyes as if trying to look into my soul. There was nothing to do but stare back into those alluring green eyes. The warmth of her hands traveled through my body like a wave going all the way down to my feet. My loins were on fire. Nothing could penetrate the cloud of her scent. She kissed my lips once more. It was euphoric.

When she pulled away, it felt like the end of the world. The devastation of being away from her made me want to die. I'd never feel pleasure again without her. Chills trembled through to my bones. I needed her told hold me again or I'd freeze to death. I moaned, unable to even form words.

Marina pulled me to my feet. They felt like Jello and buckled under the weight of the rest of my body. She caught me under my shoulders and dragged me to the sand.

"P-p-p-l-e-a-," I pleaded through the frigid tongue in my mouth. The world was fading on me. The moon's reflection against the water disappeared. The sky dulled like a thin film blacking out the sky. The waves crashing against the rocks sounded like the ocean roared at us. Never in my life had I ever felt so horribly dizzy and out of control. The idea of her spiking her own flask with LSD or some other mind-altering drugs passed through the haze of my blurred thoughts. *Beautiful women don't need to roofie men to get them into bed.* If it wasn't obvious, I was more than willing to spend the night with her. Maybe she wanted to get high and have mind-altering sex. If that was the case, she never gave me a warning.

It could have also been the effects of two straight weeks' worth of binge drinking taking its toll on my body. It made more sense to my body to shut down instead of allowing me to continue forcing alcohol down my throat. My mind zipped back and forth between believing I'd been drugged or drunk to the point of blackout collapse until I realized it didn't matter. I needed help.

"Home…" I murmured, feeling exhausted in the effort. Marina didn't hear me. My inability to communicate should have been a clear indication of the loss of my faculties. The idea of Marina ignoring me seemed sinister. Then again, I had only known her a few hours. I didn't know her from any other stranger with nefarious intentions.

Once we were out of view from the beach, she set me down in the sand and rearranged my arms to rest at my sides and spread my legs open. It was a sweet relief to feel the ground again. It felt even better when she climbed atop me and kissed me again.

For the rest of my life, nothing will ever be comparable to the feeling of her lips on mine. Sexual madness is the only way to describe how it felt. I kissed her back as ferociously as my paralyzed state allowed me to, wanting to swallow her whole while shoving my tongue down her throat. She laughed as I bit her lip, not caring if I drew blood. Then as quick as it started, she pulled away and climbed off, fading away into the darkness. My mind felt uncoupled from the rest of my body. Every part of me buzzed, throbbed, and pulsated, wishing for more.

The sound of scraping caught my attention. Tiny sparks flared through the air, disappearing once they hit the ground. Another scrape, more sparks, and then a fire burst into view, illuminating Marina. Smoke erupted from it like shadowy tendrils roiling across the sand. It brought tears to my eyes as it loomed in my direction like it had a will of its own, gravitating toward me. The smoke burned my throat and lungs. A coughing fit wrenched through me. Spittle covered the sides of my mouth.

Marina then made a noise like Styrofoam squeaking through a megaphone. It made me want to rupture my ear drums to never have to endure it again. The ocean responded to her outcry crashing harder against the rocks on shore. She stared in the direction of the water for God knows how long until she turned back in my direction. She removed her dress and top, revealing her bronzed, naked body in its invigorating glory. The only blemish upon her perfection was a set of three birthmarks or tattoos, I couldn't tell which, on the both sides of her rib cage. A mischievous smile crept across her lips. She tossed her clothing into the fire, feeding the flames. The spectral light flashed for a moment, revealing several figures beyond the reach of the light. There was an audience watching now and they were ready for the main show.

She mounted me again, bringing her lips to mine. The sweet madness of lust and adrenaline made me roar. There was unexpected numbness in my arms. My arms slapped at her belly, missing the birthmarks by inches. A flash of pain ripped through me like an electrical current. My body sparked to life, convulsing in a freakish dance like a bucking bronco trying to throw off a riding cowboy. Nerve endings fired all over, going haywire until I lay still on the sand.

Marina didn't blink as she resumed slurping on my lips and tongue. Her mouth was cold. Colder than any human being could have been. Purple spirals appeared in the whites of her eyes. They bled into the green irises, which seemed to be melting and mixing with the purple spirals and forming a new glassy eye like a snake's eye.

Everything was different about her. Her lustrous hair was falling out. It fell from her head, lifeless and dull. Her breasts didn't heave with her labored breaths. The birthmarks were clearly not birthmarks. They overlapped each other, opening and closing like tiny mouths drawing breath when she inhaled. The skin around them overlapped making it near impossible to see them if she wasn't breathing. They weren't birthmarks at all. They were gills.

The world came crashing down around me. My vision blurred and unconsciousness was about to release me from the reality of a creature disguising itself as a human, shoving its cold tongue down my esophagus. Another shock to the system brought me back from the brink. There was no escape.

Marina needed me awake for what was to come. She undressed me from the waist down and smiled, displaying multiple rows of sharp teeth. It was like the mouth of a great white shark. She took me into her hand and brought her lips to my crotch. She kissed and flicked it with her tongue, sending earthshattering shockwaves through the sensitive tissues and nerve endings. Euphoria overcame me. Stiff and ready for action, Marina went to place me inside her.

Gathering the last of my courage I reached up, trying to push her from me, and found myself grabbing her breast. A giggle sounding like a gargle escaped her throat. She leaned forward and hissed into my ear.

"Don't move too much or they'll kill you."

Marina opened her mouth to kiss me once more and it smelled like the dumpster at a seafood restaurant on the hottest day of the summer. I swallowed back the vomit in my throat. She straddled me and inserted me into her. It was cold and dry. The lack of lubrication made it feel like I had a condom made of sandpaper on. Noticing my discomfort or feeling her own, I couldn't tell but she alleviated the situation by reaching into her open gills and scooping out a thick purple jelly which she rubbed onto me.

After applying a generous amount, she swayed her hips from side to side, forward and back, like music was playing. Marina was dancing again and the whole world faded into the background. All the attention in the world belonged to her. Even the chorus of hisses and gargled coos coming from the figures in the shadows dissolved into the background. The fire pit exploded into an array of overpowering colors. A spectrum of blues, greens, and purples with no business in existence, curved and angled, lighting the distorted figures at the edge of the shadows. Nothing in the world made me want to look at them. Marina was the center of my universe. We were one.

Time slowed to a grueling halt. Man and creature together. Marina's skin changed. So did my level of participation. She morphed from bronzed and toned to a pale, scaly maggot white. The rest of her long, beautiful dark hair fell out in chunks onto my chest, revealing a shiny bald head with eyes too bulbous for her head like a surprised Japanese cartoon character. Her moans shrilled like the thunderous screeches of a prehistoric animal in heat until the moment she roared with climax. We both finished at the same time. The screech echoed over the sound of the crashing water. Marina fell down on me in exhaustion.

With a satisfied sigh, she dismounted me and reached down. With a wet slop, she brought a webbed hand to my face. She touched me, then lifted the hand into the air, displaying it to the witnesses of our consummation. There were a few hisses from the crowd before the sound of splashing could be heard. With the show concluded, it was time for everyone to go home.

What if she was like a mantis or a black widow? They kill their mates after finishing with them. *Or if she was like a bee?* Their cocks explode after they finish. Mine was still intact but who could be sure of what was to come later. Those sharp rows of teeth were definitely not for eating tofu and salad. The thought of getting eaten alive posed a strong possibility. My friends and family would never know what happened. They would assume I'd drowned in the ocean or disappeared. There wouldn't be a body left to bury. Being digested in the stomach or stomachs of this creature terrified me to the point of tears.

Marina's satisfied grin ran away from her face. Deep lines appeared where her brows would have furrowed if she had any. I saw shame.

She cradled my head between her scaly breasts and cooed like I was a child. There was no warmth or comfort to her embrace. She was cold and rough against my skin. A layer of the slime on her hand stuck to my face. I trembled and cried.

Marina pulled my face to her breast and squeezed my nose shut. She smothered me against her chest, shoving her breast into my mouth until I was forced to try to breath and swallowed liquid instead of air.

She ran her fingers through my hair to comfort me as I unwillingly nursed from the creature's nipple. My vision blurred and the world was spinning once more. Reality slipped away and my eyes could stay open no longer.

* * *

My mouth was slimy with the taste of fish on my tongue when I awoke the next morning to the daylight. It shined between the gaps of the boardwalk overhead. Droplets of water trickled between the tiny gaps soaking me from head to toe with water. My teeth clicked together with the chill in the air. Despite the pounding headache pulsating through my skull, I burst into tears, happy to be alive and whole.

My pants were still around my ankles. All the fluids were dried and crusted except for the drips of water wetting my lower torso and pubic hairs. My stomach turned with the nauseating smell wafting into my nose. Bile filled my mouth, forcing me to turn over and heave into the sand. The taste of

Marina's breast milk, alcohol, and the remnants of the previous day's food returned. It disappeared into the sand, leaving behind only the acrid stench and a couple of lumpy chunks.

Trudging through rain-soaked sand felt like marching through a field of mud. Every part of me ached from sleeping in the sand and savagely vomiting my guts out. The water was my first stop before heading back home. Cupping a handful of seawater into my mouth got rid of the taste of fish and vomit. The taste of salt was the lesser of two evils. Cleaning off the rest of muck on me could wait until I got home.

The walk back home was a lonely one with all the shops on the boardwalk closed. The time of day and the rain kept the dog walkers, joggers, and morning folks inside. The ongoing downpour soaked me from head to toe, making my pants slosh with each step I took. It felt refreshing despite the awkwardness of the damp clothes sticking to me. The rain mixed with my tears as I cried at the sound of Frank Sinatra's booming voice inviting me to come fly away with him. My own personal walk of shame.

The house was peaceful with silence. None of the boys or girls would be up for hours. I didn't wish to see anyone anyway. I grabbed two Gatorades from the fridge, chugged them, and jumped into bed without showering. I didn't care how foul I smelled or how much blood and crusted fish jelly there was on me. Shutting down to sleep off the hangover was the priority. The moment my head hit the pillow, I was out once again.

* * *

"Time to hit the gym, jerk-off!" Anthony shouted through the door. He pounded his fists, shaking the doorframe. My digital clock claimed it was five in the afternoon. I'd been asleep for close to ten hours. There was no way in Hell I was going to work out.

"Go without me, I feel like shit!" I replied, hoping he would leave.

"That chick from last night wore you out? Bro, you are outta shape! Come on man, you gotta get your swell going for round two! We're hitting up Seaside and Skeletor is probably gonna be gunning for us!" Anthony persisted. Marina handling Skeletor the previous night rushed to the forefront of my thoughts. It explained a lot.

"I got plans!" I shouted back.

"Plans? Don't tell me you're wifing up already!" Anthony chided. Ian shouted for him to shut up from down the hallway. He must have still been nursing a hangover, too.

"Don't worry about it. I just gotta take care of something!" I shouted, dismissing him.

"Suit yourself, pussy!" Anthony barked. His heavy footsteps walked away from the door. Once he was gone, I jumped onto my laptop and searched for the address to the nearest urgent care center. It was next to the diner we had eaten at when Anthony took Skeletor's girl for a ride in the back of Ian's Explorer. Gathering myself together didn't take long. I don't know why I changed my shirt considering my pants and underwear were damp, covered in sand, and worn for over twenty-four hours. Grabbing Ian's car keys from his room, I almost managed to slip out of the house before I ran into Brooke. She was wearing some of Larry's clothes and her hair was a mess.

"Hey…" Brooke greeted, averting eye contact.

"Hi," I greeted back. "Have a good night?"

"Um. Yeah, you could say that," she replied blushing. "Rough night, yourself, huh?" she asked, examining my disheveled and sandy clothes.

"Yeah, you could say that," I replied, shaking the sand from my pants onto the floor. I did not wish to elaborate. Who the hell would believe me?

"When did Marina leave?" Brooke continued questioning.

"She didn't come home with me," I replied.

"She's really hot," Brooke confirmed like she was revealing a big secret. "Never wanted to be with a girl before but after she kissed me it was like. I just… lost it."

I nodded, knowing exactly what Brooke meant. "I'll let you get back to Larry. I'll see you later," I excused myself and headed out the door for the hospital.

* * *

Making sure I was clean was the least I could do. I don't want to end up being patient zero for some new strain of gona-sypha-herpalies or some flesh-eating disease. The possibility of catching some unknown disease to science or medicine was in the realm of possibility after the night with Marina. I thought that even if science didn't know what I may have, if it was caught early, they could cure me.

I was quickly ushered into an office. Once the nurse finished taking my temperature and heart rate, the nurse asked for the purpose of my visit. On my ride over to the hospital, I came up with a cover story and put it into action. It was simple. Someone drugged me last night and I woke up with blood and "residue" on my genitals. I had no idea how it got there and wanted to make sure everything was okay. The nurse wrote on the chart and then handed me an empty cup and told me to piss into it. After we finished, the nurse told me to wait until another nurse came to check me.

Half an hour later, a male nurse entered the room and asked me to lower my pants. The thought of making a joke of it crossed my mind but I didn't. He took a sample of the residue, holding his breath, while he poked and prodded, the residue congealed from my shaft to my balls. Once he was satisfied, he drew two vials of blood, then waited for a moment to make sure I didn't pass out. At least he'd have a fun story to tell his friends, family, and fellow nurses for the rest of his life.

The doctor came in almost an hour later. With all the other real patients to attend to, a drugged up tourist was the least pressing matter. He introduced himself and got right to the point. The urine test came up negative for drugs. The doctor chalked it up to my metabolism taking care of the problem and the dosage of the drug being marginal. With nearly twenty-four hours having passed it wasn't rare to find a system was clear. He said the bloodwork may reveal more, but it would take a week. The samples of the residue were sent to another lab to identify since the doctor had no idea what it could have been. He asked if I was in any pain and since I was fine, my consultation was finished. I was told to go home and relax then left the urgent care facility, hoping all the results would come back negative.

When I walked into the beach house, Anthony and Larry were cooking on the stove while Ian tidied up the living room. Their expressions turned sour when I entered.

"Where you been?" Anthony asked, turning away from the boiling pot of pasta to me.

"Just checking out some spots in town," I lied. All eyes were on me. They knew something was up.

"Did one of those spots happen to be an urgent care place?" Ian called me out. They caught me.

"Yeah, how did you know?" I asked.

"Browsing history, bro. Learn to clear it," Larry replied.

"Not even. You left the window open on your laptop," Ian added.

"What's wrong with you?" Anthony asked.

Keeping with the same story I gave the urgent care place, I told them everything except the part about Marina's transformation into a monster. As far as they knew, one of their best friends was drugged and didn't remember the rest of the night. It wasn't far from the truth. Whatever was in the flask had paralyzed me. Her breast milk knocked me out. Her kisses were an aphrodisiac. Everything about Marina was intoxicating. After leaving the club, I blacked out and woke up in the morning by the water.

"What a cunt!" Ian shouted once I finished.

"Let's go find her. We know she's prowling the clubs," Anthony suggested.

Everyone was on board except for me. The idea of encountering Marina again shot a shiver down my spine. The thought of those rows of serrated teeth grinding my bones to powder didn't sit well with me. I didn't want to press my luck. Surviving one encounter was miraculous. Chasing her down was suicidal. Especially because she wasn't alone. The other creatures that watched us were also out there.

"Let's forget about it. I'm fine. Let's not let it ruin our summer. I just need a day off and I'll be back to business," I requested. There was a quiet exchange between my friends and they appeared to agree with each other.

"I'll call you when the food is ready," Anthony stated, turning back to the pot of pasta and adding in salt. I marched off to my bedroom and jumped into the shower to finally clean myself up. The warm water would have been the most incredible feeling in the world, if it hadn't been for the ecstasy of Marina's kiss replaying over and over again in my head.

After finishing my shower, I took the underwear, pants, and dampened, sandy bedsheets and tossed them into the trash. Nothing would have ever gotten the smell out. I don't know if Anthony ever tried to get me for dinner. I laid down in bed to rest my eyes and fell asleep until the next morning.

After the encounter with Marina, my life took an even stranger turn. The fear of having caught a disease seemed justified as my body started to act as if it was fighting off an infection. The lack of energy, the inability to sleep, and an elevated temperature all contributed to my misery. My nights were spent tossing and turning with the discomfort of alternating hot flashes and insufferable chills down to my bones. Everyone chalked it up to having caught a cold after being left out overnight by the ocean and walking back home in a downpour.

My daily activities took a major hit. Hanging out at the beach and having the sun beating down on me all morning was out of the question. Something about being out in the heat crippled me. My skin felt as if it was sizzling like bacon cooked in oil. For all intents and purposes, the summer was over for me and I was a freakin' vampire. Nothing but air conditioning and low lighting for me. I tried to go out at night but even that had its problems.

My energy prevented me from leaving the house for too long. It was exhaustion to the point of fainting spells and needing to sit for long periods of time before being able to stand up again. Alcohol was also off the table. As soon as a drop of liquor or beer hit my lips, it was game over. Nausea and dizziness came instantaneously and vomit would make an inevitable appearance. The idea of getting dressed up and heading out to a nightclub became unappealing. Watching everyone getting tipsy and having a marvelous time while I was sipping on a Coke didn't sit well with me.

The guys understood I wasn't ready to go out again for the first couple of nights and even stayed in with me to show their support. They had questions which I tried to answer honestly but there were obvious details I omitted. Having Alexis and Brooke over satisfied the quota for girls but it didn't last. On the fourth night, the squad tried to get me out of the house but I couldn't. Resuming the non-stop action from our first couple of weeks wasn't something I could physically do. I made it clear it wasn't personal and declined to leave the house. It continued for the next couple days until the end of the week. That's when they stopped asking me to go out.

When the phone call from the lab came, my heart sank into the pit of my stomach. My expectation was confirmation of an unknown illness and being called back to the hospital for evaluation. To my surprise, the caller said everything was okay except for my cholesterol being a little high. *How could nothing be wrong with me?* There should have been something there. They probably couldn't identify it if they didn't know what they were trying to find. It wasn't as if I could lead them in any direction without looking like a crazy person. I didn't trust the results.

The rest of the conversation went quick. The fluids on my

penis were semen, vaginal lubrication, sweat, and specks of sand. The jelly was inconclusive. He said they would pass it on to another lab for further analysis. No one ever called back. I imagine the slides of jelly have been passed around from lab to lab with each scientist scratching their heads and wondering what the heck they were examining.

With the final week of the rental upon us, the boys were partying extra hard without me. After having felt like I'd abandoned the group, I pushed myself to make an effort to allow myself back into the fold even if I couldn't participate directly. I volunteered to chauffeur them to the clubs and pick them up at the end of the night. They appreciated my services and we managed to bridge the gap again. Going out at two or three in the morning to pick them up didn't bother me since sleeping was near impossible. Vivid nightmares of Marina taking me underneath the boardwalk began to overwhelm my nights. Waking up screaming started becoming normal. Luckily, the guys were always out partying or blacked out and passed out so no one ever heard me.

On the second to last day of our rental, the boys decided to hit up Seaside for the last hurrah down south. They invited me to join them but as much as I wanted to go with them, I declined. A dull ache in my testicles had been bothering me since that morning. When I checked them in the bathroom, they were swollen and looked ready to burst. As much as I did want to join the guys, I stayed home watching movies and then flopped into bed early, hoping nothing serious was wrong with me.

The clock said it was one in the morning when the urgent need to urinate awakened me. I jetted from the bedroom to the bathroom, feeling like I was about to explode and when I tried to pee, I couldn't. The ache in my testicles turned into a full-fledged agony like someone stabbing millions of needles into the sensitive tissue. My urethra burned like a river of molten lava was pooling in the shaft. I could only groan and cry while holding my cock, trying to force myself to piss. With no other idea on what to do, I opened the faucet and drank until my stomach was sloshing with water. I didn't think I could have felt worse but the water made everything even more excruciating. Chopping off my cock seemed like a good idea.

With each deep breath and push, something felt like it was working its way out. I leaned over the toilet and braced myself against the wall, aiming toward the water of the toilet bowl. With a final push, whatever was clogging my plumbing burst. It felt like an explosion from the inside out happening over and over again. Something was coming out of me like peas covered with needles being passed through a straw just a little too small. I screamed until something gave out in my throat and I collapsed to the floor, holding myself in grueling pain.

It must have been twenty minutes before the pain subsided. I picked myself up from the bathroom tile and peeked into the toilet, expecting to see bloody kidney stones. Instead, I was met with hundreds of tiny, glowing purple eyes staring up at me from the inside of transparent bloody eggs.

Time stood still. The synapses of my brain must have misfired, overloaded with shock. The eggs floated on the surface, bumping into each other and bouncing away. A popping sound followed up each collision. The eggs burst open and the larvae inside fell beneath the surface of the blood and urine mixture. The toilet bowl wasn't going to sustain them all. With a pull of the lever, the toilet rumbled and all the purple glowing eyes began to swirl around the toilet and disappeared down the drain.

Hours later, I awoke to the sound of the guys calling my name.

"Dom, where the fuck are you?" Anthony called out. He sounded pissed.

"In the bathroom!" I croaked, clutching at my aching throat. I shut the door and locked it with my left hand. My entire right side had fallen asleep and the painful tingles of blood recirculating ran through it.

"You were supposed to pick us up!" Anthony shouted, startling me with a heavy pound on the door.

"Sorry, I felt really sick," I whispered hoping it wouldn't further agitate my throat. Anthony was a bad drunk. I could smell the booze on him through the door.

"You're always sick!" Anthony replied. Larry and Ian called him to the kitchen. He punched the door once more before his footsteps faded away. If only Anthony knew what had happened on the other side of the door. Not wanting to get into a confrontation, I jumped into the bathtub and took a long shower. I let the warm water envelop me and relaxed for the first time in weeks. The tension fell off my shoulders and disappeared down the drain.

When I finished up in the bathroom, everyone was already asleep in their beds. It was a blessing not to have to confront Anthony, Ian, and Larry. A few hours of sobering up would do everyone well.

Hours later, when everyone was gathered at the door for our final foray of the summer, I was right there with them in my bathing suit and with my towel under my arm. I had gone outside earlier that morning and felt okay standing out in the sun. By their reaction, I could tell the guys were still upset with me.

"Guys, listen. I'm sorry about last night. You wouldn't believe how sick I felt. It's not an excuse but I take responsibility for not letting anyone know I wasn't coming," I began. "Ever since I got drugged, I haven't been feeling myself. I can't explain it but I've been feeling so damned weird for the past few weeks, like I was in a depression or something. I know I should have talked about it but I needed to clear my head. I'm sorry."

Each of them stared at me without a change of expression. It felt like my apology had fallen on deaf ears until Larry smiled.

"No worries, man," Larry said, and all was forgiven. Anthony and Ian smiled too and went out the door. I followed them out, closing the door behind me and headed out for some much needed fun in the sun. Everything went fine the rest of the day. All the symptoms vanished. I had a ton of energy and guzzled down three beers without puking. It was such a relief. Alexis and Brooke joined us and it felt like nothing had ever changed.

It was a fine way to end our summer. The walk back to the house in the evening was full of laughter until Alexis and Brooke told us they were leaving. We invited them to spend the night one last time, especially since Larry had developed some sort of relationship with Brooke, but they declined our invitation. Since we were going to be getting up early in the morning to leave and they wanted to sleep, our goals were incompatible. Personally, I think Brooke wanted a clean break from Larry. We said our goodbyes while the Frank Sinatra House played "All My Tomorrows." We never saw Alexis and Brooke again, unless you count pictures of them on Facebook. Alexis still parties hard and Brooke is always in the background, babysitting.

The next morning marked the end of the summer hunting season. We loaded up the truck with our stuff and headed out back onto the highway, leaving Point Pleasant the way we came in. There would be no more Frank Sinatra, sand, or salt water. Best of all, no chance to see Marina again, wherever she was. It's hard to admit it but perhaps meeting Marina was the best thing to ever happen to me.

After getting back from the Shore, I decided to take a long break from the party scene. Getting my life together took over the majority of my time. Wasting away in the clubs and taxing my liver into cirrhosis lost its appeal right along with the one night stands.

Before losing touch with Ian, his father put me in touch with some of his business partners and I was presented with a lucrative job offer. The rest of the guys didn't follow my lead.

It is what it is.

Life has changed for the better upon moving into the city. Getting married was never in the cards for me until I met Sharon a few years ago. We met online off a matchmaking website and hit it off. She became my best friend, my partner, everything and all. You know how that type of shit goes.

A few years later, we got married. It was the most wonderful day of my life. Only to be topped when she informed me a few months later she was pregnant. I wish I could say I've been excited, but every few weeks since the shore I've pissed one or two eggs through my urethra. Deciding to have kids was a really hard decision. Saying I was hesitant would be an understatement.

Today was all my fault. The ultrasound. Sharon's difficult morning sickness. To think I could ever move into a life beyond my poor choices in college. The techs didn't know what to say when they put the wand on my wife's stomach.

None of us did; and I'm the only one who knows why my wife's belly is full of eggs.

Manliness

My Time Is Very Valuable

By J.D. Patrick

I was fresh out of high school in 2005 and about to begin college. I had no idea what I would be getting myself into and, honestly, hadn't even selected a major prior to enrolling. I knew what to expect—to a point. The parties were great, the campus was awesome, but the courses were a little harder than I thought they would be. I was a straight "A" student all throughout high school and recorded near perfect scores on my SAT and ACT without studying once. But I had done the required work and no more. Halfway through my first semester in college, I realized I was on track to earn at least one "B" and possibly a second.

That, for me, was unacceptable; I started to grasp at straws. I had no idea how to study in earnest and study groups seemed like a pointless waste of time to me. That's when I met Mike. He was the perfect student. He aced every subject he took, seemed to have the social life of Tony Stark, and was on several student committees. How he managed that sort of lifestyle was something I couldn't comprehend. I hoped he would be able to help me. He was actually working on his second degree. He was a senior, but we were in the same dorm, as he was one of our "senior sponsors" along with a few other upperclassmen, and his room was directly across from mine. I managed to catch him one day after my classes ended and struck up a conversation with him.

Mike was awesome. He was into *Halo*, a huge *World of Warcraft* fan, and, as it turned out, we were actually from the same hometown. We had a lot in common. He invited me to a dorm LAN party that night. *Halo 2* had come out and we were going to play all night long.

I was outclassed all night; the guys had a reaction time that I couldn't even gauge. Whenever I thought I had them caught in a trap or ambushed them I would suddenly find that I had been the one lured into a trap. I watched helplessly as I was pinged with sniper fire only to find that I had backed straight off a ledge into the waiting arms of another enemy player with a rocket launcher and an itchy trigger finger. In the same game I watched a sticky 'nade fly the entire length of Ivory Tower and land on the back of one of my unsuspecting teammates; took down the entire team.

We switched up teams throughout the night. I was afraid that when I finally managed to get onto Mike's team that everyone would have to play bodyguard. Instead, they worked me into their scheme; they found my strengths and weaknesses within seconds and posted me where I fit best. It was amazing. I had never fit into a team that well. Video games or otherwise.

As the hours drew on, some of the people left. Mike and his friends decided that we should play a few ranked matches online. Our opponents kept complaining that we were modding—this was back when it was easy to get away with and X-Box Live was new. Winning fifty to nothing, game in and game out seemed to get monotonous for Mike and his friends. After a handful of games we went back to playing each other and the field was much more even and interesting.

I thought I saw Mike pop an Adderall or some sort of other pill at one point in the night, but it was so quick and so perfectly executed that he may have been eating a chip and I just interpreted it incorrectly. I had heard of Adderall only because of college, and considered it an option. The rumors were that the pills could make anything seem interesting. Especially studying.

No one seemed to get tired among Mike's friends. By four in the morning I was an absolute wreck. I had quit drinking beer around midnight, as I had no tolerance back then, and I was working on my fourth or fifth soda in a futile attempt at staying conscious. Everyone else seemed to be going strong. I somehow managed to stay awake until six in the morning when a few people muttered something about needing to leave for classes soon.

That's when it hit me: I had a class in an hour and I had an exam that day. I was truly screwed. I stood up a bit too fast and the lack of sleep caught up to me; I had to grab onto the table to keep from falling over.

I saw Mike looking at me as he extracted a lone pill from his pocket. "Here, take this. It'll give you a little extra boost today, and you look like you need it." He handed me a small white pill with the number "1,000" indented in the surface. I took the pill with a swig of soda without a second thought. Hopefully Mike would think I was cool.

I started to feel better within seconds. I felt like I was thinking more clearly. It was amazing. The world may as well have been in slow motion. I thanked Mike and went to take my exam.

The exam was a breeze; it was stuff that I had been struggling with all semester, but suddenly it clicked for me. I was answering questions that should've taken half an hour within minutes. I was done in less than an hour while having the remaining time to check over my answers. With all that time left I decided to just leave. I knew my answers were correct. The experience was surreal. That one exam was enough to bring my grade up from a "B" to an "A."

I spent the rest of the day crushing my remaining three classes, then I went to the library, where I stayed until the librarians made me leave. I didn't have any other exams to study for, so instead I finished three papers, all of the required readings for all of my courses, and two assigned take-home exams that weren't due until the end of the semester. I was flying so high above cloud nine that the International Space Station was within reach. The weirdest part was that I actually wanted to do all of the extra work. It was fulfilling on another level. I wanted to go climb a mountain, and I knew I could; I wanted to write a book, and considered it; I could feel the itch to start reading ahead for the next semester.

Around midnight that night I finally got back to my dorm and saw Mike again, doing his regular checks on everyone to make sure no one was being too crazy. He asked me, with a slight grin, if I was feeling alright. I almost didn't know what to say. I was still at the same altitude that I had reached nearly eighteen hours prior. I thanked him profusely, of course, and I decided that it was time to get back to my room and go to sleep. I had been up for a long time. As soon as my head hit the pillow I was out.

I slept eight solid hours and woke up with the most bizarre sensation. I wasn't "coming down," or anything like that, I was already there. I didn't feel hung over or tired, I just felt normal again. I felt unprepared, vulnerable, and jumpy. I threw my door open and went to knock on Mike's. Before I could, the door opened and he was standing there with something in one of his fists. I knew it was another pill.

Mike began, "Listen. This is some personal stuff. I can't just keep giving these to you on the regular. I'm gonna have to get you in touch with a guy. He's never said no to me in the past, but it's on you to keep up your end of things."

"Yeah yeah." I didn't really have words. I just knew that I wanted the sensation to return. Normal wasn't where I belonged. I thought of the night of *Halo* and I was convinced Mike wasn't the only one taking the pills. I was at the cusp of another world and I wanted in.

Mike studied me for a moment. "Alright. How bad can it be? That's what you're thinking, right? Yeah. It's not bad. I started in middle school and haven't looked back. It's worth it, man." Mike tossed me the pill he was holding in his closed fist. I missed the catch and had to chase the pill across the floor as Mike started to close his door.

"Wait, what's your guy's number?" I asked, anxious.

Mike looked around the hallway. "Hey. Tone it down a notch. He'll know you. Don't worry. He'll meet you when you're ready once I tell him who you are. Go on; take the pill and chill." Mike calmly shut his door behind him as I fumbled with the small white pill. It read "10,000." That was more than "1,000."

I thought about knocking on Mike's door. I wanted to ask him about the extra zero, or the potential side effects. I stood there a moment, in the empty hallway. Complete silence. Then I decided I cared more about what Mike thought of me than I did the potential repercussions of taking more than I was supposed to of a drug I knew nothing about.

I swallowed the pill and reentered the clouds.

"10,000" meant it lasted ten times longer. I was invincible. I went four days without sleep. Classes blurred by me and I set myself up for perfection. A few days later I found a note that had been slid underneath my dorm room door. It was from Mike, telling me a place to meet him and his friends if I wanted to go camping with them. I went.

Mike had the type of smile that would make the Cheshire Cat jealous. It was infectious and intriguing at the same time. An intelligent smile.

The camping trip changed my life: booze, women, and one particularly interesting incident involving a raccoon entering one of the tents in the middle of the night that I may or may not have had a hand in.

I was still going strong after the trip, even though I had decided to sleep on the fourth night. I didn't feel like I needed to. I did it just to do it.

I went to class that Tuesday and after my second class of the morning I was waiting outside of the campus library for a friend from what already seemed like a previous lifetime. Instead of meeting the person I was waiting for I heard an unfamiliar voice call out to me. Out of habit I was briefly surprised, but, at the same time, I knew who it would be and I knew exactly what he was there for.

"Daniel. I hear you're interested in working together." I was almost surprised, but my newfound confidence had prepared me for anything. The man's face was one that could blend in with a crowd in basically any scenario, and his attire was a very light tan suit that, for some reason, didn't seem at all out of place on a college campus.

"Yes," I said, "I've seen some promising results and I'm only on my second dose." I saw that the man briefly paused but quickly masked his expression with a reassuring look of satisfaction. I quickly surmised that Mike probably wasn't supposed to give me two pills. The last thing I wanted was to get Mike into any kind of trouble. The pill must have begun to wear off. A few hours prior and I would have never made the same mistake.

"The exchange we make relates to time. You provide me your time and I provide you the supplement." He bent over and raised a backpack from behind a bush next to us. He gently placed the backpack in front of me. I looked down and then up to the man. I unzipped the bag, revealing tied off plastic baggies full of pills.

"I don't know that I can afford all of these," I said. I was, after all, not exactly wealthy at that point in my life. My parents weren't covering the college bills, and my scholarships only went so far. I had only planned on getting just enough pills to skate through college. I looked at the bags. I found myself looking at a path of success that would most likely have to continue to be supplemented by the pills. A high GPA would lead to the need for me to be just as successful in my first career, then the pressures of performing for promotions. I imagined the amount of money that would be required to sustain such a successful life.

The man interrupted my thoughts, "I only need your time. As long as I receive your time, you receive the supplements. Just be sure you're more careful with your supplements than Michael is with his. We've had incidents in the past that caused more trouble than the time is worth. Fulfill your potential. Don't squander it."

"Are there side effects? Doses?" I asked.

"Take one when you feel the previous one wearing thin. You will not overdose, but for your own sake, do manage your time as best as you can. If you run through too many too fast, we may have to reconsider our arrangement."

"Arrangement?"

"My name is Gregory. If you need me, I'll find you if you have the time."

The entire interaction took five minutes and suddenly I had a backpack stuffed with enough pills to bring Elvis back to life and kill him again. I needed to get back to my dorm.

It's really easy to look suspicious when you're trying very hard to fit in. I hadn't worn a backpack in years, and suddenly I was wearing one that sounded like it contained thousands of beads knocking against bags of birdseed. It was also pretty heavy.

Needless to say I was more than a little concerned to find campus PD at my building. That concern deepened when I noticed that they were also on my floor. Concern turned to utter fear when I saw them directly outside my dorm room. *Had I been part of a drug bust? What if "Gregory" was actually an undercover cop?* My mind raced until I realized that the PD wasn't actually in my room. They were inside Mike's room.

"Son, we're gonna need you to wait back here." Someone in uniform was speaking to me. I couldn't concentrate. My eyes were locked to the ground. A hand was lying on the floor, sticking out of Mike's open door. I froze and I also remembered that I had an entire pharmacy's worth of pills in a backpack.

"My room's right across from his. What happened?" I

stammered out as best as I could. I sounded like a lost child looking for his parents.

"You a friend of his?" The officer looked me over once or twice as I nodded meekly. "We'd like to talk to you. Wait here."

By that point, the bricks had been shat, and I was pretty sure that Gregory had sent some sort of hit out for Mike as soon as we'd finished talking. Mike's door had been shut when I had left for class in the morning. I didn't know anything, but I probably looked so guilty.

I was about to fess up to the pills and hope for the best when inspiration touched me. I knew that if I took a pill I could talk and reason my way out of the hallway. I could do anything, solve any problem. The officer turned his back, giving me a quick opportunity to get a pill out. I did my best to move just one hand behind me to the side of my backpack. I had a habit of zipping my bag all the way to one side. The habit saved my life that day.

In one swift motion I thrust my hand into the bag, tore a bag of pills open inside the backpack, removed a single pill and brought my hand out, zipping the backpack closed. The pill was in my mouth when the officer turned back around. I must've had enough of the previous pill in my system that I was able to execute the maneuver without making too much noise. It definitely took more concentration than it would have even one day earlier. I was having a little trouble swallowing it, but managed to get it down before I was required to speak.

The officer turned to me. I probably didn't look the greatest at the time. "Why don't you have a seat. I'll be with you in a few minutes. Sorry about your friend." The man sauntered back to the open door as some paramedics came down the hallway with a gurney. They placed Mike on the gurney and covered him with a sheet.

Minutes turned into nearly an hour, and I was invincible by the time the officer returned to talk to me.

I didn't technically even have to lie about anything. I was asked a variety of questions ranging from how long I had known Mike, how well I had known him, and if he'd been involved in anything illegal. I was the perfect model student as far as they knew, and, according to me, so was Mike.

I played it perfectly: I was crushed to learn that my senior sponsor had died so suddenly, and I made sure to be concerned for my own safety as well; if someone died right across from my room, was I at risk of being next? The conversation quickly morphed into the police assuring me and providing their empathy regarding the situation.

The interview lasted all of fifteen minutes and I was then allowed to access my room later in the day. I could immediately see that it had been searched.

It couldn't have been the cops. It would have been mentioned and they would have needed a warrant without any type of probable cause. It had to have been Gregory. I decided against hiding the pills in my room. It was too risky.

I decided to keep most of the pills in my car until things

blew over. There was no reason to arouse suspicion, and I had a floor cutout that previously housed a speaker in my car that I could use to easily store what I needed to. I waited for a few minutes in my dorm before leaving again. I headed to a local grocery store and purchased the largest container of vitamins they carried.

That would hold enough pills that I could leave some in my dorm and the rest in my car.

As I left the store I saw an unassuming man in a tan suit standing beside my car. Again, he seemed to fit right in, even though it was the part of town one expected to see a man wearing a suit only if he was accompanied by two women on either side of him.

"Daniel. You did well today. I'm sorry you had to witness that, but I want you to know that it wasn't us. Michael was simply out of time. He didn't stop to understand the consequences of his actions. We know what you saw, and we're quite thankful to you for not doing anything foolish. You've made the right decision," Gregory said. I nodded in agreement.

"Did you know he was dead when you were still talking to me?" I didn't have much to say to Gregory, but I wanted a few answers.

"No, we actually found out when you did. You, of course, were followed back to your room to ensure that you didn't do anything that could jeopardize our operation. It's standard procedure for each new subject. I assure you that after today it won't be needed anymore. You made smart choices and we feel that you can be trusted. You haven't been followed since you made it back to your dorm. You were a smart young man, and you're smarter now." He turned to walk away.

A small part of me wanted to follow Gregory, but my brain, or maybe something else, warned me that nothing good would come of it. I got back in my car and returned to campus.

The following week, I was informed that Mike's heart had stopped as he was trying to leave his dorm for classes. There was no preexisting condition, no defect, and no particular reason for it to stop, according to a campus PD officer who was nice enough to follow up with me. They also told me, after a few well-placed hints, that it wasn't drug related.

From there things returned to normal. Well, as normal as it could be when I was ten times better than pretty much everyone else around me. I chose a double major in computer sciences and computer engineering. I could see that things were blooming in that prospect and I knew I could take advantage of it. I continued to maintain a perfect GPA, only occasionally scoring below one hundred so I could appear normal. I started the practice after a professor accused me of cheating in her class because, in her words, it was "impossible to get a perfect score on every test" in her class. Not true. I did so quite easily. After the academic equivalent of "court," I proved my innocence and she was asked to leave the university by the Dean. I had made a rather compelling case for myself, and I wasn't afraid to let her be a lynchpin.

I continued to take a pill every four to five days for a while, noting the numbers on the pills.

Near the end of my first year I noticed that it took only two to three days to wear off, then every day, then every twelve hours. I started to get worried until I opened the next bag and it contained pills labeled "50,000."

I was relieved for a time. Then I began to consider the dependency I was developing. I decided to perform a test and go a week without taking a pill.

It wasn't awful. I didn't turn into a babbling idiot, I didn't start having withdrawals, I wasn't all shaky, and I didn't feel like I needed the pill to function. I did, however, feel like I needed the pills to function at the level I was able to achieve when I was using them. I was a lesser man without them. A normal man. I was naked without the pills. A soldier in a war zone with a water pistol.

After week of testing, I was satisfied and immediately resumed my consumption. I wasn't addicted. No apparent side effects. Just as promised.

From that point on I never missed a pill. I soared through the remaining semesters like I had written the courses myself. Occasionally, I would let myself get the better of a professor who I thought needed taken down a peg or two, but I always did so in a manner that portrayed me and my fellow students as the innocent martyrs being persecuted by the dictator of Econ 305.

With time, my physique also changed. I was never

particularly athletic before the pills, but the pills changed that. My musculature became more defined. I didn't gain weight like a body builder; more like an Olympic swimmer, or a free-solo climber. By the time I became a senior I had a solid eight-pack and looked like I hit the gym seven times a week.

School had become easy. I took a few positions throughout the student organizations but, to me, they felt rather boring. I did them mostly to fill the extra time. Soon after, the university itself offered me a position. I became "that guy" that everyone wanted to be, I had a cheerleader for a girlfriend, a job with the university that paid more than most people would make even after graduation, and my professors loved me. Maybe out of fear more than interest in mentoring a young up-and-comer.

Just over three years after I took my first pill I graduated with my perfect GPA intact, the highest honors and a full-time job lined up where I'd be making nearly 80 grand a year. I had the potential to be making over six figures within a year if I didn't disappoint. I knew I wouldn't, and the low start gave me a goal to reach for.

The night after I turned in the final exam of my collegiate career I threw a complete rager that would've made National Lampoon jealous. I was somewhat worried that I was being careless with the number of people in attendance but I had a feeling that I could make everything work and still enjoy it. All in all I had representatives from nearly every graduating student body and seemingly from all walks of life. I would love to say that there were so many people that I couldn't count them all, but that would be a lie. I counted 1,324 people at the party.

It was incredible. It was the culmination of everything I had hoped college would be when I had graduated from high school. Beer pong, shots, pools (because one just wasn't enough), a hot tub, and more alcohol than anyone could shake a breathalyzer at. The best part was that I was king of it all. I fit in with all of the social groups. I could hang with the nerds, impress the academics, and drink with the best of them. I even drank the starting nose tackle for the football team under the table that night.

I popped my second pill of the day around midnight, even though I didn't feel like I needed it. It may have been the alcohol, but I didn't want to miss anything. After about thirty minutes I didn't feel drunk anymore, but in a good way; I wasn't hung over and I could start drinking again with no ill effects, which I absolutely did.

"Daniel." The voice stated from about ten feet behind me. I knew exactly who it was even though I hadn't heard the voice in over three years. I turned to face him and saw the man who'd given the startled teenager a backpack containing thousands upon thousands of pills of pure awesome. He wore the same tan suit.

"Spending your time well I see. You took two today. Does it feel good?" Gregory was sitting in a foldable chair with his feet propped up on one of the numerous kegs. No one else paid any attention to him. "I hope you remember Mike. I would encourage you to spend your time wisely. All we have is time." Gregory grabbed one of the cheap beers from the table near him and sipped it briefly before placing it back with disdain. "Surely you can afford better than this colored water." He stood, turned, and walked into the crowd. I once again had the urge to follow him, but it was quickly quashed by the rational side of my brain. My pill-fueled brain. I remained and finished out the party, albeit somewhat more sober and a little less carefree.

The remainder of graduation went off without a hitch. I began work the following week at my new job. Within six months I was in line for a promotion. Within two years I was basically my own boss and only reported to the CEO when he explicitly asked to see me. My first bonus was nearly half of my yearly wages in pay and by the time I had received it my salary had doubled. I enjoyed the money, but I wasn't stupid with it.

I was engaged by that point, to the former cheerleader, and wanted to have a big wedding and a fantastic honeymoon. Some people questioned why I chose Alice. I chose her because she was what I wanted: a brilliantly adaptive mind, and someone who actually made me think a little to hold a conversation with her. She never questioned my intelligence or my confidence, but I could tell that she was certainly impressed by them and had come to know and love me for them. I was smarter than her, but it was her potential that I loved. When I met her, she was the cheerleader. It didn't take long to discover the depth of her mind. I was impressed.

Our honeymoon took us to Hawaii. Two weeks of bliss. It was the first time I was able to put everything aside and focus my entire attention on pleasure. It was refreshing to truly have no cares in the world. I still took my pills, and I was glad I did. On the third day we were nearly mugged. Well, that's not entirely true—I spotted the muggers following us from a few hundred yards away and directed us through a different route back to our hotel.

The detour happened to take us right by the police station. In passing I was able to alert a local policeman that we were being followed without looking overly suspicious. The men were questioned and were found to have the wallets and belongings of several other tourists in their possession.

Once we returned home Alice began working at a research position for the state university while she completed her master's. I continued to rapidly ascend the corporate ladder. I wasn't cutthroat, I wasn't cruel, and I wasn't harsh. I was smart. I did things the right way. I just did them better than everybody else.

A few years passed without any particular incident until the CEO of the company I worked for had a stroke. That was the event he needed to make a change. He was in his late 60s at that point and hadn't been in the best physical health to begin with. He decided to retire and sail around the world with his wife. I bought as many of his shares in the company as my investment portfolio allowed, with his blessing, and became top dog in my own right. I had arrived. I was 27 and making over one million a year. I gave to charities, supported my alma mater, and was active in my community. I didn't need more money, and I didn't want it. My goal wasn't necessarily to be the CEO of the year or to turn the company into the next Microsoft. I wanted control.

Throughout this time I continued to take my supplement. The pill was something I never let go of. I stored them in the same backpack and only took out another baggie when my jar ran out. Each bag was stronger than the last: "50,000" led to "100,000," and eventually on to "1,000,000."

Two weeks ago I ran out of pills in my jar and went to refill it from my backpack. As soon as I undid the zipper I could tell that the last pill I had taken had already worked its way out of my system; I was surprised, and honestly terrified, to see that I was down to my last bag of pills. I had incorrectly assumed that I had at least a dozen more bags, and yet there I was staring at the bottom of the barrel.

I asked Alice if she had taken any and she informed me that the only pill she'd taken lately was birth control. I began to worry. *What if Gregory didn't find me in time to refill my supply? Would I become a blathering idiot?* It had been years since my experiment with the pills and I didn't want to go back to being normal. I wasn't ready to relinquish my stranglehold on life. I began to dig through my old university records to try and find some trace of Gregory.

I found nothing at first. Then I found a name. It was

Gregory's real name. I didn't have much else to go off of aside from an old roommate of his. The roommate's name was Marco. Marco was a large man. If he wasn't six-foot-four he was taller, he was probably pushing 250 and very athletic. He would've intimidated me if it hadn't been for the pills. I never knew for certain if he took them too or not, but I was always under the impression that he did.

I called into the university pretending to be a prospective employer trying to get in touch with Marco. Within a few minutes I had weaseled his email out of the receptionist, and had sent out the message I'd drafted while on the phone. Thankfully, he was apparently in the market for a new job and had emailed me back within the hour. I technically wasn't lying to him either; if he was taking the pill he'd know. I did have a position I could hire him in. It was similar to what he was working at the time and would almost certainly benefit both my company and his wallet.

After setting up a meeting time for the following day I decided I should count my remaining pills; if nothing else, I could ration them to last as long as possible if I only took them when I knew I absolutely needed to be functioning at max capacity. I wasn't prepared for what I found. Two dozen pills marked "107." Ten million seemed like a huge dose, but I had been taking the pills for long enough to not worry about the dosage.

A lower number seemed like a mistake. I popped one and felt an immediate effect. Like it was my first time.

I slept like a baby that night. It had been a while since I had two pills in my system like that and it felt great. I actually got up early and ran a few miles to start the day. One of the perks of being in charge was that I could work whenever I wanted. My first meeting was the meeting with Marco. I was able to finish the run, shower and get ready and be relatively on time.

My company leased three floors of a high-rise for our business. There were ups and downs; it took a while to get to the 42nd floor, but upon arrival I was always met by my staff who were willing to keep me comfortable and functioning. I was usually met by a receptionist and an assistant within seconds of walking in the door. My assistant, James, was an older man who was very intelligent, but had several serious character flaws: he liked to gamble, and drink, and he'd managed to get divorced seven times since 1998. Granted, at least one of those divorces was the result of the aforementioned drinking and gambling in Vegas.

James was always shoving some sort of paper in my face or setting up a client meeting. If there was one thing he was good at, it was managing my time. The record for the longest I'd gone without seeing James in the morning was seconds, not minutes. He was nowhere in sight on that day. The same could be said about the other dozen or so employees I was expecting to see before I made it to my office. The lights were on, but no one was there. I did, however, notice a large figure waiting in my conference room. The silhouette told me that this had to be Marco. I breathed a slight sigh of relief as I tossed my briefcase in my office and hurried off to meet him.

As I made my way back to the conference room I took note that the office was still inexplicably quiet. My mind screamed that something was wrong, but I couldn't figure out why, and the possibility that I could return to some sense of "normal" by meeting with Marco outweighed my mental objections. I quickly opened the door and took my usual seat at the head of the table.

The look Marco gave me wasn't one I was expecting. He looked frozen, and he was completely still. At that moment things began to click, and a familiar figure stepped into the room behind me.

"Daniel, Marco. Marco, Daniel," Gregory said. "Marco isn't much of a talker. At least not anymore he isn't. That stopped about five minutes ago." Gregory hadn't changed a bit; he looked just as confident, the exact same demeanor, and the exact same suit.

For the first time since I'd started taking the pill I was genuinely worried. At once I saw a million scenarios play out in front of me comparing the different ways that the scenario could end. I quickly decided to concentrate on a path with low chance of success, but a high probability of avoiding jail time.

"Stop." The smile was gone. Gregory no longer looked happy, more disappointed if anything. "You won't be calling the police. Your cell won't have any reception, and if you did try to make it to one of the office phones, I could stop you."

My alpha-male mind told me that I could easily take Gregory one on one, however, the pill told me otherwise. I was more inclined to trust it at the moment. I tried to relax. *Plan B.*

"I need more. I'm almost out." If I could reason with him, maybe he'd take Marco. Well, his body. *Was I spending my time poorly? Was I making myself too busy and too inaccessible?*

"You don't have the time. Neither did Marco. He was not one of our success stories. Things didn't go as smoothly for him as they did you." It was true. Marco looked rough. He had deep bags under his eyes, was nearly bald, easily fifty pounds overweight, and not nearly the collegiate linebacker he was supposed to be. The fact that he had been desperately searching for new employment, rather than running a company made me begin to question the pills for the first time. If they hadn't been wonder drugs for everyone, maybe they only emphasized what already existed in someone. A potential unlocker.

Gregory interrupted my thinking. "Stop thinking and be present. This is important. I am taking Marco. You may want to step back. This isn't always pretty." Gregory motioned to two people who had somehow eluded my notice up until that point. The first person stabbed Marco's body in the neck with a syringe. The second was poised directly behind Marco as if waiting for the body to try to escape.

A growl began to emerge from Marco's throat. He had appeared dead for the moments that I was in the room, but he was suddenly making noise. Marco stood bolt upright and tried to grab the man in front of him with the syringe. That's when creepy-guy-number-two leaned in and put Marco in a wrestling hold. Marco growled again and finally relented.

"It's all about time," Gregory said. He seemed to feel very superior in that moment. Marco's eyes were completely white. There appeared to be nothing behind them, no brain, no thoughts. "We do not normally warn people, but you've done your part and it would only be fair of us to let you know that you're almost out of time. You may want to go enjoy what little you have left." Gregory silently walked away with the three large bodies following him. As he did I began to notice life creep back into the office. James was on me before I knew what to do, asking how I'd managed to sneak past him, and I was suddenly holding a stack of papers that needed to be signed before lunch. I quickly excused myself and made for my office. I spent a few minutes in the office before deciding that I had to leave.

I raced home, and it felt like the pill wasn't working anymore. *How much time did I have left? Were they going to kill me?* I needed another pill. *Definitely needed another. Maybe I would take two.*

I took out a hedge turning into my driveway, but I didn't slow down. Inside I found my pill bottle nearly empty save for two pills rattling around. I grabbed one to examine the strength, but it was a number I hadn't seen before; "4,392." That was odd. I looked at the other one and it read "10,000." That too was odd; they were both very low compared to the other pills I'd taken recently. I looked back at the first pill and it read a different number than it had a moment before: "4,381." I knew what it meant, but I couldn't accept it. I could still feel the previous pill in my system. I watched the counting pill.

"4,380."

"4,300."

Eventually it dropped below "4,000."

My heart began to race, and the counter moved faster.

I didn't move. I could barely think. I quickly popped the pill marked "10,000" and felt nothing. I held my last three-thousand-something heartbeats in my hand.

All that time wasted. I tried to think about where the time had all gone.

Gregory was suddenly standing next to me, the two large men and Marco in tow. Gregory looked pleased. "Let's not drag this out. We will use your time well."

I threw the last pill down my throat like I had done so many times before; no water, straight down. I felt tired. For the first time in many years, my body hurt. Everything ached. I could feel a lifetime of pains that I had been able to ignore come over me all at once. Arthritis that I would have experienced at sixty suddenly set in deep. My chest hurt and my left arm went numb; somewhere along the road I was due for a heart attack. Finally my head started pounding. It was the worst of the pain, very localized, sharp, and throbbing. I guess I was destined to die from a stroke.

I drooled and looked up at Gregory.

As my world faded I wondered what could have been, what I could have done without the pills. If only I'd had more time.

Gregory bent over to speak, "This isn't the end. You may quite enjoy what comes next. Though, I must admit, I am very surprised you took the pill. If only you had thought of the decision a little more. I'm not here to hit you over the head with your decisions. This isn't a pep talk. Just let go. It's time for something new."

The world went black.

Ambition

Birthmarked

By J.L Spencer

There were a lot of things that Lynne was and that Lynne had become, but never once were any of them normal. What fate had composed for Lynne from the time she was born was a life of forced introversion. Her pustulated and scaly features marked her as a target. A target for ridicule, a target for curiosity and a target for sympathy. She knew, from being told so often as a child, that there was no such thing as being normal. That normalcy was an illusion, brought on by society and its own insecurity. However, she never felt that way.

The people in town knew her as the freak, the shut-in, and the monster under the Lake Pointe Bridge. The house she lived in did her no favors to argue the rumors. It embellished them. Nestled quietly beneath an overpass was the Waggoners' home. Submerged and bound by ivy and weeds, the shack was unrecognizable as anything other than a pile of forest debris.

The Waggoners had seen their fair share of unwanted visitors despite their property's appearance. The house was a mainstay of dares for the children of Lake Pointe. It wasn't uncommon for rocks to come soaring through their front window or for them to find dead animals lying on the walkway. It was from those experiences that Lynne's mother had decided her daughter was safer indoors, where she could be protected. The world wouldn't and couldn't understand Lynne's condition.

When Lynne did leave the house, it was for appointments with specialists who all wanted to try their hand at fixing her. Each specialist had a theory of cause and cure and each, time and time again, proved themselves wrong in the case of Lynne. Her skin never hurt, she would say, but it occasionally tingled. The condition baffled doctors, which resulted in countless cream and lotion prescriptions. Failure after failure brought Lynne a life of sorrow, hopelessness and adverse reactions so harsh that oatmeal baths and Benadryl were introduced as part of her weekly regimen.

On her seventeenth birthday, Lynne chose to surrender to her condition by tossing her medicines in the wastebasket. She spent weeks in the attic, silently debating how to break the news. Telling her mother wouldn't be easy, but hiding it among the small confines of their shanty home was no longer impossible for her. She nervously paced the same stretch of floor in the attic until she had worn a lackluster trail in the oak.

It took her several days to find the courage, standing at the top of the overused staircase, and even then she couldn't look her mother in the eye. Instead, she bellowed down to her mother's bedroom, taking in a harsh breath before belting out as clear and distinct as her shaking voice could manage, "I don't want to do it anymore!"

When she mustered enough bravery to walk and stand

under the threshold of her mother's room, Mrs. Waggoner was sitting calmly in her rocking chair, holding the paisley-printed book which contained hundreds of photos of Lynne from the time she was born. Unlike most families' photo albums, it had served a purpose beyond preserving memories. Overflowing with before-and-afters of Lynne's condition, they had taken the photographs every week between regimens for nearly a decade, hoping to capture a glimpse of progress.

Positioning her hands demurely in front of her and preparing to speak, Lynne quickly found that words had failed her and for a moment there was only silence between the two of them. Mrs. Waggoner moved her fingers gently across the pictures, giving no acknowledgement to Lynne's presence, instead keeping her eyes fixated on the book in her lap.

Finally, Mrs. Waggoner spoke, her voice hovering just above a whisper, "Open your eyes. You're too much like me. I can't fix you. I've tried, but I can't. I'm not perfect. And neither are you."

It was everything Lynne needed to hear and the perfect summary of everything she had spent the last week alone in the attic forcing herself to accept. A soothing mixture of relief and victory swelled in Lynne as she sunk down to the floor, curling her knees to her chest in heaves. There would be no more fight to resolve her appearance, but there would also be no more hope. No more Benadryl or oatmeal baths. No more doctor visits or photographs. Relief and emotion washed over Lynne. The battle was over and the monster had won. Mrs. Waggoner had known it just as well as her daughter had. Mrs. Waggoner fell to Lynne's side, shushing Lynne rhythmically against her chest until Lynne's sobs turned to snores.

Lynne awoke groggily to her dusty bedroom. The familiar peeling wallpaper lulled her awake and a light breeze rolled through the room, bringing the smell of her mother's cooking with it. It was Wednesday and Mrs. Waggoner was throwing together the last of what they had before William would arrive to drop off the family's groceries. William had been the only visitor they'd ever come to welcome in all their years of living at Lake Pointe. Mrs. Waggoner had grown so fond of him that she began paying him nearly four years ago to deliver their groceries every Wednesday, and it was Lynne who ran eagerly to collect them. As she'd swing back the big cedar door, sweat would build unwillingly at the base of her neck and her cheeks would glow embarrassingly bright. William had quickly become her first and only crush as well as the highlight of her week.

Comfortable under the warm quilt, thinking of William, she had almost forgotten the events of the night prior. It wasn't until she rubbed her raw eyes that she had remembered. Although she always considered herself condemned by her appearance to a life of perpetual misery, the sentence had never felt more absolute until that particular morning. All of it changed, dramatically, when Lynne pulled herself to her feet and walked into the bathroom. That was the day the mirror became Lynne's best friend.

Examining her reflection, with a toothbrush protruding

from the side of her mouth, she saw a girl who bore the same perfect features as the dolls she had played with as a child. Every inch of her skin without so much as a blemish. There wasn't a single pimple, blackhead or scar. All signs of suffering removed, miraculously. No ridges or pock marks left for her or anyone else to gawk at. Her pale, nearly translucent skin revealed a flawless network of cornflower veins.

"Impossible." Her fingers traced the curve of her jawline before moving down the stem of her neck, pulling her shirt to the side to showcase a positively smooth shoulder.

Minutes went by as she studied herself and Lynne held onto every second, taking careful breaths while listening to her mother's quiet hums emerging from the kitchen downstairs.

And for the first time in forever, a genuine smiled took form on Lynne's new face. There would be no giving up.

Later that day when William had arrived, Lynne eagerly lunged at the door, nearly ripping it from its hinges throwing it open. He stood with bags in tow, smiling brightly just as he had every Wednesday before. William had never regarded Lynne the way most had when brought face-to-face with someone so painfully deformed. He had always been kind and greeted her with a genuine smile that exposed all of his brilliant teeth. That day was no different, despite the obvious change in her appearance. Blushing, Lynne politely took the groceries and turned to head inside when William stopped the door with his hand.

"You look great, Lynne," he said, still wearing his smile.

Lynne played nervously with the half-moons of her fingernails. "Yeah? I think so, too. About time something worked, right?"

Although conversation between Lynne and William was not unfamiliar, something about it felt new. The small talk between them went on for a few minutes, and before long, Lynne felt a nervous blush spread across her face. The kind of blush that most girls would fight to hide when talking to a boy of interest. Lynne embraced it. She could see the color of her cheeks as they brightened in the reflection of the small mirror that hung next to the door. Its shade deepened when William had asked to take her out on a date that evening.

As Lynne made her way into the kitchen, feeling light as air, she noted the old dining room table where she had sat during the autumn months to watch the leaves on the maples deteriorate from the wind. The entire house seemed less like an enclosure and more like a home. She placed the groceries atop the table and sat, waiting for her mother to serve the tea.

"I heard you with that boy." The way Mrs. Waggoner said it made William sound like an overused dish rag. Something dirty that should have been discarded long ago.

Lynne let her mother go on without interrupting, though she had an idea of where the conversation was headed and bit her lip hard to keep quiet.

"Nothing good can come from that, you know. People don't understand. You're a thing to them. A circus act. A curiosity. They don't see you as a person. Especially boys. I know firsthand."

Her voice trailed and it forced a twinge in Lynne's stomach, compelling her to leave the table. She knew what her mother was getting to. Lynne's father was rarely mentioned in the household, and for good reason. Having left them before she was born, Mrs. Waggoner had always believed, deep down, that he had loved her. But only in the way that a person would love a dead bird brought to their door by their pet. Since Lynne's birth, her mother had struggled not only to raise her daughter alone, but with losing the one man she had hoped to spend the rest of her life with. Seventeen years later, Mrs. Waggoner couldn't cope. Most days she rejected Lynne for looking so much like her father, even through her asperous skin. He had promised Mrs. Waggoner forever, and in Lynne, kept half of that vow.

"You can't just assume the worst in everyone. William is kind; considerate. He's never treated me as anything less than normal. He's a friend." Lynne paused, watching her mother's jaw tighten as she poured the tea, its steam curling toward her face. "For once, can I just feel normal?"

"You have never been and you never will be. Cursed or cured!"

Mrs. Waggoner leapt from her seat, flying across the table to grab Lynne's arms, shaking them until they went limp.

"You can't expect to be loved or understood by these people. With or without your scars!" Lynne knew what her mother meant. Lynne would always be a freak in one way or another. If she bore the scars, she was a freak for having them. And if they stayed gone, she was a freak for ever having had them at all. It was an extreme flip in temperament from the night before, but that was the life that the Waggoners lived.

Lynne's mother's voice and grip stayed firm as she continued, "And believe me when I say, the damage you've worn outside is nothing compared to the damage boys like William can do to you on the inside. Though you might think you're strong enough to wear them with pride someday, I can promise you that you'd never be more wrong."

Despite all the truth Lynne knew her mother's words contained, only a few weeks earlier, she had been sitting in the same room, tracing her blemishes with her fingers and imagining herself walking to the deli on the corner. She would smile and wave at everyone she passed and they would greet her just the same. That was the world Lynne had wished herself a part of for as long as she could remember. And now it was hers for the taking. For Lynne, the miracle meant she had a chance to be as close to human as she had ever wanted, but to her mother, it meant her daughter was one step closer to leaving, just as Lynne's father had.

Later that afternoon, while Lynne studied the blooming welts on her arms that had begun to resemble bruised peaches, Mrs. Waggoner walked into the attic holding a slice of butter pecan cake on one of their ivory tea saucers.

With her peace-offering, Mrs. Waggoner made an attempt at coaxing Lynne into understanding things the way she saw them. The risk outweighed the benefit, if the benefit existed at all. For each point Mrs. Waggoner made, Lynne had a counter argument. The two of them went back and forth and eventually Lynne's mother surrendered, allowing her daughter one night out and no more. Certainly Lynne would see things for what they were. One night was plenty of time for her to figure out what Mrs. Waggoner already knew to be true. When Lynne heard her mother's footsteps descend the staircase, she buried her face joyfully into her pillow and screamed with joy.

* * *

That evening, when Lynne was getting ready in front of the mirror, she felt like Cinderella. She imagined walking through the front door with William standing next to a large golden carriage made from a pumpkin pulled by white horses. She had spent hours piling her hair atop her head, pulling down loose tendrils with the same precision she had done for years with her dolls. Sorting through her mental checklist, everything was in place. Chores had been finished, regimens had been completed; creams, lotions and a makeup compact tucked away neatly in her purse until she was finished. She stood, admiring the princess she had become, and swelling with excitement over experiencing her first adventure.

William stood on the stone walkway of the battered house, listening to the traffic pass overhead. Lynne looked stunning. Narrow, flowing strips of blue chiffon hung from the bottom of her blouse and they quivered in the wind as it blew from the movement of the door. After compliments were exchanged, William slipped his hand into hers and they were off.

They had decided to go to a movie instead of just dinner and as they walked to the theater, William carried on about the plot and how action-packed it would be. Lynne had never gone to a movie, nor had she ever seen the inside of a theater. When she walked in, she found it overwhelming. The rich, buttery thickness of the air from the popcorn, the way her shoes stuck to the floor from spilled sugary confections. The endless rows of chairs as they walked down the aisles that cradled them and the soda-stained upholstery that smothered each seat. It was a dream to her, and she found it was easy to push thoughts of her mother from her mind with so much excitement happening around her. That night she was not the monster under Lake Pointe Bridge. That night she was just a person, like everyone else in the theater.

When the lights dimmed for the movie to begin, Lynne gasped. The opening credits played on the screen with a drum-heavy beat, and the noise came from all sides. Each bass note delivered small vibrations into Lynne's back and feet. It was so loud. And all of it made Lynne feel more alive than she had ever felt.

Thirty minutes into the movie, she watched nervously on as a woman hid beneath a desk to escape silently from a man who was looking to take her hostage. Lynne's anxiety grew and she dug at her leg through her pants, pushing her fingernails deep through the cloth. At first, she didn't notice the scaly bump that had risen on her thigh. The cotton was thick enough and the movie distracting enough that she didn't think twice about it. But then, as the woman on the screen emerged from under the desk unharmed, Lynne's attention went back to what she felt beneath her fingers.

With fear, she rolled her hands over the skin of her arms, then desperately pulled at the skin to reveal what looked like the bark of a tree. Her hands fumbled around her purse to retrieve the compact she had tucked away in a small side compartment of her purse. Turning to her left so that her back was to William, she checked her reflection. The monster peered back, its appearance more savage than she had ever seen it before. Its cheeks were like tightly wrapped coils of dirty rope; its chin like flesh-colored gravel. Lynne rose from her seat and ran from the theater room. She could hear William scrambling after her, but she had already reached the bathroom before he was through the exit door.

Taking the nearest empty stall, Lynne hurriedly locked the door and flipped her purse over to empty it of its contents. The white-capped bottles spilled out onto the dirty tile and she frantically searched the labels. Her crying made it hard for her to read any of them. Track marks stained her cheeks from all the tears and even with her skin as tough and ugly as leather, she had never felt more fragile. Sorting the bottles desperately, Lynne started with the one she always did at home in front of the mirror every night. The thin, sloshing liquid poured into her hands like milk and she began scrubbing her face. Her nails dug at her cheeks and throat, building a frothy mucous on her ridged skin. It wasn't working. Instead, it seemed to be making it worse.

Within moments, she had removed all of her clothing and started on bottle number two. Its liquid was thick and slow, like cold honey. Using as much strength as she could manage, she scrubbed her arms and torso vigorously. Forcing her nails to work the mixture deep into the scars until they started to tear. Streaks of crimson blood pooled around her fresh wounds until they turned pink with the lotions. She worked through the pain until, eventually, there was none at all. In its place was panic, driving her to hysterics and numbing all feeling. By the end of bottle number three, she looked as if she was molting. Slivered strips of flesh fell softly to the floor, like the last remaining leaves from a tree in the dawn of winter. She tore at herself until there was nothing left to tear and until she couldn't anymore. She had ripped and shredded herself to pieces until each torn sliver hung from her the same way the strips of blue chiffon did when she had stood in front of William earlier that night.

Lynne's remains were found by a group of teenage girls who had walked into the bathroom shortly after, alarmed by the sudsy maroon pool that escaped from under the stall. When they peered through the open gap between the stall door and the stained ceramic, they saw the disfigured heap, mauled by its own hands and resting amid a literal bloodbath.

It is said that when her mother was delivered the news, she was completely devoid of emotion. Her expression stoic and impassive as detectives crossed the walkway toward the Waggoner's home, stepping over the dead animals that littered the cobblestones.

Vanity

Given Form

By S.M. Piper

Walking through the homes of the rich never got less weird with practice. Everywhere I went, I was surrounded by fine art and high ceilings. Like stepping into a movie, only I was reminded of how real it was every time the host spoke.

"I acquired the monolith from a very influential associate of mine," Alaine Clemont informed me as he led me through the halls of his mansion. Though he wasn't quite tall enough to come up to my shoulders, his gait was such that I still felt rushed. I took in the sights as best I could; on every wall hung a painting, in every alcove sat a vase, and each of them looked priceless. "It was discovered on the ocean floor only a few miles from the Solomon Islands. Heaven knows how long it's spent down there, but it cost a small fortune just to retrieve it, not to mention the amount I had to spend purchasing and having it shipped here."

Clemont led us to a large spiral staircase set into the floor. "I'll be honest, I've never worked with, or around, ocean damage," I said as we descended. "Marble's resilient, but—"

"That won't be an issue, Miss Fields," Clemont assured me. His shiny, black leather shoes made a distinct click against the concrete floors as we walked. "The piece is in pristine condition, and I believe you'll find every tool you could possibly want at your disposal. I'm assured they're all top-of-the-line."

"Of course," I said. The basement seemed to be as big as the house itself. Thick beams supported wide-open rooms, and I couldn't help but wonder if I wasn't standing in the start of some sprawling underground community.

We reached what was to be my studio. Plastic sheeting had been laid down across the entire floor, and just as he said, the walls were lined with tables containing every sculptor's tool I'd ever seen. It was smaller than the rooms we had just walked through, which made the centerpiece that much more dramatic: a massive, seven-foot-cubed piece of marble dominated the room, drawing attention almost exclusively to itself. Clemont was already beside it, running his fingers along the surface.

"Come feel it. A true find, and a marvel of any collection. Untold decades down there on the floor of the ocean."

Intimidating though it was just to approach the piece, I stepped forward and touched the white-blue stone. "You've polished this already."

Clemont's eyes went wide, and he gave me a look of practiced indignation. "I certainly did not!"

"Someone did," I muttered, gazing up at it. "Marble doesn't come out of the ground this smooth."

He huffed. "Are you implying I can't control my staff? I'll have you know that—"

"I'm implying that someone's polished this." I didn't bother masking the exasperation in my voice. "But it doesn't matter, it's not like it's unworkable. I can make something great with this."

Clemont's disposition cheered immediately. "Wonderful! And speaking of which, I was having a look through your portfolio, and I thought something like A Song in Pearl, on a larger scale of course, might go very well with this. At the very least, I want something grand, something that tells the storied past of the stone, something…"

"Something that looks expensive."

"Exactly! Yes, exactly right. Oh, I was told you were good."

Looking up at it with my hands on my hips, I tried to picture what was inside the marble. "You know, there's a saying that sculptors don't create anything, just free whatever's already on the inside," I said aloud.

"Romantic," Clemont said in a clipped tone. "I'll let you get started on setting my masterpiece loose, then." He strode from the room, his click, click, clicking fading rapidly.

"All right, big guy. What've you got for me?" My question filled the room, echoing off the concrete walls a half-dozen times. I had worked with marble before, of course, but this felt like another beast altogether. Picking up a power drill from one of the tables, I returned to the piece and began to shear off a corner, vague ideas already taking root in my mind.

What I'd told Clemont wasn't entirely sentimental.

Whenever I have chiseled, carved, and drilled, I have slowly closed a window of malleability for each piece. I have found that it's bad practice to rely too much on the gut instinct changes.

I approached every piece previously with precision and used rationality over my gut whenever possible. Until the sea marble.

It wasn't even as though I had a clear image in my mind of what I was doing, just the feeling that every action I took was the correct one. Every hole drilled was the perfect length, every chunk of marble that came off was never going to be part of the finished piece. The feeling went beyond a flow state; I wasn't just creating, I was creating perfection.

Clemont came in every few days to see how it was going. It was strange, but I almost enjoyed working in front of him, showing him what I was doing, what he couldn't yet see in the marble. Each rough outline of the finished piece was as much a surprise to me as it was to him, but the feeling of pride in my work never went away.

A few days in, Clemont got my attention as I was drilling on top of the stone. Cutting the power to the tool, I pulled my earmuffs around my neck.

"What is this here?" he asked me, indicating the corner I'd begun on.

"Well, it's rough, it'll look better at the end, but it's a guy kneeling?"

"Is it?" he asked, picking up on my inflection. Honestly, I

wasn't sure why I'd framed it as a question either. For the first time I was seeing it as a whole, rather than a series of corners and contours. But, unmistakably, it was a man on his knees, head raised up and arms outstretched in front of him, facing the center of the stone.

"Yeah," I said with more confidence this time. "Yes, that is what it is."

Clemont seemed skeptical, but kept any reservations he may have had to himself. He ran his forefinger along the man's bare back, then pressed it to his thumb as if displeased with the residue.

"It will look better in the end," I repeated.

"Mmm." Clemont stepped back and gave a small nod. My ire piqued, I slid down the small ramp I'd made for myself and approached my employer.

"Did you have something you wanted to say?" I felt odd, as though the words I was choosing weren't quite my own. "Do you not appreciate what I've done for you?"

Clemont held his hands up defensively, backing against a support pillar. "Well, it's certainly no favor, of course, you're being compensated very well for your time."

He was right, of course, but I felt compelled to press. "You couldn't make what I can," I said. "You're not an artist." For added effect, I held down the trigger to the power drill still in my hand.

"Miss—" he startled, taking a short breath to compose himself. His eyes were trained on the tip of the drill. "Miss

Fields, renown though you may be, I am certainly not a man you want to threaten."

"And I'm a woman you can't afford to lose." I gestured toward the sculpture with the still-spinning drill. "Nobody else would know what to do with this anymore—and besides, what a blemish that would be to your collection. Think of what they'd say at parties: 'Oh Mr. Clemont, why couldn't you get Ellen Fields? Was she too expensive?'"

Clemont visibly bristled at the idea; a poker player he was not. "Fine." He stormed past me while giving a wide berth to the power drill. "I expect a masterpiece!

"You should have from the beginning," I said to myself. Approaching the kneeling man Clemont had sneered at, I spent the next several minutes drilling deep holes into its head, and a feeling of catharsis rolled over me in waves.

* * *

From then on, except to eat, sleep and use the restroom, I didn't stop working. When the fatigue started to set into my joints, I took painkillers to keep going. It was too exciting to stop, too interested to not see what would come of the sea marble. The stone called to me, and I couldn't wait to answer.

In what felt like no time at all, it was fleshed out far beyond a single kneeling man. There were eight of them ringing the center, and during my brief respites I noticed that each of them seemed to have some sort of affliction. One man had rough boils all across his back; the side of another's head was concave. There was a man who knelt on legs cut off at mid-shin, and there was a man who had deep lacerations over his body.

I barely remembered carving any of it.

The center was the largest part still left unworked, though with a sculptor's eye it wasn't hard to see where it was going. A figure stood, towering over the supplicants with its hands on its hips. Its hair was the only defined feature, flowing dreadlocks that whipped through the air as if blown by a powerful breeze.

"You're looking pretty today," I remarked aloud one morning as I stepped up on one of the kneeling men to reach the head of the centerpiece. "Are you doing something different with your hair? Oh, are you moisturizing? You are, aren't you?" Chuckling to myself, I started chiseling away at the face, concentrating on every grain of powder I scraped off. It had to be just right.

The eyes and nose were roughed in, and the whole thing was starting to look familiar. I wasn't sure quite where I'd seen the face before, but I let instinct guide my hand. Working intently on the slope of the nose, concentrating on the gradual curve, I wasn't at all ready when my footing gave out underneath me.

At first I assumed the noise I was hearing was just my head ringing in pain. I lay crumpled between two of the kneeling men, still reeling from the shock of agony, but a long, shrill noise demanded my attention. I crawled off the base of the sculpture and lay on my back, clutching my head, but the noise persisted.

I don't know how long it took me to notice, but finally my eyes fell on the face of the sculpture. When I'd fallen, the chisel had gouged out a small hole in the nose, and the statue was screaming. I had gone too far, chipped away a part of the actual statue, and it was screaming in pain.

"Stop it!" I yelled back, getting to my knees. The shriek rang inside my skull, bounced against the back of my eyes, and pierced my brain so sharply I thought my skull might split open at any moment. "Please, stop! I can fix this! I can fix it, goddammit, stop!"

Frantically, I scoured the base of the statue, looking amongst the supplicants for the missing chunk, but it was nowhere to be found. Only dust and pebbles, jagged shreds of excess that dug into my hands as I swept back and forth across the stone, looking for the missing piece—all the while, the statue screamed.

"Stop it! Stop it! I said I'd fix it, just stop!" My pain gave way to rage, and I yelled at the statue, staring into its coarse, emotionless eyes. "What do you want from me? Huh? I slipped. What do you expect?"

Perfection.

The screaming hadn't stopped, but the word unmistakably entered my mind and took the wind from my sails. It was right, of course. This piece deserved perfection, and I was capable of that, but I had failed. There was a blemish on the statue, right on the flawless face I'd been crafting with painstaking detail. Tears welled in my eyes as I thought about what I'd done. What I could never undo.

It occurred to me that I might just walk away. The intensity of the screams had varied with proximity, and it seemed as though I might be able to simply outdistance them.

I walked to the entryway, and looked down the long corridor. Other assorted works of art lined the hall. My work would never be among them. It would gather dust, unfinished —or worse, completed by some lesser artist—and I would have to live with that knowledge.

You can't.

"I can't." My voice was a whimper as I retreated to a nearby table, lifting a small ice pick Clemont had, for some reason, bothered getting.

As the screams rang in my mind, I approached the statue. My head was bowed in reverence, the ice pick clutched firmly in my grip. Climbing onto the sea marble, I raised my gaze to its own one last time, placing the tip of the pick pointed upward against my throat. I considered the action only briefly. Something in the back of my mind made me feel so dramatic. Rationality took over and I fixed my eyes on my mistake.

Glancing up at the wound, my breath caught in my throat.

I could fix it. I gripped the ice pick with both hands and opened my mouth, reaching in to prod one of my molars. The pick slipped a few times, but after some doing, I got a good hold on the tooth and pulled for all I was worth.

The agony shot through my skull, mixing with the screams of the statue into a transcendent tone; a sound of love. A sound of acceptance, of divine approval. The statue had been trying to speak to me. My mind just wasn't used to the voice.

I doubled over in pain, yanking on my tooth with all my strength. Every centimeter of progress felt as though my skull was splitting open anew, and blood was starting to trickle out of my mouth, dripping onto the statue.

Once the tooth was free of my skull, I wasted no time in filling the hole in the statue and the screaming stopped immediately. The gouge was filled perfectly; a little bit of smoothing and nobody would ever know the difference.

I spent the next hour collapsed at the base of the statue, sobbing in relief.

* * *

I heard Clemont coming before he arrived. I was eager to have him see the piece, as it had been finished for days. The centerpiece had become a woman in a long, sleek dress that flared out at her ankles. Her hands were held a foot away from her hips, palms facing forward, and she stared into the distance, seemingly unaware of the worship of the men around her.

She was perfect.

So it was of no surprise when Clemont rounded the corner

to my workspace and, laying eyes on my art for the first time since its completion, regarded it with a look of awe.

"Isn't she beautiful?" I spoke with an unpracticed lisp, and it caught my employer's attention. He looked up at me and gasped. Before he could say more, I nodded and waved my hand dismissively. The moment wasn't about me, or what I had sustained and endured to create such a masterpiece. The moment was about the art. Clemont stammered, unsure of where to begin, so I continued. "I kept… I kept messing up," I admitted, working on favoring the left side of my tongue. "First it was her nose, then a part on her arm here, and then I kinda, well, I got this hooked gouge into her side." Each spot I indicated was as smooth as the rest of the sculpture. "And I couldn't figure out how to fill the wound."

"Miss Fields, are you feeling all right?" He sounded genuinely concerned for me, but I dismissed the idea with another wave.

"I'm fine." Clemont looked down when I limped, and held a hand to his mouth.

"Your foot!"

"As I was saying, I kept making mistakes, but I think she wanted me to, so I could grow as an artist. The side wound was easy, once I thought about it." I displayed my tongue to Clemont, showing him the half that remained.

"Jesus Christ. Where? Where did you put it?"

I showed him the spot with my finger. "It's here, but you won't see it. That's something else she wanted to teach me."

Together we looked down at the statue's foot, and Clemont tested it with the tip of his own shoe. It remained firm, acting just like the marble it had become.

"Miss Fields, you understand if this is all a little hard to believe." He glanced around the room as he spoke, doubtlessly looking for my discarded body parts. "You understand if I cannot take the word of a madwoman who has descended into self-mutilation."

Smiling, I retrieved a small chisel from my tool belt. "Observe," I told him, approaching the statue. The agony of her screams hadn't lessened with practice, but I wanted to show him what I had created. Bracing myself, I carved a three-inch gash in her shoulder and was overcome at once by her keening. I looked up to Clemont, who did not appear to be reacting to the screams.

No matter. I set my jaw and dug the chisel into my shoulder, peeling off a small strip of flesh. Mr. Clemont grimaced at the sight and tried to say something, but his words were lost on me.

Holding the strip of skin up to the statue, I gently pressed it into the wound and beckoned Clemont closer. He approached, and together we watched as the marble accepted my skin. It was a slow process, but already the edges were hardening, taking on the white-blue appearance of the rest of the stone.

"My god…" Clemont muttered, his voice once again audible since the screaming had stopped. He looked me up and down again, taking stock of my injuries. I had small scars up and down my arms and legs, but none as major as my mouth and foot.

I shrugged, very pleased with my accomplishment.

Clemont matched my expression, looking back at the statue.

"That's remarkable. You have done a tremendous job here, and it does look flawless." He looked down at the kneeling supplicants and seemed as though he was about to say something more before changing his mind. "Come, come. This is just in time."

Clemont had gone on ahead, and my limp was slowing me down a little.

As I walked up the stairs, several large men followed down the stairs and walked quickly. Some were carrying a variety of tools.

When I arrived at the top of the stairs, Clemont was there to greet me. He had a white dress in his arms and quickly ushered me to follow one of his staff members.

I followed and was quickly changed into the dress and adorned. When I was finally given a mirror, I looked beautiful. Just like the sculpture. Just like my art.

I could hear the crowd before I limped around the corner. Clemont was there waiting, my masterpiece the center of the room.

The eyes in the room quickly turned to me. The missing body parts, scars and bruises my cross to bear for my art.

Some eyes looked on me as if I was the only contributing body. I wasn't enough for the piece. If only they all knew just how many other people it took for the masterpiece to truly become what it was.

No one could speak to me that evening, because I wasn't able to hear above the screaming of my masterpiece. She kept repeating herself all evening, asking me to add more to her, to finish her because she wouldn't be perfect without more than me.

At midnight, I obliged her.

It took five men to finally stop me.

Pride

Dammit, Janet

By Ashley Franz Holzmann

Here Janet is, being alive. Waiting in a line. Chewing bubblegum. Being human—waiting to die, just like all the others around her. Some are probably waiting for Heaven. Others are waiting for nothing. The rest are waiting to go get stoned again—it's that kind of rough neighborhood.

She is bored.

Human existence feels a lot like a long waiting game. Wait until school is over, wait for a child to come to term inside a belly, wait for a driver's license, wait for a war to end or an election or a movie to be released. It's all about waiting. She feels like her entire existence is defined by waiting. She lets her mind wander around the idea like a child in a forest.

Janet feels like some kind of robot. Like the ones she used to watch in the cartoons her brother liked. He always tried to get her more involved in his boy stuff. She's just standing here, inputting useless knowledge into herself from her phone. Every few minutes she takes a step. Oh, she also keeps breathing, but that's a subsystem function. Blink the eyes, breathe, keep the oil flowing through the joints. Receive input.

The idea of robots reminds Janet of a thing she saw on TV about a girl who was seventeen or something and way too into makeup. The girl would dress herself up and do her makeup for hours and her hair for hours and her nails for hours and when the hours were through she would take pictures of herself with wide and empty eyes and she would look just like a life-sized doll. The thing on TV was concerned about how the photos were being passed around and how it was a fetish. The mother was largely unable to prevent her daughter from spending four or six hours doing something like that—maybe she had soap operas to watch or something. Maybe the mom was like the people around Janet.

Janet wonders what it would feel like to know that many guys jerked off to pictures of her. It's an interesting question. She thought about it a couple times in high school and wondered how many of the boys in class thought of her like that, but ever since then she had forgotten about the rush of trying to figure it out. To have it happen on a national level feels like a form of destiny. Like a goal that all actresses and models want to achieve. They all had to know that that's really what they were reduced to when they became that popular.

Janet looks down at her watch. Time isn't moving very fast, but it does keep passing her by. The world thinks California is some type of magical place—it really is nothing special. North California is a different world from Southern California.

How many lines has she wasted her life in over the years? How many times has the wait been because there was some eighteen-year-old behind the counter not giving a shit about everyone standing and waiting on them?

How many times has it been because she decided to go shopping on pay day? Or because she was waiting for a friend so they could eat lunch together? How many times was it a technical error, or—well—she doesn't care enough to keep thinking about it.

The pharmacy she is standing in is the closest to her home on the way to and from daycare. It sits next to some fast food places and is a frequent stop after dropping the children off. The kids. Sometimes Janet has to lie to the daycare and say the kids aren't sick.

Janet is going through top ten lists on her phone about things that she will never remember again. Ten ways to improve sex, best purses, other things that she compares herself to. She just wants to fill the prescription, but it's taking forever. Janet has to think for a moment to remember where she is. Some drug store. A mom and pop place. Yeah, that's why the neighborhood is sketchy.

Janet gets off her smartphone and looks around at the others in the line with her. They all look worthless. Some kid on his smartphone is next to her, trying to disassociate himself from the group. The kid smells like french fries and looks a lot like one of the regular register kids from the fast food place next door.

It looks like everyone else here in the pharmacy enjoys the fast food nearby more often than Janet. Most of the group isn't in shape—unlike Janet.

Janet may not be rich, but she knows how to carry herself and she exercises.

There is an old man with a limp making a fuss with his fat wife—Janet assumes she's the guy's wife.

"Now, Mr. Sumpter, you behave yourself this night," says one woman behind the counter.

So the couple are regulars. The husband calms down right away, so that's at least nice. Janet hates to hear arguments and screaming. Janet is generally annoyed by a lot of things. Inconveniences. The world is a great pool of inconvenience and everyone is supposed to soak it in and dive in head first.

The wife probably needs the meds because of her obesity. If only all the people in the room took care of themselves. Most of them wouldn't have to be here.

Janet is different. She isn't like the rest in her neighborhood. She knows it. She is a damn good catch: she has the hourglass figure down, and she has herself an ass that she works hard to shape in the gym. Janet has mastered makeup and cooking and all the girl things she is supposed to be amazing at.

She is pretty.

On days when Janet needs to feel popular again, she puts on her yoga pants and heads to the drug store wearing her furry boots, her hair up but not done, with a pair of large glasses that look more expensive than they really are. Sometimes she wears them inside the store. It makes her feel above the others—alone in her bubble. Untouchable. They all want her or want to be her.

In high school, Janet was very outspoken about most things. She was social and she was popular. Things were going her way and she was going to be rich and famous. She didn't have a real plan for how it would happen, she just knew it would.

Janet is still waiting for her moment—to be discovered, to be recognized for being the person she knows she is. It will happen. She can wait around for that too if she has to.

It is finally Janet's turn at the counter. The lady behind the counter has a face that looks like stacked mud, but a nice smile. The mud lady is actually cute in her own way. Janet wonders what the lady looked like before age and food got to her.

"How can I help you, sweetheart?"

Janet hands the prescription for one of her kids to the lady behind the counter.

* * *

Something has to change. Janet is in the car on another morning that is just like all the other mornings. Driving the kids to daycare so she can get back home and watch some streaming movies she has downloaded.

It is the summer. Hot and humid and yellow.

She doesn't have a lot of reasons to be a stay-at-home mom. She is able to clean and cook with the kids. They are mobile and they love to play together. Janet just feels the need for space.

Soon the kids will be in public school and the government can raise her children for her.

Janet tries to think of the lost time. The wasted parts. How she manages to still feel bored with everything. Life was supposed to be exciting and wonderful and free and love was supposed to last forever.

Movies and songs had told her that. Her parents weren't great examples, but Janet was—at a younger age—convinced that she would be different.

Janet got into partying in high school and she liked older boys. If they had a job and a car, she was attracted to them. Something about the power of freedom was addicting.

She is easily addicted to things involving emotions.

Janet thinks about the first time she met Francis. They were at a house party. Francis had been looking at her for a while. Janet liked that kind of attention, but only so much. At a certain point, if the guy wasn't attractive enough, it became creepy. She didn't like wasting her time when she knew she was out of someone's league. She was pretty—that's all she needed in life.

Francis kept staring.

They fucked that night.

Janet lied and said she was sixteen—legal. She wasn't, but she liked the attention and it was her first time—she was ready and she wanted the moment to happen.

Francis really was a good guy. He figured out her age and

tried to make it right with her parents, who were happy a boy with a job was the boy who got Janet pregnant. Janet's parents didn't have very high standards.

The ring was the most beautiful thing she had ever seen. Francis was a romantic and he was attractive enough to keep around. At that point, Janet had already dropped out of school and was low on the social totem pole she used to reign above. Saying yes to that ring essentially defined the next eight years of Janet's life.

Janet had liked the idea of being married.

Francis worked construction. Lot of room to excel. He was unionized and he was a hard worker and had strong hands. Janet loved his strength. After a few years he made foreman. It wasn't easy, but he would wake up early and work extra hours to afford the SUV Janet drove. Francis drove an old beater truck. She knew he liked it.

Sometimes Francis would change his hours to help more with the kids at home.

The home, which was once filled with unpopular magazines, became flooded with children's books that Janet would never read. Francis read some of them. Sometimes he would try to tell Janet things about her body, but she rarely listened. He didn't know what she was going through. It was her body; she knew what her body needed more than anyone.

Janet snaps out of her daydream. It doesn't feel like a dream. Dreams are supposed to have more substance. Be more than the B movie. She is waiting for the real movie to begin.

Janet is at the daycare and has to drag the kids out of the back of the car. They always cry when she leaves them, but she never feels the same way. She feels relief—she isn't sure if she should feel guilty about that.

Janet sits in the car for a moment, trying to find a good radio station. Something that would be good enough. That's all she is looking for.

She clicks through a few and gives up. The effort is frustrating.

She begins driving again and tries to think about things. She usually gets so wrapped up in the daily events that she forgets to reevaluate what she is going through. She rarely does that.

Janet stops at a light and remembers a story she had once heard from somewhere. The story was about an Amish couple: a husband and a wife. The wife was pregnant and when the time came to give birth there were a few complications. Something the Amish midwives couldn't figure out and it really worried the husband. His wife was beautiful and smart and cared for him and they were truly in love.

The Amish couple's relationship had grown past the smitten love stage and they had entered into a phase of their relationship that wasn't simply a comfortable coupling—it was truly love. And that husband saw his wife in a pain that wasn't supposed to be happening during labor, so he took her and he carried her and she was strong for him and she held on to life in the back of the carriage while they rode as fast as the horses could go to the nearest hospital. The husband saved his wife's life doing that. They had a little girl that wouldn't have made it without the husband's decision.

They returned to their little settlement out in the country and they were cast out. They gathered what they had and found their way. They raised their family and still abided by many of the Amish traditions, but they were never allowed back into that lifestyle because they had gone to the modern hospital.

The husband gave up everything he had for his wife. He gave up his faith—his lifestyle—just to save the life of his wife. He knew what he was giving up, but she was worth the sacrifice. They would still be able to live together on the earth and they lived good lives after that.

The light turns green and Janet keeps driving.

Janet has never felt that feeling before: that feeling of total connection. She has never felt that she was going against everything in life and she never feels consumed with the love between her and Francis. She felt the spark during the first two years, but after that, there wasn't a lot to build off of. Just the physical and the gravitational pull of having children.

Janet often feels alone when she sleeps next to Francis. She has lived for many years assuming that love is best defined as a friendship with sex. She feels most people should marry a friend, and that love isn't a lasting emotion. She overcompensates with fitness or blowjobs or whatever to prove that the love is there.

She runs to fill in some of the gaps of her life. She has a cheap treadmill from the supercenter that Francis had surprised her with. Nothing special, but it is nice to not have to run outside. Janet is content to be inside most of her life. She runs in the room that used to be Francis' office.

Sometimes Janet would want more. She'd ask for a foot rub or for flowers. Francis would always smile while doing it. Sometimes he would surprise her with other things like chocolate.

Janet feels guilty for not being more supportive. Francis often makes her feel inadequate. Not from shaming her or being a bad guy in any way, but by being a good man. Most people make Janet feel that way. She doesn't understand how everyone could be so happy all the time—could care about others so much.

He has encouraged her to get her GED. He would try to watch shows with her on TV, talk about work. It was all boring. Janet could do any of those things any day of her life, so she grew to feel obligated to those experiences. It was Francis' role to support her; that's a man should do for his girl.

She can't change who she is on the inside. The world will have to accept that. She has to.

Janet looks down at one of her hands, rotating it off the wheel so she can consider whether or not she can get away with not redoing her nails for another day. Then she quickly pulls back into her lane, realizing she was almost swerving. Such a girl thing to do, she thinks. She turns the radio a little louder and breathes out the air in her lungs.

Janet wonders if the story about the Amish family was true.

* * *

It has been a few years of the whole day-in-day-out. Window shopping helps. So do the TV and the movie theater. She has watched a lot of movies by herself in the last year or so. Summers will come and winters will follow.

It is the winter. The white and gray of the urban footprint trap the wind into the corridors of the buildings. She is wearing her down coat with the fur around the collar.

Janet is surrounded by people but they are all strangers, living their own lives, thinking whatever thoughts they were thinking on their walks to their destinations. The snow on the ground does not make the isolation any easier.

Janet looks down at the ground. All of the footprints of the people who have walked before her have mushed into tiny mountain ranges of gray and white goo. She looks across the street and sees an old man with a walker. A tiny dog with a pink sweater is tied to the railing of the walker. To each their own. The dog has to move its legs a hundred times faster than the man. It rushes and stops, rushes and stops. Every few steps the man takes, the dog licks some of the slush off the ground.

Janet looks down at the slush she is standing in. Licking it is not an appealing idea. She looks again into the windows along the street. The world is right next to her, but it is all behind glass.

She meanders. She has some hours to kill before she has to pick up the kids from school.

She stops in front of a jewelry store.

Days seem to pass while Janet looks through the barriers at the things she will never own. Sometimes people bump into her on purpose. She is blocking their paths, after all. They have places to walk to. Janet does not. She doesn't have any direction that seems to pull her this way or that—no reason to walk, no reason to feel frustrated, no reason to go home. She has things, but not the right things. Even though she has children she feels empty around them. Janet is living a life for the sake of living.

She hasn't noticed the man standing next to her. He is dressed warmly, but also very plainly. He is wearing a hat of sorts that looks both old and stylish—along with sunglasses and a gray coat that compliments his height.

"I said, what one are you looking at?" says the stranger.

Janet is startled out of her trance. She hadn't thought that anyone would talk to her. She is used to putting up the bitch-front.

"Oh, I don't know. All of them," Janet says. The man seems nice enough. He is smiling and he is handsome.

"Well. Then let's buy them all," says the stranger. "Dave," he extends his hand. Dave has soft hands, and a chiseled face. He is gorgeous. Gorgeous the way that an older man is gorgeous. Maybe he is in his 40s. He takes care of himself. Distinguished. Refined.

"Janet."

* * *

Janet finds herself daydreaming of the new world she has been given. A perfect world. She lies in bed and imagines how far she has come in life. She knows she deserves it.

Janet is the center of the universe, and Dave never lets her think anything different.

It took only three months before Janet left her family. She did it clean. She left a note.

Francis didn't even chase after her. Never found her. If he really wanted her, he would have found her and brought her back. Janet knows it was for the best. It was what her heart wanted. A cleanse of life.

Almost ten years with Francis and she had been no closer to her dreams. Just the dreams of normal people. Janet isn't normal and neither is Dave. He gives her dreams.

Dave has opened Janet up to a life she had always known she was supposed to live. The life she had been born to live.

He teaches her things. Teaches her about true fashion. Janet had thought leopard print was sexy before. She had never realized what a joke it had made of her. She feels embarrassed to know she used to like things that Dave had later told her were not sophisticated enough. Box wine was replaced by wines from California and France and Italy.

Dave teaches her how to drink wine, how to smell the cork first, smell the wine before sipping and tasting. Janet loves it. She loves all the things Dave teaches her.

Janet has earned a new life. She had fallen so far from the top of the status totem pole. She had it and lost it. A childish mistake that ended in children.

Janet rolls over in bed and looks out the window. It doesn't matter what time it is. She can sleep in as long as she wants. She has true freedom. A true life.

Dave is a movie star and a famous one. He spends a lot of his time between movies in Northern California. He tells Janet that he likes having the separate life. He likes having the secret world that he can come to when he isn't in front of the movie cameras and on the carpets or doing the press junkets. He is that famous. Famous enough that he's been around the world a few times doing press for films.

Janet hadn't even recognized him when they first met. He looked handsome, but he also looked so human and normal. David was the name he was born and raised with, but when he made it to Hollywood he changed it to something that really took off. It helped that he was handsome—that was most of the battle in the business from what he tells Janet. That and parties and cocaine and fitness and agents and lunches and a world that he didn't really identify with. Dave was lucky that he was able to become as famous as he had without doing as much of those things as other people had to do.

Janet is happy that Dave doesn't want her to have to go through all of those things. She is his little secret. His world away from the world. And the universe revolves around her and she is happy. She has been given the keys to all of the things she has ever wanted.

Most of the days of her new life revolve around waiting for Dave. Sometimes he comes home, sometimes he doesn't. His job is so difficult to measure that she never knows when to expect him. She stays up all night some nights watching streaming movies in their enormous bed and she never feels bored. She knows she is where she is supposed to be.

She gets out of bed and decides to wear a red version of the same outfit she wore the day before. The beauty of money is being able to buy all the colors of everything she has ever wanted. She has options.

* * *

It is another slow day. Dave comes home and is too tired to do anything. Janet understands that; Dave is a busy man.

It will be a screenplay day. Dave will read through some, and Janet will read magazines in the sunroom and dote on Dave. They have spent many days like this. Sometimes shifting to watch TV. Sometimes Dave will show up on TV and Janet gets excited. Dave doesn't enjoy watching himself as much and they will have to change the channel.

Janet waits until after lunch to try and convince Dave to

work on his own screenplay. He had started it when he met Janet. A story about a woman who lived a life of eternal beauty and youth. Janet thinks the story is brilliant: it is about what every woman truly wants.

Dave works and Janet reads magazines. She loves it.

Sometimes Dave talks about work. It is rare. When he does, Janet asks questions about the women that he works with. He is always a gentlemen, but he doesn't avoid talking about the women's bodies or their lips, or their noses. Dave is a perfectionist and an artist at heart. He notices those little things.

On most days when Dave comes home they make love and Janet feels completely infatuated with him. He is everything she has ever wanted out of life. He is the object of her greatest desire.

She rubs his feet and soaps him up in the shower and pours all of herself into his happiness, like a woman should for her man.

* * *

Sandy and Susan had never known that Janet was funny. When they usually see her they see just another client who wants to be something different than what they already are.

For some reason, Janet is loose, though. The humor overcomes the nerves. Maybe it is because Janet had gone under before, knows the drill. The first surgery, she was so nervous. Janet talks about her first time. Sandy and Susan laugh —they are used to people acting silly before falling asleep. Sometimes the truth really comes out.

Janet wasn't ever considered funny. She loves the attention. Needs the feeling. Sandy and Susan egg Janet on. Janet talks about her first kiss and how the boy didn't know what to do with his tongue as if he had never seen a mouth before. Then she talks about how she had to put the condom on the first boy who she had sex with. How the condom was useless and they ended up not using it.

Janet talks about a myriad of inappropriate things until she is asked to count backward. Instead, she starts with one, two, three, four…

Francis was her first.

Her first everything, really.

Janet wakes up a few hours later. It was the last time she would have to go under and she is giggly from the gas.

The room has a fog to it that she can't pinpoint. As though her eyes are foggy and these aren't her real surroundings. The room smells like bleach. She hadn't noticed that smell before. At least this time she can use her nose still.

She can't wait until she is all healed up. Dave will get home from his latest shoot by then. Maybe they will finally make love again. They have been going through a dry spell. The last time that happened, she had waited until he would be away for a while and then she got a nose job.

When Dave came back, it worked.

He loved it and he couldn't stop talking about how pretty she was. It has been some years since they first met. Since the beginning she has gotten her eyes done, her nose, and a tummy tuck. She has reshaped her ears and given herself a less masculine chin. She wants to look like the girls that Dave pretends to fuck in the movies.

After so much money spent under the knife, she is pretty. Really pretty. Not just normal pretty. Janet has never felt more real or tangible or perfect. She has the perfect life.

Janet is driven home by her driver. She can never remember his name, so she often doesn't say anything to him. It is embarrassing to attempt conversation. She gets home and immediately heads to her little gym room.

When Dave is away, Janet runs on her treadmill. A really expensive one that Dave had gotten for her. After the boob job, she has to wear two sports bras and take it a little slower. The bouncing is uncomfortable when she runs too fast, but that is a small price to be perfect.

She has to get her workout in for the day. Even if she has just finished another surgery. It was just a small one. Something with the hairline. She doesn't really know anymore. She is just checking the boxes on the list at this point.

She takes it slow and jogs instead of runs.

* * *

She is standing in the kitchen at the island. The sky is

whatever, the air is recycled. The electricity is from the sun and the gadgets are all boring and overused within the house. Janet is staring at an invitation to her ten-year reunion. High school was so long ago. She hadn't even graduated.

Five years is a long time to Janet, considering there is no ring involved. Dave has bought her all the jewelry she has ever wanted, cars, a home, and he pays for anything she could dream up. Money isn't the problem, but Janet feels more and more marginalized as Dave delays the proposal that he continually says is going to happen when the time is right.

Life is moving and Janet is standing in the same place. She wonders how the letter has reached her. No one knows where she really is. They aren't supposed to. Maybe Francis does know where she is. Maybe he is going to rescue her from her ivory tower. She won't leave. Not even for Francis and the kids. But she likes the idea of someone finding her; chasing her. Someone who needs her more than she needs them.

Janet has started to let Dave know as subtly as possible that she isn't sure if she can wait around for the rest of her life. He hasn't even let her be seen out with him. She wants to walk a red carpet. She would do anything. She feels she already has done anything and everything. The things he likes to make him happy. She is entirely willing. She needs his love.

New teeth, new tits, new face, new hair, new body. Everyone in Hollywood has fake teeth, Dave says. She has a personal trainer, a chef, a masseuse. She is more like a piece of equipment than a person at this point. So much of her is maintained and serviced and balanced out. The oil in her joints is always lubed, the fluids maintained. All of it is high class. The same surgeons the movie stars use. The kind that can't be traced, don't use name-brand anything. Anonymity promised every time.

Janet takes the reunion invitation to the sink. She hadn't even graduated. She had left, knocked up and ugly. If they could see what she had become. They would never recognize her. She has become genuinely pretty.

Janet fumbles for where the lighters are supposed to be. She finds one and lights the invitation on fire. She drops it in the sink and lets it burn on the metal. Maybe the fire alarm will go off and she'll be able to feel something different.

The alarms never do go off, though. Janet walks back to the kitchen island. She thinks of Dave.

Every few weeks or months, the headlights of Dave's car approach the house. Dave shows up and they have sex and then watch TV together. They don't talk a lot.

They used to.

Janet sometimes wonders if the little things Francis did were because he didn't have any money or because those were really the things that made her happy: flowers, chocolates, a card, hugs, foot rubs.

She feels empty.

* * *

Janet is finally going to get married. Dave has spent some time away and gave her the good news over the phone. Told her how it would happen. She knows it will be the proposal.

A driver is sent to pick Janet up. She makes sure she wears her nicest dress. White, for the occasion.

She can't imagine it is finally going to happen.

She has done her makeup, done her eyes and her lips and her nails. She looks like the doll girl she had seen on TV so many years before.

Janet gets to the first destination and swaps drivers. The first one has a strict schedule he says, so Janet will have to swap a few times.

By the fourth driver, Janet isn't entirely sure where they are. The mountains somewhere. The vehicle is no longer a limousine; it is an all-terrain vehicle.

By the end of the journey, Janet has been driven around for over four hours. She has been excited the entire time. She is finally going to get married to Dave. Finally getting to be with him forever. He will have to take her out. Their marriage will get leaked somehow. She will walk a red carpet and share in everything with him. Not just watch him on the TV or in theaters. She will be with him.

She has done everything for him. Left it all behind to live the life she knew she should.

Janet arrives at a cabin and runs from the vehicle. The driver drives off immediately, but Janet doesn't even think for a moment about how she will leave. She wants to stay.

She throws open the door and Dave is standing there, elegant and gorgeous and strong. He is wearing a white tuxedo with a white shirt and a white bowtie, and he has a pair of roses in one of his hands—his other hand behind his back. Janet has never seen the white tuxedo. Dave looks amazing in it.

Janet hadn't even known about a cabin. It is truly a surprise.

The room is beautifully white. A white carpet under a white coffee table, next to white sofas and adjacent to a white dining room and a white kitchen. A white fireplace is yellow with warmth. It is perfect. The perfect moment.

She knew it. She knew it was going to happen.

Janet throws herself at Dave. She can feel the warmth of his body against hers. Then, suddenly the warmth in her stomach turns into a burning sensation. More than warmth, and she finds herself out of breath. Janet pulls back slightly and looks down.

Dave is holding a knife in Janet's stomach. A large one.

Janet has no initial reaction beyond the widening of her eyes. She doesn't see a ring. She looks at Dave's hands and doesn't see any ring in any of those hands. Just the roses and a knife. Dave throws the roses to the floor.

No, Janet thinks. The ring must be in the roses. Somewhere in the roses.

Janet collapses to the floor and crawls over to where the roses are. Dave had thrown them down so nonchalantly. She knows he cares, though. Knows he cares. He has given her so much.

She is bleeding quite a lot. All over the white carpet.

Janet can't find a ring. She grabs among the roses. Scratches her hands up—she feels lightheaded. She has to slow down. Calm herself. Her hands are bloody from all the grasping and grabbing.

Dave.

Dave has left her. No, he is here. He must have made a mistake. He was supposed to propose. Supposed to love her.

She is his. She is perfect. She is pretty.

Janet sees Dave's feet half a room away. Had she really crawled that far?

Her makeup is running all over her face.

"No," Janet sobs. "No."

Dave slowly walks over to Janet. She waits to see what will happen. She is feeling dizzy. Feeling tired.

Janet sniffs in some of the snot. She feels hideous doing it. It is so hard to breathe through her nose after all the surgeries.

Dave stands over Janet.

She grabs for him. Tries to hug him. She feels like she's leaking. Maybe she is. A machine leaking oil.

"No," Janet says. "We can still. There's still… I want this to be forever."

Dave looks down on Janet, the knife still in his hand. Janet grabs on to him. The carpet under her has become as red as velvet. He doesn't mind that the white rug is stained, that he will never be able to wear the white tux again. He can change everything in his life to blue if he wanted. For now, Dave sees the red in the room and is happy.

Dave raises the knife. It isn't a ring.

"This is forever," Dave says.

Here Janet is, waiting to die.

She doesn't think about Heaven. She doesn't think about anything beyond wanting to live.

Janet passes out before anything else can happen. She never wakes up, but for a brief moment she does dream.

Janet sees her children and her first husband: Francis and Joey and Samantha. Her first kiss was awful, but she remembers the butterflies she had when it happened. Her first time was painful, but she remembers how the boy hugged her so tightly. How Francis hugged her, how he kissed her, how he was the first. She sees the births of her children and the looks on Francis' face when each were born. Janet thinks of the help and then she thinks of the Amish story. The love the husband had for his wife. How he would do anything.

If people could cry in their dreams, Janet would.

Janet's body is rolled up in the red carpet and dumped in the woods. She isn't the first to be thrown out here, but it wouldn't matter how many were found if they ever were to be found. They will lie in their rugs in the middle of the woods.

None of the women look the way they used to when they first met Dave. Dental records, hair color, bust size, none of it is the same. They are human dolls, all designed to be untraceable. All manufactured for death.

They are all pretty.

Lust

Heart Full of Love

By L Chan

Dave settled into the chair and wondered what secrets his pancreas was whispering about him. Would it complain about the late-night snacks, the sodas he snuck in when nobody was watching?

The medical aide pottered nearby. She was a small woman with a pinched face, quietly efficient in her pale frock. Her fingers danced over the readouts. Her gnarled fingertips were yellowed by the touch of cigarettes. She smiled at Dave, displaying perfect teeth. When she opened her mouth, the sound of a schoolgirl's chirp came out of wrinkled lips. "Everything looks fine, Mr. Barrows. Blood sugar's okay. Battery level in the prosthetic is holding up. You'll need to pop by in three months for a recharge. A bit early for your first checkup, isn't it? You look a little peaky."

Dave tried to smile. "Just nerves. I thought you'd have to stick a wire in me to read the data from the prosthetic. It keeps giving me these warning messages."

The aide laughed. A sound high and perfect, like a bell, but not annoyingly so. "The latest prosthetics communicate wirelessly. Even the charging can be done without opening you up. It's common for fresh prosthetics to be overenthusiastic with the warnings. Calibration issues and all that."

"Calibration issues?" Dave paused and swallowed. "What about interference?"

The aide rolled her eyes, almost too quick for Dave to notice, the flicker of movement distracting him from the light line of scar tissue around her throat.

"The latest prosthetics all have onboard processors. In your case, it would monitor your blood sugar levels and react with insulin in real time. If you had an artificial liver, for instance, the two prosthetics would communicate wirelessly so that your body functions properly. Prosthetics have to be synced to communicate with each other. There's no chance for mutual interference. She loved you until the end."

The chair squealed in protest as Dave sat up, startled. "What did you say?"

The aide looked deeply embarrassed, spots of color burning on her cheeks, visible under the thick makeup. Her hands flew to her neck protectively. "Did my voice go strange again? I only had it put in a few months ago. The doctors had to take the entire larynx out because of the cancer. I used to be a pack-a-day smoker. Should have listened to the warnings on the packets." She mimed taking a drag on a cigarette with her stained fingers. Satisfied that she had prevented further embarrassment, she turned back to her charts. "Speaking of prosthetics, your heartbeat is showing early signs of distress. We should do a deeper scan at your next visit. You may want to look into getting it replaced. The latest models are very dependable. Expensive, but worth the cost."

Dave got out of the chair and started buttoning up his shirt. "I know," he said. He swallowed and said it again, too soft for the aide to hear. "I know."

Dave mulled over the strange utterance by the lady as he made his way back to the car.

She loved you until the end.

Natalie. The girl without a heartbeat.

Things were over with Natalie. Dave was free. Free to live out his life. Free to start again with his wife, and in six months, their baby. Dave got into his car and told it to take him to his lunch appointment. The car paused, telling him that it was having difficulty acquiring a network signal. He flipped the car over to manual control. Something else to get fixed. He sighed and sped away from the prune-faced woman with the voice of an angel.

* * *

"I'm going to need something to help me sleep."

"That's easily done, Dave, but I'd like to know why." Dr. Chang was a compact man. His voice still carried a trace of the musical lilt he brought over from Hong Kong. He charged by the hour, with a healthy premium for the discrete consultations outside of his practice, like Dave was having.

"I don't know. Stress maybe? Sometimes I lie in bed for hours, like I just can't find a comfortable space. The other day

I thought I heard something." Dave related the encounter with the medical aide to his psychiatrist. "Before that, I was washing my car in the driveway. I thought I could hear the sound of Natalie breathing. Something in the rhythm reminded me of the way she used to breathe after we. Well, you know. It was just a jogger running by. Looked like a pro. Augmented lungs or something."

"Aren't you and that young lady done?" Dr .Chang never judged; it wasn't his job. Dave looked up, calm brown eyes gazed back. If not for the slight purse of Dr. Chang's lips, Dave would have missed the trace of disapproval completely.

Dave remembered the first time he waited for Natalie in that downtown hotel room, leaving sweaty palm prints on the sheets as he sat on the bed. Nervous as a schoolboy. He had texted his secretary that he had a fictitious last minute meeting, too ashamed to let the lie pass his lips. How easily that mask of semi-confidence, so secure in the boardroom, slipped off.

Natalie had turned Dave's well-ordered life upside down. When they first met, he was pushing forty and adrift, the wind in his sails but without a rudder. She had a desperate zest for life that Dave found intoxicating. Maybe her love was too much for him in the end. When they were together, there was barely a second where she wasn't hanging on to him; her soft fingers twined around his own, her breath warm on his ear. She had been close to death before, a long time before they met. It had left her with a need to constantly feel, stroke, grab; as though anything she couldn't touch would slip away.

"It is over. I broke it off. I told you last time. And the time before." It hadn't been easy. Dave had never been popular with women and the breakup with Natalie was as raw and abrupt as his awkward dalliances of his youthful days in school. He remembered how she clutched at him that night. The begging. The screaming. Then the threats.

Dr. Chang took a moment before replying. "Confucius said: If you look into your own heart, and you find nothing wrong there, what is there to worry about?"

"I don't want Confucius' words, I want yours. I run a business. I can't afford to be going nuts over some young girl. Am I going crazy? Why did the aide say what she said?"

Natalie wasn't just some young girl. There must have been some love between them at the start. She laughed a little louder when he made his jokes. She straightened her back when he walked by her in the office.

It was strange that Dr. Change would talk about hearts. Dave remembered stroking the long slash of the scar in the hollow between Natalie's small breasts. How he would marvel sometimes, when they lay in a musky tangle of limbs and sweaty sheets, at the lack of a heartbeat when he put his hand over her chest. Sometimes he would place his ear there, just to listen to the little clicks and whirrs from that alien, mechanical thing.

The heart Natalie had been born with had coughed and stuttered all through her teenage years. A random draw at the genetic lottery and she would be dead before she hit thirty.

When she was twenty, doctors opened her up, scooped out that tired knot of muscle and popped in a shiny new creation. She was still paying for it, eight years later, when she met Dave. It was the most expensive thing she would ever own.

Dr. Chang tutted and drew out a prescription sheet from his bag. He produced lines of indecipherable doctor's script with an expensive pen. When he extended the chit across the table, Dave could not help noticing how the doctor's writing hand seemed a shade less tanned than the rest of him. "A bad fall," Dr. Chang said. "Compound fracture. It would have taken at least two months to heal properly. Replaced it instead. My golf stroke is better than ever. The grip is something else." He frowned and flexed his fingers. "Except I can never get the right shade of spray-on to match the other hand. They just don't make enough shades." The doctor excused himself. The session was over.

Dave examined the sheet of paper. After a moment of squinting, he grunted with satisfaction. He thought of the abrupt end to their conversation. Dr. Chang always wanted to talk, but seemed to shy away from Dave's true emotions. The moment of earnestness always made him feel lost without a response. Maybe it was a method to keep Dave returning. Dr. Chang loved to end sessions on a cliffhanger.

Then Dave realized there was another line at the bottom of the prescription sheet.

"She would have died for you."

* * *

Dave stared at the single line of spidery text for a good while in his car before he folded the piece of paper in half. It wasn't the doctor's handwriting. Correspondence through the written word used to be one of Natalie's quirks. An anachronism in a world where phones and emails gave up their secrets to jealous spouses. Dave kept the stack of notes, cards and letters in a small box in his office, far away from prying eyes. The loops and whorls of the text identified its author even more surely than the content.

She would have died for you.

Dave's hand was halfway to the glove compartment when he thought twice about it and slipped the prescription into his pocket. His car took even longer to start up than it had the last time. His annoyance grew.

Greetings were unreturned as Dave strode through the office. He'd pick up his things from his room and take the rest of the day off. The darkness of his mood was infectious and the cubicles settled into an uneasy silence, the light banter faded. Dave was pleased by the momentary superiority. Time and quiet were things he craved.

Dave straightened his tie with shaking fingers, thoughts veering back toward Natalie as though the memory of their time together had developed its own gravity, pulling his conscious mind in again and again. Things long buried in his mind had putrefied, the corruption leaking from where Dave had hidden his darkest thoughts.

Dave buzzed his assistant to bring him a cup of coffee while he mechanically sorted through his messages, eyes open but not seeing anything. Dave's mind was far away, thinking of how Natalie and he meshed perfectly at first. A chance encounter at some corporate function or another, one thing leading to another, blind to the possibility that loneliness and lust were the glue that bound them—two otherwise incompatible puzzle pieces.

The cracks in the relationship appeared almost as soon as it began. They would fight, then make up, each too in love with the idea of a relationship to stay apart for long. The poison in their fights was only matched by the desperation of their reconciliations, the escalating physicality of both making it hard to tell one from the other.

His assistant padded into the room and deposited his coffee on the table. Dave left it untouched and left the office.

* * *

The young lady at the pharmacy was distractingly pretty. She smiled at Dave before she turned around to dial up the concoction that Dr. Chang had prescribed. Her eyes were green, reminding him a little of Natalie's. *Christie,* her name tag said.

Christie, that's the name Natalie wanted. Dave took a second to marvel that, after years of trying, lightning did strike twice. Once with his wife and once with Natalie. A flash of events and memories and moments briefly overtook Dave. Natalie and he fighting over the impossibility of pregnancy between them. Dave suggesting alternatives. The ensuing fights. The clawing. The build up until Dave finally struck her. The chase through her apartment. Natalie darting out with a knife in her shaking hands, drawing blood from his palm as he tried to defend himself.

The pharmacist returned with a small box of pills. *Christine. Her name was Christine.* Dave exhaled, a long slow sigh. Christine pushed the box across the counter. "You'll have to observe the usual restrictions, no alcohol. I don't suppose you work with heavy machinery but stay away from it all the same." She gave him a little wink. Just the same wink that Natalie used to give him. How quickly mannerisms started to grate once the love drained out from lives. It was the first thing he started hating about Natalie. He shivered and took the pills.

"Ow!" the pharmacist said, her pale hands flicking up to rub at her eyes. Dave realized too late that the pharmacist's eyes were a little too green, the whites a little too perfect. She hadn't been born with them. When her hands came back to her side, she blinked once, twice and gave him a look.

The same as the last look that Natalie had ever given him.

In that last moment, Natalie's green eyes held nothing but questions she couldn't ask. No words came from her lips, only a crimson bubble of spit, swelling and shrinking with every shallow breath. Smaller each time as her heart steadily pumped the life out of her. Spurts of blood painted the bed crimson.

Natalie's heart was the only thing left. The rest was rotting in landfills, ashes in the wind or sunken husks within the depths of the oceans. Dave had been careful.

Something stopped him from being as careful with the heart. He had balked at smashing the little mechanical wonder. He was a man of reason and destroying something worth the cost of a small house did not come easily to him.

A panic started in the pit of Dave's stomach. A strange weightlessness that flowed upward, squeezing the air from his lungs. When it reached his head, he had to blink the white spots from the edge of his vision and press his palms onto the counter to hold the world still.

The pharmacist hurried out from behind the counter, her mouth an O of concern. She must have been asking Dave something, but he could only see the relentless approach of those perfect green eyes. He lurched from the store, his medication uncollected. He could feel the weight of those perfect green eyes on him as he staggered out.

Dave yelled at the car to take him home. It started without complaint for once. He stared at the glove compartment. What did he expect? The sound of a beating heart? A slow drip of blood seeping through the bottom of the hatch?

"What do you want?" he demanded, his voice bouncing around in the enclosed space. He leaned forward, popped the catch on that little crypt under the dashboard. "This is you, isn't it? Everything. This is all you!"

The glove compartment fell open. There it was. Sitting there, slick with blood like a newborn, the clear plastic covering it like a caul. Dave seized the bag.

Dave whispered, "I loved her but it's over." Spittle spattered onto the plastic. He had to get away. Get somewhere safe. Out of sight. Find something heavy. A cinderblock would do. He remembered the skittery feel of the tip of the knife scraping off the wall of the prosthetic heart when he had finally decided to end his and Natalie's relationship. Even after all of the violence, the heart was undamaged. It was a tough little survivor.

"Navigation error," said the car. "Searching for signal."

"Oh no, you won't win. No. You always thought you were smart. You wanted to be better than me. To talk down to me." Dave put a hand on the steering wheel, holding onto the mechanical heart with his other hand. He thought of smashing the heart to pieces, of scattering the pieces to the world, just like he had with Natalie. It was the only way to gain freedom. No more strange looks. No notes from unsuspecting hands. No whispers.

"Cut to manual," Dave commanded.

"Confirmation required," asked the car, flat, emotionless.

"Yes. Yes. Do it now."

"Navigation offline. Steering offline. Collision detection offline."

Dave felt the jerk as the steering wheel returned control of the vehicle to him. He allowed himself a smile, the first in days.

He was still smiling when the other car broadsided him.

* * *

The impact gave Dave some minor memory loss and he remembered very little from the crash. The other driver fared little better.

Dave only had flashes of memory. The crushing pain in his chest from the collapsed frame of the car. The whirr of the saws as the emergency workers peeled the car off him. The paramedics wheeling the other driver away on a stretcher. Dave saw the gray rope of synthetic muscle, exposed by a long gash on the driver's leg that was still twitching.

The doctors did the best they could. It was certainly a breach of protocol, but it wasn't every day a trauma patient was wheeled in clutching the means of his own salvation. Of course there were questions later. Many questions.

How did a man come to possess an old prosthetic heart, still wet with someone else's blood?

When did this man last see this young lady?

The murder of Natalie Burnstein has a new lead; how would you like to plead?

The questions mattered little.

* * *

Dave stroked the dark, twisting scar down the center of his

chest.

It was quiet in his cell and Dave had all the time in the world. Nobody visited, his life outside of prison faded along with his issued clothes.

Dave felt the mechanical heart purr as he ran his fingertips over the smooth scar.

The heart seemed to speed up whenever Dave touched it. It didn't take long before the heart began to speak to Dave. At the end of every conversation, the heart would say the same phrase.

"She would have died for you."

Love

Sesshoseki

By Kristopher J. Patten

Should've worn heels, dammit.

I was late, but the ankle-deep rain water made me keep my movements slow to avoid sloshing the oily water onto my pants. I was walking through the Japanese neighborhood of Shinsekai and paused briefly to look up at Tsutenkaku.

Tsutenkaku was built to emulate the Eiffel Tower in Paris, but the French version—even in pictures showing the monument as a backdrop for Nazi marches—never gave off an ominous vibe. Tsutenkaku Tower loomed above Shinsekai like a blocky, nuclear-age robot. The low-hanging clouds and torrential rain that enveloped the monolith glowed with the light of Tsutenkaku's neon advertisements, as if the robot was charging its batteries for another blast of its energy weapon.

Perhaps Tsutenkaku tapped into some latent fear or desire in Japanese culture, the same feeling that gave rise to the original Godzilla movies; the macabre fascination of seeing themselves destroyed. I took my eyes off the tower and focused on getting to the little ramen restaurant where I was to meet my contact.

* * *

The restaurant buzzed with conversation, more than usual as the residents who tended to hang around the back alleys sought refuge from the downpour. From the looks of some of them, many had pooled their money to buy single bowls of soup, picking at the soup languidly to give themselves more time indoors. The salty, stale air that usually hung in the shop turned my stomach. I preferred it to the cold rain, but not by much.

The smell was tamed slightly by the biological tang of unwashed bodies huddled around small, circular tables. I walked to the counter to place my order, my flats squelched water like half-drowned swimmers purging their lungs.

When the man at the counter finally turned his attention toward me, a fixed sneer in place of the typical Japanese business owner's helpful and calm smile, I asked for shoyu ramen with seaweed, a boiled egg, and tempura-battered chicken nuggets. I ended my order by requesting chopsticks— about as unnecessary as ordering a fork with your salad at a French restaurant—carefully pronouncing the word so that "chopsticks" sounded more like "bridge." Those particular faux pas were my cue to the owner, a joint American-CIA/ Japanese-PSIA asset, that I wasn't just a typical tourist.

Of course, to keep my cover intact, the message had to seem like something a dim-witted Westerner might say. I bet the owner and his handler had a blast coming up with the phrasing.

The man behind the counter grunted, a smile threatening to defy the architectural struts of scars that ran across his lower jaw. He passed me a paper packet of chopsticks. I bowed clumsily, which widened his half smile. On the back of the chopstick wrapper, written in a tiny, perfect hand, was the English sentence, "Northeast corner, dark navy pea coat." I headed for the indicated corner, scanning the patrons in my peripheral view, careful to keep my pupils trained in front of me. There was only one man with a navy pea coat, so I slid into the chair in front of him.

He took one last slurp of his soup before wiping his chin with the back of his hand and raising his face to look at me.

"You're not Yuto," I said.

"Yuto is dead," the man said, his face stony. I couldn't tell if he was trying to be stoic about a friend's death or if he really couldn't give a shit.

I found myself silent, trying almost as hard to process my own emotions while attempting to discern my dinner partner's. Yuto was my most frequent contact, a PSIA agent who had been undercover with and maintained several assets in the Yamaguchi crime syndicate. He was a nice enough guy and we made it a habit of sharing a celebratory beer (or sake, depending on the stakes of the operation) when closing a case.

Almost a year previous, he had asked me on a proper date. I declined, giving him the reason that my superiors would have frowned on it. In truth, there was an agent back stateside that I had gotten close to. That relationship hadn't worked out;

American agents tended to have a chip on their shoulder, no doubt a calcification that grew as a result of watching too many James Bond films in their adolescence.

I thought about taking Yuto up on his offer after the breakup, but I didn't want to be known as a woman who hopped from agent to agent. I would have considered Yuto and I friends except he had withdrawn into a shell of himself since my rejection. I think he took it much more personally than it was meant. I knew Yuto well; the man he had become was a stranger. Both were gone.

The man across from me had gone back to slurping his ramen. I tried to ask him a question, but found speaking difficult. Swallowing away a tightness in my throat, I asked, "How did it happen?"

"Sumiyosha-rengo. Some faction of them. Yuto caught wind of Sumiyosha activity from one of his Yamaguchi buddies. He thought it was nothing; maybe a drug shipment or something. He was going to tip off the local police. Then this happened." The man pulled a manila envelope from the inside pocket of his pea coat, fished inside for a glossy picture, then slapped it down on the table in front of me. "Guess it wasn't drugs."

"Jesus Christ," I exclaimed, hissing through clenched teeth. I quickly swiped the picture off the tabletop and hid it, face down, on my lap. *What the hell was the guy up to?* If any Sumiyosha informants were in there and saw the photo, they would know who we were.

"Do you think this is Alice's Restaurant?" I asked. From the confused look the agent shot me over the top of his ramen bowl, I could tell he didn't get the reference. I guessed it was pretty obscure, even for Americans.

I slid the photo up my thighs a bit and used my thumb to prop up the edge closest to me like a poker player checking out her hand. The first thing I saw was blood. Blood everywhere. Dark, black, congealed blood in strips and pools and streaks and flecks. In the center of the sanguine Pollock masterpiece was a body. Most of a body, anyway. Everything above the lower jaw was gone, probably—I guessed—all over the walls and the carpet. The teeth of the lower jaw grinned for the camera, as though happy to be free of the oppressive cranial weight. A black tactical shotgun lay on the body, barrel on the chest. One of the lifeless thumbs was still trapped in the trigger guard.

I sighed and pressed the photo down on my legs. Yuto. I passed it back to the agent across from me under the table.

"Looks self-inflicted," I said.

He nodded. "It does. But that weapon was traced back to a military shipment that was intercepted by the Sumiyosha. And Yuto wasn't the type to—" he finished the sentence with his hands. The agent lifted his bowl to his mouth and sipped the last of the broth. "Unless you know something I don't. Was he the type?"

Good question. *Was he?*

"No," I said with little confidence. Yuto wasn't, but

whoever he had been during the last year may have had suicidal wishes.

The owner brought my ramen to our table. I unwrapped my chopsticks and pushed the toppings around: seaweed, a boiled egg, and diced chicken in place of the nuggets. I didn't mind the egg, but I hated the damn nori seaweed and I would have liked to try—just one damn time—something other than chicken. *Katsu pork, maybe?* I sighed and dug in.

"So," I said between mouthfuls, not slurping the noodles to enhance my tourist look, "it strikes me that Yuto's death is shitty, but probably a job for the local police. Why are we meeting?"

"Like I said; it wasn't drugs. The Sumiyosha wouldn't kill a known PSIA agent over a shipment of heroin. You know that. They would try bribery, blackmail, making a deal by trading information. If things got too hot, they would simply let the drugs get seized and use some inside contact to steal them again. Drug dealing is a sin that can be forgiven; murder isn't. Associative ties between organizations like ours and criminals like them are permanently severed by murder. No one wants that. They have fed us more information on Chinese terror cells than our own agents."

I rolled my eyes at him, realizing the type of person I was dealing with. He either thought Westerners were obtuse or women were subservient. Maybe both.

"This isn't my first job. Give me something real," I said, hoping I wouldn't have to walk. I didn't want Yuto's death to go down as a suicide if it wasn't. He deserved a star on the wall as much as anyone.

"Easy, easy. So, drugs are out. Money laundering is out. Girls are probably out. The PSIA in general and Yuto, specifically, have a sour feeling about human trafficking."

He had my interest. "So, what do you think?"

"Remember I said we know it's Sumiyosha-rengo because the shotgun matches a shipment they lifted a while ago? The organization is not a single, cohesive whole like the Yamaguchi-gumi, but is made up of," he paused, in thought. "I guess the best example is a realm ruled by a confederation of kings each with their own individual vassals. Local and international police groups have been cracking down on organized crime, which has led to very corporate-like downsizing. The Yamaguchi have funneled these former warriors into their legitimate and semi-legitimate businesses. Some Sumiyosha constituents have followed suit but others, those without businesses, have not. The band who stole the gun shipment is no longer an official member of the Sumiyosha-rengo. In fact, both the Yamaguchi and Sumiyosha have declared war on this cell because of their willingness to work with radical Chinese Islamic groups."

I nodded. It made sense. During World War II, some of the largest Italian American crime families offered their assistance to the Allied intelligence services. Hitler and Mussolini's despotic regimes were at odds with the free capitalism that allowed the Cosa Nostra to flourish. During the

Cold War and the global War on Terror, a similar cooperation arose between criminal organizations and intelligence services. Communism and religious fanaticism are bad for business. It's a simple case of siding with the lesser of two evils. Not only did the Sumiyosha and Yamaguchi families want to rid Japan of a threat to their way of life, they were likely ashamed that men they trained were using their skills against Japan.

"You think Yuto stumbled onto a terror plot," I said.

The man across from me nodded.

"Something big enough to risk an investigation," I said. "But they tried to cover it up, so that means it's not in play yet. Yuto's intervention may have even sped everything up."

"Explain," the man said, leaning forward slightly. I guess I had finally proven my worth.

"Let's say it's the intelligence community's Loch Ness Monster," I noticed he seemed confused at the analogy and paused while I racked my brain for some cultural equivalent. "Ah. Say it's the Three Imperial Treasures for people like us; a dirty bomb. We're always looking for one and we always jump to it, but it never shows up. If Yuto found information about a dirty bomb that's going to go off in a few hours—say, with the dawn of the trading day—no one would have bothered covering up the murder; they would have shot Yuto, left him in his apartment to rot for a few hours, and blew the bomb while the police were still searching for forensic evidence."

"Then they have a long-term goal."

I nodded. "Something long term enough to give us a

chance to find them."

We sat in silence while I worked my way through my soup. Two men walked in and each ordered a beer. They were nicely dressed, but not too extravagantly. Nothing about them screamed yakuza, save for the eyes. I had seen those eyes on militants in Tikrit, US Special Forces Soldiers in Afghanistan, wolves, sharks, and abused girls and boy soldiers in Africa.

"So, what should I call you?" I asked my stolid companion.

"Benkei," he said. The name sounded familiar. Maybe Yuto had spoken of him once or twice.

I smiled. "Nice to officially meet you, Benkei. I'm Stevens. Also, take a look over your shoulder. Those two guys drinking Orion back there might be something we have to worry about."

Benkei nodded. "I saw them, too. I was trying to figure out who tipped them off."

"Could have been someone outside watching for an American."

Benkei waved his hand by the side of his face to dismiss that statement. "That would still mean they were close. It's more likely they were looking for me. They could have eyes in every ramen restaurant in Osaka. No matter, though, we should leave."

"I was feeling full anyway."

Benkei and I left the restaurant, careful to smile and banter on our way out in a last attempt to shake the two Sumiyosha soldiers off our tail. We rounded a corner into a tight, covered alleyway and Benkei stopped, leaning against the corner of a building and producing a pack of cigarettes from his coat pocket. He offered the pack to me and, once I declined, peeked around the corner, flicking his Zippo lighter as he snaked back into cover. Despite his size, he seemed to move like a shadow.

"Nothing yet," he said, blowing a stream of smoke out into the rain. It didn't smell like cigarette smoke. Instead of the heavy, acrid scent that all cigarettes gave off in varying amounts, the smoke was sweet and spiced, like a mixture between a clove and a Swisher Sweet. I kicked myself for not taking him up on the offer.

"Where is the stone?"

The question boomed behind us, shouted in a low, authoritative tone. I turned hastily, sloshing in the water, to see three men standing further back in the dimly lit alley. The speaker held a pistol in his hand, pointed directly at us. The other two had their coats drawn back to reveal holstered weapons. Each one had a look on his face that said *don't fuck with me.* I could see the edge of a tattoo peeking out from underneath one man's open collar. Yakuza. Probably from the Sumiyosha-rengo group that had killed Yuto.

Benkei ducked to his right, using the motion to draw a short, thin sword that was hidden under the left side of his pea coat. The yakuza closest to him fired, but the bullet went wide. There wasn't a second shot; there wasn't the time. Benkei's blade sliced clean through the shooter's wrist.

The remaining two gangsters had realized they needed to join the fight and were pulling their own weapons. My hands were faster. I shot the leftmost gunman from the hip, the round catching him in the side and sending him staggering backward a few steps, dazed. The next shot put him face-down in the runoff.

"You're looking for the stone?" Benkei asked the remaining gunman who had moved his hands far away from his pistol and leaned up against the alley wall. Benkei's blade was mere centimeters from the gunman's neck.

"Yes," the gangster answered, his eyes locked awkwardly on the bloody steel below his chin. "They said you took it from the PSIA agent after he died."

Benkei grunted. "Not true."

With a flash of reflected neon light from the main street, Benkei's sword cut the gunman's throat. The yakuza grasped at his throat, trying to keep the blood inside. His knees began to buckle and he fell backward, propped against the wall. He slid downward as his life slipped away, drops of blood falling into the rushing water to be carried away like rose petals in a stream.

Benkei turned from the dying man and stalked toward the first gangster who was kneeling in the runoff, floating trash and leaves gathering at the crotch of his pants like a storm drain grate. He was cradling his oozing stump to his chest, making soft mewling sounds to himself. His severed hand, still

clutching the pistol, was in his lap. He must have retrieved it
before the pain and realization of what had happened fully hit
him. Not uncommon in battlefield dismemberment situations.

Benkei placed the midpoint of his blade on the man's
shoulder.

"Wait," I said. "You're just going to kill him?"

Benkei nodded. "They're looking for me; they think I took
the stone Yuto found. They don't even know you're involved.
They will if he talks."

"I'm fine with that. I've been in situations like this before."
Being a woman didn't mean I needed protection.

"No. You misunderstand me. Yes, it will be safer for you if
they don't know you're involved. It also means you can
continue the operation if they find me. They won't even know
the CIA is involved."

He had a point.

"Besides," he said with a shrug, "this is not a noble man.
Instead of remaining loyal to his organization or country, he
sided with terrorists because it was easier than taking a few
month's meager wages until a different job came along. There
may be a shortage of more respectable criminal work in Japan,
but China, Malaysia, and the Philippines are as corrupt as they
have ever been. He's a rabid animal. Only one way to deal with
rabid animals."

With that, Benkei drew back his blade and sliced through
the man's neck. The man hadn't even looked up. He knew his
fate. The body went limp instantly and splashed down like a

ragdoll. Benkei wiped his blade clean on the hem of the man's coat and returned it to its sheath inside his own.

"We need to go," I said. "Those shots probably weren't drowned out by the rain. Even if they were, I bet these guys had friends."

Benkei grunted an agreement. "We need to get back to Yuto's apartment. They think I have the stone. I thought they had it. Yuto must have hidden it. Do you have a car?"

"No, I came on the train. It's not ideal, but it might get us to Yuto's faster than driving in this mess," I gestured up at the clouds.

We walked briskly the half mile to the station I had stepped off merely 30 minutes before. A lot had changed in 30 minutes. My friend was dead. Osaka—or, hell, maybe all of Japan—was in danger. I had just witnessed a beheading and, even worse, had sanctioned it.

I scanned my ticket, happy to be safe from the downpour. Tsutenkaku Tower and the clouds that partially shrouded it still glowed with neon lights, but didn't look as mechanical as it had earlier. The tower had taken on a distinctly authoritarian feel, like a guard tower at a maximum security prison. The bright blue-white glow seemed to be searching the grounds of Osaka for someone with a guilty conscience. I drew further into the shadows of the station and directed my gaze down the tracks.

* * *

We rode in silence to Shinjuku station. I was trying to step back from my emotions so I wouldn't be complicit in any further revenge-fueled deaths; Benkei alternated back and forth between snoring and staring disinterestedly out of the tram window. When we transferred to trains heading toward Kyoto, my curiosity finally got the better of me.

"What's the stone?" I asked.

Benkei shrugged. "No idea."

"When you told me about Yuto's murder, you made it seem like you were in the dark but you didn't bat an eye in that alley. You had one of them cornered for questioning and all you asked for was confirmation that they were looking for this stone. You would have asked him."

Benkei stared into my eyes. It wasn't a look of dominance, though. More like weariness or disinterest.

"A historical item went missing a few weeks ago. I don't think Yuto knew about the theft. What Yuto did know about was the increased activity of those ronin Sumiyosha that coincided with the theft. When I learned of Yuto's supposed suicide, I suspected he might have learned about the stone, but I was open to the possibility that he may have found some other item."

That seemed reasonable, but I noticed Benkei dodged my initial question with his answer. "But what is it, exactly?"

"I'm not sure. Some kind of geologic anomaly. Looks like obsidian. It gives off an energy—radiation, electromagnetic, infrasound… Something—that interacts strangely with the human brain. It appears to suppress neural activity, especially production of serotonin. Sometimes it excites the limbic system and can lead to violent behavior. Either way, people near the stone tend to end up dead."

"How do you know what effect it has on a human brain but you don't know what it gives off? That seems like a simple matter of measuring it."

"Brain imaging technology has recently become very affordable. As for measuring the stone itself, we don't…" Benkei paused, perhaps realizing how his next statement would sound. "We're not sure where it is exactly. We do know it used to be in Tochigi Prefecture, which is where it got the name. The bodies littered among the volcanic rock on the hills of Nasu, most of them suicides, needed an explanation. The warriors and priests who investigated the deaths noticed the greatest concentration of bodies around a single, flat stone."

"Sesshoseki."

"Right. At some point in history, the story was altered such that the stone contained a malevolent spirit. Some local hero showered the stone with Buddhist blessings as it was able to resist multiple blows. In reality, the stone was probably a super-hardened volcanic rock. Like obsidian, but not as prone to shattering. Anyhow, in response to the prayers, the rock was supposed to have cracked and allowed the spirit a chance to escape. Thankful to be free of its prison, it flew off somewhere and the stone was rendered inert. That's almost definitely bullshit. The stone was neutralized and it did crack in the process. The stone was then hidden in a secret location in Japan, far away from population centers in case the stone became active again. It has never been located. Perhaps it has remained dormant. That was the belief. Have you heard of Ayokigahara?"

"The forest at the base of Fujiyama."

"Right," he nodded. "It's also known as the Forest of Suicides. Forest workers have discovered bodies in the forest every year since at least the 19th century, and the yearly count has risen steadily. Psychologists suggest the phenomenon is due to increasing popular awareness about the suicides. That knowing that others are taking their own lives makes the act seem less taboo to the depressed and also gives them a place to go to die among like-minded people. The Japanese are very collectivist, you know. Even a solitary act like suicide is more attractive when others are doing it."

Benkei smirked with that final sentence. I did, too.

Maybe he wasn't so bad. Maybe his apparent heartlessness was born out of the simple fact that he had never met Yuto.

"So when you say 'we,' I'm sure you're not talking about the PSIA," I said.

"No. I work closely with the yamabushi." When he saw no recognition in my face, he continued, "The yamabushi are priests who live away from society in the mountainous regions of Japan. Sort of like Tibetan monks. Actually, a lot like Tibetan monks. It's possible that some characteristics of both sects are borrowed from an earlier group."

"So, this might be a dumb question, but what are we looking for when we get to Yuto's? Just a rock sitting around looking like art?"

"Maybe, though probably not. I was there once already today and I didn't feel any of the effects of the stone. It's possible Yuto has it in a shielded container. Maybe he thought it was an old Soviet warhead."

"That's the other question," I said, leaning closer and keeping my voice low, "if the stone has an operating field the size of Ayokigahara, what is the plan? I mean on the part of the people who wanted this thing bad enough to pull it out of the forest in the first place. A slow attack on a small district of Tokyo? I realize there's a good potential for loss of life, but it seems like a simple knife attack like the ones we've been seeing in China would be more noticeable. More media friendly. If a group claims responsibility for a few hundred suicides, I think the public will most likely laugh at them. It would hurt the cause."

Benkei shrugged. "Obviously, I don't know their plan. What you say makes sense; fifteen very obvious, very violent deaths makes a larger statement than the secret death of ten times that many citizens. Maybe the goal isn't a large attack. Maybe they're planning to use the stone to soften the defenses of an installation where they can get something more effective. Or maybe they can magnify the effect somehow."

The train arrived in Kyoto without incident and our walk to Yuto's apartment was not a long one. A small police vehicle was parked in the front of the building, its blue lights still flashing and casting reflections on the wet pavement. The reflected light cast a ghostly pallor on the faces of pedestrians who seemed to either avoid the side of the street near the cruiser or walk more briskly past it. I pulled my agency badge out of my back pocket and had it in hand for any uniformed officers we may encounter inside.

We climbed to the third floor in silence, though the silence seemed to extend beyond my conversation with Benkei; the entire complex was quiet, an odd occurrence for a rainy Saturday before 11 PM. The hallway in front of Yuto's door was a ghost town. No neighbors, no curious children. No guards in front of his door. I thought it odd, but assumed they must have taken up a post inside the apartment.

I was wrong. The only body in Yuto's apartment was his own, covered by a bluish sheet that had soaked through with blood hours ago. And then it hit me.

"Benkei," I whispered.

He turned, one eyebrow raised.

"There should be cops. I think the suits from Osaka are watching this apartment."

Benkei nodded and let his breath out. He seemed to deflate a little.

"If that's true, they want us to find Sesshoseki for them. Once we do, they'll kill us." He snapped his fingers. "Or they'll try. You knew Yuto better; you search for the stone. I'll try to set up some things to slow them down. Once you find the stone, don't retrieve it. There may be cameras. We'll leave it until I've got everything ready."

I nodded and walked into Yuto's kitchen, keeping my eyes off the body in the center of the living room. I was on edge, but if I looked too long at those scuffed red Converse shoes Yuto always wore, I knew I wouldn't be able to hold back my tears. Yuto deserved my tears. Just not at that moment. We had to finish what he had started.

The kitchen cupboards were empty. A glance into Yuto's bedroom yielded nothing obvious, but a myriad of possible hiding places. The task seemed impossible. My own training dictated that nearly any space in a house, business, apartment, or hotel could be a useful, concealable, and accessible hiding spot. It would take us days to pull apart every room in a thorough information search. And then I stepped into Yuto's study.

The study was familiar; I'd seen it several times before. As the main agent in charge of getting information from Japanese organized crime, Yuto had to have access to several PSIA safe houses across the country. I had stayed in two, both of which had living rooms, bedrooms, or studies that matched Yuto's study to a T.

I remembered his words, "I designed this room to be as cognition-free as possible. All agents I work with have seen this room somewhere. Same with yakuza defectors and informants. Say you're on the run, maybe you've been stabbed; you have no money, but you can get to my safe house. Once you're here, you know there's a safe hidden under the southeast corner of the bamboo rug. The code is 3-2-6-3-8-2-7. From the garbage smasher from *Star Wars*. Inside is cash in yen and dollars, MREs and freeze-dried hiking rations for food, two gallons of water, and a charged burner phone. You learn it here, you see it in other safe houses, your brain knows it like the back of your hand when you need it. Saves lives."

I walked to the southeast corner of the rug and found a finger hold. Swinging up the hidden door in the floorboards revealed a thick metal safe hatch with only a small handle and a digital keypad marring the smooth, beige surface. I typed in the code, controlling the emotion that threatened to spill over as I thought of Yuto's constant allusions to *Star Wars*. He once told me he thought of the US as a nation of Han Solos: reckless, infuriating, loud, loyal, friendly, and all rolled into one package with wavy, feathered hair. I asked him if that meant Japan was a nation of patient Jedi sentinels. He scoffed, but never denied it.

The safe opened to reveal a mess of copper wire. It looked as though Yuto had tried to make his own Slinky and shoved the evidence of his utter failure into the safe. I pulled my cell phone from my pocket and shined the flashlight into the metallic wolf spider nest. Buried beneath several layers of wire, and sitting atop several more, was a smooth square of dark rock, one edge jagged where it had been broken. It had to be Sesshoseki. I left the safe open and moved on to Yuto's bedroom to make it appear that I was still searching.

I had pulled open the drawer on Yuto's nightstand when my phone rang.

"Stevens, it's Doug. I've got some bad news concerning Yuto."

Doug Miyamoto was American, but because of his Japanese ancestry and flawless command of the language he was one of principal liaisons with the PSIA. His usual jovial tone had been lost in the evening's tragedy. I knew he and Yuto were close.

"I know. I'm investigating it now. I'm with one of Yuto's PSIA colleagues."

"Seriously?" he asked. "That's fast; we only just heard about it from local PD. Who's with you?"

"Benkei. Not sure of his first name."

Doug was quiet for a few seconds. I thought he might be pulling up Benkei's file. "Is that a joke? I'm not in the mood for a fucking joke right now, Kate."

"What? No. What would I be joking about?"

"You're investigating Yuto's apartment with Benkei. That's like me saying I'm brewing some K-Cups with Pecos Bill."

I could feel the muscles in my stomach involuntarily start to clench. "Code name? Or maybe a coincidental last name?"

"I'm searching it. Hang on."

I waited, absentmindedly moving my hands through Yuto's drawer. I stopped when I uncovered a Polaroid of the two of us at one of Yuto's favorite bars in Tokyo. We were laughing. We'd just arrested the leaders of a Uighur extremist plot to steal weapons specifications from a firm in Tokyo. We were happy. It was right before he asked me out. *If I had said yes, would he be alive? Would he have asked me to help him?*

"Kate, you need to run. No Benkei in the system. Walsh and Honda aren't far. Meet them at Man in the Moon Pub. I'll text you directions. Good luck."

I put my phone in my pocket and pulled my pistol. I found Benkei still in the kitchen, near the front door, tying a piece of string. He paused when he saw the muzzle of my weapon pointing at his chest.

"I thought I heard you on the phone."

I stared at him.

"They told you I'm not with the PSIA?"

I nodded.

"That's true. I'm not. But I did tell you the truth about the yamabushi. My parents were yamabushi; a warrior and priestess. I was raised in our shrine. My sect of yamabushi are sworn to protect Japan from Sesshoseki."

"Bullshit," I said, gesturing with my gun. "You're yakuza. That why you killed those men? So they couldn't blow your cover? Pretty clever. Put that hidden blade you carry on the counter and then keep your hands on your head."

"You're making a mistake. I'm on your side. We need to get the stone and get out of here. This is costing us time."

"Sword on the counter now or I take out a kneecap. Your choice."

"Who's there?" shouted a new voice from out in the hall.

"This is a crime scene!"

The cops? Where had they been? If Benkei was telling the truth now, the apartment complex was still swarming with yakuza. I lowered my weapon and hid it behind me.

The cops came in with nightsticks drawn and glanced from Benkei to me.

"Who are you?" said one of the cops.

"PSIA," I said, holding my CIA badge up with my left hand. "Relax. We're investigating this death."

One officer walked closer to me, squinting his eyes at my badge. I noticed neither one had put their nightsticks away. Both officers were bulky with muscle and the quiet officer looked very Korean. Japanese culture is very homogenous and citizens are notoriously untrusting of most outgroups, especially Chinse and Korean immigrants. It was a sad fact, but a fact nonetheless, that seeing a muscular Korean usually meant yakuza.

I consciously relaxed my shoulders. Doing so would allow me to better swing up my pistol if I had to. I pictured myself blasting three shots into his chest as he swung his metal club at my head. Still, I couldn't just kill a police officer. What if they had really taken a short break? The Korean officer could be a fluke, or an omen of changing attitudes. And then I saw tattooed flesh show through the buttons on the officer's sleeves, the shirt too small for him.

There was a moment when we both stood in Yuto's apartment, staring. Each of us knowing the other knew. I swung my pistol up at the same moment he brought his club toward me. He moved fast, but sloppily. Instead of my head, the club caromed toward my ribs. I slung my elbow low, putting my forearm between the club and my body, and still managed to get one shot off.

My forearm exploded in pain. I allowed myself to be knocked from my feet and rolled with the blow. I was on my knees, gun in hand, in about a second. The yakuza in the police uniform was investigating the bullet wound in his side. It had gone in at the very edge of his torso, but came directly out the other side. I had done nothing more than given him a place to add a new body mod ring.

I raised my gun, fingers tightening on grip and trigger, and yelped in agony. My forearm was definitely broken. I loosened my grip, then prepared to tighten again and fight through the agony. I didn't have to. To his surprise and mine, the tip of a sword protruded through my attacker's sternum. He grabbed at it, trying to push it back through his body and succeeded only in slicing his hands to shreds.

Benkei tilted the hilt of his sword forward and the man fell to the floor. "Are we good?"

I nodded. Benkei shoved the front door closed and pulled on the twined strings he had slung around the handle and several other kitchen appliances. I stood up and saw the body of the other false police officer. Benkei was fast with that sword of his. I rushed to Yuto's safe-house-lookalike room and grabbed the stone from the safe.

"Good to go," I said, holding my injured forearm close to my body.

Right then, a hailstorm of running footsteps moved down the hall toward Yuto's door. The door was shoved open, hard, but stopped a few inches in. Benkei's twine had worked. A black ball also popped out of Yuto's emptied coffee can. It took me a second to place the object as it wasn't part of the standard intelligence and street-fighting life of an agent in Japan: a grenade.

Benkei and I ducked into Yuto's bedroom as one of the assailants on the other side of the door jutted a combat knife through the narrow opening to cut the twine. He never had a chance. The grenade exploded, splintering through the thin door and sending the team behind it flying. Benkei and I took the opportunity to rush out the ragged opening, careful not to trip over the injured bodies or slip in the blood scattered on the carpet.

I drew my pistol with my uninjured hand and kept the other under my coat, out of the fight and where it would slow me down least. We prepared for a fight. The hall was... quiet. For a time we assumed the Sumiyosha were preparing an ambush but it soon became clear they were just gone.

I walked with Benkei, not entirely certain where we were heading. We were both silent. Whether the silence was born out of vigilance, pain, or confusion, I didn't know. We ended up at the same train station we had left a scant hour before.

"Where are we going?" I asked.

"Ayokigahara."

The suicide forest.

I was confused. "Isn't that where the stone came from in the first place?"

"Yes, but it's also where we can take it to be neutralized."

He was the expert on matters concerning the stone and the strange mysticism in which it was shrouded, so I didn't question his decision.

* * *

We sat in the center of the train on opposite sides of the aisle. We talked sparingly to each other, Benkei keeping his eyes on the doors ahead of us and me on those behind.

The trip from Kyoto to Ayokigahara took us far out of our way to Nagoya and Tokyo. We boarded a bus to Fujisan Station around mid-morning. After grabbing a quick lunch at the station, we set off on foot toward the forest.

As we came to the crest of a small hill alongside the scenic drive, we could see a small, shimmering lake to the north. There were small paddle boats, kites, and anglers dotting the scene. It was idyllic. After 36 hours without sleep and rapidly decreasing blood sugar from paltry meals, I would have given almost anything to drop the stone, join some of those swimmers in their leisure, and let the Sumiyosha lay waste to whatever they wished. Instead, I pulled my eyes away from the lake and peered at Ayokigahara.

The day was bright and devoid of even sparse clouds. The forest seemed shrouded in shadow. I knew, from what I had been able to look up on my phone during the train ride, that the darker leaves of the trees in Ayokigahara were a direct byproduct of the nutrient-rich volcanic soil. That same soil made it possible for trees in the forest to grow closer together than any other area in Japan and, as such, light and sound did not penetrate far into the forest. Like a biological version of the technology used in stealth aircraft and recording studios. Though I knew the real, scientific reasons behind the dark blight of Ayokigahara, I couldn't shake the feeling that we were walking into a large, greenish-black abyss.

Benkei took point as we stepped over the threshold between Japan and the otherworldly innards of Ayokigahara. We started off following a path set by the local forestry service, but soon broke off to the southeast. A few strips of plastic tape followed us in, the remnants of hiking groups who felt the need to investigate the hidden depths of the forest—probably teens from Tokyo looking for suicide victims. It wasn't long before even the plastic tape left us behind and we walked in silence. Benkei's footsteps were so drowned out by the density of the foliage around us that I could barely hear them; he could have been speaking and it would have never made it back to me.

We passed an empty noose, its maker either having abandoned it or rotted from its embrace. I averted my gaze and pressed on, sure that the suicides would be tailing off as the distance from the entrance grew behind us. From what I had read on a forest service document, most suicides in Ayokigahara were clustered within a mile of the front entrance, far enough to seem lonely but not so far that it became a hike. That made sense; suicidal ideation and lethargy went together like sushi and seaweed, but it also meant that the other noises and the rotting skull propped up between two tree branches were even more out of place. If anything, the unmistakable signs of suicide became more prevalent as we trekked deeper into the forest.

And then we came upon a pair of femurs that had been strung from a tree like a decoration. Up until that point, the bodies littering the floor had died by their own hand and been scattered by rot, time, gravity, and the elements. Not so with this macabre wind chime. I stopped.

"What the fuck is this, Benkei?"

He studied the decoration for a moment before replying simply, "A warning. Not the last one." He continued on without so much as a glance my way.

He was right about it being the first of many, but I didn't realize how many there could be. As we trekked deeper, I spotted another femur, this one hung by a hole drilled through the center of the bone. The twine used to string the warning was crusted near the bottom where marrow had seeped from the hole. Deeper still, we encountered more femurs, but also ribs, vertebrae, and skulls strung through the nasal cavity. Oddly, the warnings seemed to serve their purpose not only for human hikers but also for wildlife; the sparse bones we first encountered had been picked clean but, further in, organic matter had dried to the hard skeleton or, in some cases, was being slowly devoured by fungus.

The warnings grew in number until it was impossible to avoid them. We shouldered past dangling fibulae, radii, and mandibles and I noted that the forest floor itself was accumulating a covering of bones. A mere 200 feet on, we were tripping and crunching over human remains. It required intense concentration to avoid rolling an ankle, but that also meant I couldn't devote cognitive resources to identifying the exact anatomy I was obliterating.

Then, all at once, the claustrophobic forest opened up. In a rough circle, the bones and dense undergrowth disappeared. The forest floor, in fact, seemed to have been meticulously picked free of almost all leaves, needles, and twigs that littered the ground elsewhere. The taller trees were trimmed such that they still shrugged away most of the sunlight trying to get through, but did not hinder movement in a six-foot space below. In the center of the circle sat a small, stone temple. It was obvious that the temple was ancient, but it was also well preserved. It appeared somewhat Shinto in architecture, but the carvings covering every flat surface were stylistically Mesoamerican. Maybe Mayan.

Though the forest had opened up, I could feel the air grow heavy. Oppressive. It felt like a large hand shoved my shoulders toward the dirt, making walking far more difficult than it should have been. Breathing was difficult, like sucking in an oxygenated pudding. I wanted to stop at a tree to rest, but the temple was almost within reach.

With a clatter, the wire Faraday cage that had been around the stone fell out of Benkei's grasp. The stone, however, did not. From the unceremoniously bent ends of wire covered in blood, I guessed Benkei had been working to free Sesshoseki for a good while. I considered grabbing the cage in case we needed it later, but I trusted Benkei to keep it if he thought it would be useful.

We walked through the temple entrance which, from a distance, had looked like a beaded curtain. Up close it was obvious the "beads" were multicolored finger bones. I didn't want to know what substances had been used in the dyeing process.

Inside the temple, sitting on her folded legs in front of a smoking stick of incense, was a woman in her mid-20s. Her long, soft-looking hair was painstakingly bundled into a nautilus design at the back of her head. Her perfect porcelain doll features were at odds with the swells of hard muscle that stretched her silk gown. Though her powerful bulk was hidden well, it was obvious she could have taken any of the field agents I trained with at Langley.

The woman's eyes snapped open at our entrance and a slight smile appeared on her lips when she recognized Benkei. "Brother," she greeted him, her formal tone antithetical to Benkei's own lazy, Western-influenced cadence. "I am glad to see your safe return. Do you bring Sesshoseki?"

Benkei raised his left hand in answer. His sister relieved him of the burden and placed it atop a lone stone altar at the back of the temple.

"We were followed," Benkei said.

His sister nodded, her face placid. I studied his face and, finding truth in his eyes, felt anger flare through my lethargy.

"Why didn't you say something? We're in a literal killing field, Benkei. This hut is entirely undefendable!" I took a breath, checking the clip in my pistol. Over half full; probably ten shots left and one extra clip. I forced myself to breathe. "We could have used the cover of the forest to our advantage. Maybe took out a few of them before we got here."

"My brother is of sound mind," Benkei's sister answered. "I am the superior warrior out of our pair. I will be able to keep you safe. And," she added, "if I am not mistaken, your safety is something Benkei holds in high regard. Do you know why?"

I didn't.

With that, Benkei's sister grabbed a spear from a weapons rack behind the door and set to honing the blade with her eyes closed.

I peered out the door. No one in view. Benkei was actively avoiding making eye contact with me, so I figured I would get him talking about something else to erase the awkwardness between us.

I gestured at the altar. "Will that neutralize the stone?"

Benkei cocked his head to the side slightly. "Short of an industrial-strength jackhammer, it's our only choice. The temple was built on an ancient holy spot; a gateway to the realm of the Oni. Like a version of Hell. We recently discovered that the portal is actually a volcanic fissure that channels infrasound from geologic movements. The altar acts sort of like a resonator. Imagine a miniature version of the Tacoma Narrows Bridge disaster. We think a similar force may have broken the stone the first time, though so much of that story has become legend it's hard to say. Still, I think it stands a chance."

"More infrasound," I said.

"Subsonic waves can be very powerful," Benkei said, simply.

We watched the stone for a short time, our attention divided between the narrow view of the forest through the temple entrance and the altar. The stone began to vibrate, first slowly and hovering right at the realm of perception. In a matter of seconds, however, it sounded like a cell phone silently ringing on a wooden desk. With each increase of vibratory energy, the air seemed to condense further around us, constricting my throat and limbs. I was forced to sit on the floor of the temple, Benkei propping a cushion under me and helping me rest my back against the rough stone.

My head began to throb in pain, a rhythmic stab of agony like the beat of some demonic drum. I felt a fullness form in my chest that rose to my throat, then the soft tissue under my tongue. It exploded into sobs and sorrow. Tears streamed down my face like torrents of rain from Amazonian thunderheads. Despair and grief flowed through my veins like congealing blood. I felt useless. Incapable of movement.

Images of Yuto's bloody, sheet-covered body entered my mind like a slide whipping in front of a projector screen. The picture of the two of us he had in his nightstand. Memories of my first sip of sake with Yuto in Hokkaido. The memories of Yuto gave way to memories of my father. He had succumbed to Alzheimer's my first year in Japan. It wasn't a surprise; everyone knew it was going to happen. Even he knew. Somehow, miraculously, he lapsed into lucidity for his final five days. He wanted to see me. His only wish. But I was too worried about what flying back to the States would mean for my career. He died without having me there to tell him I loved him.

I shrieked, overcome with emotional torment. I hoped letting out the building scream would relieve some of the pressure. It didn't. Yuto, my father, the two yakuza I shot—murdered. Something needed to release the pressure. I had to let the pain out.

Benkei appeared in front of me, holding a dagger with a feathered serpent head for a grip. He pressed it into my hand and said, "It's okay. This has to happen."

I pressed the dagger against the flesh of my wrist, knowing the slash would bring reprieve with each drop of shed blood. I pressed harder.

A loud crack reflexively jerked my head up and to the altar. The stone had cracked clean in two.

Benkei's sister jumped to her feet, grabbed a dagger identical to mine, and made a clean cut across her own throat. Her bright arterial blood sprayed over Sesshoseki and sizzled like water on a stove. Benkei's sister straightened up, stretching her arms out to her sides and inhaling deeply. She retrieved her spear from the floor of the temple and rushed out the door. The gunshots and screams that met her exit seemed miles and hours away.

"She should be dead," I whispered to myself.

"What, Stevens?" Benkei asked.

I shook my head, sloughing off some of my confusion. "She should be dead."

"I know. Infrasound can't account for that." He crouched in front of me, bringing our eyes level. "The stories our parents told us may be true."

I took pressure off the hilt of the dagger in my hand, blood swelling slowly into the small scratch I had left. "What stories?"

"The spirit. A consciousness trapped inside the stone. My sister took my parents at their word, but I tried to find alternative, scientific explanations for the tales. I didn't think she would risk her life to be imbued by the spirit but," he laughed, "I guess it worked!"

Benkei placed a hand on my knee. "That makes me more sure than ever that we're on the right path."

His hand floated onto mine, onto the fist clutching the dagger. There was something sensual about the touch as he pressed the blade closer to my wrist. Each millimeter closer to my flesh sent tingles down my spine and pressed my grief back into the locked recesses of my mind.

Luckily, the removal of that sorrow also meant the return of my rationality.

The blade touched my wrist and I writhed with pleasure that shot down into my abdominal muscles. I wanted to see what happened when the blade cleaved my pink flesh in two. I fought the urge.

I jabbed the knife back in Benkei's direction, landing a glancing blow on his right shoulder. He cried out in pain. I tried to use the opportunity to stand, to fight, but I couldn't. Without Benkei's touch, the headache and overwhelming depression started to beat on me like a boat in a squall.

"You killed Yuto," I said. Firing off the accusation was the only action I could manage.

Benkei rose to his feet, a hand covering the gushing wound on his shoulder. "Yuto killed himself."

"Like I wanted to a minute ago?"

Benkei didn't answer.

"And who's after us? Not some rogue sect of Sumiyosha."

Again, Benkei simply stared at me, his face gone stony. The realization that Benkei had used my trust of Yuto to use me against Yuto's own mission was not as surprising as it was enraging. Just as pleasure at Benkei's touch had staved off my grief, the anger was slowly filling me past brimming and pushing sorrow out. I stood.

"So you're the puppet, then. You're the traitor playing terrorist in his backyard," I said.

"I am not a traitor! My allegiance is to something greater than this country. Greater than any country. The yamabushi revere nature above all, and humanity is killing this world. We used to worry that gods would return to bring about end times with floods, earthquakes, famine, darkness, poisoned waters, and plagues that rot flesh from bone." Benkei ripped off his pea coat to tend to his injury while I teetered on the balls of my feet. "We don't need gods for that! We're doing it ourselves. Rising temperatures leads to rising water levels and more intense storms. Your own country has seen more destructive tornadoes in the last five years than the first fifteen of the 20th century. Fracking causes earthquakes daily, not to mention poisoned water. Need I go on, Stevens?"

I shook my head. I knew the statistics. "So your goal is to blow the whole thing up?"

"Of course not," he said, sounding hurt. "No. Nature is precious. That's the point. We, humanity, are the problem. Sesshoseki," he gestured to the vibrating altar, "is most effective on humans. Maybe it's the effect of infrasound on our well-developed frontal lobe. Maybe it's the vengeful spirits who have been trapped in their dark prison. Maybe it's the will of God or, hell, even Izanagi. Whatever the case, we can remove our destructive influence on nature right now.

Sesshoseki's power influenced this entire forest even while it was buried wherever Yuto and his Sumiyosha buddies found it. On the altar, it can spread far beyond that. Much larger than Japan."

"But that only takes care of some of Asia. Your real problem zones are China, the US, northeastern Russia, and parts of Europe." I reached behind me to find my pistol still tucked into my waistband. "It's a shitty plan, Benkei."

He shook his head again. "This temple is not unique. Another exists in Yakutia, Russia, and a third on the Yucatan Peninsula. The effects would be far reaching. Enough to end civilization, halt the slow death of the earth, and begin the healing process. But not so far reaching that all humans would die. Our species would continue. And maybe be more responsible the next time around. Stevens, this is important. And it's important that you're the one to start the chain. I'll stay with you."

I kept my eyes locked to his, but moved my attention to his bloody coat in a heap on the floor. I could make out the hilt of his katana jutting from the wool fabric. There was no way he could grab it in time.

"Fuck you," I said, and whipped my pistol around to fire five blasts directly into his torso.

Benkei didn't try to dodge the bullets, clutch at his wounds, or even cry out. He simply looked into my eyes like I had betrayed him. I guess I had. His knees began to quiver and he took one large step backward to lean against the wall. He let himself slide down into a sitting position, his eyes locked on mine. His breathing slowed, then stopped. Still he stared at me with accusing eyes. I could feel the grief start to flow back into me, start to sap the strength in my legs.

I took a few steps toward the altar, feeling like raising the gun to my chin would be easier than forcing my legs through the quicksand of another step. When I reached the altar, I swiped at the stone with my left hand and sent the two halves clattering to the floor.

I spun at the sound of a loud, angry wail from outside the temple, remembering that Benkei's sister had bounded out earlier. I approached the doorway, shoving aside the dyed phalanges. I wasn't prepared for what I saw. The clearing that had been so clean when we approached, a refuge from the macabre clutter that surrounded the temple, looked like a 19th-century meatpacking plant. Blood was splattered on every surface; no tree trunk or single leaf was without a congealing spurt of red. Men and women, some in suits and some in black robes, littered the ground. Or, at least, parts of them did. Arms were separated from shoulders, entrails spilled from abdomens, and heads lay yards from bodies.

Benkei's sister looked as though she had been baptized in blood. It was obvious the carnage in the clearing was the product of her and her spear, which had been broken at some point and was now being wielded as a sword. She moved fast enough that the suits—Sumiyosha, I assumed—weren't able to draw a bead on her. Some were still alive, expelling rounds desperately.

Benkei's sister saw me standing in the doorway and shrieked again. She ran directly toward me with startling speed. I raised my pistol and emptied my clip. Her dead run gave the gunners the break they needed and two or three other weapons joined my volley. Benkei's sister shuddered as the bullets ripped into her flesh and shattered bone.

She fell in a heap at the stairs leading into the temple.

Though she had to be dead, I walked toward her broken body to kick away her weapon out of habit. To my surprise, she tried to grab my foot as I stepped near her. I jumped back, kicking her face with the opposite foot as I moved.

The force of the kick lolled her loose head to the side so I could see her face. One of my bullets had hit her in the upper lip, just off center of the nose. Her teeth had imploded into her face, some forced through her tongue. Another bullet had rent the flesh from the back corner of her jaw, the bone bright in the mess of oozing fluid. She moved one eye to look at me, the other hanging dead in her skull.

"You have killed us all," she said, the words slurred and distorted by her ruined mouth.

A suited man strode up to us, raised his large revolver, and ended Benkei's sister. He shifted the gun to his left hand and offered me his right.

"Agent Stevens?" he asked.

I shook his hand, wondering if he could be PSIA and, if he was, how they found us. "Yes."

"My name is Harada. I was a friend of Yuto."

Yuto had talked about Harada before. He had defected from a smaller, more violent gang and traded information about a high-level assassination in exchange for Yuto's help in hiding him until he could change his looks and obtain forged documents from his new Sumiyosha employers.

"What code did Yuto use for his safe house floor stash?" I asked, wary of another person who claimed to be friends with Yuto. Especially after killing two of his men.

Harada's eyes crinkled in a smile devoid of any humor. In fact, his eyes seemed to glint with wetness in the dim light of the clearing. "3-2-6-3-8-2-7. From *Star Wars*."

I nodded and let down my guard. Finally. It felt good to relax.

"Yuto and I were the ones who found the stone," Harada continued. "I overheard a conversation I probably wasn't supposed to hear from someone within my organization. An archaeologist from the University of Tokyo had found a strange artifact while hiking through Ayokigahara. They wanted to either rough him up or pay him off and sell the thing on the black market. I didn't feel right about it, so I made contact with Yuto. We called up the professor and, when he started talking about it, Yuto remembered some old folktales his grandmother used to tell him as a boy. He started asking all kinds of questions and, next thing, we're out here with shovels. Yuto offered to hide the stone in his apartment until we were sure the professor wasn't going to be shaken down. The professor ended up missing instead. They found his body here, about twenty meters inside the park. Hanged. Suicide. Yuto got spooked. He thought someone had been watching us. I told him he was crazy, said the professor was probably hiking out here to kill himself in the first place and found the stone. Then… well, you know what happened to Yuto. We tracked that guy you were with from Yuto's apartment to your meeting a few hours later. I didn't realize it was you until after my guys met you in the alley."

"So," I asked, confused, "you knew what the stone was?"

"No idea. Still don't, really. The people in robes," he gestured to the clearing, "are yamabushi. They came to us when I was already tracking the guy for killing Yuto. I wanted revenge. They wanted the stone. They've got some hocus-pocus tale about this one and her brother being part of a strange branch of their religion. I don't really care much for religion of any kind. The stone can go to Hell for all I care. I just wanted to get that bastard for Yuto. He was a good friend."

"He was," I agreed. "But, Harada, there is something weird about the stone."

He nodded. "I felt it while we were hiking up here. I thought it was just nerves but no nerves can be that strong. The Sumiyosha own a business that might be able to keep it safe. Safer than out here in the mud. These yamabushi pajama guys seem to be alright with us taking it."

"What company?" I asked.

"You may have heard of them. Takahara Hachi? They're a biotech firm, but their labs are locked up tighter than banks and military bases because they work on antiviral medication and don't want to let their test viruses out into the world."

"Seems safe. Will your pajama guys allow that? They seem pretty old school."

"The yamabushi lost a lot of members today. Their entire clan was in the forest. Even if they weren't ashamed of their initial hiding job, I'm not sure they have the necessary manpower. We'll take care of it."

* * *

I reported back to my superiors that night, careful to leave out any detail that might possibly seem too farfetched. I left out Benkei's sister's berserker rage and self-mutilation, most of the backstory of Sesshoseki, and told my handler and his boss that Benkei and his sister were part of an irrational religious cult that had been whittled down to two final members. I was praised for my bravery. They even talked about giving me the Intelligence Star for my efforts in stopping a terror plot against Japan and "other friendly targets." Yuto was posthumously awarded a similar medal from the PSIA. He deserved it; there were fewer suicides in Ayokigahara the next year than the previous one, a trend I'm sure directly related to the operation Yuto put in motion.

I've since taken over most of Yuto's safe houses and keep

them ready for CIA and PSIA agents who are in trouble, modeling Yuto's preparedness. Harada generously offered to pay the rent on all properties for as long as I wanted to keep them running as safe houses. That time feels like it's rapidly running out. I'm done with this part of my life. I may not be done working for the CIA, but I want to go somewhere else. Somewhere with fewer memories.

Still, something keeps me in this island country; when I think back to the intact stone I pulled out of Yuto's floor safe, I remember a jagged edge. An edge that had been broken long ago, likely during the time of one of those fairy tales Benkei told me. Could there be another Sesshoseki somewhere in Japan?

Trust

The Sand Quarry

By Manen Lyset

The day of the incident started off like any other. My two older cousins and I woke up at the crack of dawn, got dressed, ate, made our lunches, and filled our backpacks with snacks. Meanwhile, my aunt sat on the couch, watching reruns and occasionally yelling at us to hurry up. As we opened the front door, she looked at us for the first time all morning. "I don't want to hear or see you guys until supper, is that clear?" she commanded sternly.

That was how she'd acted every time I visited in the years following her divorce. She'd shoo us out as soon as we were fed. I suppose she wanted some quiet time to recover from dealing with an extra kid, even though I was only staying for a couple of weeks. I never felt like I was that disruptive. Heck, if anyone needed alone time, it was me. As an only child, it was hard for me to adjust to the constant presence of two rowdy preteen boys. It didn't help that Parker and Joshua clearly had it in for me, partially because I was a bit younger than them, but mainly because I was a girl. At eleven and nine, they were old enough to know better than to hate someone strictly based on the possibility of cooties, but they showed their lack of maturity in the chauvinistic way they interacted with me. To make matters worse, our parents insisted we do everything together. Looking back, I can see why they were a bit resentful of me: they were essentially my unpaid babysitters, and though I considered myself an equal, they saw me as a burden.

We started by playing in the forest outside my aunt's hilltop house. By "we," I mean my cousins. Parker, the older of the two, decided they'd play Superhero. Joshua was the villain and Parker was the hero. I was told I'd be the hapless traffic cop that had to sit back and watch the scene unfold. Not that I wanted to be the damsel in distress, but I would have taken any role more involved than a mute cop forced to stay on the sidelines. After a while, the boys decided to change things up and play adventuring archaeologists instead. That time, Parker was the evil Nazi spy, Joshua was the archaeologist, and I was the servant girl, carrying their backpacks around while they swung from a tree swing and fought with twigs. I begged and whined for them to let me join, but Parker huffed and brushed me off, claiming girls couldn't fight. His brother stood behind him in silence.

I could have been a little tattletale. I could have run back to the house and told my aunt all about how her sons wouldn't let me play, but I tried that once before and it only made matters worse. My aunt cursed at Parker for half an hour, using a broader range of colorful language than an enraged thesaurus. From a hiding spot at the top of the stairs, I watched in horror as her hand slammed against his face with unrestrained force. For the rest of that visit, Parker wore a blue baseball cap to hide the mark she'd left on him. I vowed never to tell on him again, no matter how badly he bullied me. I didn't want him getting hit, and wouldn't risk further damage to the status quo. There was already enough tension between us.

The sun cycled overhead as I lamented the fact that I was, yet again, forced to sit on the sidelines while my cousins had the time of their lives. I sighed and ate the homemade cookies my aunt had baked the night before. I lost track of what game the boys were playing at that point, but it barely mattered. Whatever they were doing, I knew my "role" would be the same. Bored out of my wits, I absentmindedly traced circles on the ground. It was then that my thoughts shifted to the sand quarry. Despite being warned multiple times of its dangers, my cousins and I played there often. Not everyone agreed on why it was unsafe—locals claimed rainwater would collect at the bottom after a storm, my parents worried about old construction equipment, my aunt said it was easy to lose footing and slip—but they all agreed on one thing: never ever go to the sand quarry at night. Fortunately, it was the afternoon, so we had plenty of time to play before nightfall. Going to the sand quarry was the only suggestion I could make that wouldn't be met with contempt. The wide-open space meant I could distance myself from the boys without getting lost, and they could go ahead and keep ignoring me like always, but I would still be able to have fun in a place like that. It was a win-win scenario.

I climbed onto a boulder to get Parker and Joshua's attention, brought my hands to the sides of my mouth, and spoke as loudly as I could, "Let's go to the quarry!"

Parker and Joshua stopped in their tracks, looked at one another, and then nodded in unison.

"I was gonna say that," claimed Parker.

"Yeah we were about to go," added Joshua.

I jumped off the boulder and started scaling down the hillside. To get to the quarry, we had to go all the way down and walk about half an hour through a field of cotton. I was a chubby child and struggled to keep up with my two cousins. As we made our way through the field, I tripped on my loose shoelaces and fell in the grass.

"Wait for me!" I screamed. "Don't leave me behind, please!" I begged.

They wouldn't wait or answer. They never did. They just kept walking and exchanging idle banter while I picked myself up and ran after them in an attempt to bridge the gap. We continued like that for a while: me, falling flat on my face, and the boys ignoring my pleas for help. From time to time, however, I'd spot Joshua peeking over his shoulder at me.

"You know," Parker said, his voice loud enough for me to hear without having to strain my ears, "they say the quarry is haunted."

"What, really?" asked Joshua anxiously.

Parker nodded, "Yup. There was an accident back when the quarry was open. A backhoe loader crushed some guy. See, back then, they didn't really wear reflective vests. It was really dark that night, so his buddy didn't see him when he backed up. It was only when he heard the SPLAT that he realized what happened. You can still find blood-soaked grains of sand scattered around if you look closely. They say the dude's ghost still roams the quarry to this day."

Even from a distance, I could see Joshua's body tensing as he fidgeted nervously with his backpack. Parker removed his blue baseball cap, mounted it on his younger brother's head, and placed a reassuring hand on his shoulder.

"Don't worry, I'll protect ya," he reassured. "Besides, the ghost only comes out at night."

Joshua fiddled with the buttons at the back of the cap, trying to adjust it to fit his smaller head.

"Pft! I'm not afraid."

Parker chuckled and nudged his head toward the edge of the field. "Of course you're not. C'mon, I'll race ya to the quarry!" he said.

The two took off in a mad dash toward our destination. I tried to follow, but had no hope of catching up to them. I was forced to spend the rest of the trip waddling along with nothing but crickets to keep me company. The journey was worth it, though. I didn't know why the quarry really closed down, or what it was used for, but the result was the most amazing sandbox imaginable. Standing over the quarry was like standing on the edge of the earth. One moment, the landscape was a flat plain, and the next, it transformed into a drastic and uneven drop, revealing an impressive collection of smooth yellow sand dunes below. I imagined the quarry being the result of a giant having taken a bite right out of the valley. My cousins and I would spend hours sliding down the smaller hills as though sledding on snow, and searching through the dunes at the bottom. We'd find all sorts of things hidden in the sand: backpacks, shoes, baseball cards, rusted bikes, and other random trinkets. That was the best part about going to the quarry. There was always something new to find. Once, I'd even found a wallet full of money. As soon as I showed it to the boys, however, Parker snatched it away from me and claimed it was his. "Finder's fee," he called it.

The only place I never ventured to was on the southern wall, which we had affectionately named "Devil's Drop." Not only was it the quarry's tallest point, it was also so steep that it stood almost completely vertical. In theory, it was the quickest way back to the field, but no one had ever successfully climbed Devil's Drop. We'd exit the quarry by taking the safer and longer route around back. My cousins would often dare one another to climb Devil's Drop, but neither ever made it past the halfway point. It just so happened that, after spending several hours sledding down the dunes that afternoon, they got it in their minds to dare me to go up the treacherous hill.

"Hey twerp," said Parker.

"What?" I replied.

Parker pointed to the colossal hill. "I dare you to climb Devil's Drop."

"What? No way!" I replied, trying to hide the tremor in my voice.

Parker glanced at his brother, then turned to me, "If you do, we'll let you play with us from now on," he promised.

Joshua kept his eyes down, kicking at the sand silently. I nervously played with the rim of my t-shirt, weighing my options. I really didn't want to climb Devil's Drop, but I couldn't think of an excuse that didn't make me sound like a wimp. I couldn't afford to say no.

"What's the matter, Emily? You scared?" taunted Parker. When I failed to answer, he continued, "Yeah. That's what I thought. You're just a scared little loser. Go play with your dolls, like a little girl, you baby."

I didn't even have dolls.

I wanted to prove him wrong. I wanted to show him I was just as capable—if not more—than he was. If I could succeed where he and his brother failed, then I wouldn't be a "loser" or "good-for-nothing girl" anymore. They'd have to respect me.

I grit my teeth. "If I do it, you'll stop picking on me?" I asked.

Parker nodded. "If you climb Devil's Drop, we'll make you an honorary brother," he agreed.

Joshua frowned. "Parker s-stop. It's not funny, it's too dangerous," he said.

With a wave of the hand, Parker dismissed his brother. "There's just one catch: if you puss out, then you can't talk at all for the rest of your visit. Not a single word. And you have to do everything we tell you to do. Clear?" he said, a devious look in his eyes.

He knew he had me. He knew I couldn't succeed, but I had to at least try. Parker drove a hard bargain, but the need to be accepted by the jerk outweighed the risk of being ostracized further.

"I'll do it," I agreed.

I'm not sure at what point he expected me to chicken out. Before I even started? A quarter of the way up? Halfway? Whatever the case, I could feel his eyes on me as I hesitantly stumbled toward Devil's Drop, nervously examining the dangerous hill. I'm not sure if it was the peer pressure or my pride that drove me to make the first move, but I eventually started scaling the wall of shifting sand, my feet skidding back slightly with every step upward.

To be honest, I was beyond terrified. I refused to look down and check my progress. Even with the soft sand underneath to cushion me, I was sure falling meant certain doom. I could hear the boys laughing below. They were probably making bets about whether or not I'd reach the next milestone. Though focused on the placement of my feet and hands, I could vaguely hear them take turns trying to psych me out. I wasn't surprised to hear that they wanted me to fail. They had no desire to accept me into their inner circle, which served as motivation to succeed. I couldn't let them win.

As I made my way up, I noticed a pale root sticking out from the wall. It was burrowed deep into the sandy façade as though hanging on for dear life. I grabbed it to pull myself up, but as my fingertips wrapped around it, I was taken aback by the unusual surface. It was smooth and polished, not at all like a bark-coated branch. When I tugged on it, I realized it was far meeker than I'd anticipated. It snapped under my weight, causing me to tumble down, sand scratching my face and filling my mouth with a grainy texture. My stomach did more backflips than a gymnast on a trampoline, but despite the fear and pain, I dug my hands into the wall and kicked my heels in deeper. Sand cascaded into my eyes, and I had to close them to temper the burning sensation. My descent only ceased when I arrived at the foot of the hill. All that progress had gone to waste. As I coughed, gagged, and tried to regain my bearings, I heard Parker's hardy laughter mocking me mercilessly from his vantage point. I wanted to give up, to cry, to run home with my tail between my legs, but then something unexpected happened.

Joshua ran over to me, a concerned look on his face.

I was taken completely off guard. I expected him to stand by his brother, laughing it up with him. Instead, he reached for my hand and pulled me to my feet. I could feel small streams of blood trickling down my face.

"Are you okay?" he asked, using his shirt to soak up some of the blood on my face.

I nodded, "Yeah…"

"You can stop now, okay? You don't need to do this," he said. "I promise, we won't ignore you anymore. We never wanted you to get hurt."

My cousin probably had no idea how much his words meant to me. I found myself getting a little teary-eyed, even through Parker's disapproving grunts. A swell of motivation surged through me, giving me the boost I needed to finish the dare. I was going to conquer Devil's Drop, though not out of spite or desire to impress others; I wanted to do it for me, to prove to myself that I could succeed.

"Just watch me, Josh. I can do this. I'm getting to the top even if it kills me!" I said.

"Wait, seriously?" Parker asked in disbelief. "You're really gonna try again?"

"Yes," I answered.

"Be careful, okay?" Joshua said, giving me a thumbs-up.

Parker averted his gaze and added, "Try not to fall on your ass this time."

I smiled and nodded, before charging toward the wall of sand. I started climbing again, more aggressively than the first time. My fingers dug deep, reaching a cold under-layer of clay I didn't know existed. I managed to get a good foothold as I passed the halfway point. My Achilles' tendons burned in protest the farther up I went, but I continued until my hands touched the grassy surface at the top of Devil's Drop. I could hear Joshua cheering below. With one last kick, I pushed myself over the edge.

As I stood victoriously at the top of the hill, I felt proud of myself for the first time in my life. With the setting sun off on the horizon, the view seemed even more breathtaking than ever. My gaze travelled down to the quarry, where I saw Joshua bouncing excitedly, and Parker clapping in disbelief, his jaw hanging so low I could have sworn he'd dislocated it. I took a moment to savor my accomplishment, and then slid down a safer path to rejoin my cousins.

"I gotta hand it to ya," Parker said. "You were kind of impressive… for a girl."

He didn't look quite as enthused as his younger brother, and I could sense a hint of reluctance in his voice, but it was progress.

Joshua looked at me. "That was amazing!"

I smiled, feeling like hero.

They bombarded me with questions and actually listened when I replied. As the minutes wore on, I became aware of the dimming light. Nightfall was just around the corner, but I didn't want the day to end—I was still swimming in the adrenaline rush. I felt like I had enough energy to move mountains. Joshua, however, began looking a little nervous.

"We should get back, we're not supposed to be here this late," he said.

Parker snorted loudly. "Don't tell me you believe that stupid ghost story I told ya."

Joshua shook his head quickly. "N-no. I'm just tired. And hungry."

"Watch out, the ghost of the quarry is gonna get you…" taunted Parker, stretching his arms out in front of him and wiggling them in his brother's face.

Joshua puffed his cheeks and slapped his arms away. "Shut up! I told you, I'm just hungry!"

Amused, I took a seat in the sand and watched the two bicker as the sun finished its daily rounds. I was beside myself, when a clunky noise resounded in the quarry, followed by the telltale sizzle of electricity. The area became bathed in the bright beams of two large floodlights, remnants of the mining operation from years ago.

We all paused and looked to the lights.

"They must be on a timer," said Parker.

"Or solar-powered," justified Joshua.

The blinding light cast a veil of darkness on anything beyond its reach. The air felt different somehow, not crisp and cool like it usually did at nightfall, but heavy and thick with dust. I could feel the sand beneath my feet shifting as though the earth was quivering in fright. A tingling at the back of my neck made me realize just how exposed we all were. It felt as though we were being watched, yet couldn't pinpoint by who, or by what.

"We should probably get out of here," I murmured.

"Not you, too?" said Parker, rolling his eyes. "You two are such chickens."

But Parker had to also be able to feel everything just like we could. One quick look at Joshua, clinging to Parker's arm, told me that at least one of my cousins felt the same sense of apprehension and dread as I did. There was something off about the quarry. Something that twisted the familiar landscape into a stomach-turning, unnatural version of itself. I had felt irrational fear many times before in my life. Back home, whenever I crawled out of bed and trekked down the dark corridor to get to the washroom late at night, the hallway looked like an abyss, trying to reach toward me and suck me in. A flick of the light, however, and the feeling would go away. That moment in the quarry was different. The fear was more potent. It wasn't the mind of a little girl afraid of things that went bump in the night; it was my body's own warning bells alerting me of very real danger. It was the difference between recoiling in juvenile terror, and becoming charged with the energy needed to flee or to fight. I didn't understand what I was supposed to fear or flee from, though.

Then a scream erupted at my side. My head snapped toward my cousins just in time to see them dive to the ground. Like an anxious sprinter mistaking a pin drop for the starting pistol, I darted toward the quarry's exit, leaving my cousins behind. There were no thoughts behind my actions, just a primal reflex demanding I run. With each step, my stalled brain tried to catch up and, before I even reached the exit, I realized the boys weren't following. I spun on my heels and saw Parker pulling Joshua with the force of a strongman in a tug-of-war. Something was dragging Joshua down the dune we'd been standing on. Joshua kicked and screamed at the thing that had latched onto his ankle, but couldn't break free. I hurriedly shuffled back to the duo, only to see a skeletal hand holding onto Joshua's leg. It didn't seem possible. I knelt down next to Parker, grabbed Joshua's arm, and helped him pull.

"Hang in there!" I bellowed.

Joshua only screamed and begged for help.

"T-the hand. Get the hand!" shouted Parker.

Following my cousin's instructions, I moved toward Joshua's feet. As soon as I let go of him, his body was jerked down violently, and his lower legs disappeared under a blanket of sand, the skeletal hand disappearing with them.

"I don't see it!" I screamed.

Parker's face was turning red, and I could tell by how his arms were trembling that he wouldn't be able to hold on much longer. As though on cue, his arms flew back like elastic bands snapping in two. Joshua dug his hands into the sand, clawing at the surface like rakes in a Zen garden. Another tug, and he was submerged up to his waist. I dove toward him, grabbing hold of his arm, but the arm kept slipping out of my sweaty palms. Thankfully, Parker recovered and caught Joshua. Now it was three against one, but Joshua was still sinking.

"Help me!" he screamed.

We were trying. We were pulling with all our might, but the deeper in he went, the harder it got to pull him out. Sweat and tears poured down the sides of my face. Through gasping breaths, I repeated Joshua's name as though it were a mantra capable of turning the tide in our favor. But, as the bony appendage crawled out of the sand and up Joshua's back, followed by a second arm, it became clear that there was nothing we could do to save him. We weren't about to give up, though, even as the creature pulled Joshua deeper in and farther down the dune. Though my hands slipped multiple times, Parker remained steady, never letting go of his brother.

Watching it all unfold was torture. I could only imagine the kind of terror Joshua must have been experiencing as he was pulled in waist-deep, then up to his chest, and to his mouth. The sand muffled his screams. Soon, only his hands remained above ground. We held them, we pulled and pulled, but we couldn't get him out. Then, when they became submerged, they seemed to dissolve. It wasn't as though they slipped out of my grasp. One second, I had a vice-like grip around his wrist, and the next, I was holding a handful of dirt. I pulled my hands out and quickly pawed at the ground, trying to clear away the sand to find Joshua, but it was in vain. Parker dug like a dog trying to get to his bone, panting breathlessly as he screamed his brother's name.

Joshua was gone.

I put my hands on my knees, looking at the ground in shock as Parker continued his pointless endeavor. It didn't matter how deep he dug, his brother wouldn't be found. Our tears dampened the sand, creating splotches of mud. I didn't know what to do or say. Everything felt so surreal. Parker's efforts slowed to a stop, and he was left pounding his arms on the ground.

Then, it came back.

A few dunes over, I spotted the pallid arms that had

ripped my cousin from my grasp. Its fingers twitched menacingly before it started crawling toward us. Like before, my body reacted before my brain could even analyze the situation, and it's a good thing it did. I grabbed Parker's arm and yanked him to his feet.

I didn't make sense. All I was able to say was, "Now!"

Parker didn't answer. His tear-stained face stared at the empty hole he'd dug. Holding onto his wrist tightly, I ran toward Devil's Drop. There was no other choice: if we took the regular route out of the quarry, we risked getting caught by the ever-approaching hands. Thankfully, with a bit of encouragement in the form of violent tugs, Parker's body followed behind. The skeletal hands slid through the sand, poking out like a shark's fin in a wave. The hands were gaining on us.

At the foot of the hill, I pinned Parker to the wall and pushed him upward. "Climb!" I ordered.

He obeyed blankly. He knew how to make it halfway up on his own, and I fully intended to push him the rest of the way. As we reached the midpoint, I noticed the odd twig I had broken earlier. I don't know how I didn't recognize the shape of a humerus when I first saw it. I'd learned the shapes and names of the larger bones of the body in class just a few months before, but I suppose I overlooked it because it wasn't something I expected to see latching onto the hill of a sand quarry in the middle of nowhere. I briefly thought of some stranger unsuccessfully trying to escape the monster like we were. I rammed into Parker's behind, trying to help him up as quickly as possible.

I was exhausted. My arms and legs growing tired as the adrenaline wore off. *Just a bit farther,* I thought to himself. We were almost at the top. I could see the edge clearly against the darkened sky. Out of breath, out of energy, and with every muscle in my body aching, I pushed Parker over the edge, then threw my arms and felt the cool grass against my skin. Just as I was pulling my torso over, I felt a tug on my foot. I glanced over my shoulder and saw not just a hand, but an entire upper body had emerged from the sandy depths. I shrieked at the sight of it. Tendons and bits of flesh still clung to parts of its anatomy, giving it the appearance of a mummy dragged several miles over gravel. There was no way I was letting it get me. Using my free foot, I knocked off the shoe it was holding, and thrust myself onto solid ground.

Parker was on all fours, having not moved since he'd been thrown topside. There was a vacant, traumatized expression on his face. My heart sunk a bit for his sake, but we didn't have time for breaks. We had no idea if the monstrous form could reach beyond the quarry, so we had to keep going. We had to live. With a missing shoe and a catatonic cousin to drag along, I trudged through the field of cotton, looking over my shoulders nervously for any signs of the skeleton. Thankfully, it didn't pursue us.

I didn't feel safe until the door shut behind us. My cousin's condition didn't seem to change once we reached the safe haven. The look of shock in his eyes was still very much present, and he acted as though he was in a trance.

"You're late," my aunt said from the kitchen.

When we failed to respond—me because I was busy catching my breath, and Parker because he didn't seem even remotely present—my aunt peeked her head out into the hall, and examined us for a moment. She must have sensed something was wrong, because her disinterested gaze suddenly morphed into a semblance of worry.

"Where's Joshua?" she asked.

Parker staggered back, bumped into a wall, and slid down to a seated position, where he maintained absolute silence. I broke down in tears, but tried my best to explain what had happened. The quarry, the skeleton, the way poor Joshua had been dragged under. I'm not sure how much of it she understood through my sobs and barely coherent babbling, but she understood one thing: Joshua was gone, and with that realization came anger. Her eyebrows arched, her nostrils flared, and her body tensed. In that moment, I was more afraid of my aunt than of the skeletal being that I had barely managed to escape.

Without a word, she grabbed the phone and pounded the numbers 9-1-1 as hard as one would with typewriter keys. She demanded they dispatch a full rescue team for her missing child, never once catering to the one that had returned.

The police were quick to arrive and immediately started asking questions. What happened? How long had Joshua been missing? Where did it happen? I tried to answer, but my aunt kept pushing me behind her, as though shielding me from the uniformed men she herself had called. She explained her son had gone missing in the sand quarry, leaving out the parts about the creature we'd seen. We were whisked away in the back of the squad car and driven to the quarry.

As soon as I got out of the car, I could sense a clear shift in the atmosphere. The air felt and smelled better, and the quarry seemed calmer. Normal, even. The floodlights, which had announced the arrival of night, had burned out in our absence, leaving only the red and blue lights of the squad cars to illuminate the sandy landscape.

"Where did you last see the boy?" asked the officer who'd escorted me there.

I peered at the sandy hills, pointed to the one where we'd been attacked, but I couldn't see Joshua's drag marks in the sand. It was as if it never happened. My eyes wandered from dune to dune, but everywhere I looked, I could see only smooth and undisturbed sand, like the beach on a deserted island.

My aunt ran into the quarry, followed by a small army of flashlight-wielding officers. They combed through the dunes all night, shouting Joshua's name in the hopes of finding him. All the while, Parker stayed in the back seat of the police car, staring blankly at the quarry with lightless eyes. His mother searched desperately for her missing son, never stopping for a break or a drink of water. Even as the officers began to lose hope of finding the child alive, she continued to dig and scream her son's name, her hands bleeding from handling the coarse sand and rocks.

By morning, a group of volunteers had assembled and scoured every last inch of the sand quarry, but couldn't find a single trace of my cousin. As the days wore on and the search party thinned, the authorities were forced to call the search off. It was concluded that Joshua had been engulfed by a sinkhole, and that his body would be impossible to retrieve.

My grieving aunt watched as the last of the officers drove away. As soon as their taillights disappeared on the horizon, she stomped past me and toward her motionless son, her face turning red and contorting in a look of grief-stricken anger.

"It's all your fault!" she said. "You were supposed to be watching him!"

Parker stared blankly, unmoving. My aunt grabbed him by the shoulders and pulled him to his feet.

"Are you listening to me?" she screamed.

She shook him violently, but didn't get a reaction out of him.

"You're just like your damn father, you know that?"

Her arm reared back. I wanted to say something, but the words were trapped in my throat and my body was paralyzed. Unable to watch, I closed my eyes and cringed as she slapped Parker across the face so hard it left a red mark. I couldn't even imagine being in Parker's shoes. The only thing keeping me from crying was the fear that my aunt would hear me and direct her anger at me instead. She threw Parker against the wall and hit him again and again, while I watched, powerless. Just when I thought she'd never stop, Parker let out a weak whimper.

"I-I'm sorry…" he said.

A few teardrops soaked into the carpet at his feet. My aunt's arm froze as she realized what she was doing. Mascara started running down her cheeks. She wrapped her arms around her son, buried her face against the top of his head, and collapsed on the floor.

"M-mom. I'm sorry," whimpered Parker.

She shook her head and ran a hand through his hair. "Shh. It's going to be all right," she said.

Parker, who was always the most rough-and-tumble member of our trio, looked as fragile as a porcelain doll in his mother's arms. They sat there for a while, holding one another and crying. Even long after they both ran out of tears to shed, my aunt continued to rock Parker as softly as a newborn child.

My parents arrived later that day and took me home.

I haven't seen Parker or my aunt since that day. I heard Parker moved in with his father a few months later, after Child Protective Services deemed his mother an unfit parent. It seemed that someone—a teacher, most likely—had been building a case against her, having spotted signs of abuse. Once Joshua disappeared, it completed the file and Parker was free of her.

Parker had a few rough years, but he eventually went to

college, got a job, married, and had a few kids of his own. I also heard that, after many counseling sessions, he reconciled with his mother and even let her babysit her grandbabies from time to time.

I lived my life like anyone else would, but I could never shake the feeling of guilt I felt at Joshua's death. The constant nagging sensation that there had been a solution—a way we could have saved Joshua. Holding him tighter, or being stronger and not so out of shape.

A few days ago, I decided to go back. It was the first time since the incident that I had seen the quarry. I guess I needed the closure. Decades later, and there it was. The quarry was still untouched. I walked down into its depths, afraid, but determined.

As I made my way across the dunes, I spotted something sticking out of the sand.

It was Joshua's—or rather, Parker's—blue baseball cap. That's when I remembered all the trinkets we'd found in the sand, and realized just how many souls the quarry had taken. I never saw Joshua. I never saw anything like the skeleton again.

Chauvinism

Chaucer's Horses

By Christina Ferrari

When Bee walked into the office Hugo was already drunk. A tower of unread manuscripts teetered on his desk as he pulled open a drawer and rummaged through the contents. He picked up a book and read the title slowly, "Chaucer's Horses." He then peered over the cover at Bee; she said nothing. He stared intently at her for a moment, then continued, "By Margaret M. Margaret." Bee had chosen her publishing name on a whim; she liked its absurdity, Hugo thought it banal.

"There is a problem," he said.

"Is that so?"

Hugo poured more Scotch. "Remind me how you came up with such an original idea."

Bee crossed her arms, tapped her foot on the leg of his desk and regretted telling him the truth. "I was visited by the Muse."

"Ah, the Muse, how delightful, if only she would be gracious enough to visit me every once in a while." Hugo raised his glass and drank.

The inspiration for the novel was certainly unusual. One night as Bee slept she dreamed a strange version of Geoffrey Chaucer's *The Canterbury Tales*. In her dream the horses, not the pilgrims, did the talking. When she woke she typed the tale exactly as it had appeared. She presented the manuscript to Hugo who read the first page and decided to publish. "We shall call it, *The Canterbury Tails*," he declared with a flourish of his hand. Bee scoffed at such obviousness and insisted upon *Chaucer's Horses*, the same title that had floated, in golden letters, through her dream.

Hugo squinted and looked at Bee with bloodshot eyes. "Have you heard of Tornaquinci T. Tornaquinci?"

"Should I have?"

"Madam, are you familiar with the name?"

"It's fake, obviously."

"Obviously." Hugo swirled the remaining liquid in the bottom of his glass. "A nom de plume with all the brilliance of Margaret M. Margaret."

"He has a charming sense of humor whoever he is," Bee said.

"Tornaquinci T. Tornaquinci has written a novel called *Chaucer's Horses*."

Bee raised an eyebrow. "A coincidence." She lit a cigarette. Bee smoked only when she was anxious; medication for the artistic temperament she called it.

"Madam," Hugo ran his finger along the inside of his shirt collar, "it is not the simple matter of a common title. You have each written the same story without the slightest deviation." Hugo drank and Bee smoked.

"I suppose I should be flattered that someone plagiarized

me." When Bee tapped her packet of cigarettes on the desk, the tower of papers collapsed. Pages fluttered to the floor while others spread across the surface; they both ignored the mess. "It's very odd that someone would be so blatant about ripping off another author."

"Yes, very odd." Hugo put his glass to his mouth and threw his head back.

"We will just have to expose him." Bee said as she stubbed out her cigarette.

"We can't, I'm afraid. The man is dead."

"Dead?"

"Tornaquinci T. Tornaquinci died in Italy three years ago. *Chaucer's Horses* was written in Italian. There has been no English translation, not officially at least," he said as he slowly tapped her book. Bee grabbed the glass from Hugo and took a deep slug, then put it back.

With a sweep of his arm Hugo tossed a heap of papers to the floor and uncovered a book hidden beneath them. "This arrived today." He placed the texts side by side; Bee gasped. Both covers featured the same enlarged image, the illustration of Chaucer sitting on a horse, taken from the Ellesmere manuscript. On the cover of Bee's novel, "Chaucer's Horses" was printed in gold letters across the top; "Cavalli di Chaucer," also in bright gold letters, adorned the other. Bee reached for Hugo's glass again, but he moved it away. She picked up the bottle, drank, then wiped her mouth with the back of her hand. Hugo loosened his red bowtie and handed Bee a letter.

Dear Mr. Carter,

"Chaucer's Horses," by Margaret M. Margaret, is a direct plagiarism of "Chaucer's Cavalli" by Tornaquinci T. Tornaquinci, published by The Bovolo Press. We insist that all copies of the novel by Margaret M. Margaret be removed from sale immediately. The matter has been referred to our Attorney…

Bee scrunched the paper into a ball then threw it at the wall. "I don't speak Italian nor do I read it, the story is different. It has to be."

Hugo's hand shook and he dropped the glass; dark amber liquid spilled over crumpled manuscripts that would remain unread. "I'm ruined," Hugo said as he stared vacantly at the empty glass.

"You give up far too easily, Hugo," Bee said as she waved a sternly pointed finger at the man sitting slumped over in his chair. Bee left the room, determined to restore her reputation.

* * *

Bee did not like Venice. Others saw a dazzling city; she saw dirty lagoons. Bee looked down as she crossed the Rialto Bridge and noticed refuse floating in the canal. Her situation had to be sorted out quickly, or she would be an infamous and unpublishable ex-writer, washed up and discarded like the muck below.

The family of Tornaquinci T. Tornaquinci lived rather well on the legacy of Tornaquinci's writing. Despite his death by drowning in the Grand Canal, his name remained permanently on best-seller lists. His novels, which mostly focused on Renaissance-era alchemy, were popular with Italians who were acutely aware of their heritage and the symbolic alchemical elements embedded in the art that surrounded them. Many believed that Tornaquinci was an alchemist himself, such mysteriousness added to his allure. From time to time the family would release previously unpublished manuscripts discovered hidden in the labyrinthine "Bovolo Palace" that was the family home. The public clamored for each new novel.

Bee went to the Tornaquinci home directly from the train station with her suitcase in tow. She went to explain the situation to Tornaquinci's son, Antonio, and his wife, Mirella. They would probably throw her out, but Bee had to try to make them understand; there was no other option. When Bee knocked on the door, she reeked of desperation.

There was a long pause as Bee waited on the stoop. It seemed quiet out there, despite the bustle of the city. The home was not quiet on the inside.

"First, she has the nerve to steal my father's book, then she turns up here, what else is she going to steal, the silverware?" Antonio asked his wife.

"If she thinks she can appear from nowhere and charm us

into dropping the lawsuit she is wrong," Mirella said as she wiped her wet hands on a crisp, white apron. Born into a rural southern family, Mirella, despite her expensive clothes, carried herself like a woman familiar with hard work. "These English, you have to watch them or they will steal your shoes while you are still walking." She removed the apron, patted her perfectly coiffed hair and nodded at a servant who then opened the door. When Mirella entered the room she wore the mask of a gracious hostess. "Buon giorno signora Margaret, welcome to Venice."

"It is an honor to have someone so talented in our home," Antonio said. "Please," he gestured for Bee to sit on an opulent red-velvet couch, "it once belonged to a doge." Like so many other items in the room, the wooden frame was smothered with gleaming gold leaf.

Bee noticed the abundance of gold. If old Tornaquinci was an alchemist, she thought, he had been a very good one. "I believe your father discovered the alchemist's secret," she said. Mirella pursed her thin lips tightly and twisted the apron in her lap.

Antonio leaned forward until he was uncomfortably close to Bee. "What do you mean?"

She picked up a small golden figurine from the marble table in front of her and turned it around on her palm. "One might think he had the power to turn base metal into gold."

Antonio straightened up but still leaned slightly forward. "Perhaps he was an alchemist of a sort. The stories he imagined have sold very well; you could say he turned paper into gold."

"I wonder if Mr. Tornaquinci and I are kindred spirits," Bee ventured to add. "Like him, I am a writer and we clearly share the same sense of humor. My name is Bee Chambres; Margaret M. Margaret is my nom de plume."

"You are mistaken, signora. Tornaquinci T. Tornaquinci is the name on my father's birth certificate."

"A peculiar name."

"My father was a peculiar man." The Italian couple smirked at each other.

Bee twisted a silver ring on her finger. "I have come to Venice to resolve the issue of *Chaucer's Horses*. There has been some sort of mistake."

"Si, a mistake." Mirella nodded then looked sideways at Antonio.

There was no other way to say it; Bee had to tell the truth. "I have never read Tornaquinci's work. It is quite strange really, but I can't have copied it. You see, the idea came to me in a dream, nocturnal inspiration you might call it."

Mirella and Antonio stared.

"A dream?" Mirella asked.

"Yes, a dream." Bee reached into her purse for a cigarette, fumbled through the contents, then gave up.

"She had a dream, Antonio. A dream, it was miracolo no? Some words sent down from the heavens. Tell me, signora Chambres, have you contacted the Vatican? They are always interested in the reporting of miracles."

"The Vatican would not be interested," Bee murmured.

"Of course it is, you go to sleep, you dream, you write best seller, miracolo!" Mirella persisted.

A portrait in a heavy gilt frame caught Bee's eye. A distinguished-looking man posed on the doge's couch. The artist had rendered his subject with a mischievous gleam in his eyes. Mirella broke the silence. "My late father-in-law. He was very, how you say… unique." Before Mirella could elaborate, Antonio picked up a golden box and offered Bee a cigar.

"Thank you but I can't stand cigars, they make me sick," Bee said as she waved the box away. Antonio removed one and eased himself back into his chair without taking his eyes off Bee.

Mirella and Antonio watched Bee with suspicion, the way a cat eyes a mouse.

Bee leaned back into the couch that once belonged to a doge but no longer appreciated its grandeur. She felt like a small fish twitching as a hungry shark approaches, sensing the presence of evil but not understanding the nature of it all. Her hasty dash to Venice had been a mistake. She tried to stand but felt dizzy and the room began to spin. Antonio lazily puffed his cigar while scrutinizing Bee. "You are tired; we will take you to your hotel so you can rest. We can meet again later to discuss the misunderstanding."

"No hotel, you must stay here. You are not well, signora," Mirella said. "We talk when you are feeling better." She nodded to Antonio, a gesture that he perfectly understood. He stubbed out his cigar, stood, bowed silently to Bee, then walked briskly from the room and instructed the maid outside the door to make the necessary preparations.

Left with the visitor, Mirella didn't speak; she caressed the string of milky baroque pearls around her throat and gazed at the portrait of her father-in-law.

"The hotel is not far, I should go there," Bee said.

Mirella turned toward her. "No," she said in an authoritative voice. "You are unwell, you stay." She stood up. "We talk no more." Her heels clacked across the white marble floor as she walked from the room. "Amadeo will come for your bag," Mirella said as she closed the heavy door.

Antonio waited for his wife in the hallway. "No good will come of this, she is going to cause trouble."

Mirella shook her head from side to side. "An entire novel from a dream? I don't like this Antonio." She pointed her finger at the sitting room door. "This problem has to go away."

"I agree, but it needs to be handled carefully." Antonio stroked his chin as he spoke.

"Just take care of it." Mirella tied on her apron then walked away.

Alone in the sitting room, Bee was troubled by the uncanny sensation that everything was not what it seemed. Something disturbing bubbled beneath the surface; exactly what, she did not know. To leave would insult the Italians and destroy her chances of resolving the situation. Bee would spend the night in the curious place. "What choice do I have?" She asked the question out loud, despite already knowing the answer: none.

"I hope you don't mind ghosts," the genial Amadeo said as he walked up the exterior spiral staircase with her luggage. "The palazzo is haunted, which should come as no surprise; this is Venice, everything is haunted." Bee was not easily frightened; her novels often featured incorporeal beings in eerie settings. Amadeo stopped and looked down at Bee. "Do you believe in ghosts?"

"I write about them so I suppose I do, not that I have ever seen one for myself."

"You will," Amadeo said as he stepped onto a dark landing. He walked down the empty hallway then stopped in front of a white door. The paint was tinged yellow; Bee had been sent to the back of the house, where unimportant guests were relegated.

The room was damp and had only a small window which looked out to a dingy canal. The view was not at all picturesque; no gondolas brimming with excited tourists travelled along the slip of muddy water. The neighbors had hung laundry out to dry. Large orange underpants waved at Bee as the breeze caught them, the same breeze that lifted an odiferous scent from the canal below and caused it to waft upward; she scrunched her nose.

"Buona notte," Amadeo said as he closed the door, "have good sleep." Bee heard him laugh as he walked away. She sat down on the bed to consider the situation. Mirella and Antonio controlled her future and she was not sure it would be possible to reach an amiable agreement with the strange people. Her future looked very bleak. The unusual feeling of fatigue that assailed her before had returned. Bee stretched out on the bed and fell into a heavy sleep.

Antonio knocked on the door early the next day. When the sound woke her she opened her eyes, jolted upright, then realized she was still dressed and had spent the night on top of the covers. She opened the door in a disheveled state.

"I apologize for disturbing you, signora," Antonio said in the charming voice he only used when Mirella was not around. Bee slid a hand over her hair to smooth it down. "Unfortunately, I have been called away on an urgent matter."

"Would you like me to leave?"

"There is no need. It is not the Venetian way to turn a guest out." His blue eyes sparkled when he smiled. "The palazzo is full of history, signora Chambres, and you are a woman who writes about history. I am sure you will find much here to capture your interest."

"Mr. Tornaquinci, I am enchanted by your home, but I could not poke around in your absence."

"This house was derelict until my father purchased and restored most of the building. My wife and I only use a small part. Many beautiful rooms remain empty. I am sure they long to have someone visit and give them living company." Bee was amused by the way Antonio spoke of the house as though it were alive. "Later we will talk about Chaucer and his horses, I am sure we can find a solution that is agreeable." He took her hand and kissed it. She blushed. The prospect of touring the palace appealed to her curious nature. Bee was excited. When Antonio left she hurried back into the room and prepared for an adventure.

Amadeo stood in the hallway with his hands in his pockets, waiting. "Buon giorno, signora," he said when the door opened. Bee gasped and dropped her purse; Amadeo looked down at the scattered contents then up at Bee. "Mr. Tornaquinci wants me to show you around." Bee picked up her notepad and pen while Amadeo watched. When the purse was refilled, he ushered her down the hallway.

"The first point of interest is the magnifico exterior spiral staircase, the snail, as it is called on account of the twisting shape, like the shell of a snail," he said, mimicking a tour guide. A serious look came over his face, "A ghost horse who walks up and down the stone steps is often heard here, signora." Bee did not believe it but he promised her it was true. "You can ask anyone in Venice."

The palace had once been home to a nobleman who rode his mount up the staircase to his private apartments every day, it was said that in death he did the same. Bee stood and listened for a moment, but did not hear spectral steps, only sounds from the calle outside, children playing and dogs barking.

"Amadeo!" Mirella called from the end of the hallway.

"You are needed. Now!"

Amadeo yelled, "Sì, signora," then put a hand on Bee's shoulder and pressed firmly, nudging her slightly forward. He pointed toward the worn steps. "You will continue." He walked toward Mirella, then stopped to look back. Bee stepped onto the staircase and took a few steps down. When she looked behind, Amadeo was gone.

The prospect of wandering alone in a mysterious building incited in Bee the dual pleasures of fear and excitement; she felt propelled—against her better judgment—to explore. The thrill of the danger that might be encountered on such an excursion prompted her to venture into the tantalizing unknown. She had vicariously experienced such adventures through her characters who frequently found themselves wandering in grand castles—all of them haunted. It was her turn to be delighted by the prickling sensation of her hair standing on end.

The winding stairs were a splendid example of gothic architecture but on them she encountered no otherworldly phantasms. When Bee reached the bottom she faced a black door which stood slightly ajar. Fixed in the center was a glittering, golden snake. Her breathing quickened.

The serpent, making a circle and biting its own tail, shone brightly as though illuminated from within. "Ouroboros," she said in a soft voice. "The symbol of alchemy." Bee was fascinated by the coiled snake motif which had been appropriated by alchemists in ancient times. To them it

signified the real purpose of alchemy—the quest for
regeneration and eternal life. Full of curiosity, she ran her
finger over the image. The door creaked open to reveal a
darkened tunnel. Exposed electric light bulbs hung from the
wall. Bee flicked a switch and the lights spluttered on. She
looked back at the sunlit staircase. She could go back; that
would be the sensible thing to do, but not the sort of thing Bee
would do. She went inside.

The tunnel ended at a second door. Bee brushed aside the
thick cobwebs that covered the handle then pushed it open.
The room she entered contained a not-entirely-unexpected
sight: an alchemist's laboratory. Stone tables stood in the
center of the room; glass jars, chunks of rock, metal fragments
and opened books crowded the surfaces. Water trickled down
the walls and formed large puddles that made the wet floor
glisten like polished crystal in the orange light. The cavernous
room was warmed by fires burning in several smelting ovens
along one of the walls. The air smelled of sulfur; Bee
remembered the odor the breeze had delivered to her room.

Tornaquinci T. Tornaquinci sat on an old leather couch
smoking a cigar. He looked remarkably like the portrait
upstairs. "At last, they have sent me some company," he said
with a grin, then gestured for Bee to sit in a heavy wooden seat
that reminded her of an electric chair. She stood still. "I insist."

There had not, until that point, been any reason for Bee to
be hesitant or afraid. No reason for her to question
Tornaquinci's legacy or family or the circumstances beyond

face value. However, there was a shift once Bee was in his presence. Something had changed entirely, and while she did not yet understand it, she did feel uneasy. She lost some of her confidence in that moment. The reality of the situation began to settle in. Tornaquinci really was in front of her. Her journey was no longer a game.

Bee considered running from the room, then she noticed a misshapen shadow hovering near the entrance; she sat down with a sullen look on her face.

Tornaquinci wrote on a piece of gold-edged paper, lifted a small metal door in the wall, slid the note inside then pressed a button; a mechanical sound erupted. "Antonio is eager to hear that you have arrived." Bee couldn't hide her surprise. "Tell her to explore the haunted building, I told him. A writer can't resist such temptation." His self-satisfied grin repulsed Bee.

"Your son lives in luxury in the palace above, while you languish here on the water floor, why?"

"One can't live forever you know. Not in the public eye, anyway," he said matter-of-factly. Bee heard a slight sound by her chair, she turned to see an emerald green serpent slither by, then disappear through a missing stone in the wall. She blinked.

Tornaquinci watched her, the way a scientist studies the captive subject of an experiment. When Bee caught him he picked up a book and opened the cover. A florid signature adorned the paper: "Margaret M. Margaret." It was the first novel she had written, *Apopis*; a dark tale about the Egyptian demon. Tornaquinci's choice of novel was not lost on Bee, she knew that the ancient Egyptians used the Ouroboros to represent Apopis. To them, the endless snake served a dual purpose—it could invoke curses or serve as a talisman for protection from evil.

"You see, I am a fan," Tornaquinci said. "I stood in line for hours just to get your signature, not an easy thing for a man as old as me to do."

A thin film of perspiration coated Bee's face. "You speak of your great age. I presume you wish me to believe you have discovered the great alchemist's secret, the elixir of life. Immortality is a fairytale, Mr. Tornaquinci."

"It is no fairytale, signora. Sadly, I am condemned to hide in this cavern because people like you will never understand." Tornaquinci poured a drink from an ancient decanter, and offered the glass to Bee. She declined. "Three years ago the imbeciles upstairs had the clever idea to confine me to my laboratory. People had begun to talk about my longevity and those two," he looked upward and waved his finger at the ceiling, "who have only a few brain cells to share between them, forced me down here to hide, like a rat. I have to admit that I agreed with their reasoning."

"But your death. The body in the canal…"

"A terrible accident," he said, then shrugged, "or so it was said. A man who had the good fortune to share my fine looks, shares them no longer." Bee saw the same gleam in his eye she had noticed in the portrait. "My son is very fond of money, but is not willing to make his own. I remain here, expected to write new stories which my only heir then publishes." Tornaquinci picked up a half-smoked cigar from an ashtray and blew heavy tendrils of smoke in Bee's direction. "May I offer you a cigar?"

"You may not," Bee replied. The alchemist blew a heavy cloud of smoke toward her; Bee coughed as the smoke strangely massed around her face and felt unbearably thirsty.

"You might be wondering, signora, why you are here." A smirk spread across his face. "When I read *Apopis*, I knew you would be perfect." To his right, on a side table, sat a rock-crystal flask, ruby liquid glimmered within. "Discovering the elixir of life is not my only great achievement; I am also a magus, one who is skilled in the art of magic."

Bee was not about to cower before the puffed-up charlatan. "Magus? Is that Italian for old man locked in the basement by children who no longer want him around?" She knew it was petty, but she often allowed herself to be ruled by her emotions. It was freeing and she felt more in control.

Tornaquinci ignored her. "Due to my current circumstances, I am in need of a suitable… vessel. You are just what I want: a writer with talent, but not too much, just enough to transcribe my words as I transmit them, but without the cleverness to add thoughts of your own. I might be trapped in this room but you are not."

Bee opened her mouth to issue a vitriolic response when an image caught her attention. An Ouroboros was painted on the floor near her chair, the head of the snake pointed down. It was an ominous symbol. The downward Ouroboros was used by Egyptian sorcerers to invoke curses against their enemies. Incredibly, the image began to move, uncoiling itself then moving toward her.

Tornaquinci continued to smoke as he watched Bee squirm; the intense orange glow of the fires cast a diabolic light over him. "*Cavalli di Chaucer* was an experiment. I used magic to take command of your mind as you slept, but the process is very tiring for an old man, far too tiring to be repeated."

"You could have sent me a new, unpublished story."

"Then you never would have come. I had to ruin you to lure you here," he opened his arms wide to encompass the underground room, "to my lair."

Bee wanted to flee, but once again she felt leaden and couldn't stand up. "There is no need to leave, signora; we have only just begun to become acquainted." Tornaquinci drew a vial from his pocket. "Now that you are here, I can finish what I started; it will be so much easier once you drink the potion." The room seemed to close in around Bee. "I am old, imprisoned, and let's not forget: dead." Tornaquinci winked at the woman sitting helplessly before him. "My family cannot continue to find manuscripts. Eventually the public will start to ask questions, difficult questions, unless you and I can make an arrangement." The black liquid in the bottle throbbed as though it were alive. Bee knew she was beaten. An unquenchable thirst took hold: she drank.

* * *

Hugo was sober when Bee walked into his office. Stacks of manuscripts were neatly arranged on his desk. "The prodigal author returns," he said. "The plagiarism scandal, I am thrilled to say, is over." He adjusted his navy bowtie, opened the drawer and pulled out two glasses. "I believe we deserve a drink." He poured the Scotch, made them both doubles, and handed one to Bee.

"The Tornaquinci family issued a statement. Apparently, you were given permission to translate T.T.T's original gem into English; a remarkable achievement for a woman who neither speaks nor reads Italian." He waited for a response from Bee but she offered none. "The official story is that an unfortunate and regrettable error was made when the printer failed to credit old Tornaquinci for the original."

Bee adjusted the scarf around her neck. "Where did you get that? It's hideous," Hugo said.

"Italy," she answered. "I think it's lovely." Bee made sure the Ouroboros symbol printed on the silk could be seen clearly.

"The official version is a complete lie," Hugo said. "How did you convince them to cover up your appropriation—to put it nicely—of the original?"

"I charmed them; I am a very charming person." Bee winked, opened his cigar box, removed the last Cuban and enjoyed the look of pain on Hugo's face. She produced a

glittering gold cutter from her purse and snipped it. After she
lit the cigar she took a long, satisfying drag.

"You don't smoke cigars."

"Nonsense; I love them, always have." She blew a large
puff of smoke toward him. "I'm here to talk about my new
book, a gothic novel set in a spooky Venetian palazzo. It has it
all: ghosts, the arcane arts and my favorite—alchemy."

At that moment in the Bovolo Palace, Tornaquinci T.
Tornaquinci completed his masterwork. A gothic novel, it had
it all: ghosts, the arcane arts and his favorite—alchemy."

Diligence

Biserka

By Kristopher J. Patten

Javor Markovic watched the long belowdecks passage flex and twist, each movement accompanied by a deep, sickening growl of metal on metal that he could feel in his gut. This view used to make him sweat, hyperventilate, run to the crew quarters to get a different view of the container ship's travels. Even then, though, he couldn't shake the image of the ship cleaving in two like the Titanic, leaving long, thin strands of jagged metal exposed on both ends like caramel inside a broken candy bar. The cold, blue death of seawater would flood into both halves and pull them down, sinking like anchors. Javor would die, trapped belowdecks and unable to escape. Or maybe he would make it out of the ship and tread water for days before running out of energy and giving up. Either way, he would breathe in the chilling, salty water. It would fill up his lungs until they burst inward like cheap water balloons.

But that was before he learned to be afraid of being exposed. Of being caught unprotected in the streets where the hunters spied you through their glass and metal tubes, the other end not even glittering in the stormy skies so you knew which way to run, and let death rain down. Now, Javor knew the pliability of the ship was preferred to the alternative. The movement allowed the hull plates to expand and contract as the temperature of the ship and the surrounding sea changed. It allowed the ship to absorb some of the force of the incessant sea swell. A rigid ship could be weakened by these things. Not to mention that a ship, especially the bowels of a ship sitting feet below the ocean surface, was far from any sniper nest.

Javor would have felt at ease in the crew cabin, smoking and playing cards with the Russians, Greeks, and the pair of Turks, but he often preferred being alone. Stano told him he spent too much time with his thoughts, that he let them tear away at him until, someday, nothing would be left but a shell of a man. Javor stared ahead toward the point where the passage, just tall enough for him to walk in without stopping though his hair brushed the matte white steel above him, came together in a point. If he crouched a little and concentrated on the bends and dips of the walkway, he almost felt like he was racing through a tunnel on the makeshift street luge sled his brother made when they were kids. The front of the ship dipped drastically—they must have been at the top of a large swell. As soon as Javor processed that information, he felt the truth of it; he staggered forward as the ship pitched downward, leaving his stomach somewhere behind him. He almost felt the old, familiar fear again when his radio squawked.

"Markovic, finished with your check?" the captain's burly Russian accent called out from Javor's hip. Behind the captain's question, Javor could hear the rush of wind. Perhaps a storm had blown in while he was making his rounds.

"We crossed paths with a squall. Best to come topside," the captain ordered.

Javor climbed the long staircase that hugged the engine cowling. It was loud in this area. Loud enough to damage his hearing. The standard procedure was to wear ear protection headgear; pairs clung to the railing on every level in case anyone forgot their personal set. Javor never wore his ear protection; he found the thrum of the engines therapeutic. The low-frequency rumble cut into his incessant inner monologue like soap breaking up a clot of grease. By the time he had climbed high enough to escape the noise, his hearing had attenuated to the intense environment and rendered him deaf to all but shouts.

Shouts, however, were the only levels of speech being used in the top decks. Crewmen rushed past Javor, deeper into the crew cabin, to lash down loose items. Other men rushed the other way, making last minute checks of the mass of shipping containers stacked in front of the ship. This was more activity than Javor expected.

"What the hell is going on?" Javor called to Michalis, a short Greek who was trying to force his chubby legs to carry him faster than their limit.

"One of the cranes' lines came unhooked. It's whipping around down there and destroying the cargo containers," Michalis said quickly.

Javor pictured the steel cable, as big around as his leg,

thrashing with each wave and careening into the metal containers like a giant, metallic scorpion caught in a jar. A few well-placed strikes from the cable could crack a container like a soda can and allow cargo to escape into the sea. Though the shipping company had insurance against such an occurrence, the company would expect payment for services lost from the crew of the ship. None of them could afford the steep fees the company charged for "incompetence." Instead, the only option was to send men like Michalis out onto the deck where the possibility of getting pulverized by the wild cable—or, worse, being knocked overboard into the water to die slowly and alone—was very real.

"Jesus," Javor said, shaking his head. "Be careful."

"No worries, my friend! We're just going to cut it loose. If we lose it today, good riddance. We'll pick up another at port." With that, Michalis hurried out the hatch, puffing again as he attempted to run.

Javor made his way to the bridge. Things were calmer in that part of the ship, but no less tense. The reason was clear: one weather radar screen showed nothing but gradations of red, the highest-density storm. Rain from the squall pelted the windscreen with such force that it was almost impossible to discern the water running down the glass from the churning sea around them. It was also difficult to tell the difference between sea and sky through the mess on the windscreen. Javor hoped the steadily rising line of dark against darker wasn't that cutoff point.

But it was. The bow of the ship cut into the wave, heaving the whole vessel downward like a forceful punch on the opposite end of a teeter totter. Then the swell rose under the hull and raised the ship vertically, the plane of gravity rapidly shifting from down to the aft of the ship. Then they were on the crest. Javor rushed to an open hatch and thrust his head out to gauge the scene. He hoped to see an end to the storm in the distance or spot calmer waters ahead. Nothing. He kept his eyes locked on the water around the container ship as it lurched over the crest like a roller coaster hurtling down its track.

In the few seconds before Javor needed to slam the portal shut and seal it against the sea spray, he peered into the next wave building ahead of them. What paltry sunlight made it through the clouds illuminated the wave from behind, outlining a strange shape caught up in the swell. Javor considered a few common alternatives, but the shape was far too expansive and solid to be seaweed. It was too amorphous to be a shark or other such creature. It had to be detritus of some sort. Perhaps another ship had been caught in the squall and ripped apart.

"Captain!" Javor shouted. "Debris in the water, might be heading toward us!"

"Size?" the captain called.

Javor turned his attention back to the wave, now dangerously close to the bow of the ship. The shape was gone. At that moment, the ship bucked downward in the front again and then popped up the wave. Javor slammed the port closed until the ship was out of the salty rain that was ripped from the crest of the wave in sheets.

"Unknown, sir. I lost it."

The captain cursed in Russian. "Alright." He sighed, then picked up the microphone that connected to the ship's intercom system. "Debris in the water. Prepare for possible collision." The captain repeated the message in Russian and very broken Italian.

The bridge lapsed into silence again. Men manning necessary pieces of equipment strapped their seatbelts on. Those who were merely assembled to watch the storm unfold retreated to lower levels or braced themselves against bulkheads. Javor didn't move. He wasn't frozen out of fear, but lost in thought.

He wondered if this would be how he died: the container ship jolting violently, then listing while the crew tried to bilge the incoming water, and finally sinking to the bottom. Would he die from that old fear? Now that it loomed so near, he found he didn't mind. In fact, it would be freeing. When he sat alone belowdecks, he replayed the gunfire and spilt blood that had brought him to this ship. It was torturous, each time worse than the last as he found new memories over which to cringe and cry. It was his penance, and he would continue until he felt he couldn't. Whatever that meant; he wasn't sure. If he died now, bludgeoned to death by a snapping steel bulkhead, he would be released. And perhaps be able to find out if his parents' beliefs were true.

A loud growl cut into his thoughts. He looked around the room, seeing the faces of the other men doing the same. Each looked expectantly at one or two others, hoping they had some explanation for the noise, then—finding no answers—checked their surroundings for clues. The ship continued the gut-wrenching climb and fall.

The captain stood, an odd look of suspicion in his eyes before he closed them and pressed the side of his face against the wall. He jumped back with a start, as if the wall had suddenly become electrified, and dropped to his knees. Again he placed the side of his face on a surface, though now he chose the floor. He stood and looked off into the distance, through the rain-streaked windscreen, through the squall, through everything and deep into the heart of despair.

"The engines have stopped," the captain said quietly.

Now that it was spoken, Javor noticed he couldn't feel the familiar slow tremble that gave the ship's floors life when the engines were running. She was dead in the water. It didn't have a bearing on surviving the current storm, but it would be a problem later. Without the engines charging the batteries, the climate control and ship lights would soon drain the last of the power. With them would go sonar, radar, and radio. The only option they would have to call for help would be the emergency radio, powered by hand crank. The range of the emergency radio, the captain knew, was shit.

"Zubov! Cut power to the shipping containers. Markovic,

get down in your nest and look for leaks. Take two others with you, but split up and be quick."

"Aye, sir," Zubov and Javor said in unison.

Javor raced back down the stairs into the belly of the ship, two Italian crew members in tow. Perelli clicked on his flashlight and peeled off from the group onto one deck, casting the circular beam on the massive steel panels. Bello stepped out onto the deck below. Javor took the lowest, coldest deck. He took a first pass with his light on, relying on his eyes to single out dents, cracks, or—God forbid—leaks. When he reached the bow, still pitching up and down violently in the storm swell, he switched his light off, letting the passage fall into a darkness so absolute it was almost palpable.

Javor walked forward slowly, silently, the rubber sole of his boots making contact with the grating of the passage without even the faintest reverberation of metal. He ignored his now useless visual sense and turned his attention to his ears, stretching out to both sides. He listened for the trickle of the water and the popping of rapidly cooling metal. He used the technique when he checked the cargo for loose lashings though, with the engine noise, it was only useful in the front third of the ship. Now, however, with the ship quieter than it had ever been, he could walk the entire length and complete his multisensory check, pausing only when the gargantuan waves outside sloshed against the hull.

In the distance, toward the engine, Javor spotted a faint blue glow. He closed his eyes and shook his head slightly to reset his vision. It wasn't unusual for him to experience visual hallucinations of sparkling colors when he was belowdecks in the dark; he assumed it was his eyes trying to make sense of the information-poor environment. The glow seemed to persist when Javor opened his eyes, so he closed them. He had to keep his attention on the sounds reaching his ears.

A few paces down the passage, Javor's boot slipped on the metal grating. Not a good sign. It meant there was water down here. He opened his eyes and reached for the flashlight in his pocket but, before his fumbling fingers could free it from his pocket, he noted that the water in the passage was glowing.

He cursed softly in Croatian, a swear of wonder. Though the prospect of water leaking into the ship was frightening, he had never seen bioluminescent bacteria in real life. One of the Greeks—Javor couldn't remember his name but he walked the deck with an old American camera around his neck at all times —had shown him snapshots of the glowing particles that had been taken from the top deck of the ship. Those pictures had cut through Javor's permanent melancholia, reawakening the feeling of childish wonder that had evaporated, much like Yugoslavia, with the fires of the Bosnian War. Javor had felt guilty for temporarily hanging up the heavy cloak of his penance while he looked at the old Greek's pictures, but he had enjoyed it at the time.

Up close, the glowing puddle stunned him in the same way. The ship could have been tearing itself apart around him. He could die, choking on glowing liquid, but he left his

flashlight in his pocket and knelt to get a better look at the
puddle. Javor felt a smile contort his features. He extended a
finger, tentatively, and tapped the surface of the water. The
glow intensified, rippling out from the point at which it
contacted his finger until the entire puddle shone and reflected
on the walls of the keel. He reluctantly stood, still watching the
glow ripple around the puddle like an electric wave, and
searched for glowing drips running down the walls.

Finding nothing, he flicked on his light and searched the
plates in the usual way. Still nothing. Where in the hell had that
puddle come from?

Javor continued down the passage, listening for the trickle
and, now, looking for the glow of a leak. He found another
puddle, this one somewhat smaller than the first and glowing
less brilliantly. Like the first, however, Javor found no
indication of a leak. Continuing down the passage, Javor found
three additional bioluminescent puddles, all without an
identifiable source.

He reached the engine without finding any problems with
the ship. Shining his light up to the next level, he saw no
evidence of Perelli or Bello. Perhaps they were still making
their rounds; the perimeter grew as the decks rose. Javor
entered the engine section, checking both the hull for water
and dents and the engine for leaking oil and coolants.

Javor's head involuntarily jerked to the left as he heard a
drip. Looking around, he found a small rivulet of water
running toward the front of the ship as the craft shot down yet

another wave. Javor backtracked to the stairs and raced up to the level from which he thought the water might have dripped. He pressed the plastic lens of the flashlight to his chest to quickly cut the beam and was met with the eerily beautiful glow he had tracked in the lower passage.

Instead of small puddles as he had seen before, there was a large standing pool of water in front him, atop the ship's drive screws. It looked like the glowing bacteria were not just in the water here; the handrails of the walkway glowed blue, as did the hull and the engine cowling. Javor knelt to get a closer look at the pool of scintillating seawater. A brighter glowing thread seemed to lay in the water and run back behind the engine, like a string of dental floss draped in the condensation of a soda. Was it something from the engine? Javor knew the engine belts were rubber reinforced with cotton thread. Perhaps a belt had become overtaxed and snapped. That would be an easy fix.

Javor clicked off his light, shifted all of his weight to his right leg, and gingerly extended his left toward the thread. He nudged it to test its rigidity. It moved. But not like a floating shoelace. It jerked away from his touch as if it were alive.

Javor almost lost his balance and fell toward the thread with a gasp. He stood and stared at the thread, now floating in the puddle again. He wondered if the strange movement had been caused by some sort of strange chemical reaction, picturing a bartender dipping his finger into Javor's beer to dispel the foam. Javor prepared to nudge the thread again when a second thread emerged from a small, claustrophobic passageway over the drive screws and behind the engine. This thread moved fast, the bioluminescence giving it the look of lightning. It caught Javor on the neck and shoulder and then both threads quickly disappeared into the dark.

Javor recoiled from the hit, his exposed flesh instantly burning. He ran toward the staircase, hoping Bello—the stronger of his two companions—had returned from his check to help him back to the crew quarters. Javor's flesh seared in pain. His head began to feel light, his cheeks hot. Javor fell a few feet short of the stairs, his legs unable to keep him stable. He lay there for a few seconds, finding it impossible to call out, before the world went dark.

Javor remembered voices speaking in Italian. Glimpses of metal stairs passing below him. He emerged in the ship's medical suite, which quickly morphed into the ruined, cold streets of Sarajevo.

* * *

It was raining. It seemed like it was always raining lately. And when it wasn't raining, it was freezing. It wasn't uncommon for Javor and his Croat unit to find the bodies of civilians frozen to death inside their apartments, the wood fire they had been burning in the middle of their living room inadequate to stave off the gnawing, gnashing cold. Electricity in Sarajevo had been spotty since the beginning of open hostilities between the belligerent Serbs and the reactive Bosniaks and Croats.

Javor's unit had been tasked with destroying a Serbian radio transmitter at the top of an apartment building in the middle of Sarajevo. In the middle of Serb territory. As the runner in a sniper hunter unit, Javor was used to sprinting through the bombed-out ruins of grocery markets, video stores, and restaurants and hurtling over Yugo-sized chunks of concrete that had been blasted from structures by tank mortars. He was used to being shot at; the large caliber bullets hitting the pavement near his zigging feet and zagging calves, shooting up stinging debris. Still, something about climbing an eight-story building in full view of all Sarajevo's deadliest shots seemed suicidal. He was used to sniper alleys, not shooting galleries.

Still, Javor was the fastest man in the unit. He was the obvious choice. He had the natural skill and he didn't complain. His brother, God rest his soul, had never complained. He did his job up until the day the Serbian armed forces filled him with rounds from a barely functional, rust-crusted AK-47. Javor owed it to his brother to do anything he could to beleaguer the Serb army.

The plan was for Javor to scale the building from the ground floor, avoiding the Serbian populace lest they alert the snipers to his location. He trotted across the open expanse between the apartment and the grocery in which his small unit huddled, his shoulders hunched in perpetual expectation of a bullet ripping through his back and exploding through his chest, taking with it blood and bits of organs. Javor slid into cover like an American baseball player and waited for cement to explode behind him from a last-ditch shot taken as the sniper figured out Javor's trajectory. No shot came. He was astounded. This section of the city held snipers the way a stagnant pond held mosquitoes.

Or maybe there was an eye on him. A very well-trained eye. Only inexperienced snipers fired on their targets out of frustration before they fled to cover. The Serbian Army had a lot of green blood, a lot of unemployed young men who wanted to fight their way out of poverty any way they could. Javor knew, though, that an experienced sniper would not give away his position for anything less than a guaranteed kill. Perhaps someone was out there waiting for him, some grizzled old vet of the Red Army who fought in Afghanistan before the Soviet Union dissolved like a tablet of antacid, releasing its constituent parts into the acidic outside environment. Javor pictured this man, creased brow peering through his scope, scarred finger resting lightly on his trigger. Javor would die when he tried to scale the apartment. If, indeed, he was right about the sniper watching him, he was far too experienced to be flushed out and eliminated by Javor's unit before Javor tumbled lifeless to the streets of Sarajevo from the third or fourth floor of the apartment building.

That option was out. Javor spotted a dirty wool coat folded into a corner along with some household trash. He tore off his own olive drab coat and traded it for the tattered, dirty rag. It had a foul smell to it and flecks of something—

something biological, Javor guessed—stuck to the elbows. He assumed it was vomit but, with the weather as hostile as it had been lately, the likely answer was that the owner had been killed. Coats were valuable commodities, even soiled ones. Javor rubbed his hands in the dirty crevice into which the coat had been tossed and rubbed them through his hair and over his face. The fatigues he wore on his bottom half were a problem, but only because they were well-kept. Javor dropped to his knees and scooted back and forth until the reinforced fabric gave way to friction and frayed apart. He rubbed a leg in the grime and then decided he was good to go. A war refugee without money to escape into Western Europe.

Javor beat on the common door that led into the complex.

"Help!" he yelled, slurring his words. "The fighting is coming this way! They'll kill me for certain this time." He continued yelling until his voice was hoarse, his vocal cords raw and swollen in his throat. An old woman finally arrived at the door and peered at him inquisitively. Her lips curled into a sneer as she took in the state of his shabby coat. He didn't belong here. Even with the threat of mortar rounds looming over the city like an ever-present storm cloud, it was a middle-class area.

"Please," Javor begged, "the Croats burned my house as they marched through. Our own soldiers shot my wife in the chaos as we fled. I don't want to die!"

The woman considered his words for a moment, her features softening in light of his supposed hardship. She sighed, then heaved open the heavy door. Javor felt a pang of regret for lying to the Serbian woman as she helped him in, taking his hands in hers. He truly was not at war with her; she probably supported General Ratko and President Milosevic no more than he did. He eased his conscience by assuring himself his efforts were taking steps toward a quicker end to the Serbian military oppression—an oppression that was felt by Croats, Bosniaks, and Serbs alike.

Javor gave his gushing thanks to the elderly woman, supplicating himself in front of her. She shooed him away, embarrassed by the gesture. Javor left her in the walkway, walking slowly and mumbling to himself until he was well out of earshot. When he deemed he was safe, he climbed the first set of stairs he found, ascending until he was panting. He emerged on a middle floor and walked slowly to the opposite side of the building as his breathing returned to normal. He ascended the rest of the way, but found access to the roof blocked. Every stairwell, every elevator, every access hatch; locked.

Javor scanned the top floor again, walking briskly, looking for another avenue to the roof. No fire escape, no maintenance lifts. And then he saw the flowers. Flowers in vases flanking a new-ish welcome mat and, above, a floral wreath attached to the wooden door. Javor knelt in front of the display and pulled a small, worn photograph from among the flower stalks.

Srdan and Milica,

There has never been a more perfect couple than you. Your presence will be missed in this building, though you will not miss us. You will spend your days in bliss as perpetual newlyweds until we are lucky enough to join you.

Peace and love.

Javor replaced the photo, giving a silent thanks to the handsome young couple who peered back at him. He said a silent prayer, then crashed against the door with every ounce of strength he could muster. The wood splintered, but didn't give way.

Someone would have heard the crash. A nosy old neighbor in reading glasses and a headscarf was likely already on their ambling way to their own door, and would soon catch Javor breaking into the dead couple's flat. He needed to avoid that. He could probably resume his homeless character and escape being held for the Serbian army, but that wouldn't get rid of the radio tower. Javor grasped the door jamb, tensed his thighs, and heaved his shoulder into the door again. With a dry crack, the thin wood holding the bolt in place snapped, peeling away from the rest of the inside jamb like a ripe banana.

Javor straightened the wreath on the door, pulled a chair from the couple's dining room table, and used it to hold the door closed. To anyone glancing around quickly for the source of the racket, Javor's destruction wouldn't be obvious. A closer inspection, Javor was sure, would reveal cracks in the door. But he would be gone before that became an issue.

The living room looked out onto the surrounding city. Once—barely eighteen months ago—Sarajevo had been a shining jewel of the former Yugoslavian state. A gateway through the Iron Curtain from the popular Western tourist destinations of Greece and Italy, the Soviets had poured money into the Yugoslav capitals. A casual tourist would have seen what the Soviets wanted him to: modern glass and steel towers of business and politics, opulent high-rise apartment buildings, and bountiful markets stocked with produce from the surrounding fertile lands. What wasn't apparent was the lack of purchasing power that afflicted most of the populace like a plague. There was food to be had, but no legal means through which to obtain it. Bread and potatoes rotted in dumpsters, waiting to be pillaged by men in suits on their way home to high-rise apartments.

In such hard times, the citizens turned to religion; congregating as secret, silent flocks under the eyes of holy men who remembered the sermons they gave before the choking hand of Moscow reached their Balkan towns. Christians and Muslims, both worshipping the same God, met independently, formed tight-knit and polarized groups, and grew apart from one another. When the Soviets left, almost overnight, the gulf between religions and ethnicities widened, each group untrusting the other to govern them more justly than the Soviets. Each group convinced that their plight was due, in some part, to the others.

Javor took in the vista of that mistrust; the roads pock-marked with mortar blasts, the government buildings belching smoke and flame from unquenchable fires. He thought of the torched homes, the mass Croat and Bosniak graves the Serbs haphazardly dug as they slaughtered whole villages, and the assassinations of which he had been a part. It used to be such a nice view from points like this. Now it was a bleak, apocalyptic wasteland.

The windowpane slid aside easily, leaving a screen that Javor popped out and caught before it fell to the rubble-strewn street below. A falling object was as salient to a sniper as raw beef to a starving dog. Javor was taking a massive risk climbing out the window. He hoped he was above the snipers' positions, but he didn't want to give them a reason to take their eyes off the road. Though he was at the top residential floor, he still had eight feet of building to scale. He guessed there was a level of duct work and maintenance areas situated above the living space. He climbed quickly, easily, moving with the vertical sure-footedness of a lizard.

Javor flipped himself over the small ledge that ran the perimeter of the roof, seeking refuge from the sniper round he was sure was speeding toward him. He pulled his rifle from beneath his shabby cloak and scanned his surroundings for a soldier guarding the radio tower.

Clear.

Explosives firmly planted at the base of the rusted metal

tower, Javor raced back to the ledge and swung out into the open. He had just planted his boots on the windowsill of the couple's apartment when the explosion shook the entire complex. He slipped inside and took cover with back pressed against the wall.

As the rumbling concussion of the initial blast faded away, Javor could hear a low groan, punctuated by loud pops. He jumped inside the apartment as the groan rose into a sharp, metallic shriek. The radio tower dipped from the roof, slowing some as it came into view through the window. It hung precariously, swaying in the light breeze. The freedom with which it moved made it obvious that there wasn't much holding it in place; a heavy glob of chewing gum hanging from a thinning strand. The stressed metal gave way without a sound, letting the tower fall freely to the blacktop below. It landed on a small yellow car with a deafening crash.

Javor ripped off his shabby coat, grasped it by the moth-eaten collar, and draped it over a corner of the open window. The cloth jerked inward from a central point as a framed painting on the wall exploded into shards of glass. The coat jerked again, this time punctuated by a dull thud from the front door. The destruction of the radio tower had caught the attention of the snipers hiding out in the surrounding buildings. The dry cracks of their rifles made their way to Javor's ears a few moments after their hastily fired rounds.

Javor dropped the coat, knowing the snipers wouldn't fall for the ruse a second time. He had caught them in a panic.

Now he had to rely on his speed and the rest of his team below. The rifle blasts were their call to action; the pair of counter-snipers would be moving to one of the potential perches they had identified as the rest of the unit laid down suppressing fire. Javor knelt into a runner's crouch; he needed to provide one more point of origin so the counter-snipers could do their jobs. His feet pressed into the wooden floor of the apartment, the toes of his boots slipping slightly on account of the grime they had picked up on the roof. Though he had lost a bit of traction in the initial burst, Javor tore across the apartment with Olympic speed. He sprinted diagonally through the small space, around the couch in the center of the room, then cut back the other way and dropped to his hip, allowing his momentum to carry him in a baseball slide.

Javor came to a stop on his back next to the chair he had wedged against the apartment door. He remained still for a few beats of his heart, letting oxygen make its way back to his limbs. Automatic weapons popped outside in bursts, punctuated by louder, more final explosions of long-range rifle fire. The Serb snipers had other things to worry about. Javor kicked the chair out of the way and jogged out the door.

Javor didn't meet a single person on his quest down the stairwell of the apartment building. The residents had hunkered down in the safety of their flats, sitting on the floor in whatever space put the most furniture between them and the direction of the gunfire. It was an unfortunate and common practice. Javor wondered how often stray rounds found their way through thin walls and into a noncombatant. Probably more than he wanted to know.

As he reached the ground floor, the gunfire continued. That was unusual. Engagements with snipers usually lasted seconds; minutes at most. Snipers, once located, either fought to their swift death for the glory of Serbia or beat a hasty retreat. Javor pressed the lock bar of the door open with his hip and glided silently into the street, his rifle at the ready.

Green uniforms swarmed in the rubble to the west of the apartment Javor had just exited. More took up firing position behind the twisted rat's nest that had recently been a radio tower. They weren't the light olive uniforms of his unit, though; these were darker, nicer. The forest green of the Serbian forces that had been financed with foreign money. Javor remained unnoticed in his position slightly behind the Serbians. He could run around the building and link up with his comrades, though he could be shot in a sprint across open ground. Attacking the Serbians hidden in the crumbling, but still inhabited, tenant building was suicide. The small contingent of flanking troops at the radio tower, however, he could manage.

Javor took aim and let his bullets tear into flesh and canvas, leaving dark red smears behind. The men were dead before they even had a chance to figure out what was happening. Javor ducked behind cover near the apartment building, certain the remaining Serbs would be gunning for him. He provided cover fire for his own men who took advantage of the chaos to move up and use the tower as their own cover. With that one action, Javor had turned the tide of the skirmish; unable to defend from two directions, the few Serbs left to retreat pulled back into the building and it became a game of—as Javor's commander would say—*Let's Make a Deal.*

"I'll take door number one, Monty!" the commander yelled as he kicked open door after door, finding families huddling in fear. The few times the door opened to reveal a Serb troop, the unit erupted in joyous shouts so loud they drowned out the sound of their near-simultaneous pulls of the trigger. Enemies died in hails of gunfire that didn't cease until their bodies had been ripped apart and spread out on the tile floors.

Fueled with hatred of the Serbs and adrenaline from the battle, some of the men in Javor's unit pulled young women from their apartments and led them to secluded corners of the building. Javor looked at his commander hoping he would put a stop to the depravity, but the older man simply looked on at his shoulders with paternal warmth.

A young recruit named Sacha tugged at the arm of a sobbing woman and shoved her toward Javor.

"A special prize for the hero of the day! She's the prettiest Serb whore I've ever seen!"

Javor kept the girl from falling to her knees. "I'm alright," he said through a tight mouth.

"You deserve it, Jav!" the boy called, then whooped and clapped his hands as another man dragged a woman behind him with a strong grip on the collar of her blouse.

Javor smiled sheepishly and shook his head.

The commander had taken an interest in the conversation and swaggered over to Javor, ripping the girl's hand away from the young recruit and shoving him off toward the other troops. Javor saluted as the commander drew near, but the tall, imposing older man didn't return the gesture. Instead, he grabbed Javor's wrist and pressed the girl's elbow into Javor's hand. He held the position until Javor's fingers clasped around the girl's flesh. Then he leaned in next Javor's ear and spoke lowly so that only the two of them, and maybe the Serbian girl, could hear.

"I don't care what your reason for declining this piece is, Javor, but I will not have you souring the mood of these men. You single-handedly kept us all from our early graves today and they want to see you rewarded for that. If you need to picture the thin, inexperienced body of a teenage boy to help you finish, then so be it. But you will go in that room and you will take the reward those boys are giving you. There is no ultimatum, no 'or else' on this because I will only accept one outcome.

"If you're feeling soft for these wretches, remember that they ordered their troops to rape our women. And the Bosniaks. Their military doctrine was to spread their Serbian seed throughout the region to secure an ethnic majority. Serbian militiamen were instructed in ways to make rape more horrific to cause the dissolution of families and instill in those broken bands a desire to leave Bosnia forever. My own daughter was raped until she bled to death internally. Show these dogs no mercy. Show them we can play the same game."

Javor stared into space as his commander rose to his full height. He could feel the colonel staring down at him, detected the itch in the center of his forehead as the man waited for Javor's assent. He didn't move his eyes to look at the commander when he spoke.

"My mother and sister were raped, too."

"Then you know what I mean better than anyone," the commander growled. "Get to work."

Javor did not nod, nor did he salute or acknowledge the commander had spoken in any way. He turned on his heels and slowly walked to the room his men had emptied for him, dragging the girl along behind him.

Javor's commander was right, he knew the destructive force of militarized rape first hand. Unlike his commander, though, Javor wanted an end to the war and he knew fanning the flames of hatred would not bring that end any time soon. He wanted the Serbian war criminals like President Milosevic dead, thought publicly executing them as Mussolini had been at the end of the Second World War would go a long way toward rebuilding Serb-Croat relations.

As he envisioned war criminals hanging from the twisted steel skeletons of government buildings in downtown Sarajevo, he could see his own commander swaying next to the fat form of the Serbian president. His commander's tongue had swelled with black blood and looked like sea slug escaping the bowels of the dead man. He smiled at the macabre thought. His commander wasn't fit to lead; he deserved a violent finale to his military career so someone with vision and purpose could take up the position.

Javor realized the Serbian girl was still sobbing loudly, crouching in a corner of the room and drawn into herself.

"Hello," he called, but got no response.

Javor rose from the bed and the girl flinched as if he had flung his boot at her. The anger-fueled adrenaline evaporated from his veins as he watched the girl; the sense of justice he felt at imagining the faces of his commander and President Milosevic burning in a mass grave froze over. All he felt was pity and a duty to protect the girl. A drive to uphold the responsibility to protect the citizens of his nation against all threats.

"I won't do anything to you. You remind me of how my sister must have felt when the Serbian military marched through our village. I can't bear to inflict that type of horror on someone. Not before all this and certainly not now. You don't have to cower over there."

The girl lifted her chin and Javor could finally see her face. She was beautiful, even with the puffy red eyes and running nose. If the Soviets had still been in control, she probably would have enjoyed a posh life in Moscow as a propaganda model. If Yugoslavia hadn't descended into bloodthirsty depravity, she could have travelled to Italy to be a fashion model or the United States to be in movies. But she was stuck here, in Bosnia, with flecks of drying blood polka-dotting her flawless skin. What had she been through?

"Are you hurt?" Javor asked.

The girl said nothing, but her sobs had faded away.

"Your mother and sister," she asked, "what happened?"

"Dead," Javor said.

The girl lowered her eyes from his gaze and nodded. "My aunt and uncle were killed by your men."

"I'm sorry. What they're doing out there isn't," he paused, trying to put his feelings into words, "it's not war, it's insanity."

"They are trying to get back at us for what the Serbian military did to your people. They want to out-genocide the architects of genocide. This is Hell. We are in Hell."

He wondered what would happen to this morose girl once his men left. If she was with her aunt and uncle, it was likely her parents had been displaced or were dead. Would she end up a corpse on the frozen roads out of Sarajevo or a drug-addicted prostitute in Bucharest?

A shrill scream from outside the room sent shivers into Javor's bones. The shriek cut off prematurely at the sound of a single pistol shot. Javor could hear murmuring followed by uproarious laughter.

So they were killing the women they had raped. Javor looked at the pretty girl, knowing his hope of leaving the building knowing she was alive had washed away like the eroding bank of river. And then a thought occurred to him:

they could escape. He could climb out through a window, talk the girl along her way, and they could leave the area before Javor's commander came looking for him. He would be a deserter, but he wanted no more of this perversion his commanding officer called a war.

The window in Javor's room looked out onto the killing ground where the Serbian forces had made their ambush earlier. The bodies, rubble, and radio tower would hide their escape. Possibly Javor could even steal an unbloodied Serbian jacket for the girl to make her less obvious in the gloom.

"Let's run," Javor said to the girl.

She looked at him with a knitted brow.

"I'll get you out of here. Out of the city altogether."

"Those men won't let you take me out of here moving. I doubt they'd let you wander off alone despite the story you give them."

Javor shook his head. "Out the window. We can make it out of this square before they know. After that, we've got a whole city to hide in." Javor's mind flashed back to the vacant apartment in the building across the street. "I know somewhere safe we can sleep for the night once they leave the area."

The girl's face had eased some, her eyes brighter with the hope of life. "My great uncle is a Russian; he captains a container ship based in Ukraine. I can get you on his crew. From there, you can deboard wherever you want."

Javor allowed himself a moment to imagine the life he

could have if he could convince the girl to disembark with him. He'd have plenty of time to try on their way to the Ukraine and once they were on the ship. He smiled at her pretty face. She smiled back, possibly imagining the same life.

"Before we go, what is your name?" the girl asked.

"Javor. And you?"

"Biserka," she replied, her smile widening and crinkling the soft skin around her eyes.

Biserka. Pearl. It fit her perfectly, a speck of beauty in an otherwise hellish landscape.

Javor led Biserka by the hand to the window and quietly slid the pane of glass aside.

A quiet creak announced the presence of someone at the door to the room. Javor whirled around from the window to find his commander staring at him with flaring eyes. The commander kicked the door shut and pulled his chrome pistol from his holster.

"You're letting her escape now, Javor?" the commander asked in a slow bass growl. "Are you a Serbian agent or just too weak to follow orders? Your heroism today be damned, I will break one bone in your body for every second it takes you to end this whore."

Javor clenched his jaw. He wanted to wait the colonel out, make him back down from his threat or carry it out and let morale wash out of his troops like blood in a stream. He wouldn't let this girl die.

"Javor," the commander said, letting the growl in his voice

be menacing enough that he needed no spoken threat.

Javor pushed Biserka behind him and stood at attention. "Sir, I disagree with this order. These people are not combatants."

The commander's scowl softened as he listened to Javor's words. When Javor finished, he laughed, a harsh, deliberate bark. "Not combatants! You think they are not combatants? Everyone in this country is a combatant. We're fighting for the future of our people. They're fighting to end us."

"She doesn't care! She doesn't care who lives. None of them do. They just want to go back to the way things were, to making dinner with their families. They want their biggest worry to be if the television signal is too weak to see *Three's Company*, not which army is shelling their homes."

"Javor, you are a boy. You know nothing. This bitch has brainwashed you." The commander lowered his pistol. "I remember when I was your age; a pretty face could make me do anything. I stole from a jeweler in town once because a girl on my block wanted a silver ring. I was caught. The jeweler bloodied my face and threw me in the garbage pile behind his shop. You cannot let your intellect be tainted by your desire for her flesh. Keep a cool head and take what you want from her.

"Javor, my boy, I feel sorry for you. You are a good soldier. You'll soon regret the course you're on. I can't let that happen.

With that, the commander raised his weapon and fired a

shot over Javor's shoulder, striking Biserka in the head. Her blood coated the window like a ripe rose.

Javor screamed and drew his own pistol. He didn't know how many times he fired, but the commander fell, clutching his throat.

"Sir!" came a shout from outside the room. The door handle rattled. The commander must have locked the door after he entered, not wanting his lesson interrupted.

The door bulged with a well-placed kick. Javor's own men would enter and be forced to gun him down.

He looked down at Biserka, her long hair covering her ruined face, but the rapidly widening pool of blood around her head like a halo over a Madonna indicated otherwise. He tossed his pistol toward her open right hand and said a prayer for forgiveness. To God. To Biserka.

The door burst open and Javor raised his hands. The troops were upset, but a course of events other than the obvious never entered their minds. Javor was a loyal soldier.

As the company trudged back to their operating base through the cold, gray streets of the torn city, Javor dropped farther and farther back in the group. No one questioned his lethargic pace, assuming he was dealing with his guilt that Biserka had reached his weapon without his notice. Working through his feelings of culpability in the colonel's death. As he passed, some men nodded to him, showing that he held no grudge. It could have happened to anyone.

Though no one had been paying close enough attention to

the commotion in Javor's room, he couldn't shake the feeling that someone would recall the loud, large caliber shot had preceded the small pops of his own Tokarev. Every glance and nod from his men as he dropped back felt like an accusation, a suspicion that he was a traitor to his own blood. He had no question he would be killed if someone put the pieces together; he did wonder, however, how long it would take him to die. As the column rounded a street corner, stepping over another of the near-infinite piles of rubble, Javor snuck away. He ran as quickly as he could without the loud clomp of his boots giving him away. He hid in the back of a smoldering delivery truck for a few hours, then snuck back to the apartment he had planned to use as a hideout with Biserka.

The next morning, he headed southeast through Sarajevo. He had shed his military uniform and donned the dead Srdan's clothes. He looked like a young shop owner. Despite his unassuming appearance, he felt both sides were gunning for him now, like he had twice as many sniper scopes boring into his back as he walked. The feel of those eyes on his skin made him duck into any crevice, jump through any shattered window he approached. He only felt safe when he was cloistered away in some sodden urban cave. Sleep only reached his body when the outside world was completely shut out. He traveled that way for weeks, feeling like he was hemorrhaging sanity with each step but also feeling justified each moment he went without being torn apart by a sniper round.

It wasn't until Javor had reached the Black Sea that he

realized he didn't know the name of Biserka's great uncle's ship, much less the port at which it docked. He slept on the streets of Odessa for weeks, looking for work on the docks in the day and shivering in the cold rain at night, having chosen his sleeping arrangements for protection from visibility rather than the elements.

And then a beat-up hulk lumbered into port. Javor's heart leapt at the Cyrillic letters on the bow. Biserka. Pearl. He approached the dock and waited eagerly for the captain to disembark. Unlike most ships that docked in Odessa, the Biserka was looking to expand her crew and the captain seemed to take a liking to Javor, especially when he learned of Javor's previous employment as a deckhand on a shipping vessel in the Mediterranean. Though the captain did not have a great niece in Bosnia, Javor took the ship as a sign and boarded, committing himself to two shipments. In Turkey, Javor opened an international account for his payment, left the Biserka behind, and found a job on an oceanic vessel.

* * *

Javor awoke on a small canvas cot. His mouth felt like it had been dried with an absorbent cloth. As he ran his tongue over the roof of his mouth, he could feel each scratching taste bud. Javor blinked into the bright, white light that shone down on his face and realized he was in the medical suite, a few decks below the bridge. He tried to speak, but a tugging sensation in his leg—that he now noticed had been present since he woke up—gave way to searing pain. It felt like a construction nail was being pulled through his flesh and leaving sharp slakes of metal filing embedded in its wake.

The pain ebbed and a green-masked face came into view. Though the man was mostly covered, Javor knew the ice-blue eyes and bushy blond brows of Petersen well. As a young man with few prospects in his native Denmark, Petersen joined the French Foreign Legion and fought with the UN Multinational Force in Lebanon. He trained as a battlefield medic, hoping to find his way to a better career when his tour ended. Perhaps sensing a common history, Petersen took kindly to Javor and understood his need to be in tight, dark spaces.

"You're back!" Petersen shouted, giving Javor a shove with his elbow. "I have to tell you, Javor, when they brought you up I thought we were all dead. Jellyfish stings said to me that there was a tear in the hull. We prepared for the worst, even checking through the cargo manifest to see if there was anything in an accessible container we could use for flotation. Then the storm passed and we were still afloat. Perelli and his buddy—the one with the nose, you know—restepped your area again and found no leak.

"I don't know how the hell you got those stings, Javor, but I'm happy to be pulling these threads from your leg instead of drowning in a freezing sea right now. You should be, too."

Javor couldn't answer—his creaking voice sounding more like a sick goat than human speech—but even if he could, he would have indicated nothing but confusion. Jellyfish? The last thing Javor recalled was heading belowdecks after the engines stopped.

Petersen handed him a small Dixie cup of water. Javor made a move for the cup with his right hand, but found it too swollen and painful to move properly. He shifted his weight, grimacing against the agonizing movement, and took used the other hand. He gulped the water like a shot, trying to wet his throat. Petersen refilled the cup and handed it back to Javor. This time he let the cool water swirl on his tongue, taming the felt-like texture of his mouth back into something comfortable.

"What do you mean jellyfish?" Javor asked.

"These spines," Petersen said, gesturing to Javor's bloodied and swollen leg, "and the ones in your arm. They're from jellyfish stings. I usually take them out of boys coming back from time off at the beach… Not sure where you got 'em."

Javor cleared his throat. The ship was eerily calm. He didn't expect the doorway to be packed with his fellow crewmembers come to check on him; he didn't even expect to see anyone on this deck. If the storm had turned too ugly after Michalis left to jettison the crane, most of the crew was probably working on either taking it down completely or relashing it. The rest of the crew was likely involved in cleanup and repair of any damaged containers. Still, there was something quiet about the ship. Something in the background Javor couldn't identify that gave him chills.

And then he had it.

"The engines are still off," he said.

Petersen nodded from his position back over Javor's leg. "Yep. Not sure what's wrong with them, but the engineers can't get them to start. Ageykin is investigating each component piece by piece and has no estimate of when we'll be underway."

Petersen tugged another spine out of Javor's flesh and tapped his thick clamp against a steel bowl until the clear thread fell in. "Ageykin did say that he found glowing water on the gantry near the engine, though. Can you imagine? Probably bioluminescent bacteria, but how did it get belowdecks?" Petersen laughed gruffly.

At the mention of the glowing water, Javor recalled tracing several puddles back toward the engine decks. He remembered squeezing behind the engine cowling and seeing the end of a glowing tentacle. It wasn't the hair-like appendages of a jellyfish, though; it was an honest-to-God tentacle. Javor remembered the tentacle coming toward him and then falling into a fever-induced dream of his memories of Bosnia.

"You have to get Ageykin out of there," Javor croaked.

"What?" Petersen asked.

"It's not a jellyfish. He's in danger."

Javor attempted to rise from the surgical cot, but Petersen blocked his movement with a sturdy forearm. "Javor, relax. We need to get these spines out of you. Any movement could release more toxins and undo all my work. You're full to brimming with antivenom already; any more and you could be at risk for a heart attack."

Javor allowed himself to be pressed back down, but continued to protest. "Petersen, listen to me, there's something down there!"

Petersen set his instruments down on a gleaming metal tray and began rubbing a vinegary-smelling pad of gauze over Javor's leg. "These toxins are bad news, my boy. They kill a man, cripple him for life. In lower doses they can cause comas and hallucinations. Powerful hallucinations.

"Perelli went over every inch of the lower decks and found nothing. Ageykin is fine. You just need to rest."

Petersen wrapped Javor's leg tightly in gauze and Coban. As Javor tried to convince himself against what he had seen by the engine, Petersen placed warm, wet cloths over Javor's injured limbs and the searing, perpetually cutting pain began to fade. With it, Javor fell into a restful sleep.

When he awoke, Javor could tell the engines were still off. Finding himself alone in the small medical bay, he ascended the stairs to the bridge. Each clang that reverberated back to him underscored the unnatural silence of the ship; even when the engines ran at only two-thirds power, the sound of boots on steel melted quickly into the fray of noise.

The scene on the bridge was calm. The captain sat in his command chair, poring over the shipping manifest with a visible sneer. Javor guessed he was checking shipping deadlines against new arrival estimates from Ageykin's crew. Michalis was attempting to expand the range of the emergency radio by wiring it to the internal mast of the powered radio.

"Markovic!" the captain called, the hint of a smile breaking through his gloom. "Glad to see you're up and about."

"Thank you, sir. Any luck with the radio?" Javor asked.

"That damned storm blew us pretty far off of the shipping routes, but we were able to make contact with a Hanjin freighter. They relayed our message to shore; if we aren't able to get our ship underway and communications back up by the time they get to port, they'll send something out. Obviously, I'd rather not have to pay for a rescue on top of all the losses we've already got," the captain backhanded the shipping manifest with more force than necessary to make his point, "the Takahara company will already have my balls for letting their container get damaged in the squall—but that might be out of my hands."

"Let me know if I can do anything, sir."

"According to Petersen, you're supposed to be resting. Why don't you head back belowdecks? I know you're not a fan of the open air, anyway."

As strange as it was, Javor hadn't experienced his familiar dread as he climbed the metal stairs to the bridge. He cast his eyes out over the calm sea before leaving the bridge and felt nothing. No, nothing wasn't exactly true; he felt a tug of interest, like he could look over the blue waters of the Atlantic all day. As he returned to the medical bay, he thought of the whales Perelli had seen earlier in the voyage and hungered for a discovery of his own. His life had been dictated by negative emotions up to this point; fear of drowning cutting his first attempt at seahand short, anger at the Serbians pushing him to war, paranoia of a sniper's bullet making any normal life impossible. The one time he had tried to let a positive emotion guide him, Biserka ended up dead, her blood on his hands. Even so, the brief elation he had felt imagining a life with the beautiful Serbian girl was unlike anything else. Perhaps it was time to let positivity guide him again.

Javor passed the landing that would have taken him to the medical bay. He continued on to the lower decks of the ship, past the lowest deck where electrical lights still shone in the cavernous hull. Most decks had been thrown into darkness to preserve battery power for the shipping containers that needed to be climate-controlled. Javor found himself back in the lowest deck of the ship, hands brushing the cold steel of the keel to keep himself upright in the lightless expanse. He wasn't overcome with the sense of calm at being protected by the void; he felt a freeing anticipation. Javor realized he wanted to find more of the bioluminescent bacteria. He wanted to discover what had stung him. A simple jellyfish as Petersen insisted, or something else? He had to find it.

Javor searched the decks, wandering slowly in pitch black so he could detect any hint of the glowing water, for hours. He skipped meals, eating granola bars he found in his coat pockets in order to continue his investigation uninterrupted. He must have walked the entire ship twice and found nothing.

As exhaustion threatened to claim him, Javor caught a neon blue gleam out of the corner of his eye. The bacteria glowed underneath the lowest walkway. Though the floor was grated to add traction in wet conditions and allow deckhands to check the hull for leaks, there was no space between the keel and the walkway. Javor sprinted to the bow where the walkway became too wide to continue into the ship's wave cutting point. His plan was to use the precarious vertical ladder than ran the depth of the ship from just below the main deck to access the tight crawlspace where he had seen the bioluminescence.

And then she appeared.

A young woman, seemingly nude on account of her smooth curves, stood on the walkway mere feet in front of him. Javor could see her in the inky dark by the white-blue glow that shone from her skin, the same unnatural emission as the bioluminescent water. She stood, unmoving, staring at Javor with a placid expression.

Javor skidded to a halt, nearly falling backward. Once he had steadied himself, the girl took a slow, deliberate step toward him. Javor's pulse quickened, the beat of his heart loud in his ears. What was this? Another hallucination from a toxin-induced coma? A stowaway who had been stung by the same odd creature Javor had seen near the engine?

She took a second step, then another. Finally, Javor was able to discern her features through the gleam.

"Biserka?" he asked.

The glowing girl did not respond, though she did pause in her stride.

"Biserka," he said again. "How?"

She smiled a little, the corners of her mouth turning up invitingly, and spun on her heel. She raced down the gantry with astonishing speed, plunging Javor into lonely darkness. When the last vestiges of her glow had faded in the distance, Javor took several breaths. Internally, he warred with himself; logical thought reminding him that he watched Biserka die, emotional thought telling him to chase after her. Externally, his body was already poised to sprint. There was no question what his actions would be. Though they has known each other for all of twenty minutes, Biserka was the closest thing to family Javor had.

He ran, his injured left leg protesting the movement. By the time he reached the bow of the ship, his thigh had cramped to the degree that it was a rigid stump impeding the power and speed of his struggling right leg. He reached the vertical passage, swung his legs over the railing, and—knowing he wouldn't be able to navigate his way down the short ladder— let himself fall the distance to the hull. He followed the glowing streaks on the keel like a trail of breadcrumbs, walking in a crouch that burned his cramped leg. He tried to press through the pain, but his leg protested more strongly with each step. Before long, the leg had gone numb. Without feeling, he easily tripped over pipes and found movement impossible.

His eyes watered with frustration. His arms ached to hold

Biserka, but he knew she was gone. He knew he had been hallucinating.

"Javor," a whisper floated to him through the darkness.

He looked in the direction of the voice, expecting to see nothing. Instead, a glowing blue hand extended toward his. He stretched for Biserka's fingertips but found his reach just centimeters too short. He pulled himself along the hull with one arm, the other outstretched to catch the ghostly fingertips, but the gulf between them widened. The arm moved smoothly, fluidly back down the cramped corridor.

Javor used his arms to propel himself along, using his remaining good leg to lift his torso over obstructions. Like his injured leg, his left arm soon grew fatigued; his grasp falling weakly into the grating of the walkway above him, his biceps burning with each pull. And then came the cramp. His arm was useless, his movement stopped.

Javor stared into the darkness, wondering if he was properly stuck. No one knew where he was and he hadn't brought a radio with him; calling for help was useless. He couldn't move. Maybe if he let his muscles rest he could, but he could feel the vertigo of sleep begin to overtake him. If he fell asleep and couldn't move by the time he woke up, it might be too late. He had already gone a full day without water and not much food.

And then his whole world became bright. Tilting his head back, he could see a glowing, undulating form moving toward him. Unlike Biserka, who seemed transparent, this new creature was opaque. Under the glow, Javor could tell its flesh was silky smooth, like that of a dolphin or squid. Skin made for moving fast in an aquatic environment.

The creature propelled itself along the hull with tentacles, the same muscular tubes he had seen near the engine. Javor knew he should have been terrified, should have tried to escape, but he didn't. He wanted to learn more about the glowing creature, wondering if this was what Biserka brought him here to see. Though he had never directly learned about oceanic species, Javor knew the glowing beast coming his way was a completely unknown species. He was the only human who had ever seen this graceful beauty.

A thought occurred to him: Maybe he was the only living human to have seen the creature. The deliberate pace at which it stalked toward him was not born of curiosity. Like a lion hunched into Savannah grass, the creature moved like a hunter. Javor tried to move, but the paralysis in his injured limbs had spread to encompass his abdomen and neck. His right arm was beginning to cramp.

With a swirl of bioluminescence, Biserka appeared above Javor, lying on the grating of the walkway. She smiled down at him with tired eyes, lids half closed.

"Don't worry," she whispered.

He stared at her face, almost forgetting the fate that stalked toward him.

"Sleep," she said. "You just need rest."

As a glowing tentacle reached over his paralyzed body, he

noticed there were no suckers which he knew were common to squid and octopi. Drawing on Biserka's strength, he resisted the urge to panic and instead marveled at the strangeness of the creature. He regretted he didn't have more time to learn its secrets.

"Sleep," Biserka said again, as his vision began to fade.

He was overcome with the feeling of accomplishment. Of heroism. He had saved her. He had saved them all. He had not failed all of those people.

"Sleep."

And then, as he felt—painlessly—something sever the flesh in his forearm and crunch through bone, he heard a second voice. A voice without the soothing hush of Biserka's. A voice devoid of all emotion, save for the most basic desires.

"Eat."

Curiosity

The End

Letter From The Editor

I am currently sitting once again in another country, away from my family, but busy with work that I find fulfilling and worthwhile.

This project truly began a year and a half ago and lasted longer than it ever should have. There were ups and downs and stops and restarts. By the time you read this, the project will have been a little over two years in the making. I believe the project has benefited from the timeline and process.

I sit in places like the place I'm in now and I try to encourage myself when I think of all of the months that have piled up. I tell myself that this will pay off. That the money I'm investing into this will come back. That I'll be able to pay bonuses to the writers involved beyond their advances. I tell myself that the money I will be spending on advertising and the marketing plan will be worth it over time.

I tell myself that most of the major publishing houses have similar timelines for their publications. Here I am, doing this in my spare time while working a demanding job by day, completely unrelated from these projects. I remind myself of the quality of the product and how we truly want to create something worth reading. I really do hope this experience was worth your time. It's been such a constant part of my life over these months that I'll be honest with you when I say that the day this book is finally published will be an absolute relief to me.

That's also how most creative endeavors feel. At least for me, they do. They're a burden and a total joy. The joy of creation versus the labor of creating. A divide, just as the themes of this collection are counter to the other. The vices and the virtues of existence: both may lead down paths we are unsure of.

Much of this started after the *All In Good Time* event, which is also experiencing a long journey toward publication and should be coming out in a few months—get excited. If you are unfamiliar with that, it was an attempt to create a viral series of stories. It was a lot of work, but also a lot of fun. Everyone involved in *All In Good Time* wanted to work on something new. A few projects grew out of that desire. This was one of them. I had published my first book, *The Laws of Nature*, and I had finished leading the *All In Good Time* event. It seemed logical to take the lead on a new project.

People came on board, people got busy, I deployed to a foreign land, came back Stateside for a few months, was deployed to yet another country. Life stalled a few aspects of the project. Many of the writers involved in this have experienced their own ups and downs.

Luckily, the group never gave up hope and we trucked through and came out the other end with what we believe to be a really solid collection of stories.

A lot of ideas were tossed around when we first started

writing for this project. There were ideas about making it a novel in the vein of *All In Good Time,* where we would work even harder and closer together to form a cohesive plot through a variety of perspectives and characters. It was deemed too much work with the group of twenty writers we had begun with. Eventually, the idea of writing about something polarizing came up. *Vices and Virtues* quickly evolved from there. The opposite sides of a spectrum would form the basis of a collection.

As the editor of the collection, I was the project lead from beginning until end. I fulfilled more of a producer role in helping to refine stories and taking care of all of the behind the scenes business, like a project manager. I have organized the marketing and worked directly with Amber, our faithful story and copy editor, to bring the stories to light.

A tradition of mine has been to include music that I listened to during the writing and preparation of a project. Each song represents a month or two of constant playing on repeat throughout the process. Once I finally get over a song, I move on to another and keep it on repeat for weeks. Looking at all of these lets me see just how long this collection took to bring together. The songs I listened to throughout this project are as follows:

Sprawl II (Mountains Beyond Mountains) by Arcade Fire
Babyfin by Jonathan Keevil
Holocene by Bon Iver

Walking the Cow by Daniel Johnston
DARE by Gorillaz
Some Things Last A Long Time by Lana Del Rey
Deportee (Acoustic) by Elvis Costello
Hazy by Nathan & Eva
Sometimes Around Midnight (Majordomo Version) by The Airborne Toxic Event

You have hopefully enjoyed these stories as much as all of us enjoyed writing them. I can tell you that I am truly proud of this book on a personal level. It has been a labor of love. I (and we, collectively) hope that bled a little into the words as you read it.

I encourage you to go through the author section and follow everyone's social media. Send them a message or an email if you found yourself truly moved or frightened or disturbed by a story. Sign up for everyone's email lists in order to get updates on individual projects.

The best thing you could do right now is leave a review for the collection on Amazon and any other platform you may frequent. Reviews are complete gold for authors. Truly. We would all be eternally grateful. Again, thank you for reading, ladies and gentlemen.

Ashley Franz Holzmann
October, 2016

Update:

Man, these projects take a long time. So many things have happened throughout the course of pulling this together. I cannot thank everyone involved enough for the enduring support. We did it, everyone! We did it.

Thank you for the patience and thank you for purchasing something that has been years in the making. I cannot believe this day has finally come.

I updated the above text and added *Deportee* and *Hazy* to the list of songs (in case you were wondering how *Hazy* could possibly be on a list written in October of 2016). *Sometimes Around Midnight* was a late edition for when I was rushing within weeks of publication to get Advanced Reader Copies out to some of you folks for reviews and quotes.

Besides the deployments, I have been busier than I thought I would be with some of the other projects in my life. Of note was the creation and launching of -30- Press, a publishing company Raff, Jake (published within this collection) and I formed. It's been a wild ride, and I'm glad I was able to still find the time to do this project justice.

This ends a massive amount of effort.

Can you tell I'm having a hard time saying goodbye to this thing?

Let me know what you think. Let the authors know what you think. They put in an amazing amount of work.

Feel free to contact me about the vices and virtues of each story. Or if you have questions about the project. I'm always reachable. As are several of the writers with their links in the About the Authors section.

Ashley Franz Holzmann
Southern Pines, NC
September, 2017

Special Thanks

Ladies and gentlemen,

This book is dedicated to the folks of NoSleep for a reason. Without them, most of us wouldn't be writers. Most of us wouldn't have audiences. Most of us wouldn't find a reason to keep creating the things we create. That includes this collection. On behalf of everyone involved in this project, thank you.

I would also like to give a special thanks to the writers who were involved in the secret sub that churned out this creative endeavor. Not everyone completed their stories, but many participated in helping the stories in this book to become the stories that they are. You all know who you are and we cannot thank you enough for the amazing contributions.

A special thanks must also be extended to the families of the writers and creative minds behind this collection. Your love fuels our souls.

Of course, I couldn't have edited this book to completion without the amazing talents of Amber. Thank you for being such a rock to lean on and confidant to rely on. This project would have fallen flat without your diligence and insight. You're a wonderful editor.

Thank you all.

Ashley Franz Holzmann

June, 2017

Adam Gray

Adam Gray posts occasionally to Reddit as /u/ AtomGray.

Ashley Franz Holzmann

Ashley Franz Holzmann was born in Okinawa, Japan, and raised in a variety of countries while his parents served in the Air Force. He considered attending art school, but is instead a graduate of West Point, where he enjoyed intramural grappling and studying systems engineering and military history. He majored in sociology and is currently a captain in the Army. He currently lives in North Carolina with his wife, two sons, daughter and their two dogs.

If you have enjoyed Ashley's contribution, check out his website: asforclass.com

C.K. Walker

C.K. Walker is an American author out of Phoenix, Arizona. Some of her popular tales include *Borrasca, Mayhem Mountain,* and *The Lost Town of Deepwood, Pennsylvania.* While writing mostly horror, C.K. Walker also enjoys writing in the thriller, mystery, and science fiction genres. Walker has been published by Jitter Press, The Altar Collective, Sanitarium Magazine, and the Thought Catalog. She received media attention in 2014 when one of her stories made national news. Much of C.K.'s work has been adapted for audio by Chilling Tales for Dark Nights, the NoSleep Podcast, and other independent producers.

Or you can follow C.K. on:

Facebook: facebook.com/ck.walker00

C.K. has previously published three books on Amazon, titled *Cold Thin Air Volume I, Cold Thin Air Volume II,* and *Cold Thin Air Volume III.*

Christina Ferrari

Christina Ferrari is a high school teacher from Melbourne Australia who now lives in Sandpoint, Idaho. She has a Master of Arts degree in English Literature. Her fiction has appeared in *Bewildering Stories*.

Christopher Bloodworth

9 books, 2 podcasts, a feature film, and a possible tv show. Keep your head down and keep shipping.

J.D. Patrick

J.D. Was born in southwestern Pennsylvania in 1987. He has been a resident of Florida since 1999 and graduated from the University of South Florida in 2011 with a B.S. in Civil Engineering. He has always had a very vivid imagination, and began to put that to good use in the fall of 2013 when he began writing and posting to /r/NoSleep on Reddit. In the beginning, he was full of stories, sometimes writing so many that he had a backlog that couldn't be posted quickly enough. Times have since changed, and life has gotten a lot busier. He still writes and posts to Reddit—often on Writingprompts and sometimes revisiting NoSleep.

J.L. Spencer

Jessa Williams is an author, wife, tea-snob and designer based out of Tacoma, Washington. Raised in the Midwest and being as much the animal-lover as she is the introvert, you can expect to find her somewhere at home, under the endless sea of pines and clouds or amid her six cats. She spends most of her time devouring books, happily tending to her aqua gardens, or painting badly.

Kristopher J. Patten

Kristopher J. Patten graduated from Arizona State University with a PhD in cognitive science. His fiction work has been featured on the Nosleep Podcast, the Kernel, and Ibexian. On the rare occasions he follows the narrow slit of light beaming under his office door and leaves behind his computer, Kristopher can usually be found hiking, playing disc golf, or pretending he's a cowboy at the Valley Bar in Phoenix. His fiction work can be found on the world wide internet of things at kristopherjpatten.wordpress.com.

Or you can follow Jake at:

Facebook: facebook.com/profile.php?id=100013312507823

Twitter: @KJakePatten

L Chan

L Chan hails from Singapore, where he alternates between being walked by his dog and writing speculative fiction after work. His work has appeared in places like Perihelion Science Fiction, Metaphorosis Magazine and Liminal Stories. He tweets occasionally @lchanwrites and can be found on Facebook at facebook.com/Straydog1980.

Manen Lyset

Manen is a Canadian horror fiction writer and sock puppet connoisseur. Manen's writing has been featured on Thought Catalog, the Nightmare Collective anthology and on Reddit.com/r/NoSleep as /u/manen_lyset. This sentient blob of flesh can also be found on twitter (@manen_lyset) or in your bathroom mirror at exactly 12:35 PM on the full moon. If you have enjoyed Manen's contribution, check out their website:

Or you can follow Manen on:

Facebook: facebook.com/lyset.manen

Twitter: twitter.com/manen_lyset

Manen has previously published a book on Amazon, titled *From the Ashes of Pompeii: and other dark tales by Manen Lyset.*

Rafael Marmol

Rafael Marmol hails from a dark crevice on the Jersey Shore and is author to over 130 stories found across Reddit's NoSleep, ShortScaryStories, and DarkTales forums under his handle, /u/Human_Gravy. Several of his stories have been adapted into audio dramas by The NoSleep Podcast and narrated by several popular YouTube personalities. When he's not being creative, he enjoys watching television shows, sampling craft beer, or walking his dog. Let's Go Mets!

Or you can follow Rafael on:

Facebook: facebook.com/HumanGravy

Reddit: reddit.com/r/Human_Gravy

Rafael has previously published a book on Amazon, titled *Horror d'Oeuvres - Bite Sized Tales of Terror*. All proceeds from that book are contributed to the Scares That Care charity.

Rona Vaselaar

Rona Vaselaar is a Minnesota native and grew up surrounded by local urban legends. She was introduced to horror at an early age and quickly grew attached to the genre. Most of her reading and writing centers around gruesome tales. She is an alumni of the University of Notre Dame and is planning to attend the University of Johns Hopkins for graduate school.

Or you can follow Rona on:

Facebook: facebook.com/ronavaselaar

S.M. Piper

S.M. Piper posts occasionally to Reddit as /u/ StealMyPants.

Other Works

Ashley Franz Holzmann has also published a short story collection of just his writing titled *The Laws of Nature*.

Exclusive short stories by Ashley have also been included in the following books:

Horror d'Oeuvres - Bite Sized Tales of Terror

The Creepypasta Collection, Volume 2: 20 Stories. No Sleep.

Ashley was also the primary editor for:

The -30- Press Quarterly: Issue One

The -30- Press Quarterly: Issue Two: 2016 Annual Edition

Ashley's Mailing List

Go to asforclass.com and sign up for Ashley's mailing list to receive a free and exclusive novella! Have your read Ashley's first anthology The Laws of Nature? Then you remember his story The Stump.

Ashley has revisited the story and expanded it. What was included in The Laws of Nature is now just chapter one.

To receive chapter one and also chapters two through five, go to asforclass.com and sign up.

It's the best place to receive the latest news on new releases, exclusive content, and special offers!

Printed in Great Britain
by Amazon